The MAN I Really Was

The Twelve Labours of Heracles
in his own words

Jeffrey Peter Clarke

The MAN I Really Was

The Twelve Labours of Heracles
in his own words

FICTION4ALL

Jeffrey Peter Clarke

More books by this author

THE DEVIL IN EDEN
THE MAN WHO SOUGHT ETERNITY
SHADOW OF THE BEAST
RETURN OF THE HERO
THE SINGING STONES
I, MEDEA
ELECTRA
TITAN
ROGUE PLANET
HIDDEN WORLDS Volumes 1 and 2

The MAN I Really Was

Prologue

When I was granted the opportunity to interview Heracles, this most famous and illustrious of men from distant times, it involved a virtual descent into hell. Now in earlier ages, in *his* day, hell might mean different things to different people and much of it didn't seem too bad at all. In later times, as we know, hell came to be regarded by many as a subterranean realm of eternal fire and damnation. Even if this latter day interpretation had been true I dare say that after a while, certainly an eternity, most of us precipitated down there would sooner or later have gotten used to it; eternity is, after all, quite a stretch in time.

The ancient Greeks, however, had varying opinions on where they might end up when having slipped or been precipitated through the loophole of life. And as hell is eternal and, as things turned out, multi-dimensional, you could, if and when offered that rare opportunity, enter it at any time and place that took your fancy. *If*, as I say, you were offered the opportunity.

I confess I was becoming obsessed with the life of this most prolifically documented hero of old but so much was contradictory, if not utterly confusing, I considered a great pity he'd never been able to speak at any length for himself. And revered as he was, there is no record as to where his mortal remains were laid. So how did *I* get to meet Heracles, later known to the Romans, by the way, as

Hercules. Well I have to say it was a virtual experience even though utterly realistic. Virtual, yes. Or was it.

Fully engrossed by thoughts on the subject, I one night fell into a dream about Mycenaean Greece, the period during which Heracles is said to have lived; thirteenth century before the Christian era, that is. The bedroom was warm – too warm. I turned over to push down the duvet and lay on my back. It was then I noticed a hint of perfume in the air. Most odd as this was quite unfamiliar or at least different to anything my wife wore. More than that, there was a presence. It was not my wife as she was away and staying with her dear mother for a few nights; an invitation I had, as so often before, declined to accept. Perhaps a scented female burglar had entered the house. I opened my eyes and found smiling down at me a warmly illuminated, golden-haired young woman in a pale, flowing gown with fancy edging. I held my breath as she announced in a soft but compelling voice, 'Have no fear, I am Athena and I am here for you.'

'What - who?' I gasped, staring wide-eyed. I of course was familiar with the name but not right then, not at *any* time, had I contemplated a visit from her. No, not even in my dreams. Athena, you see, was one of the great Olympian deities, regarded by people of those ancient days as a goddess of war but one who fought only in righteous causes. She restores order and so she is also a bringer of peace. She embodies also the spirit of truth and divine wisdom and is devoted, generally, to the interests of mankind. I believed at once it really was her and I was certain she knew my mind.

'You wish to speak with Heracles our immortal hero do you not,' she whispered, leaning over me as I squirmed to prop myself up on the pillow. Her eyes shone, her other-worldly perfume was quite intoxicating and her warming closeness made me shiver.

'Oh, er – yes please, wouldn't mind one bit,' I muttered, this being the only response I could summon.

'Then you must arise and follow me,' she said.

Thinking myself still adrift in a dream I felt I ought to do as she asked and so I slipped naked from the bed while mumbling, 'Better put some clothes on hadn't I; a decent shirt, thick socks and outdoor shoes – no time for a shave.' As I groped in the bedside drawer for my underpants I was wondering if I'd be warm enough on the way to hell as this *was* October. Last, but I considered most essential, dreaming or no, was the pocket sized, digital voice recorder I frequently relied upon to capture ideas for future use in my novels when away from the computer. Fully charged it would be since, as always, I'd plugged the thing in before going to bed.

Athena waited in silence with her back turned to me as I dressed and crammed the recorder into my left side trouser pocket then, with a rearward, smiling glance, she stepped, almost drifted from the room. I followed, no longer sure for some moments what was going on, but then did it matter if this was only a dream? Soon, however, it was starting to seem very real. Too real! Especially when, in the darkness, I bashed my elbow on the kitchen door. I don't recall what I imagined was next to happen but as we departed the house I was much aware of the cool autumn breeze. In the light of a half moon I glanced at my wrist to see what time it was then saw I'd forgotten my watch, as I had that essence of life, my mobile phone. I hesitated but dared not go back for either. We were on a path that was obviously my own back garden because there was the old shed, now with its door standing ajar.

The goddess entered like a drifting spectre and gestured for me to follow her swaying form, so I stepped inside pushing by the lawnmower, this and all else within being illuminated only by her heavenly radiance. I suppose accessing the route to hell via the garden shed made more sense than clambering down a gaping hole in the lawn, especially since we'd had new turf laid during the summer. Athena was most considerate. So on we went, but down where never before had there been a down. Ever down into darkness through a rocky passage with my footsteps echoing ahead. It hit me right then that should I meet Heracles I'd be going back in time well over three thousand years and maybe should have grabbed up the liquid soap dispenser and a toilet roll! Then another concern: I stopped suddenly and called, 'Wait! Er, I don't know any Greek do I, ancient or modern. I won't understand a word he says and he won't understand

English.' This was something I ought to have mentioned before we set out.

She hesitated, smiled and said, 'Oh, that is no problem. I have blessed you both with mutual understanding. Heracles will think you are speaking his language and you will hear his words as though in yours.'

'But what do I call myself?' This had to be important.

'As you are from a strange land,' she assured me, 'it will matter little to him that your name is strange. In his world there were many languages spoken.'

All very handy, I thought, so we continued on down and my mind was once again occupied by thoughts of where we were heading. Some time ago I'd gathered from an English translation of several Classical Greek authors just what an odd place Hades could be. Firstly, it is named in honour of the one who rules over it and his domain is rightly called The House of Hades. Hades himself is another of the twelve Olympian gods, though not at all popular, and as ruler of the underworld was said to live down there in a sumptuous palace. On learning this I wondered if his residence might have double glazed windows. Probably not as his name means, 'The Unseen,' and I imagine the place would be pretty dark anyway.

His subterranean realm was not to be entered unless, as with most people, I did say *most*, you happened to be dead and therefore a spirit. There you would continue your existence as a counterpart of what you'd been on Earth. If you were smiled upon by the gods for being a really decent sort, or recognised as a hero like Heracles, you most likely would end up living amidst pleasant countryside with decent weather, that land of pleasures known as the Elysian Fields where you might cheat death altogether and remain in most other ways a mortal. On the other hand, had you proved unworthy or a real undesirable you'd probably end up in the basement, Tartarus, a real dump of a place where you wandered forever in perpetually dismal surroundings. Among the various torments you risked encountering in Tartarus were people you never liked in the first place and didn't have time for you. Not much fun from the sound of it.

Getting to Hades even when you'd qualified, however, sounded pretty tricky. According to the ancients, the way in was guarded by a monstrous three-headed dog called Cerberus. Cerberus was placed at the entrance to prevent anyone sneaking back out to the upper world or prevent anyone getting in there who wasn't supposed to. Did no one take it out for a walk, I wondered? Then you'd find Hades was surrounded by five rivers including Lethe, the river of forgetfulness. Best known, however, was the Styx, across which Charon, the ferryman carried the souls of the dead. A coin sometimes placed inside the mouth of the deceased was intended as payment to Charon otherwise he wouldn't take them across and they'd wander the netherworld between him and Cerberus forever begging, so I imagined, for loose change. Heracles, it was claimed, got past the dog, threatened Charon with his club and had himself rowed over the river free of charge.

By now I was beginning to harbour second thoughts and slowed almost to a standstill. This could no longer be a dream. No, *definitely* not! Athena turned and once again smiled. She knew my misgivings but I nevertheless voiced them. 'Look here, I don't like the idea of this damn great dog with three slavering heads. What if it wants to start sniffing me somewhere embarrassing, or worse? I don't like being licked by dogs, even those with only one head and I don't have any loose coins in my pocket for crossing the Styx, so, er…'

'Don't worry,' she reassured me, raising a sacred finger, 'being a goddess I can avoid Cerberus and the rivers and take us through a short cut. It is also the way we will return.'

A short cut! That was something of a relief so we carried on until the gallery levelled out. Then we turned off to proceed along a narrow, winding passage that curved this way and that and after a while had me feeling it must be endless. I was beginning to worry once more when over her shoulder I noticed a vague light ahead that grew ever larger as we approached. Closer still and I could make out a small clearing part surrounded by trees that receded into utter darkness, except for a further light that flickered some way deeper within or a little beyond their crowding trunks and branches.

'It is early evening here,' she informed me, 'but being the Elysian Fields it is pleasantly cool now - but there will be warm sunlight tomorrow. There is rain only when it is requested.' With the weather forecast, if only ours was like that, Athena actually seemed more real than she had before we set out.

The main source of light proved to be a fire that burned bright and before it was seated a large figure whose features I was just then unable to make out.

'He *is* expecting you,' assured Athena, gesturing me to step by, 'and after a day's hunting he occasionally, even after dark, relaxes in front of his fire. I told him you would appear and would be dressed in a stranger manner than almost anyone he had met before and he assured me he wouldn't mind.'

'Oh, good – yes, brilliant,' I muttered, staring across. Me, strange – of course, I suppose I would be to someone from that far back in time. 'Tell me,' I asked, 'how do I address him – I mean, does he have a title like, Your Lordship or just, Sir?' There was no reply. When I turned to ask a second time, she'd disappeared. I stood for uncertain moments, took a deep breath then stepped forward to meet the one who, relaxing in his high-backed chair, looked me up and down as I approached.

Before his tunic-attired form the log fire spat and flared. Close to this was another sturdy wooden chair into which he gestured with a wave of his hand for me to sit. Propped up against a tree only two steps away to my left was the formidable club and on the ground next to it lay his bow and an elaborately patterned leather quiver containing arrows. Nearer still was heaped a pile of small sawn logs. To my right stood a modest sized, heavy-looking wooden table upon which rested an ornately carved jar of sorts containing, as it turned out, red wine. By the jar stood two golden goblets, already filled to the brim. Just as well I wasn't teatotal as by then I certainly needed a drink.

Beyond the comforting warmth of the fire I could see little else other than the glow I already mentioned, but no matter because, though in numbed silence, I sat before the figure of the one I'd been bought here to interview. My initial enthusiasm was shadowed by a rising degree of nervous agitation and I hoped this would not be too obvious. I'd had, however, the presence of mind to transfer the recording device to my shirt pocket when I approached him and to reach and switch it on as I moved to sit before his imposing form. I was about to record his words by a method that would be utterly incomprehensible to him and for that reason might provoke his confusion or even anger. I would behave as if the recording machine existed not at all and that I, in truth, knew precious little about him other than the wild and conflicting hearsay from ancient times.

Now I waited in silence.

Chapter 1 - Heracles Speaks

'The good lady Athena told me last night you were soon to call by,' he declared in a deep and imposing manner. 'Aye, from some distant land in the endless sea that stretches forever westwards beyond our own is what she said. She said what you were expectin' of me but I'll 'ear it again from you.'

I cleared my throat and began, 'W-well, sir, there are many in my homeland who know of your fame through the tales of others but they would much prefer to hear your own words through myself. Once I'm back with my people I will write everything down.'

'You got that good a memory then 'ave you?' he asked. 'It'll need to be good an' I mean *real* good. It sounds better than that of anyone else I ever 'eard of.'

'I have been blessed with a memory like no-one else's in your land,' I replied, 'so that your words will pass from me to others *exactly* as you have spoken them. This I promise.'

'So you're a kind of bard are you? An' will your people understand what I'm all about?'

'Oh, they will indeed Mister Heracles – I mean…'

'Did you say, "Master?" he interrupted, 'I've not been called Master since I was a kid.'

'No, "Mister," – it's a polite way of addressing other men when you put it in front of their name.'

'No need for fancy names - call me Heracles like everyone else or if you like, put the word you just mentioned in front of it. And what are you called? I know she mentioned it but I was tryin' to get this fire lit at the time and 'ave since forgot some of 'er words.'

'Sounds as if she visits you often,' I said.

'Aye, she an' others drop by on the odd occasion an' tell me more of the world I once knew but when they do it's often as an ordinary person and not always one I'd recognise; a friend rather than one of the 'igh an' mighty. So then - your name.'

'Oh - er, Peter I'm known as.'

'Oar-peter,' he grinned, 'what sort've name is that?'

'No, sorry, I mean it's just - *Peter*.'

Muttering, 'Still sounds odd but I'll anyway stick with, "Mister," as it's the polite way in your world.' He slid a goblet of wine my way, splashing a little of its contents onto the table, then picked up his own. I glanced at his hands. They looked twice the size of my own, much like the rest of him. At last, though, I could hope to relax as I added, 'My people will understand very well because they have been taught much about your world if not about your true self. So may we begin with you explaining to me, a complete stranger, who you are and what you look like in your very own words.'

'Aye, if that's what you want. My name, Heracles, means somethin' like, Glory of Hera, but you'll see the irony of that an' you'll know more of

17

'er soon enough. As you see, I'm a big man, muscular and strong. You'll note I've got curly black 'air and a lately-grown longer but not too bushy beard to match. I'm sharp-eyed – always 'ad to be didn't I – an' there were those who made out I was a bit on the ugly side, though they'd 'ave thought twice an' more before they'd let me 'ear 'em say it. I suppose the scar on me left cheek didn't 'elp. I was seen as aggressive, too, because I'd usually carry a club an' sword around when I was out an' about, and on occasion my bow an' arrows or a spear instead. Aye, *the* club, the one you see restin' there. It's a treasured possession, Mister Peter, even though I no longer 'ave any use for it.'

He gestured to the club and it looked as if I'd have a job even lifting it, certainly with only one hand, let alone applying it to split someone's cranium, which I was soon to hear he'd been rather good at. I assumed the club, together with the bow and arrows, had been placed there in advance to impress me. I took up my goblet and drank. The wine wasn't too great and it didn't taste particularly strong. Watered down, perhaps. In the brief silence that ensued I became aware of running water and realised there must be a stream close by.

He leaned aside to take hold of a log which he dropped casually onto the fire, then said, 'Alright, Mister Peter, let's talk some more before I take you to where I live. Your people 'ave 'eard somethin' of me then, as most everybody else 'as. Most of 'em think I'm 'ero of sorts because of all the challenges I've faced – not most of 'em by any means of my choosin' an' that's the truth of it. Over the years, I've been hearin' from those who visit 'ere all about the amazin', all the impossible things I'm supposed to 'ave done. Aye, the people I'm supposed to 'ave conquered or murdered when most of 'em I'd never 'eard of. My name an' my alleged exploits must 'ave been a convenient justification for a lot of other people's actions.'

He downed what remained of his wine, refilled his goblet, glanced at mine but seeing it still over half full he set the jar down.

'Now you might think I went about lookin' for trouble,' he continued, 'but that's not so – it's trouble usually came lookin' for me, though I'll not deny some of it was my fault. That's when the old club came in 'andy. A tap round the 'ead with it usually had 'em seein' sense when they woke up - *if* they woke up. Then there's the lion skin I took to wearin' a good time back. It's 'ead fits right over mine so I could stare out from between the jaws an' shout loud. Aye, sometimes I'd roar. It usually created an impression but I'll come back later to explain 'ow I got 'old of it - the lion skin that is. Now I'll agree I've sometimes rough manners an' careless speech so for your sake, Mister Peter, I'll try to improve both – at least me speech, though I'm sure you'll excuse the occasional slip. You see I wasn't spendin' enough of my time in any of them - I mean *those* classy places such as palaces, except for one, even though, and you'd better believe this, I do appreciate the finer things in life and experienced a fair bit of it when I was first married.'

I hoped I wouldn't have to discuss Knossos with him because he'd know it well whereas in my own day I'd seen it only in ruins and reconstructions, some of which were regarded as inaccurate or fanciful.

'Years ago, when I was growin' up in Thebes,' he continued, 'I learned, for instance, to play the lyre – taught by a man called Linos. He was the brother of the famous Orpheus who, accordin' to some, was 'imself taught to play by the gods an' was said to enchant all who 'eard him perform. I've listened to 'im here often enough an' I say it's true.

His brother was different – down to earth, very precise, aye, that he was, but pale as a ghost and not one to enchant anybody. He set about me once, though half my size, accused me of laxity and punched me repeatedly in the chest like he was trying to beat a drum. I'm inclined to lose my temper as the man should've known and I did so right then. I grabbed the lyre and as he dashed off in panic I threw it at 'im. Too hard as it 'appened because it whacked 'is head an' killed 'im. Got me off, though, when others agreed he'd started the trouble.' Heracles gazed at me for some moments while firelight flickered in his eyes, then he said, 'As for you, Mister Peter, you look a bit pasty as well, like you've 'ad an easy enough life unless I'm mistaken.'

So he thought I looked pasty did he. Well I didn't look pasty compared with most other people back home. And I thought *he* looked pretty odd with his less than refined features, especially his nose.

This appeared to have been struck a hard blow at some time in the past but I considered it unwise to make comment. As to his age – my best guess was fifty-something or maybe a bit older. At least that's how he looked then.

'So now to the very beginnin', he went on. 'It's well known unless you're an outsider, and maybe most of your lot hearin' this seem like they might be, that Zeus, chief of the Olympian gods, wealds more power than all the rest of them on high put together. He's also fond of his women, mortal or otherwise, and *that's* an understatement if ever there was one for never did he let sanctity get in the way of lust. His lust, that is. On many occasions he'd descend from Mount Olympus under one guise or another, often as an ordinary man, sometimes not, to take his pleasure with whoever he fancied.

But Zeus had and still has a wife of 'is own, Hera of course, herself one of the twelve Olympian gods, the greatest feminine divinity and regarded throughout the land as Queen of Heaven. Very important you see and, well, what more could any woman want. And she's got temples and monuments dedicated to 'erself all over Greece and beyond – aye, more so than any other deity. And how about this – some of our priests claim that Zeus wooed Hera disguised as some kind of bird to beguile her with 'is song and have 'er in the mood to meet him when he finally appeared in human form. Now I can't say if many people believe this, if any at all do, and I'm convinced the priests don't, either. And let me say this - I'm sure the priests themselves don't believe much of what they preach to others. I doubt they ever did and most likely never will. But bein' a priest makes 'em appear important and keeps 'em well fed. I wager they'll be like that where you come from – am I right?'

'We've had our share,' I replied.

'Tell me, Mister Peter,' he asked, 'which of the gods d'you look to for favours?'

'Helios,' I replied, surprised at my own spontaneity.

'And does he shine on you often?'

'Er, not quite as often as we'd like, Mister Heracles.' Memories of dull, drizzling days drifted through my mind.

Heracles gulped the remains of his wine, glanced again at my goblet, still not empty, and refilled his own, saying, 'A bit too strong for you is it, Mister Peter?'

'Not really,' I mumbled, picking up my goblet and thinking I might have preferred it if the contents had been full strength.

'Hera nagged 'er almighty husband often enough over his debauchery,' he went on, 'but Zeus wasn't taking too much notice. Never did. Being a god's very useful when it comes to pullin' women though he's said to have consulted his wife for advice on less controversial matters. Aye, Hera might've known, no, *had* known what 'e was like all along but bein' wife of the top god wasn't to be sniffed at in spite of all their ups an' downs. And they'd argue about anythin' an' everythin'. The priests tell us, though don't ask me 'ow *they* found out, that Zeus and his wife argued over who enjoyed sex most. Hera made out he, like mortal men did, whereas he argued that she, like mortal women did. This pointless dispute was submitted to Tiresias, a mortal and a seer who claimed to have lived a part of his life a woman an' so understood both. Our Queen of Heaven was none too pleased when Tiresias told her she was wrong and 'er 'usband right, so driven by malice she deprived him of 'is sight.'

'A part of his life as a woman!' I grinned, recalling certain situations lately prevailing in my own time and place. 'How did he manage that?'

But Heracles had lost interest in the subject of Tiresias, or didn't really know, and continued, 'Yes, the wife of almighty Zeus *is* inclined to be vengeful. Not just vengeful but a total bitch and very much so in my case.' He hesitated to pass a hand thoughtfully down his beard then went on with a broad smile, 'Aye, Mister Peter, she 'ad it in for me good and proper but better if you don't say too much about this when you're outside in case she overhears and turns you into a frog.'

Outside alone in this strange land was somewhere I had no intention of going just then as it was far too dark. And a frog! No thanks.

'As for others,' he went on, 'the ones it's alleged fell foul of her spite; they were mainly Zeus' female conquests and their offspring. Their fates were many and varied, though for now I'll name but two. There was Io, a beautiful priestess of Hera herself at her temple in Argos. It's said Zeus saw Io wanderin' by the river picking flowers and at once took a fancy to 'er; a frequent trait as I've already explained. He appeared before Io in 'er dreams to express 'is feelings but she can't have been too impressed since he didn't get much of a response and even joked about it to others, so we're led to believe. Being King of the Gods though, Zeus wasn't inclined to give up and in the guise of a mortal, caught up with her as she returned sometime later to the river. There he called down a dark cloud to cover the affair up and she being impressed, he finally got what he wanted. Hera had noticed the cloud from on high and bein' ever suspicious of 'er dear husband when 'e was down on Earth she now dropped by, peered under the cloud and realised what'd been going on. Accounts vary over what happened to Io; some priests claim Zeus turned her into a cow to hide her from Hera, others make out the bovine transformation was Hera's doing. Whatever the truth of it, if any truth at all, it seems she galloped off at a pace but was later restored to her former, youthful self by Zeus, who I've no doubt would've expected the woman to show due gratitude.'

What total, utter nonsense I thought his account was as I took mouthful of wine. But then look at what some people still believe in my own world despite centuries of scientific progress.

'Semele,' he continued, 'was another mortal beauty who succumbed, this time willingly and with greater discretion to Zeus' advances. She from the beginning believed he might be a god and the thought of it appealed to 'er vanity. On this occasion Hera didn't realise what had been goin' on until Semele was obviously carrying a child. Her divine husband's. The celestial wife was furious as ever; perhaps more so. By a cunning act of trickery, Hera appeared before the girl as a friend. She persuaded Semele beg her almighty lover to appear before her as 'is true self as she and Zeus walked in open woodland. As the all powerful bringer of thunder and lightnin', Zeus was, we're told, reluctant to express his truly dangerous powers as Semele might suffer a miscarriage. The girl, in her avid insistence, can't have had any idea just what she was in for when Zeus rose up to 'eaven and the display began. The skies darkened almost to night beneath rollin' dark clouds. Thunder boomed, billowed and shivered the very ground. Lightnin' split the darkness in crazed confusion and rain began to fall, here and there at first in large ponderous drops that soon became a deluge. I've seen it that bad, many times, Mister Peter. It had Semele headin' for shelter beneath a tree and that was the end of 'er. A mighty, ripping streak of light took her from sin to sizzled in an instant. But as I said, in the end it was me – or do I mean, 'I,' who Zeus' loving wife singled out above the rest for torment; well almost the rest. In fact she just as much hated the Trojans and look what 'appened to them! But I'll talk more of her in the mornin'.'

He reached down for a stick lying close to his chair and shifted the recently placed log, causing the fire to blaze, crack and splutter. By this time I'd finished over half my wine so he reached for the jar and topped up my goblet as well as his own, which had been again empty. As he was doing this I'd glanced at the light showing amidst the trees and so I asked him, 'Where d'you live, Mister Heracles? Do you have a big house, a palace maybe?'

'A palace,' he laughed, darting a thumb in the direction of the light. 'A *palace*! No, don't need a palace 'ere, do I. Well it is the Elysian Fields as you'll see in the daytime; not at all like where old Hades lives. What sort've place d'you live in – and you got many slaves?'

'Well, it's a house; nothing special,' I replied, 'and we have very few slaves, at least in my country.'

Two questions had been lurking in the depths of *my* mind and now were stirring restlessly to demand attention, prompted by his reference to daytime. Firstly, as there was to be a bright tomorrow, and as there were trees in abundance that obviously needed light, as trees and most plants usually do, how could the Elysian Fields be underground, because that's where hell was supposed to be? Impossible! Bright stars by now peppered the sky and above us glowed a full moon. I tried fleetingly to imagine what his answer might be but instead of raising the question I decided to apply a theory of my own, influenced near as I could by twenty-first century reasoning. Initially it seems we had descended beneath the surface of the Earth from my garden shed but in that last meandering passageway we had entered some parallel universe where the Elysian Fields basked beneath wide open skies and the rest of hell really was down there below it. That theory would simply have to do as I expected Heracles would not care to analyse the ways of the gods in that respect. My second question had to be less problematical: 'Are there other people living with...I mean, do you have company?'

'Aye, I have company. As good company as I need, 'as, you'll find. Now then, Mister Peter, d'you want a bite to eat? You look as though you need somethin' to 'elp fill you up. There I go – language slipping again. You'll have to bear with me.'

'A bite to eat?' I responded, downing a little more wine. His own goblet was empty again. 'Well, yes, but where – how - ?' In pursuit of my interests back home I'd learned how little was known about the Mycenaean diet. Turning his attention to the light amidst the trees, Heracles raised two fingers to his lips and let out a shrieking whistle that went right through me and caused some nocturnal creature in the bushes nearby to scamper away through rustling bushes. Moments of silence passed. Looking about, I noticed the light from amidst the trees waver, dim slightly then resume brightness as if momentarily obscured. A pair of figures were approaching and as their features became clearer by virtue of both moon and firelight, I held my breath in mute surprise. Two young women stopped before us, their full red lips bearing wide smiles as they appraised the odd sight that was myself. Heracles smiled at them, then turned to grin knowingly at me with a slight sideways nod toward the new arrivals. The fire cracked again but this was of little distraction as I assessed their presence. The style of their attire – their overall appearance, had me thinking their origins to be New Kingdom Egypt, a part of which was contemporary with Heracles' own times, and their ages but a year either side of twenty. And whilst ancient Egypt was a keen interest of mine, it wasn't Pharaonic history that occupied my thoughts just then.

'This is Tiye' informed Heracles, gesturing to the nearest, then to her companion, 'and her friend Mayet, The good Athena called 'em over in the same way as she did you. And this 'ere,' he added, eyeing them and wafting a hand towards me, 'is Mister Peter.'

Tiye and Mayet smiled as one, each saying in only slightly accented English, 'Hello, Mister Peter, how are you?'

That both were slim and beautiful there could be no doubt and as each smiled wider still and raised a delicate, bejewelled and nail-polished hand to me, I judged from their refined appearance they must originate from the upper echelons of court life in their home country on the Nile. In the presence of Heracles, a rough and ready man born of a less urbane culture, they struck me as quite out of place. And though they bore vaguely similar features they did not strike me as being twins. The fire, burning brighter now as the new log settled, was reflected in their dark eyes. It sparkled in the precious stones embedded in headbands that were fitted about their long, braided hair. It glinted on the moon-disk earrings. Jewels were set amidst the deep and elaborate pectoral necklaces and the finely wrought gold bands that enhanced their upper limbs. Their ankle-length, almost form-fitting dresses of sheer white linen, covered but did little to conceal their figures beneath. That people of more refined class in the Egypt of those days abhorred all body hair and took much care to remove it was accordingly evident. Was I taken aback by the sight of them? I certainly was! But why had he summoned them? Was it his intention to impress me with the benefits on offer to him in these Elysian Fields?

My thoughts were interrupted when Heracles addressed me in a matter-of-fact manner, 'Time we went indoors – you ready? My attendants will serve what I 'ope will please you so follow us now.' I wasn't sure what I was ready for as he arose from his seat like a large bear to loom over me. 'You and I' he added, 'will talk a little after dinner then we'll take to our beds. In the morning we'll begin again and I'll tell you plenty more. The girls 'ere will keep you company through the night during your stay unless you wish otherwise.'

Keep *me* company! I tried to conceal an incredulity soon to be sidelined by enthusiasm. 'Oh, er, sounds fine, Mister Heracles,' I muttered as I arose from the seat.

'I take it,' he grinned, 'a man of status such as you in your land will always 'ave such girls on call.'

'Oh, er, yes,' I responded, 'any time, day or night.'

No longer, it seemed, was this just to be an interview with the great hero. I was being drawn ever deeper into a world of - of fantasy, I was about to say, but this was all *too* real and I was again feeling unnerved. With thoughts of dinner I instinctively glanced down to check the time but my watch, of course, wasn't there. Heracles strode by the fire stooped to grasp the club which he swung over his right shoulder as though it was no more than a broom, then he said to me, 'Grab those other bits will you, Mister Peter.'

I was to carry his bow and arrows, these almost as famous as his club. The empty wine jar and goblets would remain where they were. Heracles set off with casual, rolling stroll towards the light beyond the trees. The Egyptian girls followed with sensual sway and I trailed close behind, my eyes fixed upon them while I fumbled awkwardly with a free hand inside my shirt pocket to switch off the voice recorder so as to save battery power. The recorder was equipped also with a small solar panel which I hoped I might be able to use at some point. The girls glanced back at me with one of them, Mayet, hesitating so as to be by my side, sharing her smile, her warmth and her perfume as she slipped a hand about my arm. 'I will be with you now,' she said softly, and seeing this, her friend Tiye likewise slowed to join us, saying, 'I, too, am with you; we three will be together if our presence pleases you.'

My mind wavered again; perhaps after all it was a dream, but one I had to see through. I had formed no idea as to where or how Heracles might reside or his nocturnal diversions but in this bizarre realm that was so possessing me, there had to be more surprises ahead.

The lights grew brighter as we passed through the trees to where they thinned out to reveal, on a low rise, his dwelling. I'd not given too much thought over what sort of place he might live in until we'd set off. Could it be timber, wattle and daub or perhaps mud-brick? Something relatively basic in spite of our female guests' refined appearance? No, they surely would require their accustomed comforts. Of the several possibilities that had passed through my mind, none were to prove correct. Even before gaining a full moonlit view it was obvious that ahead of us stood something quite substantial. As already hinted, I was familiar with Minoan architecture, having twice visited the Palace of Minos at Knossos on Crete where had thrived the advanced and far reaching culture contemporary, though in many ways superior, to that of mainland Greece in Heracles' day.

We approached a two storey residence going back some distance with to one side of it a couple of outhouses, one of wood looking like a stable. All the others were constructed of white painted dressed stone with the main building graced by some of the features to be seen at Knossos. The porch boasted a pair of typical Minoan downward tapering stone columns painted bright red with black capitals. We passed through the porch to enter a part sheltered courtyard.

To one side of this a log fire burned vigorously with further illumination provided by moonlight and a number of ceramic oil lamps placed upon level surfaces above the smooth flagstone floor. The wall spaces between door openings were painted with rustic scenes that depicted a variety of trees and wild animals. There were various bronze weapons, mainly spears and swords, mounted between some of these frescoes but what drew my attention more than all else hung on the wall opposite the fire. This was Heracles' famed lion skin with its white-toothed jaws agape. Had it now been consigned to a place of retirement? Two figures in plain white tunics, one male, one female, both of middle-aged appearance, waited in shadow by one of the inner doors for Heracles' summons; evidently the attendants, or at least two of them, he had earlier mentioned. In one corner a stooped figure, seated upon patterned cushions, dispensed melodic notes from his lyre.

'This 'ouse,' Heracles declared with a sweep of his hand, 'Aye, this 'ouse is one of the finer things in life – at least in mine, and it's where I'll spend the rest of my days.'

And although there were marvels of their day that I was yet to witness in the home of Heracles, dinner, as I would consider it, was to manifest itself first.

In the centre of the courtyard stood a solid wooden table set with decorated ceramic dishes. These contained a choice of food to include diced beef and some kind of bird meat, already sliced, together with figs, green vegetables and olives. There were also what proved to be wheat cakes topped with honey and not to escape my notice either, was another jar filled with wine. Those seated at the table would reach to select and eat their food by use of a bronze knife or tongues.

We sat, with Heracles' bulk perched upon a large, sturdy chair to my right and with Tiye and Mayet placed closer to me. Regardless of all else, their presence intruded strongly upon my thoughts.

'We don't like to eat so late,' Heracles informed me with a passing hint of displeasure. 'Middle of the day's what we prefer but you being brought 'ere's altered things this time around.'

"Oh, sorry," I muttered peering at the food. I couldn't help but wish for a side dish of slightly overdone French fries but the discovery of potatoes was still many centuries away in unknown lands.

The girls' delicate, almost fastidious approach to their food and drink contrasted with that of Heracles who appeared to be far hungrier than we and he accounted for considerably more wine. His beard and his tunic soon acquired evidence of food that would not progress far enough to enter his digestive system. But I'll not labour to much over the details of our dinner as this was not the essence of my visit and a continuing account of his life was to take place the following day. But of course there was the later evening to come.

I did at times have to judge with care my answers to his questions about my homeland, my life and our gods who the two girls, adding comments of their own, considered must be many and varied as were those of Egypt. During this time, for reasons I could not explain, images of my own home on rainy days and of red double-decker buses in traffic jams passed momentarily through my simmering mind. Perhaps I was trying to reassure myself as to where I actually belonged.

'The girls will show you around further,' announced Heracles with a loudly satisfying belch and a sharp-eyed glance at me, followed by, 'And be out and about by sunrise, Mister Peter. I'll be waiting.' Then silence. I'd been tempted to laugh at his overt manners but thought better of it though one of the girls giggled and discreetly squeezed my arm. It was obviously time for us to leave the table and that the three of us should retire together. We left with one of Heracles' attendants, or did I mean menials, leading the way from the courtyard; a slender, bald, stooping man who tottered ahead of us as if in need of a walking stick. It turned out the man had been ordered also to show me, together with Tiye and Mayet, other parts of the house. I still considered the girls' presence totally out of place, but wasn't everything odd and out of place here, especially me.

We passed by the aged lyre player who ceased his music to offer me a largely toothless grin through his long, grey beard then we entered a short corridor that led to further rooms. What I was to witness, to experience in this house, would be like a dream within a dream but I decided to cover only the essentials in order not to drift too far from my intended purpose. This was not so easy.

With the girls close behind grinning and chatting in whispers to one another in a language I took to be their own, we first entered what was obviously a bedroom, this also illuminated, though far from brightly, by a small number of oil lamps. Leather covers were pegged over glassless windows and the generous sized bed itself draped with what appeared in the gloom to be decorated woollen covers. Here, too, were cushioned chairs and a bronze-banded, wooden storage chest.

'It is good for us here, Mister Peter, yes?' said Tiye, slipping a hand onto my shoulder.

'It looks fine,' I replied, 'but please, my name is not *Mister* Peter to you, no, it is just, *Peter* – understand?'

'Yes, we understand,' Tiye smiled and Mayet nodded her agreement with both probably wondering why I was addressed in the former manner by Heracles.

From this room we stepped along the corridor past another then to one on the opposite side, far better lit from lamps positioned on wall shelves. This proved to be a bathroom. Yes, that's what it was, and more. I was of course familiar, via reconstructed scenes, with the so-called Queen's bathroom and the toilet facilities at the Palace of Minos. Such facilities as these we think of as modern yet they are known to have been in use, perhaps invented at Knossos well before even Heracles' time. I was seeing here a more modest but closely derived version. The upper section of one wall bore marine frescoes with leaping dolphins but the main feature of the room lay beneath this, a baked clay bath, its colourfully decorated sides rising higher at one end than at the other. From the wall close above the bath projected a kind of bronze valve meant to facilitate the entry of water; a similar device known from the palace on Crete. Now I'd heard that even this far back in time a kind of soap was in use – fats boiled with ashes, was the sum of my knowledge but a flattened lump of some stuff resting in a small bowl by the side of the bath was to prove just that. Noting my interest as I peered up from this to the ceiling our attendant said, 'Floor above 'as tanks collectin' rainwater. Some've this is piped out an' 'eated in separate tanks for't' bath down 'ere then it's let out into the river after it's done with. Lord 'Erakles 'as a room like this 'e can use as 'e pleases an' there's 'is woman. Aye, she's a big woman from 'Aattusas far to the east. She's more the master's size, but doesn't like bein' seen by strangers so keeps out of the way.'

He meant Hattusas, the ancient Hittite capital in what is now Anatolia. I supposed at the time that living in the Elysian Fields you could order people and goods from almost anywhere but I was to learn a lot more about the woman later. I nodded my thanks but there was more within this room to command my admiration. In an alcove to the left side of the bath, part concealed by a moveable wooden screen, stood a carved limestone toilet bowl with wooden seat and a valve positioned low down for flushing the bowl and washing the user with hot water. 'All mod cons,' I concluded, with some of my rather basic concerns alleviated.

At an adjacent wall to the right of the bath was a window at present covered like that in the bedroom and set before this a delicately carved wooden table with a padded stool tucked beneath. Most obvious on the table was a circular, highly polished bronze mirror on a finely carved wooden stand. I approached to find items of feminine usage placed close about it, set there for Tiye and Mayet. There were small ceramic bottles, golden pots and seashells that held pastes and colours for the adornment of face and body. There, too, awaited jars of perfumed oil, hogs-hair brushes, bronze tweezers, razors and nail files, also pumice stones to smooth the skin before oils and perfumes were applied. Was the use of all this comparative luxury sanctioned by Heracles? In his more, shall I say, basic approach to life I doubted the girls' further enhancement with make-up would impress him to any degree.

Then a notion struck me – had Athena really troubled to introduce Tiye and Mayet for my sake only? Perhaps they were considered better looking than those even from Crete where women of the royal court trotted about bare-breasted but appeared overdressed below the waist. If so, how very thoughtful of the goddess; as already stated, a true friend of mankind. I thought briefly about tomorrow when I would be expected to meet up with Heracles at sunrise. I hoped next day would offer enough time for him to deliver a sufficient account of his beginnings before my voice recorder battery began to lose power.

I looked around to find our attendant had left us. The Egyptian girls stood silently by, glancing with amusement at me then to each other with unspoken yet, I was certain, mutually intelligible thoughts. They stepped close, linked their arms into mine, enticing me by their sensual warmth and Tiye said with ear-tingling whisper, 'Peter, dear, we must continue with the rest of our evening.'

'Yes we must,' agreed Mayet as they coaxed me to turn about. This was room service par excellence.

Sorry, reader, but this tale is about Heracles and not about me so we'll rejoin the great man tomorrow at sunrise.

Chapter 2 - Heracles' Rise

I awoke to find I was quite alone. My companions of the night, Tiye and Mayet, had left the bedroom without my hearing them yet their perfume lingered. I twisted aside to see the cover had been removed from the window and although brighter stars were still visible, the sky beyond was beginning to lighten. I lay a short while wondering if the two girls might return but when I saw they had taken away their dresses and the valuable decorative items they had been wearing I concluded they might be getting ready elsewhere. There were cries from beyond the window. Familiar cries. Chickens! There were also sounds from close within the house. Echoing laughter. I clambered from the bed, muttering, 'Don't have much time do I,' and looked across to see my clothes draped over one of the chairs where I'd left them with my slip-on shoes close by. Also laying there was a pale woollen gown of sorts that I thought would be convenient to wear when heading to the bathroom. After pulling on the gown I checked my shirt pocket to confirm that the voice recorder was where I'd left it. So far, so good, but where *were* Tiye and Mayet? It had to be the bathroom because that was from where the laughter came but I would hold back a while for the sake of good manners. The laughter stopped but still I waited. I waited until I considered I ought to hang back no longer. I crept along to the bathroom and peered cautiously inside. Finding Tiye and Mayet were gone I took advantage of its facilities quickly as I could so as to dress and join Heracles by sunrise.

Freshened up, I made my way to the courtyard but as there was no one around I continued to the portico from where I stepped out into a cool morning breeze. The sun peered from over the horizon like an inquisitive eye. In fields, already aglow on the other side of the busy stream, really a more modest river, grain was ripening, pigs, goats and sheep I could see, tended by people. Further woodlands lay beyond. Were the people I observed allocated to the Elysian Fields through acts of heroism or service to the gods? I thought not.

'They'd be kept down below if they didn't agree to tend my livestock and crops,' came the voice from behind as if in answer to my unspoken question. I spun about and there he was in sunlit glory, draped in the lion skin with his grinning face peering from between its white-toothed jaws and the great club held resting on his shoulder. He laughed loud enough to split the morning air with a roar that scattered nearby birds then announced, 'Thought before we eat you might be interested to see 'ow I looked an' sounded when dealin' with awkward buggers. Enough to make some people shit 'emselves. Aye, somethin' else you'll be able to tell 'em about when you get back 'ome.'

I was suitably impressed then he turned away, saying, 'There'll be food and beer waitin' for us and I'll 'ang the lion back up before we carry on talkin'.'

It seems the passage of night had compromised the promise Heracles had made to refine his speech but perhaps it didn't suit him. I followed, reaching into my shirt pocket to switch on the recorder while regretting I'd not had some means of capturing his lionised image. We strolled back to the courtyard and Heracles, having replaced the intimidating garment on its hook, joined me at the table. Two attendants stood by the inner doorway awaiting his call. Tiye and Mayet were not to be seen, nor was his furtive Hittite wife. Apart from the jar of beer and large goblets the somewhat meagre offering for breakfast consisted of figs, grapes and olives plus a few honey-topped wheat cakes left over from the previous evening. How I regretted Athena could not grant me a bacon sandwich! He grasped the jar to fill up our goblets, carelessly splashing beer onto the table.

'Had a good night, Mister Peter?' he asked with a roguish grin. 'Managed to get some sleep, did you?'

I noticed his somewhat uneven teeth as I replied, 'Most agreeable, thank you,' and that's all on the subject he was getting out of me.

'Very well then,' he declared, diving fingers into the olives, 'let's get started.'

'Yes, let's,' I responded, helping myself to one of the wheat cakes before sampling warm beer.

'So how did it all begin?' he continued. 'You'll 'ave heard different accounts, a lot of 'em exaggerated beyond reason by people who never set eyes on me; aye, exaggerated to a point where I 'ardly recognise most of those 'appenings myself.'

'Amazing, isn't it, Mister Heracles,' I said, 'what a reputation can do over time. We have in my land tales of a hero king called Arthur whose travels and deeds are many and varied, yet there is no proof he ever existed. We talk of a hero called Robin Hood who defied tyrants by stealing from the rich to give to the poor yet he's no more than a fleeting name. Yes, the less people know of something, the more they will make of it. We have an old saying, "All that told it added something new, and all who heard it made enlargements, too," but that's not the way I work.'

'That's good, Mister Peter, so you'll stick only with what *I* tell you as an' when I get around to it.'

'Oh, I will,' I assured him.

'Very good,' he muttered, taking another gulp of beer, 'my supposed grandfather was Electryon, King of Mycenae. He 'ad a daughter named Alkmene, said to be a woman of great charm and beauty. She'd no desire in 'er early days to get married, though she was openly admired by Amphitryon, a man of some importance in Mycenae and claimin' to be a descendent of Perseus, 'imself a son of almighty Zeus.'

'What d'you mean by your *supposed* grandfather?' I asked.

'That'll all be clear soon enough,' he responded.

I gathered from the tone of his voice that I was not expected to interrupt at that point.

42

'Durin' a religious ceremony at Mycenae there was a raid from over the border by a well organised gang who 'elped 'emselves to a large number of Electryon's cattle. His five sons, Alkmene's brothers, were out huntin' at the time an' witnessed this. They attempted, though not suitably armed, to turn an' drive some of the cattle back. Unfortunately they got 'emselves killed - their 'eads chopped off, by the rustlers who must 'ave known who they were.

Alkmene was distraught and Electryon, bein' 'imself no stranger to a round or so of violence, organised or not, rode off with his pals, all of 'em well-armed, intendin' to sort things out, avenge the deaths of his sons an' regain the cattle. He gave Amphitryon the responsibility of runnin' Mycenae's affairs while he was away and knowin' the man's desire for the woman, promised 'er in marriage to Amphitryon if he proved 'imself able to make a proper job of the given responsibilities. Amphitryon, anyway, considered he'd now be in line to take over the throne of Mycenae since by then there was no-one else left alive to claim it. That bein' so, Alkmene insisted he took responsibility for avengin' the deaths of 'er brothers. Amphitryon had learned, meanwhile, that most of the stolen cattle had fallen into the hands of another party, the Eleans, who were not particularly warlike and 'ad paid in silver for 'em.

Amphitryon took off with his own armed men, all experienced warriors, struck somethin' of an enforced bargain with the easily persuaded Eleans

43

and 'ad the cattle driven back to Mycenae. When, eventually, Electryon arrived home empty-handed, only to find most of the cattle returned, he was suitably impressed. But not at all impressed when Amphitryon asked to be paid back what it had cost 'im to recover them. Electryon was furious and made it clear he'd no intention of payin' for the return of what from soon enough would be Amphitryon's and that was that. But it wasn't. Amphitryon threatened to 'ave payment from 'im by whatever means since Electryon still had many years ahead of 'im as ruler of Mycenae. And so their animosity smouldered. Accordin' to witnesses, both men 'ad been drinking 'eavily at an inn when the subject of payment for the cattle erupted again but this time it resulted in violence. It began as a brawl with punches bein' thrown then Amphitryon in drunken rage seized and 'urled a stool at Electryon, striking him so 'ard on the skull that he was instantly killed. Witnesses claim that Amphitryon, on realisin' what he'd done, cried out repeatedly, "No – no, I didn't mean to kill 'im!"

But Electryon 'ad been popular with the citizens of Mycenae an' through the followin' days, in spite of Amphitryon's readily expressed regrets, it became clear that anger, fuelled by the priesthood of Hera, was growing throughout Mycenae. When another man, Sthenelus, stepped forward to seize the throne, Amphitryon realised he'd soon need to flee the city. Alkmene, not well respected because of 'er association with Amphitryon, determined to leave Mycenae with 'im.'

Jeffrey Peter Clarke

'So Amphitryon considered his own life to be in danger,' I commented as Heracles, drained and refilled his goblet before topping up mine, while I munched on the remaining wheat cake.

'That he did. He and Alkmene gathered together their belongin's and one moonless night, loaded 'em into a four-wheeled chariot then with two 'orses taken from the stables, they left Mycenae via the Lion Gate.'

'The famous Lion Gate,' I said. 'Were they not challenged by the guards?'

'It seems not, or maybe Sthenelus, now established as king, told the guards to let 'em through. They took with 'em a slave who was familiar, in sheer darkness, with the long route to their intended destination, Thebes. The slave was eager enough with a promise of silver and 'is freedom upon their safe arrival.'

'Why Thebes?' I asked.

'Why Thebes - because Creon, their king, was on good terms with warlike Mycenae and 'ad got on very well with Amphitryon during a visit there some years earlier. Amphitryon was welcomed at Thebes for other reasons. When he explained to Creon what'd gone on at Mycenae they did a deal: Creon would give Amphitryon and Alkmene a good place to live and he'd oversee a grand weddin' for them if Amphitryon, who he regarded as a leader of men, would assist in puttin' down a few of Thebes' own enemies. To this Amphitryon agreed. After fleein' Mycenae he was most keen to prove 'is mettle.'

45

'I take it, Mister Heracles, this suited Alkmene also.'

'It did in more ways than one, Mister Peter. Alkmene was married to Amphitryon in a lavish ceremony with all the food, wine and entertainment promised by Creon, but after it came a big disappointment for Amphitryon. On their weddin' night she refused to allow consummation of their marriage until he'd complied with her demands to set off and avenge the deaths of 'er brothers.'

'She appears to have planned well ahead for that,' I muttered. 'Sounds as if she was a pretty determined woman.'

'Aye, that she was. What 'appened to 'er brothers 'ad continued to play 'ard on 'er mind and all along she'd regarded the bellicose Amphitryon as a means of carryin' out 'er wishes. Had he realised 'er intentions, I ask? Maybe not but it seemed for both there were rich rewards to be 'ad for him playin' his part at Thebes if this proved successful. Creon allowed Amphitryon enough men of 'is own to ride off armed to the teeth and sort out the Taphians, those people responsible for the gang who'd murdered Alkmene's brothers and who were also sworn enemies of Thebes.'

Heracles drained his goblet once more, peered at mine, saw it was still far from empty, refilled only his own then went on, 'It was some days after Amphitryon's departure when Zeus flew in to take 'is pleasure with Alkmene, disguised as 'er 'usband and claimin' to 'ave done for the cattle thieves once an' for all. As far as *she* was concerned *he* was who he said 'e was and that homely visit resulted in me. It's since been claimed by Zeus' priests that Alkmene was the last mortal woman 'e possessed for pleasure but I never believed it.

Amphitryon turned up the followin' mornin' and soon after did his business with her. It's said Alkmene was greatly puzzled by 'is enthusiasm because as far as she was concerned they'd been at it the night before while to Amphitryon it was 'is first time.

Now you'll understand, Mister Peter, how the circumstances of my birth ended up such a complicated affair. I was born of a mortal woman yet fathered by the Almighty an' this angered Hera beyond measure. Aye, she wanted me out of the way before I got beyond screamin' and wettin' the bed. I also 'ad a brother, Iphicles. He *was* the true son of Amphitryon an' we were born a day apart. Zeus, and of this the priests also assure us, decreed that I was destined to become the mightiest and most famous hero that ever trod the earth because *he*, the wielder of thunderbolts, was my true father. Lucky old 'Eeracles you might think. Zeus 'ad determined that the first child born that day by our mother, namely me, would also become a great ruler, of Mycenae, most powerful city in the Peloponnese, but Hera, knowin' of this, contrived to 'ave another born first in order to thwart her mighty 'usband and ensure I never achieved the promised status as king. But it was *not*, however, Iphicles - he was only a co-incidence. This new arrival 'ad to be, like Amphitryon, a descendent of Perseus, who as I

said, was another offspring of Zeus. King Sthenelus
of Mycenae fitted the bill with his ancestry and 'is
wife, Nicippe, bein' pregnant, was induced to give
birth to the child a short time before I was born and
so buggered up my chances of kingship. They
named the boy, Eurystheus but we'll return to 'im
later.

Those around some days after Iphicles and I 'ad
arrived on the scene tell me a pair of serpents –
large snakes if you like, appeared in the cot
occupied by the two of us, sent so they insisted, by
Hera to finish me off. Those lookin' after me said
Iphicles panicked while I did for the snakes good
an' proper - strangled 'em both with my own 'ands
and that proved who was to be the 'ero. I wouldn't
remember it too well though, would I; not at that
age – just a gurglin' kid. But if people choose to
think it true then that's fine by me. What most likely
persuaded Zeus to let 'is dear wife have 'er way on
this occasion was her promise to overlook some of
his more obvious sexual transgressions.'

Reading the above might have you confused by
it all; I certainly was feeling that way but by this
time it seemed Heracles was convinced I'd
remember everything he told me. Or maybe he
wanted to relate his adventures to a willing ear just
to get them off his chest. That suited me as long as
the voice recorder behaved itself. But doesn't it
show how closely the gods of those days were
believed to interact with humanity.

'So that was it, Mister Peter,' he continued,
'I've described what made my birthday somethin'

of a drama so I'll go on from there. I'm told by the priests, bless 'em, that Hera, angered at me doin' what I did to the snakes, visited my mother at night, in 'er dreams and instilled 'er with mortal fear an' a lingerin' death if she didn't take me from the 'ouse and abandon me in the woods to act as dinner for whatever lived there. If that's true then maybe you can imagine what Alkmene must've felt. She did as she was told, 'ad no choice did she, but first she prayed and made sacrifice to Athena to spare me from 'arm. Athena, as you probably know, is 'erself one of the twelve Olympians, backs righteous causes but is *not* to be messed with. That worked for a while because the goddess, in all innocence and thinkin' it the right thing to do, is said to 'ave whisked me off to Hera herself to find me somewhere safe and secure back on Earth. Hera soon enough realised who I was but not wantin' to upset Athena, who could have appealed to Zeus, made some excuse or other an' said to give me back to Alkmene and Amphitryon an' tell 'em it was all a mistake.'

'Some mistake!' I exclaimed. 'Enough to give your poor mother mental health problems.'

'Metal what problems?' he asked, with the goblet hovering close before his beard.

'No, not metal – *mental*. Mental health problems. They're very popular nowadays where I come from. They help some people to get off with all sorts of things.'

'Do they now,' he breathed.

Heracles explained to me how Amphitryon continued for some years in Creon's service, achieved success and gained honours in keeping back Thebes' enemies and increasing for a time the security of the city.

'One thing Amphitryon did for me, in my earlier years,' he added, 'was 'ave me learn how a chariot *should* be used in warfare. I mentioned earlier about Linos an' my lessons on the lyre but during those years at Thebes I also learned to wrestle down any man who'd challenge me. I practised with the bow and arrows to gain as good a score as the best of 'em and as for the sword – why, I'd cut down in battle any man who'd raise his blade against me.'

'Sounds like multi-tasking,' I was tempted to say, but thought better of it.

'I usually preferred the club, though,' he continued, 'much more direct and saved a lot of messin' around. No need to sharpen it, see.'

'And what became of Amphitryon and his wife?' I asked.

'Amphitryon eventually fell in battle and 'is tomb stands proud in Thebes. Alkmene lived on to a great old age an' died in the city where they later regarded 'er as a goddess. With Amphitryon gone the enemies began to close in an' demand tribute or they'd take Thebes by force. Creon might 'ave given in to 'em but by then I was of an age to step forward and do somethin' useful. I rallied the Thebans, even had 'em take down all the shields an' spears they'd left hangin' in their temples for many years as offerings to the gods and 'ad them put to proper use. Aye, under *my* leadership we defeated the greatest of Thebes' enemies and forced *them* to pay tribute to *us*.

In his gratitude to me, and in fear I might be plannin' to clear off to settle elsewhere, Creon offered me 'is daughter, Megara, in marriage. Already eighteen and lookin' like a goddess 'erself, yet still unaccounted for, she was surrounded by wealthy suitors, droolin' at the mouth at the very sight of 'er, and vyin' for 'er attention, so I wasn't about to turn the offer down.'

'Didn't that make you unpopular at court?' I queried.

'Aye, my friend, it did an' just before the ceremony there was a plot against my own life by three of 'em until I found out. One I caught an' dealt with, if y'see what I mean, and the other two Creon 'ad executed. All three bodies were 'ung from the city wall to rot and 'elp feed the birds. Life after that looked to be set fair. The omens were good. I 'eld high office at Creon's court an' I'd gathered together a close-knit group of followers I could rely on. Among them was a lad called Iolaus who knew all about me although I'd never heard of 'im until then. I learned soon enough he was the son of Iphicles who I'm sure you'll recall was born to Alkmene around the same time as me.'

'I do indeed, Mister Heracles,' I said, wanting to reassure him over what a brilliant memory I possessed, 'just as I recall you were a result of a visit to Alkmene by Zeus and Iphicles the result of

51

Amphitryon turning up a day later, so you were half-brothers.'

'That's right, Mister Peter. In other words, young Iolaus was a nephew of sorts and 'ad become a member of the Theban royal court! Aye, we soon became good friends and he'd be with us when our group set off huntin' together. I'd show up with my men in full strength at those towns where rumours of trouble stirred and he'd be with us then. We'd keep Thebes safe for her citizens an' ensure respect for the king. When problems arose on our borders we'd gather, we'd arm able men of the city and we'd set out to confront whoever was lookin' to give us trouble. At such times the ever cheerful Iolaus proved himself a born leader. But more than that, my life with Megara was honey-coated. For the first time ever, Mister Peter, I experienced true fulfilment. We 'ad three sons but one died while still a child. The surviving two I began to raise as warriors at an early age but never did I neglect their education in some of the things where I myself 'ad fallen short. One of the pair 'ad more a thirst for battle than the other, even 'is toys were weapons and he'd got 'is own small chariot. The other boy I thought would aspire to nobility and in my mind it seemed to me that he'd one day take the throne of Thebes. Iolaus, being well educated, helped both of 'em in that respect better than I could.

All appeared well, yet I should 'ave known all along there was one up there watchin' an' layin' 'er plans against me. Aye, she was doin' exactly that, and one day it 'appened.'

Heracles set aside his goblet, bowed his head and, consumed in thought, stared down at the table in silence. I wondered then if he'd lost all awareness of my presence, if I ought to leave him alone, switch off my recorder and maybe wander off to locate Tiye and Mayet. I decided, however, to remain where I was.

Chapter 3 - And His Fall

Heracles looked aside at me and still bowed, asked in a low voice, 'Tell me, Mister Peter, 'ave you ever woken up thinking you're still havin' a nightmare only to find it's no nightmare at all because - because it's real?'

'Not as I recall, no,' I answered.

'Well it 'appened to me,' he sighed. 'Aye, it 'appened to me it did.'

This sounded portentous and I suspected from the ancient writings of others what he might be about to reveal even if those accounts varied or disagreed entirely in many details. There was a further spell of tense silence as he eased back and closed his eyes in contemplation.

Then he resumed. 'I'd gone to our bed with Megara that night, tired but contented, when the dream began. I was standin' naked in a featureless, dim room. Didn't know where I was or what I was doin' in the place. There was a small window, high up – little else other than a couple of flickerin' lamps to see by. Opposite me was an open door and outside I could see it was night. I was about to step forward, to go outside, when there was a breeze come through the room. The lamps wavered an' went out. Then she was there, in the doorway, little more than a silhouette. Somehow I knew who it was an' I asked, "What is it you want with me?"

"Oh, how you have defied me," she answered coldly, her voice a sharp-bladed knife cutting through my mind. "From the very day you were born you have defied me. Zeus, my husband, also has defied me and by his own admission he now owes me recompense. I stand before you now to claim a part of it."

'Anger arose deep within me, Mister Peter, an anger unlike anythin' I ever knew. She may 'ave been one of the immortals but I didn't care, I was going to seize 'er by 'er fuckin' throat an' even if I couldn't kill 'er I intended she would suffer. But part way across the room I fell to the floor, struck down by a sudden weakness in my limbs an' I could no longer speak. Unable to rise I rolled aside to find her starin' down at me, a grin of triumph on 'er face, her eyes blazin' fearsome red. Still 'elpless I watched 'er leave the room then vanish into the night. Only then was my strength returnin'. I rose to my feet but the anger still 'ad a grip on me; a burnin' anger that possessed me an' drove out all reason. It 'ad to be vindicated. If ever this anger was to leave me it 'ad to be spent. Aye it 'ad!'

Heracles banged his fist hard upon the table, shaking its contents and splashing beer as he relived those moments. He gazed across the courtyard then turned his attention back to me.

'As I emerged from sleep,' he resumed in a calm but grave manner, 'I thought for a moment life was returnin' to normal. But it was not. I was alone, still naked an' no longer in my own bed. I was bewildered, aye, utterly so. Through the small, high window there was daylight, but where was I? My flesh was damp an' crawlin'. I felt unclean. The

55

very air stank of shit and I was layin' on a woollen blanket beneath which was a bed of straw. I tried to rise but I ached all over an' my arms felt bruised. My 'ead was sore as if someone 'ad whacked me with 'ard object. I looked about an' saw the room was much the same as that where Hera had stood before me in that damned dream. I got to my bare feet to tread on cold, 'ard flagstones. Close to the oil lamps stood a pottery jug that looked to contain water an' by it were two dishes, one with scraps of food in it, the other empty. I stepped over to the door an' found it locked and as the window was beyond my reach it meant I was a prisoner - but a prisoner of who, and why, though I might 'ave guessed 'ad I not been so mightily confused. But right there an' then it was no dream. No, Mister Peter, it was no dream at all!'

Heracles sank back into his chair and once more closed his eyes. He was gathering his thoughts and I knew I must wait in silence for him to speak again. It was, after all, due to my presence that he had dragged these best forgotten memories to the surface as stirring bones from a deep and mouldering pit.

He resumed his tale once more with, 'Aye, a prisoner I was and I realised it must be mornin' because the light comin' through that window was grownin' brighter. Tell you the truth, Mister Peter, I'd no memory of anythin' other than gettin' into bed after sunset with Megara. Despair might've taken possession of me 'ad I not heard a bar bein' drawn back outside the door. With my strength almost as I felt it should be I stepped closer to confront whoever was about to enter. The door swung in on grindin' sockets, fresh air spilled through an' there were three men pressed together an' peerin' in at me. All were armed, one with his sword drawn and ready to use should I move closer. Still they stared at me as I asked, "What's goin' on and what am I doin' 'ere?" They continued to gape then the man holdin' the sword at me said to the others, "Sounds like 'e's almost with us again. What d'you think?"

'With no clothes and no weapon to 'and I resisted the temptation of goin' for 'em with my fists only. I demanded once more they 'ave me know what this was all about. Where was Megara an' where were my two lads? The man grippin' 'is sword glanced to one of the others an' said, "Go and tell 'em at Athena's shrine the prisoner seems to be 'imself! Fetch the priestess, quick!"

'Off the man went. I stood there ardly' able to think but the two left at the doorway had no intention of sayin' more or of lettin' me out because they slammed the door shut an' slid back the bar. They'd referred to me as a prisoner – me, Heracles! I stood there for what seemed a very long time an' I listened 'ard. At last there were voices outside then the bar was bein' drawn back. The door swung in and morning sun flooded past the figure of a finely robed woman. She stood facin' me with a white woollen gown of sorts clutched in 'er arms and asked, "Heracles, who am I?"

"You – you're Leucippe of course." I replied, "Leucippe, a priestess of Athena. Why d'you ask me if I know who you are when you oversee the sacrifices I make at 'er shrine an' where we talk together often? What's 'appened, tell me - 'ave I been lost to the world by a sickness, and why do I find myself inside this – this, whatever it is? And why's my wife or at least one of my boys not 'ere with you?"

"Heracles," she answered, holding out the gown, "you have not been and are not still the man you would care to have others see. I will tell you all that has to be told but first you must cover yourself with this gown. Follow me quietly to the temple pool where I will have slaves wash the foulness from your body."

'I did as she asked and in the light, as she stepped back, I looked down an' saw just 'ow much I was in need of clean water. I followed 'er, my eyes troubled by the bright sun, with the three men close behind, their swords at the ready, but desperate as I was to know what'd happened to me I said nothin'.

Washed clean, dried an' bodily refreshed with warm olive oil and wearin' a fresh tunic, I rejoined 'er alone in a quiet space at the rear of the temple where food an' beer were set on a table before me. As she eased 'erself down opposite, Leucippe wore an ominous expression unlike any I'd ever seen as she spoke. "Heracles, Athena has redeemed you at last and you are with us once more. What I am about to reveal will not be easy for you, nor will it be for me in the telling, but you must know all that happened before you go from here."

'I nodded my willingness to listen further and she waited while I took a long, welcome draught of beer. Leucippe leaned closer to me and with tearful eyes fixed upon mine she said in a low voice,' "Heracles, you were stricken with madness by Hera. She placed a demon within your head as you slept so you no longer knew who you were or what you were doing and this I tell you *is* the truth. And while it was in full possession you did terrible, terrible things. You arose from your bed that night and you turned upon your wife intending to kill her.'

"No!" I cried, jumpin' to me feet. "This can't be true – not Megara! I could never do wrong to 'er!"

"Heracles, *please* hear me. It was not *you* intending her harm, I swear! It was not you but the demon within that possessed you as an instrument of Hera's cruel vengeance. This you *must* believe."

'Aye, Mister Peter, that's what she said an' whatever else I might 'ave expected from 'er, this was only the start of it as she carried on. "Heracles, you would have strangled your wife to death but in the struggle she cried for help. Your two sons answered her call and tried to restrain you while she fled the room. But you turned upon the boys and killing one with a single blow you next beat the other until he, too, was dead. Megara had summoned the palace guards and although you struck down one of them, there were too many even for you, and you were not armed. They rendered you unconscious with cruel blows. They dragged you from the room, they took you outside and carried you still helpless to a place aside from our temple; the very place where sometimes the condemned or deranged are confined, often until they die. When Creon was told what had happened he would have had you put to death but I, in the name of Athena, prevailed upon him to let you live because our good goddess knew the cause of your madness. So you were kept where you were but fed by armed men each morning. In there you prowled back and forth like a wild beast for seven days, crouching in a corner when the men entered. Iolaus was much concerned and came hoping to speak with you but you did not know him. You would have turned upon him with murderous violence had not the guards prevented it. Here at Athena's temple we prayed and made sacrifice for your return to sanity. It was Athena herself who appealed to Zeus and had him compel the evil thing to leave you, Athena who in the end completed your release from madness by a single touch upon your head."

"And you - you say I'd meanwhile slain my own sons. I do *not* wish to believe you but I know I must for why else would you speak of it. And what about Megara, is she...?"

"Your wife is safe and presently taken care of by Creon," Leucippe assured me, "but she is utterly grief-stricken."

"Then I must go to 'er," I said. Aye, I was desperate to try an' explain in my own way.'

"No, Heracles," she insisted, "you cannot do that! The bond between you both is broken. Megara has denounced you forever, though even this, too, may be the work of Hera, and Creon will not allow you to approach her."

'I leaned back a while in frenzied thought before askin', "then – then what must I, what *can* I now do?"

"Though innocent," she replied, "you can no longer continue as you were in Thebes. Others will not understand or appreciate what happened and their respect will no longer be yours to command. You must go to Delphi and there consult the oracle over your future. There is no other way."

'I tell you, Mister Peter,' he said, wagging a finger before me, 'It took me quite a while to come to terms with the idea. We lived in violent times as you're well aware but it was my own family I'd destroyed. And madness or no, Leucippe was right about respect. I was soon made aware Creon would no longer call upon my services an' although others I encountered were polite enough, some treated me with caution whereas others looked aside or avoided me altogether.'

'So you had no choice, Mister Heracles. You had to leave Thebes and find your way to Delphi.'

'Aye, Mister Peter, I 'ad to go *all* the way to Delphi.'

Dear reader, you will have noticed how Heracles' pronunciation had by this point lapsed entirely to its former carelessness but under the circumstances, when relating those memories, I'm

sure you will appreciate why, so we must take him
as he was.

Chapter 4 - The Oracle at Delphi

He drank deeply, drew a sleeve across his mouth then turned to me once more. 'I left via the palace gate well before sunrise that mornin' in a cart pulled by a single 'orse. It was an ordinary, stout workin' cart, nothin' fancy about it, nothin' to give away what it contained, and I wore a plain, dull tunic with my knife concealed safe beneath. I'd no desire to attract attention once away from the city. With me in the cart were small possessions of value, maybe to trade or donate at Delphi an' I'd as much in silver and gold as I thought necessary. Beer I carried, too, in a pair of earthenware jars packed with straw. I reckoned this would 'elp me keep clear of anywhere I might be recognised until I was well away from Thebes. My club rested out of sight on the floor.

There were a good number who watched me pass by on my way to the city gate, mainly citizens and traders of the town. Some looked up at me, puzzled, others stared and gathered in small groups to speculate and air their opinions while a few made a point of ignorin' me altogether. At the city gate an' beyond it was mainly peasants I encountered, 'eaded to the market an' gettin' in my way as they shuffled along with pigs, sheep an' goats or baskets hangin' on mules full of whatever fruits and vegetables they'd been growin' in their orchards an' fields. Once amidst 'em I attracted less notice as maybe they'd little idea as to what'd been goin' on in Thebes.'

'How much time would your journey take?' I asked him.

'From Thebes three days, maybe more as some of it further north could be rough goin'. I'd visited Delphi before, like everyone who could make it there, but not by this route. Small numbers of bandits 'ad for some time been reported as spotted in a few areas, on the lookout for what they saw as easy pickin' but I'd the means to defend myself should any of 'em care to try their luck. I nevertheless 'ad consulted the priestess at Athena's temple who told me my destiny was assured, which I took to mean I'd reach Delphi in one piece.'

'What about your companions of old, Mister Heracles, could some of them not have made the journey with you?'

'I never considered it. After all that'd 'appened my relationship with them could never 'ave been the same. No, they'd not 'ave looked up to me as they once did.'

I understood what he meant but considering the lawlessness outside some of the cities in those times, Heracles was leaving himself pretty vulnerable.

'So, Mister Peter, I was leavin' a way of life I'd come to value an' take for granted, followed by a few days of madness that'd destroyed it all, aye, inflicted on me by one filled with unendin' hate. But Athena 'ad done what she could to preserve me and I 'oped she be not too far away when I set off.

The day was fine and before long I was leavin' the fields and grazin' land behind. I 'eaded west over hilly country toward Thespiae, a town noted for its worship of Eros, then after passin' it by I'd carry on north.

It was gettin' on for late mornin' on my second day under a scorchin' sun and in fairly open country when I stopped for a drink. I spotted three men on 'orseback who'd appeared on a rise some way over to my left. They stopped an' were obviously watchin' me. I carried on as normal but very soon I saw they were followin', raisin' dust an' gettin' closer. I didn't imagine for one moment they were out to wish me luck on my journey. I goaded the 'orse to go on quicker but bent low to get ready my bow an' my arrows. When I glanced over my shoulder they were closer and spreadin' out so as to go for me at each side and from behind. The three were shabby, long haired an' full bearded an' the one gallopin' to my right had a spear ready to do its business. I'd fitted an arrow an' raised my bow at the same time as the bugger cast 'is spear. He was pretty good, I'll give 'im that, but he must have seen me takin' aim because he should 'ave slowed down or come in closer. Now shootin' an arrow from a moving cart on rough ground isn't the best way to go about it but I'd plenty of experience, especially while out huntin'. As the spear struck and split the side of my cart I let fly at 'im. I'll admit luck also was on my side for the arrow went into 'is right shoulder as he went for 'is sword. I didn't 'esitate to see if he fell because with poundin' hooves close to

my left I ducked down to grab the club. Just as well
I did for I heard the swish and felt the wind of 'is
sword as he leaned across to strike me down. He
cursed aloud, tried to steady 'imself on 'is mount
an' raised the sword again but I swung the club at
arm's length an' struck 'im full in the face. He let
go the sword, screamed an' fell back from 'is 'orse
with hands graspin' 'is mouth. If he'd got any teeth
before, he couldn't 'ave too many left in the broken
jaw I'd just given 'im. Seein' the fate of those two
the third man, who'd not wanted to get in the way
of his pals, fell back an' slowed to a standstill. An'
so did I. I picked up the bow once more, stepped
from the cart, fitted another arrow an' took aim as
he was still within range an' I was now steady on
solid ground. I saw the arrow hit as he turned to
gallop off but since it didn't stop 'im it may only
'ave grazed the bugger. The first man was
scramblin' about, trying to get up with one hand
graspin' the embedded arrow while the second
rolled about the ground clutching 'is face, chokin'
and howlin' aloud. I considered grabbin' my club
an' walkin' over to finish 'em both off but then I
thought, no, a quick death would be too easy a way
out for the bastards though death was surely to be
their lot. The sun was well above by then so I
climbed back into the cart, took another drink an'
continued on my way.'

'A fair day's work, Mister Heracles,' I said,
though I thought the whole episode sounded pretty
dreadful as I added, 'Perhaps Athena *was* with you
all the way.'

'P'raps so – aye, p'raps so. The priests assured me she was there when I drove back the enemies of Thebes but maybe she was otherwise occupied when I needed 'er later. Does any particular god in your land 'elp you out at times, Mister Peter?'

'Er, well, none ever helped me personally unless we count Athena who brought me over to meet you. But some people think they get help from one god only and others swear they know him without any proof whatsoever. Our religions have created problems different to yours but often with the same results – strife and bloodshed through the ages. But please, let me hear more of yourself and Delphi.'

'Aye,' he breathed, 'then I'll carry on. Around sunset I found myself in rougher country where in an area surrounded by pine trees I came upon a stream. There I ate and settled down to take my night's rest on a bank of soft grass where I thought 'ard over those days before and after I was stricken.'

'Were you not concerned about bears, lions and that sort of thing?' I asked.

'Never crossed my mind, Mister Peter. After dark, lookin' up at the stars, I wondered if that cursed wife of almighty Zeus had 'er eye on me and was plannin' further mischief. The sound of runnin' water I found restful an' listenin' to the stream I 'eard suddenly an' almost above me, I swear, the call of an owl. A welcome call it was for the owl, a personification of wisdom, is sacred to Athena who 'erself values truth and justice. Did you know that,

Mister Peter? I think that night Athena *was* keepin' her eye on me.'

'I do know how highly the owl was regarded, Mister Heracles, because its image was shown later on - ' I stopped and cleared my throat because I'd been about to add, '- the coins of Athens,' when I realised in Heracles' day they of course had no coins and trade was mainly by barter.

He glanced at me questioningly but I fell silent and so he carried on. 'The stars were fadin' when I awoke. I felt chilled by the night air even though wearin' the woollen tunic but all around me was still an' quiet except for the stream chucklin' away. I found a spot in the stream where I could easily bathe and I tell you Mister Peter, that water was damned cold. By the time I'd got dry, fed an' watered the 'orse, and 'ad a bite to eat an' drink, the sky was brightenin'. I'd then to get across the stream but that wasn't so deep that I couldn't manage it where the channel was wider an' shallower, then I was on my way again. Soon after sunrise I was clear of the woods but the way was becomin' hillier and the land risin'.'

'No more bandits, though,' I remarked as he hesitated to take up his drink.

'No more bandits, Mister Peter, just an odd sight of people goin' about their business or tendin' their land so I carried on without further trouble. It was late that day, in cooler air, when I approached the slopes of Mount Parnassus beneath which lay remote Delphi, considered by many to be the centre of the world. There's a stone there, the Omphalos, they clam to be the navel. Many cities and towns 'ave their temples an' others even a treasury there. Some buildin's are in ruins or partly so through occasional earthquakes an' rock slides. By that time, of course, I knew well enough where I was an' took a familiar route along which other visitors were comin' an' goin'. Next I'd to find a place to stay, to stable my faithful 'orse an' to secure the cart and belongin's. I found a suitable lookin' tavern among many others further down the valley from the temple I was to visit. You won't be surprised to learn that because these taverns 'ave a year-round demand from suppliants an' pilgrims able to pay an' needin' somewhere to put up for a few nights, the buggers charge whatever they think they can squeeze out of you, and more. I persuaded 'em though, aye, I persuaded 'em to accept the amount in silver pieces I thought was fair to cover my food, my stay and the proper care of my 'orse.'

I imagined, dear reader, that Heracles' approach in obtaining their agreement was not altogether polite.

'After that' he continued, 'I'd to arrange for my meetin' with the Pythoness or the Pythea as these women were referred to as a group. Whichever of 'em was in attendance at the time 'eld also communication with Apollo, another of the Olympian gods; this one concerned with the promotion of poetry and music. I'd never been keen on poetry myself an' never, havin' killed my teacher, 'ad I truly mastered the lyre. Anyhow, there were two, sometimes three of the women, dependin' upon demand, but this was no easy matter and would take some time as I'd found out all those years before. You didn't just walk in and out, no, you'd need to give three days notice. For a start I went along to the main temple where was to be found the oracle, this situated in a wild and rocky glen. There I was taken before the top priest of Apollo to make my appointment. He knew of me, of course, but made no comment. Maybe he'd 'eard too much. I didn't want to 'ang about three days but it was that or nothin'. Food an' wine served up in the tavern was reasonable enough but then they'd not care to give me cause for complaint.

Durin' those three days I made conversation with other visitors to Delphi, many of who related their own encounters with the Pythoness. Some of 'em appeared satisfied with what they'd been told while others admitted they weren't sure what the answer meant or it contained only vague meanin'. Otherwise I wandered the woodlands beneath Mount Parnassus with the club restin' over my shoulder, though I never met any trouble.

When findin' somewhere quiet to sit I'd listen to the birds and ponder over what I might end up bein' told. Later on in the third full day as I waited by the temple, minus my club, the priest appeared and confirmed the time 'ad arrived for my meetin' the oracle. I already knew I'd need to wear a laurel wreath an' fillets of wool before bein' allowed entry to the inner sanctum because that's what they always insisted on; don't ask me why. A sacrifice would also be demanded so before settin' off I'd

collected my knife an' visited a dealer to find something suitable. There were goats, young deer, other small animals an' various birds to choose from. I selected a goose because it would give me less trouble but whatever I'd chosen would most likely end up as food for the priests.

After this brief but bloody business I was conducted to the temple by another gowned an' cowled priest, a skinny old grey-bearded man who walked with a limp. He would be in direct service to the Pythoness. Before entering the holy of holies the man turned, looked up at me and croaked, "You must keep a respectful distance from her and speak only after *I* have spoken."

'I followed 'im through the stone portal and bein' taller than most men I needed to beware of grazin' my 'ead. From there we descended a short way by steps to a lower level with only modest light filterin' down. Aye, it brought back a few early memories. The air within was warm, still and oddly charged when we stopped before the oracle, the Pythoness 'erself. Here was one of only a few women I'd seen since my arrival at Delphi, though there are a number available for involvement in temple rites. My eyes were soon accustomed to the semi-darkness of this eerie yet most holy of places. I stared up at 'er as the old priest announced in tones that reverberated within the chamber, "The man I bring before you is Heracles, once the defender and hero of Thebes but stricken by the wrath of Hera and cast adrift from the town and all

71

he cherished there. When he has spoken have me gather your words and impart them to him."

Perched very still upon a soft-cushioned tripod of polished bronze, she was young and fair, her slim form draped with a fine diaphanous gown, 'er head partly covered an' over 'er right shoulder a shawl of the same material. I was so taken with the sight of 'er that I could 'ardly get the words out when the priest called on me to speak. It felt now like there was nothin' else in the world beyond the chamber where I stood, as though nothin' but 'er sacred presence mattered. "I - I attempted to slay my wife, Megara," I began, "a woman most dear to me. I killed my own two sons who I also loved but I knew nothin' of it, no, I knew nothin' for many days after until freed from that shroud of insanity cast about me by Hera. I wish to know the path I must take to regain the life that once was mine."

'I tell you, Mister Peter, only once before 'ad I felt so diminished an' that was when madness struck me. I was beggin' to be told my future because I'd nowhere else to go. The Pythoness remained motionless, 'er gaze concentrated upon a bowl that rested in 'er left 'and while in 'er right she 'eld a sprig of laurel taken from a tree sacred to Apollo. As I waited my attention drifted to the narrow crack runnin' across the stone floor beneath the tripod. From this arose tenuous wisps of pale vapour that carried a sweet aroma. And in that otherwise silent chamber I could hear from within the fissure a sound of water runnin' deep below. The girl continued to peer into the bowl as if entranced but now 'er lips were movin'. I'd been told years earlier how the vapour was said to affect the Pythoness, to enhance 'er powers of prediction an' to call forth 'er prophetic utterances. It was said also that the bowl contained a quantity of sacred water from that which on occasion welled up from beneath the ground. Aye, through the gap where the tripod stood. She began to speak; sometimes softly, sometimes barely audible, sometimes in a chantin' voice an' now 'er eyes were closed. The priest, his 'ead tilted back, his eyes closed also, was mouthin' in unison with her. She rocked gently on the tripod, 'er head noddin' from side to side, her voice risin' and fallin' but the tone was no longer hers – no, it was a harsh, gratin' voice I recognised from before the madness took me an' I knew, yes, I knew who it was an' I knew it should not have been there! After a while the Pythoness was silent. She leaned forward, relaxed, as if the pronouncement, obscure an' impossible for me to understand, had been of some effort to 'er. Moments later she was again still an' poised as before in other-worldly contemplation.

"The Pythoness has spoken," declared 'er priest but he must have known it wasn't just her voice we heard. "We are now to leave her presence and I will speak with you outside."

'Have you ever felt, Mister Peter - 'ave you ever felt you're some place where don't want to move? You just want to stand somewhere quiet, to close your eyes, to think an' take in the essence of the place. Then I saw she was lookin' down at me an' I knew I 'ad to go. With much reluctance I followed 'im up into cool, fresh air and a late afternoon sunlight that did nothin' to ease my thoughts. And there, as we stood face to face some way from the temple, castin' long shadows, I asked, "Well what did it all mean? None of it made sense to me."

He looked down a while then stared directly into my face. "To fully redeem yourself," came 'is reply, "you must go to Mycenae and there present yourself to her king, Eurystheus. You must follow his instructions whatever they may be."

"Eurystheus!" I responded. "No I'll not do that! There must be more to what the Pythoness told you. Out with it!"

Heracles fist descended hard upon the table, causing some of the smaller items there to clatter.

'Eurystheus was a weak ruler,' he continued 'one of little consequence in spite of his alleged descent from Perseus. He was kept in power by 'is generals as a figure'ead, though a very convenient one since they ruled in 'is name. As you'll remember, Mister Peter, his birth was brought forward by you-know-who for no other reason than to deny *me* the kingship of Mycenae. To be obligated to such a man was somethin' I could 'ardly bear to think about. The old priest eyed me sternly then added, "Should you choose to disobey what has been revealed then the wife of Almighty Zeus' may once again plunge you into madness." I was tempted to wring 'is skinny neck for sayin' what he did but a voice inside, or maybe it came from outside, persuaded me to think again. I'd go back to the tavern, rest quiet an' consider in the night what'd be best for me to do.'

'I really sympathise, Mister Heracles,' I said; knowing his anger as I picked at the remains of my food. 'It's pretty obvious this was some kind of cruel game Hera was playing.'

'Aye, it *was* a game to 'er - a game of spite pursued for 'er own satisfaction! Athena had done what she could to 'elp me but it seemed even she'd been overruled by Zeus so as to placate 'is bitch of a wife. Then she'd be off his back for a while so he'd be able to get on with what gave 'im most pleasure – makin' it with other women. Anyhow, next mornin' in the tavern I prepared for the journey to Mycenae, takin' care to top up my beer supply. Clearly hopin' to see the back of me, the tavern owner offered to provide a detailed explanation of how best I could get to Mycenae so I'd be gone from 'im all the sooner. I managed a smile as I informed 'im that as I'd made the journey from Mycenae to Thebes years before comin' to Delphi I'd no need of 'is generosity. I checked my cart an' its contents where they'd been secured at the rear of the stable, hitched my 'orse an left Delphi behind. I'd 'ead south-east along the coast of Boeotia thinkin' maybe I'd stop a while at Thespiae, maybe not, but either way I'd reach the town of Plataea south-west of Thebes an' there stay the night.'

'How long altogether would your journey to Mycenae take?' I asked.

'Oh, seven, eight or more days I'd reckoned. I was doin' what was expected of me but no one 'ad

75

placed a time on it so why hurry. After Plataea I took a westerly direction, the only one I could by land, across the fairly level Isthmus of Corinth where at the other side lay the town of that name.'

'No bandits so far, then?'

'No bandits, Mister Peter, no, but on crossin' the Isthmus, a wide and well-trodden route, somethin' strange did 'appen.' He took another drink, thought for some moments then continued. 'I'd not gone too far when I spotted a woman ahead of me, stoopin', carryin' a load on 'er back. I'd seen a good few people that day but as I drew closer she stopped and let slip the canvas bag, droppin' it to the ground as if findin' it too 'eavy. About to pass 'er by I took a closer look. She was no land-begotten, sun-darkened, skin wrinkled peasant ploddin' 'er bare-footed way to who knew where but a paler-skinned, good lookin' young woman with bedraggled black hair an' a look of anguish on 'er face. The gown she wore was that of a city dweller and 'er dusty shoes were never intended for rough ground. I stopped an' asked, "What're you doin' out 'ere and how far are you goin'?"

"I've come from Plataea," she answered with a forced smile that soon was real. "I'm going to Corinth."

"Walkin' all the way to Corinth!" I exclaimed, thinkin', at first there were a number of small villages on the Isthmus to one of which she might have been 'eaded. "Well carryin' that, whatever's in it, you'll not be close to Corinth before darkness. I can go by Corinth easy enough; I can take you there because I'm on my way to Mycenae." My cart had very little spare room but I was ill inclined to leave the woman an' I doubted she'd ever get to where she wanted on 'er own.'

"You're very kind," she responded with 'er smile broadenin'.

'I clambered out of the cart and 'elped her on board to where she could sit on a wooden box containin' valuables of my own then I found a space for the bag she'd been carryin'. What it contained I couldn't see because it was knotted shut with a cord. My bow and arrows an' my spear would've been visible to 'er in the cart but my club was out of sight beneath other stuff. When I was back up there with the reins in my grasp an' the cart rumblin' on I turned to ask 'er, "How come you're on your own tryin' to walk all this way? It's too far – didn't you know that?"

"Because I have to, that is all."

"Very well then, if it's none of my business I'll not ask again. There's beer in those two jars and a cup somewhere down there. If you're thirsty, dip in an' 'elp yourself."

"I'm sorry," she said, looking up at me with tears in her dark, engagin' eyes, "I will tell you. I left my home through fear. My father wanted me to marry a man who I detested because this man's wealth was considered important to our family. My father is a violent man and threatened me with harm if I continued to disobey him. I left his house this morning well before the sky began to lighten and started on my way with clothes and those few possessions dear to me that I was able to carry. My father has horses, servants and slaves but no one would have dared defy him by agreeing to help me escape. I have an old friend in Corinth who knows what my father is like and she will keep me safe."

"Then it's fortunate I was passin' by."

"Yes, very fortunate. And what, sir, takes you to Mycenae?"

"Oh, it's a personal matter," I answered, "it'd be of no interest to you." We didn't talk for a while after that but I'd already told her to keep an eye open for anyone on horseback who might be followin' us. I'd know how to deal with 'em if that 'appened. Aye, Mister Peter, she was a beautiful woman, that I didn't doubt, but oddly, I felt I could never 'ave felt desire for 'er. As for touching 'er - again, no, I'd not want to do that either.

It was late in the day when we approached Corinth, seein' first the Acrocorinthus, the great rock that towered above the city as a citadel. We close approached the nearest entrance in the city wall where I reined in the 'orse an' turned to ask the girl if this was a good place to leave her. She didn't answer but was already climbin' down from the cart with 'er bag. Steppin' away she turned to look up at me, her face illuminated by the lowering sun, an' said, "Farewell Heracles." Her face bore a smile that was no smile of gratitude. It struck me as more one of triumph. Had she 'eard enough about me to have guessed my name? Maybe she 'ad but I knew I'd not mentioned it. And 'er expression – that partin' smile! It bothered me. I watched her walk

78

away to enter the city gate but she never looked back.'

'Had you not asked her name?' I queried.

He remained in deep thought for a while then replied, 'No, it never occurred to me. I hoped for a time it might've been Athena 'erself but why in the guise of such an unfortunate woman with such an unlikely tale – then there was 'er expression. No, it was not Athena. The ideas came an' went but maybe one day I thought I'd figure things out or somethin' would 'appen. I'm inclined now, talkin' of it to you, to believe it was Hera wantin' to gloat as I 'eaded on my way to meet Eurystheus.'

'I think, Mister Heracles, it was who you now suggest and that she'd influenced your mind with her powers.'

'Hm, maybe you're right. Well I wouldn't reach Mycenae before dark but there were many taverns not far from the city wall that surrounded the core of the town. I found one that suited my purpose with a place for my 'orse and cart. From the landlord I hired a slave, a big man from somewhere south of Egypt, to take good care of these for as long as I needed an' promised 'im silver to do that. Takin' my club and silver with me I joined others in the tavern for a bite to eat and earned myself a few odd but silent looks - then I went up to the room where I managed some sleep.

I'd not covered the window so when I woke up I could see the stars were not altogether faded. By the time I'd readied myself and eaten, the sun was just risen but the sky was streaked with thin cloud. I now 'ad to make my way into Mycenac. D'you know anythin' about Mycenae, Mister Peter?'

'Not very much,' I answered, though I was familiar with printed reconstructions of the city and thought I knew quite a bit about it. But I wanted to hear and to record a contemporary description in his own words.

'Well,' he began, 'Mycenae I knew was the most powerful city in the Peloponnese. It occupied a steep rise amid a fertile plain; it was easily defended an' well positioned to control routes to an' from the sea. Its formidable walls, with an inner walkway around most of the city, consisted of great irregular stones that they liked to tell visitors were constructed by the Cyclopes, giant men with only one eye in the middle of their 'eads. But I say not. I say ordinary men built those walls like only ordinary men build everythin' else. Have some more beer.'

'Oh, thanks,' I replied as he tipped enough into my goblet to spill over the rim.

'I set off up the steep hill on foot, approachin' Mycenae from the north because on that side stood the main gate. There were many people, most with their goods an' wares, passin' the same way, all with lots of chatter, an' a small number of others comin' out. There were children playin' about an' birds circlin' overhead. There were small groups of armed men watchin' it all an' keepin' an eye open for trouble. These each wore an 'elmet made of bronze or from interlockin' boar's tusks stitched onto a leather cap, an' each carried a spear. Maybe you've 'eard of armed men like that.'

'Yes,' I answered as he picked up his goblet, 'it can't have been too good a time for boars though, can it.' I realised as I spoke that perhaps I ought not say any more as he went on.

'Most merchants an' farmers lived outside the city whereas those people with influence lived inside. Anyhow, this main entrance was known as the Lion Gate because above it an enormous stone slab supported a carvin' of two lions, one standin' either side to support one of those downward taperin' columns – same style as you saw outside 'ere. I passed beneath the Lion Gate with the guard'ouse to my left. To my right as I ascended the great ramp was a big grave circle where'd been buried the worthies of Mycenae in earlier days. The ramp passed up toward the south of the city where it swung left to approach the acropolis an' there at its summit stood the royal palace. Guards positioned outside the entrance eyed me an' the club with stony expressions an' crossed their spears to prevent me goin' any further. When I informed 'em I was expected by King Eurystheus they summoned a slave to go an' tell 'im. When the slave returned with 'is message they insisted I leave my club with them before they'd let me through. This took some doin' as I was reluctant to go without it. But I'd no choice when two more armed guards were called upon to escort me further inside.

The palace buildin', where was located the megaron, the great hall an' social heart of the palace, was approached by a grand staircase. I recalled from my early years how the whole place struck me as a dazzlin' fantasy. Having passed between a pair of brightly painted columns I stood before the megaron. This was an extensive flagstoned area where every surface of its walls was colourfully decorated with geometrical designs but where greater space permitted, mainly the walls, with images of livin' creatures from land and sea. These in turn were interspaced with arms and armour captured from Mycenae's enemies durin' 'er frequent conflicts an' wars. Toward the far end a square entablature was supported by a further four columns. Above these the ceilin' was open to the sky but directly below lay a great circular hearth from which smoke from burnin' logs arose. Beyond this stood the scalloped marble throne upon which sat the fancily robed King Eurystheus lookin' more like a peacock than a man. Close by 'im were grouped three guards and a number of gowned officials, some also armed, who appeared more dignified or purposeful by far than did Eurystheus. Seein' them I'd no doubt who was really in control at Mycenae. When I'd walked around the hearth one of these men approached me with hand raised an' said, "Remain standing where you are and when you are called to step forward you must do so and bow before our king. You will say nothing until he addresses you, then you in turn will address him as Your Majesty."

'I tell you, Mister Peter, I could 'ave swung a fist an' busted 'is jaw but I 'eld back thinkin' it'd be better to get this over with an' know what awaited me. One of those standin' next to the fancy man's throne raised 'is 'and, gesturin' me with a wrigglin' finger to approach. I did so slowly while lookin' straight at the one perched on the throne. Eurystheus was watery-eyed, even paler than you are with dark 'air pokin' out from underneath a kind of jewel encrusted domed crown that 'ad a red plume droopin' on top. He'd no sign of a beard an' 'is cheek bones were prominent. Worse, though, aye, what I saw then was that he 'ad lip-colourin' an' make-up more like a woman. I was tryin' not to let my expression give away my feelin's when the bugger spoke. He might've been my age but still 'ad not the voice of a grown man as he said, "Ah, who do we have before us – Heracles is it not, the greatest hero ever to walk our land; am I correct?"

'I managed only a bow of my 'ead while sayin' in as measured a voice as I could, "Thank you, your majesty; how fortunate I am to find myself standin' before one such as you." My thoughts were quite different an' went somethin' like, "I'd like to cut yer balls off if you've got any, fry 'em an' make you eat 'em." Then I imagined if I dashed up to 'im an' bawled into 'is ear how he'd most likely shit 'imself before the guards could step in. Just as well he didn't know what was in my mind an' I was careful to aim my gaze downward so he wouldn't get the idea. I swear, though, out of the corner of my eye I noticed one of the guards lookin' fondly at 'im - if you know what I mean.'

'Just as well you remained as calm as you did, Mister Heracles,' I remarked as he gulped his beer. 'I do understand how angry you must've felt.'

'His tarted-up majesty summoned over a robed an' cowled, stern-faced woman who'd been standin' alone by a column. In 'er 'ands she held a rolled-up parchment. This she offered to me, sayin' in almost a whisper, "I am a priestess of Hera and I am summoned by our king to present this to you. The king holds another parchment identical to it. I assume that if you are unable to read then you will have someone to do it for you. You must come and speak with me as soon as you have left here."

'She turned and swept off around the hearth with 'er robe billowin' then Eurystheus said, "It is my command that you take upon yourself the twelve labours set out on the parchment you have been given. I of course will need proof of each task when it is completed. You may now leave us and prepare for what is demanded of you."

'He reached out an arm an' with hand palm down, waved his bejewelled fingers dismissively to indicate that I should depart the royal presence. Well that was a quick visit after all the trouble I'd taken to get there so clutchin' the parchment I turned my back on the arrogant bugger an' left the megaron.'

'But why,' I asked, 'did one of Hera's priests not deliver the message to you directly?' though I'd realised perhaps why before he answered.

'Yes, Mister Peter, that was to belittle me by havin' to first obey the call of someone as unworthy as Eurystheus - no more than a puppet who'd occupied the place of kingship that should all those years before 'ave been mine. And there was much worse to come, as I was about to discover. I 'eaded off at once to Hera's temple, within the city wall an' not far from the palace. I located the priestess who took me aside into a private chapel.'

"You will have gathered," she said, "that after each of these labours you must return to Mycenae and go before Eurystheus as he says with proof that you have succeeded.'

'Aye, this'd been determined by Hera. That sad bastard Eurystheus was there to make it sound official an' believed by all that it was only *him* I was obeyin'. I stood lost for words then she added, "In the end, our great goddess assures me she will require nothing more of you." I took that to mean I might not get through in one piece all that was expected of me but what alternative did I 'ave. Knowin' what Hera was capable of I asked, "And if in the end I do succeed - what then?"

"Should you do so then glory will be yours and Almighty Zeus may grant you the ultimate gift."

'Well that sounded to me like Zeus' damned wife *was* certain I'd never make it. I returned to the tavern with my parchment of destiny an' there, with a good supply of wine set by, I studied it until the wine took me over. Just as fortunate, I thought, that all of it was on parchment and not inscribed on clay tablets like almost everythin' else that needed to be written down.'

The MAN I Really Was

Heracles closed his eyes, relaxed back in his seat for a time then sat up to look at me, saying, 'The sun's pretty well overhead; I'll call for food and maybe we'll eat in the shade. What say you, Mister Peter?'

"Yes, fine by me," I agreed, while before my eyes drifted a fleeting image of gammon ham, two eggs, chips and fresh garden peas. Just a thought.

Chapter 5 - The Lion and The Hydra

We'd finished our food, a generous meal, main one of the day that included skewered lamb which I didn't mind at all and of course, olives. It was a meal Heracles relished with a degree of drama, helping it down with copious amounts of beer then wiping his mouth and soiled beard on the edge of his gown. As I'd discovered the previous evening when his table manners were less demonstrative in the presence of the Egyptian girls, serviettes, or whatever their equivalent might have been, seemed not to feature at mealtimes even in the Elysian Fields. I fished discreetly in my pocket to lift out my handkerchief. After this modest diversion he proceeded with his account.

'I was up before sunrise that cool and pleasant mornin' an' havin' eaten I sat to gaze at the parchment, takin' in what I was to attempt for my initial labour. The first six of these were located within the Peloponnese with all but the very last somewhere else. In the light of day I pondered over the whole thing; my visit to Delphi and the decision given by the oracle through the Pythoness, all under the influence of Hera, followed by its interpretation by the priest. There was that strange woman I'd picked up on the way to Mycenae then my appearin' before Eurystheus, a man who I could have picked up an' thrown from the city wall with pleasure. What I was up against could be, on the face of it beyond any man, maybe includin' me. So what if I tore up the parchment an' threw it away – what then? You see, Mister Peter, there were many who knew of my prowess, many who'd value my services to 'elp 'em sort out difficulties with their neighbours an' I'd once again 'ave an acceptable life. But no I wouldn't. S*he* would be waitin', crouchin' like 'ungry beast in the night until I was most vulnerable in my sleep, then she'd pounce as she did in Thebes. Zeus 'ad given 'er rein an' she was determined to make the most of it. The way I saw it, I might as well die in some conflict, some challenge or other than 'ave my mind taken over again.'

Heracles became silent and pensive, during which time I thought back to the references I'd consulted about his alleged life. The ancient authors who set it down, both Greek and Roman, were writing many centuries after Heracles' day and we all know how, without solid evidence, imagination, wistful thinking and fantasies will expand to fill the gaps, with the various writers contradicting one another. That might be seen as how, closer to our own times, mainstream religions have developed. My attention returned as Heracles began once more to speak.

'Aye, Mister Peter, I'd wavered, but in the end I determined I'd go ahead. First though, I'd visit the temple of Athena, which lay on lower ground outside the city. An' even though the goddess might be subject to the will of Zeus Almighty, 'er advice an' whatever 'elp she might offer, even given through her priestess, would be a consolation of sorts. I headed over to the temple, made an offerin' in silver at 'er shrine, before her elder priest who seemed to know what had been goin' on but all she could say was, "I have spoken with the lady Athena and she often will be with you."

'It didn't seem much at the time but consoled by that visit I returned to the tavern where I prepared the 'orse an' cart so as to get on my way. For my first challenge I was to 'ead to Nemea, a valley not so far away to the south-west of Corinth, so within easy reach from Mycenae. There, so it was rumoured, a larger lion than anyone ever saw – well it'd 'ave to be, wouldn't it - was terrifyin' the area, and 'ad defied all attempts to kill it by any weapon of bronze.

I travelled through that hot day until late in the afternoon I reached Nemea an' the village of Cleonae where I stopped to speak with a ragged lookin' peasant by the name of Molorchus who didn't smell too good, though I'd find out why later. Once I'd declared my intentions 'e offered to water my 'orse an' invited me into 'is hut where the smell 'ad me oldin' my breath. In the semi-darkness I noticed animal skins layin' in one corner. He informed me how this lion was ravagin' the countryside, takin' people's sheep an' cows, an' earlier that very year 'ad killed his grandson one night while the boy was on his way to offer sacrifice at Hera's shrine. The lion, so he informed me, was as big an' as fierce as people claimed an' he'd seen it 'imself though as he confessed, only from some considerable distance. It lived alone, was quite old, so he thought, an' occupied a cave in nearby Mount Tretus. He explained to me how I might get some way to the cave with my cart. It was too late in the day for me to do anythin' of the sort so I thanked the man, stepped out into fresh air an' made my way to the only tavern in the village.'

'Had you not told this Molorchus who you were?' I queried.

'No an' he'd not asked. Anyway, the tavern was such a hovel of a place that I decided to accept what food they 'ad to offer then after stablin' the horse, make my bed some distance outside, close to the cart, which I could then keep an eye on.'

'But was that not taking a risk, Mister Heracles?' I asked. 'What I mean is with this lion wandering around at night and feeling hungry.'

'Aye, Mister Peter, maybe it was a risk but I'd keep my spear an' club within easy reach an' nearby was a geese pen. If the lion or anythin' else turned up I expected their panickin' would alert me soon enough.'

So Heracles really was that night, as well as next day, prepared to confront the lion alone. I was duly impressed.

'I slept well an' woke up with the birds singin' and the sun shinin' from behind the 'ills. As when I'd slept out before, there was a stream nearby, though not much of one. Still, it was enough to 'ave me fresh and clean.'

'Very commendable,' I remarked. 'Where I come from, keeping clean is also regarded as important, at least for most of us.'

'Aye, well,' he responded, eyeing me up and down, 'when fightin' for Thebes I'd often need a good scrub-down to rid me-self of sweat an' blood – my sweat an' other men's blood, if y'see my meanin'.'

I offered an encouraging nod and he went on, 'I 'ad my 'orse pull the cart as close to this Mount Tretus as the rocky ground would allow then I carried on to where old Molorchus said the lion lived. I wasn't able to carry bow an' arrows, spear an' club all at the same time so thinkin' they'd be of little use if the lion came boundin' at me I left bow an' arrows in the cart.

Ahead of me, away from the grass, in a slopin' rock wall was a cleft almost the 'eight of a man, quite wide and as it was facin' away from the sun it looked to be utterly black within. I stepped up closer, laid aside club an' spear, picked up a large stone an' hurled it into the cave, hearin' it clatter an' echo within the blackness as I took up the spear. For a time nothin' 'appened until all of a sudden the beast sprang out into daylight an' stopped to stare as if surprised at the very sight of me. It shook its 'ead, tore the air with its roar an' pounded straight at me with burnin' fire in its eyes an' its teeth bared gleamin' white with fangs like daggers. Aye it was big, lithe an' I tell you, Mister Peter, it didn't look old to me. And I was to be its next meal! I crouched low with the spear levelled an' dashed forward to meet it intendin' to ram the blade into its gapin' mouth before it leapt on me. The lion turned suddenly to avoid this but I charged on to thrust the spear into its side. The spear pulled free as it spun about with eyes ablaze an' jaws wide to go for me again, roarin', scatterin' small stones as we circled one-another in a crazy dance of death. But maybe Athena was with me because this time, as it prepared to leap, I drove the blade 'ard an' deep into its mouth until it was stopped by bone. I was almost thrown to the ground but I quickly recovered, seized an' wrenched the spear free. With a piercing snarl the lion backed off, leapt about an' looked as if at any moment it was to take another dash at me an' wasn't ready to die. Then it spun around an' around until fallin' onto its side where it growled, jerked an' writhed before finally, choked on its own blood, it lay still. I stood an' waited to make sure it was dead - but it surely was. I collected up my club an' with the bloodied spear I returned to the cart. This I managed to back up close to the lion an' from it I pulled a good length of rope. One end I attached to the cart itself then 'oped I'd enough to enclose an' secure about the lion's body. There was enough so I led the 'orse, pullin' cart an' lion slowly back to Molorchus' hut where he stood in amazement gapin' in turn at the lion then at me.

I'd got plans though but I wasn't at all sure how to go about what I 'ad in mind. I'd need proof of what I'd done but I wanted also to make full use of the skin an' told 'im so. Luck was with me there, Mister Peter, because I'd expressed my thoughts to the right man. He agreed there and then, if I wanted, and if I'd pay 'im, how he could get to work on the lion an' do what was needed. He confirmed what I'd already guessed from the smell of 'im how he was somethin' of an expert at skinnin' an' took 'is cow hides to the tanners where he 'elped transform 'em into leather. I agreed I'd 'ave 'im do it so Molorchus went off to collect 'is means of carryin' out the job. When he returned we dragged the lion down to a level bank by the stream an' layin' it out, Molorchus began 'is work, cuttin' into its guts with a bronze knife. It was a long an' messy business but I'll not go into the details now.'

'Oh, thanks for that,' I muttered.

'Are there many lions where you live, Mister Peter?'

'Not many nowadays.' I answered, 'just the odd one.'

'What'd puzzled Molorchus when he'd got started was the spear wound in the lion's side. "That doesn't look enough to kill a lion outright," he remarked while peelin' aside the skin. "How did you..."

"Strangled it!" I responded without a thought. I might 'ave told 'im the truth but he stopped what he was doin', eyed me up an' down with a look of disbelief then finally asked, "Who are you, sir? No man, even a man of your size an' strength could 'ope to strangle such a beast unless you're – unless you're a man I've 'eard much about called 'Eracles."

"I *am* Heracles," I informed 'im, thinkin' I'd say nothin' about how I'd really done for the lion. I'd let him an' anyone he spoke to think what I'd told him was true an' I'd no doubt the word would spread, especially as I was known of one way or another throughout much of the Peloponnese. It was late in the day when Molorchus 'ad finished an' the skin lay separated on the ground. What could be washed away went into the stream an' what couldn't be we'd leave there for night-time scavengers. I bathed an' washed myself upstream before we left. The skin would take many days to clean an' dry but it was overall a long process. I promised the man he'd be paid well in silver if he'd do whatever was necessary. I returned to the tavern where I demanded the owner's room. He could sleep where he put 'is guests an' maybe learn a thing or two about 'ospitality.

Eager to see the skin finished I kept 'old of my tavern room in Cleonae for many days longer than I cared to count. Aye, far too many. I'd retained my cart but at times I'd ride out with the local men on one of their own 'orses to check their herds an' drive off or shoot at any predators we encountered. Good practice with the bow an' arrows that was, Mister Peter. In between times I'd ride back to Mycenae an' spend a day or so there, drinkin' more than I ought with others I'd got to know while takin' advantage of the ladies on offer at night. It all 'elped to pass the time.'

'Was there no time limit imposed upon you?' I asked him.

'I 'oped not,' he answered. 'That lion skin I was determined to 'ave. I was back in Cleonae when Molorchus turned up early one mornin' with the finished skin. I marvelled at the job he'd done. I pulled it on, it was quite 'eavy, and - well, you already know what it looks like. When I peered at 'im through the jaws the poor old bugger was speechless but once he'd recovered an' with my prized skin stowed away in the cart, he begged me to offer sacrifice to Zeus with 'im at their modest shrine, which I did. It was the only shrine in the village.

After this, I departed, leavin' him with the two dead geese an' well rewarded as I'd promised. I continued on to Mycenae but arrived too late to call upon the great Eurystheus. Instead I dealt with the 'orse an' cart then took myself to the tavern outside the city where I'd originally stayed. There I 'ad food an' beer an' spent my time there thinkin' over what'd passed that day an' might pass the followin' one.

'Next mornin' after I'd eaten, I took up the lion skin an' carryin' it over one arm I made my way to the palace where I announced myself to the guards who remembered me from my previous visit. When one of 'em hurried off to inform Eurystheus that I'd shown up I stepped aside an' pulled the skin completely over myself until I was gapin' through the jaws. It gave the guards somethin' to think about but right then they weren't inclined to object. They stood well back then followed in silence as I made my way into the megaron. I carried on around the great hearth an' approached Eurystheus who stared 'ard, squirmin' on his arse and grippin' the sides of his throne like he wanted to shuffle it backwards. So uncomfortable did he look that two of 'is guards stepped out to prevent me gettin' any nearer. The rest of those gathered there were lookin' 'ard at me and at each other then they started voicin' comments. The guards in front of me moved aside to give Eurystheus a better view but they kept their spears crossed in front of me.'

"Let him come a little closer," announced his glorious majesty, at last tryin' to appear as if he was in charge and risin' from his seat as I grinned at 'im through the open jaws. His courtiers ceased chatterin' an' now stared in silence. "So, er, yes," he declared in an uncertain manner, "you appear to have succeeded in your first task. May we - yes, may we congratulate you but require now that you continue at once on your way to the next." He waved his copy of the parchment at me then concluded, "You had no prior appointment with us and we now have other matters needing our attention."

'Eurystheus 'ad obviously found my appearance most unsettlin' an' that suited me. I turned to go but didn't on this occasion benefit from a dismissive wave of the royal 'and. I left the way I'd entered, slippin' off the lion skin as I emerged into daylight. I was strollin' down the ramp towards the Lion Gate when someone walkin' up the other way, a tidy-haired, beardless youth attired in the formal, belted tunic of a noble caught my attention, and I his. We stopped to face one another an' he exclaimed, "Uncle Heracles – it's you!"

"Iolaus!" I cried, graspin' 'is arm, "What're you doin' in Mycenae?"

"I'm here in the city to discuss minor matters with Eurystheus and his happy lot then I meet with a group of merchants later. And you? I well understood all about the disaster that had befallen you but I was away from the town for many days afterwards, then I heard you'd left Thebes for Delphi. And that hanging over your arm – it looks like a - ."

"It's lion skin!" I laughed. "Aye, that's what it is. Now then Iolaus, meetin' you 'as cheered me up no end. Can we talk soon?"

"Yes, we must do that. I'll not waste too much time with Eurystheus as seeing him is little more than a formality, so why not later this morning? This afternoon, as I say, I have to be elsewhere."

"Aye, later this mornin', before midday, 'ere in town at the Poseidon tavern – d'you know it? I'll meanwhile return to the tavern outside the wall where I'm stayin' an' I'll leave the skin there."

"Indeed I do know the Poseidon," he grinned, slapping my shoulder, "before midday, then."

'So we parted for a while and I was mightily pleased over our encounter. We may have appeared an odd pair to the Mycenaeans. Iolaus was your build an' almost as pale with me towerin' over 'im by a head.'

'What rare good fortune that was, Mister Heracles,' I said as he lifted the beer to his mouth and I helped myself to the last honey-topped wheat cake.

'Aye, Mister Peter, and more than just good fortune as it turned out. We met as arranged at the inn where we took food an' drink an' I 'ad the parchment with me. As we sat opposite one another, Iolaus wanted to know everything that'd 'appened to me since I'd left Thebes an' what'd brought me to Mycenae, but I insisted he first tell me what'd been going on back there. Not anythin' of great importance as it turned out but people still discussed what'd become of me an' the death of my sons at the 'and of their own father.

When it was my turn to speak, Iolaus leaned forward bright-eyed an' eager to know all. I described how I'd seen off the three bandits then I explained all about my encounter with the Pythoness an' the interpretation given me at Delphi. I told 'im about the strange woman I'd encountered on 'er way to Corinth and 'ow I'd stood before Eurystheus then been given the parchment settin' out the twelve labours created by Hera. My subsequent encounter with the Nemean lion an' old Molorchus who did such a fine job of preparin' its skin had Iolaus quite fascinated an' at times 'ighly amused. He unrolled the parchment an' read through it carefully before lookin' up to say, "Heracles, some of these challenges look ridiculous; I have to wonder if the one who prepared this knew what they were really letting you in for."

"Maybe so," I agreed, "but each one's to be pursued to avoid that damned woman cursin' me with madness again. I somehow 'ave to get around to it all then I'll be free of 'er for good, or so I'm promised."

'Iolaus was quiet for a while then looked up to say, "I'd like to be with you some of the time, Heracles; I'm willing to lay aside my other plans and I'll be by your side as I was when we were out hunting or facing a common enemy."

"Iolaus," I responded, clutchin' 'is arm, "I could wish for no other companion than you but it may bring a greater danger to both of us."

"A greater danger – how?"

"That bitch who looks down on me," I replied, "she may lay a curse on us both as a punishment for your offer an' for my acceptance. That I surely cannot risk."

'He rolled up the parchment an' pushed it across the table to me, sayin', "No, Heracles, we must think about this – really we must. Now look, as you know, I have other affairs to deal with this afternoon but will be in Mycenae overnight and at a loose end early tomorrow morning. Will you be here also?"

"Aye, I'll be at the tavern an' thinkin' over my next move."

"Then we'll both be able to sleep on it, won't we. Meanwhile, what say we take ourselves about the city for the little time I have left now and discuss your affairs further next day?"

'I saw no 'arm in that but I felt there could be little chance of my acceptin' 'is offer without callin' down retribution. The sun was low when we parted company, havin' arranged when and where we'd meet next day. I returned to my tavern where I studied the parchment further, keepin' it before me after nightfall with only oil lamps to see by. After a while the whole thing seemed meanin'less so I laid it aside, I slept an' I dreamed.

The walls all about me were gone. A young woman appeared, lit by the light of a full moon, fair-skinned an' with strikin' blue eyes that appeared to glow softly. On 'er head she wore a plumed war 'elmet an' in 'er hand she grasped a spear. It was Athena! Ayr, it was Athena in one of 'er many guises! All about 'er fell silent bolts of lightnin' that vanished as she spoke in a sweet voice that drifted over me. "Heracles, hear what I am to tell you. I have spoken with mighty Zeus who rules above all. I have prevailed upon him to offer you modest consideration throughout the dangers you are to face. Let Iolaus be with you whenever he is able. Hera may follow but she will not see and she will not hear him. She will be oblivious to his presence." Darkness returned and I slept on, contented.'

'Marvellous, Mister Heracles!' I responded. 'Athena had come to your aid as you hoped she might.'

'It would seem so an' it meant I'd gladly take young Iolaus up on his offer. Over a bite to eat I once again studied my instructions. My next labour was titled, The Lernaean Hydra. About Lerna itself I knew little, except that it situated on a river of that name some way south of Mycenae. With the details in mind I set off from my tavern in warm mornin' sunlight and 'eaded along the path leadin' up to the city. In case you're wonderin' about my club and the lion skin, Mister Peter, let me tell you -.'

'It did cross my mind, Mister Heracles, yes.'

'Well I didn't want to attract undue attention so I left both in the tavern. Anyhow, I reached the Lion Gate to find Iolaus already waitin' there.'

"You're smiling!" he declared as I drew close. "Does that mean you're to accept my offer?"

"Aye it does, so let's get ourselves a beer so we can talk over what next we do."

'We sat facin' one another in the tavern an' I said, "This Hydra that's causin' problems at Lerna – I'm supposed to kill the thing. I know little or nothin' of it so we'll need to go there an' find out more."

"Fine – you'll be well enough armed, Heracles, and so will I, and I also possess armour, something, as I recall, you never felt you needed."

'Iolaus was right, Mister Peter, I never felt the need for armour; it can get in the way of swingin' a club or castin' a spear. But as we discussed the task ahead at Lerna, thoughts of what later was to come were on my mind an' I said, "What bothers me right now is when I think of the distances I later must travel to accomplish what's expected of me. I've pondered over 'ow long all of this might take. Some places mentioned on the parchment are scattered throughout the Peloponnese but' others, almost 'alf of 'em, are so distant it'll take months to get there an' back by land an' sea. Then each time I've to

101

take before that bastard Eurystheus proof of what I've done." Iolaus was silent. I stared into my beer for a while then added, "I've tried not to think about it, unless Hera -."

"Unless Hera - what?" he asked.

"Unless she 'ad some of the dangers confront me in the realms of sleep yet still be of real consequence when I awoke. What I'm sayin' is that should I fail my challenge, even in a dream, then Hera's ultimate revenge would still be my lot. After all, the gods can make us think the unreal is real an' what is real isn't real at all. Zeus' dear wife 'ad me slay those closest to me without me knowin' of it until I awoke."

Well, dear reader, perhaps you'll imagine how that conversation had my own thoughts hopping about.

"Heracles," Iolaus shrugged, "there's nothing to be gained for now by thinking about those future tasks is there. Anyway, you were not dreaming when those awful events in Thebes took place – you were not the real Heracles. And as for your first challenge, you made short work of that didn't you, so let's see what we can accomplish together this time as we once did at Thebes. And Lerna is nothing like the distance you travelled to Delphi, is it."

'There was youthful enthusiasm for you, Mister Peter, and Iolaus put me to shame when I ought to 'ave been ready to get a move-on. "Very well then," I said, "I believe Lerna to be around three times the distance south of Mycenae that Nemea 'ad been to the north, an' that's far enough at present. I suggest we get ourselves two strong 'orses an' a good sized two-man chariot made for rugged lands. I'll 'ave most of what I don't need to take left safe at Athena's temple." At this suggestion he grinned, prodded his fist against my chest an' declared, "Good man! We can organise ourselves later today and leave tomorrow morning, can we not. Meanwhile I will secure a room for you at my own tavern. This will be more convenient for both of us." We availed ourselves of more beer then turned our attention to a group of girls in the corner who looked ready for our attention.'

That, dear reader, had me wondering now about Tiye and Mayet. Would I engage with them again this evening? I was also concerned about my voice recorder. I couldn't check the thing in front of Heracles so I had to wait until he'd left the table to relieve himself. It was running well enough but before resuming conversation tomorrow I would need to place it in direct sunlight to allow recharging. I was thrusting the thing hurriedly back into my shirt pocket when he returned to continue his tale.

'The next day we met at the stables outside the city wall where that previous afternoon I'd traded in my 'orse an' paid in silver for a handsome pair of strong brown ones. These I took to the builder an' trader of chariots situated close by where Iolaus waited. There he'd already obtained a plain, unadorned but spacious two-wheeled chariot, not built for speed or the transport of warriors into battle but suited more for travel over long distances an' the carriage of our belongin's. With the 'orses hitched to its centre pole, we were soon to set off with everythin' we needed to take.'

'I trust you remembered your club, Mister Heracles,' I quipped.

'Yes, Mister Peter,' he responded, gulping his beer, 'of course I remembered it, together with my sword, bow an' arrows and a couple of spears, oh, and an axe. Iolaus, well armed, also 'ad with 'im a bronze breast plate an' white plumed 'elmet. As you know, through the power of Mycaenae there was, unlike most of Greece, less chance of meetin' trouble anywhere around the Peloponnese. But as I'd done earlier when goin' alone to Delphi, we'd still consider the possibility. Sometime after we set off we found ourselves crossin' hilly country. There were trails of course, the odd hamlet, some deserted, but we encountered no trouble. So when late in the day we approached Lerna and the river of that name we found ourselves a grove of trees, tethered the 'orses an made camp there.

At sunrise the next day we were hitched up an' headin' into Lerna, a modest town close to a marshy area in a part of which, as it turned out, the Hydra was reputed to lurk. We approached a largish hut from within which a gabble of conversation drifted. There we pulled up, stepped from the chariot and entered to ask about the creature they were said to fear an' to learn from them where it might be found. I had the club over my shoulder but not wantin' to scare the wits out of 'em I'd left the lion skin at the chariot which we ensured would remain visible from the open door. The place was dark, full of loungers, peasants with seemingly little to do. It reeked of stale sweat an' worse. They stared at us with suspicion, as if we'd arrived there to lay 'ands on whatever they owned – which couldn't have been much. "We've come to Lerna to find an' deal with the Hydra," I announced.

"This is what we intend to do," agreed sword-tapping Iolaus with a smile I felt I ought to match.

For a time they shuffled about, mutterin' to each other before one man turned his grimy face to us. "Oh, come to get rid of the 'Ydra 'ave you; well let's 'ope you do."

"Someone needs to get rid of it don't they," added another an' by then we 'ad their full attention.

"Crawls out at night it does," put in a third, "aye, out of the marsh it comes to 'elp itself to our sheep an' cattle. We're ruined we are for fear of it; not enough to sell an' too little to proper feed ourselves or our families."

"It lives close to where the river enters the marsh," offered one man.

'Again a silence then the first man said, "Some 'ave seen it an' they say it's got more than one 'ead – five maybe."

"More than that!" cried another from the rear of the ragged group. "An' if one's cut off then more grow in it's place!"

"Fine," Iolaus responded, "so one of you here must know where it lives – yes."

"Maybe I do," said the first man. "I'll show you the place."

'We followed 'im out to where he stood starin' at the 'orses an' chariot then as we climbed aboard he set off in the direction we'd been goin' then turned to the right along a beaten path that approached the river Lerna. Before reachin' it he stopped, pointed ahead an' informed us, "See where the river widens; over there is marshland an' in it you see an island, right?"

"We see it," I said.

"Well that's where they say it comes from," he declared. "Around there somewhere, right."

"Who says?" asked Iolaus.

"The ones that's seen it," he answered.

"Then go back now," Iolaus told him, "and tell your friends we'll wait for the thing."

"Aye, do that," I added "an' maybe later on we'll 'ave good news for you." Without another word the man turned an' proceeded back leisurely the way we'd come. We stepped from the chariot and Iolaus said, "It strikes me none of them have seen anything at all except for dead animals of their own and they're too afraid to stay around at night to protect them. Could be it's wild animals doing for their sheep and cows."

"Maybe someone's put into their minds what they think is doin' it," I suggested. "If so I can guess who that might be. But one of 'em must 'ave seen somethin' an' we've got to assume this Hydra exists because it's what I'm supposed to do away with. Perhaps it came up the river from out of the sea as

106

that's not so far away." We decided to explore the area at length before returnin' later that day to where the man had left us.'

"If the water's not too deep," said Iolaus, "we could make our way across to that island and see what's to be found. We have enough food and beer to spend the rest of today and tonight there."

"And it looks to me," I added, "like there's enough scrub over there for us to make a fire."

As Heracles replenished our beer I recalled hearing how by one method a fire could be made without the use of matches or some kind of artificial lighter. They'd have a small bow with its string coiled tightly about a pointed stick. They would jerk the bow quickly back and forth with the stick shoved down hard against a small block of dry wood with kindling packed around it. With a bit of effort, friction would cause the kindling to set alight. Basic but it seems to have been effective.

'You look thoughtful, my friend,' said Heracles, peering at me. 'You takin' all this in?'

'I most definitely am, Mister Heracles,' I assured him, raising my beaker. As for the recorder, I hoped my faith in modern technology was not misplaced.

'Then let me tell you, we tested the water where the river was widest an' found it wasn't too deep to get the chariot across. There was a breeze comin' off the sea further down but the water was flowin' calm. Once across we found the island plenty large enough to keep our 'orses and chariot in good order, an' to make ourselves a decent camp.

We noted how the grassy surface 'ad been disturbed in places by somethin' or other but couldn't say what that might be. I managed to make us a fire and as a precaution Iolaus prepared in advance a rough firebrand.'

"What if nothing happens?" Iolaus asked as we sat and prepared to eat.

"Somethin' 'as to, doesn't it," I replied. "After all, the woman wouldn't mind seein' me dead long before I've done what she had that bugger Eurystheus demand of me." As darkness fell we sat an' talked over old times; about huntin' boar an' deer together, about takin' on the enemies of Thebes, about the places we'd been an' about the women we'd known. Soon there was a three-quarter moon arisen an' the stars were bright against utter blackness. With the fire replenished an' burnin' bright between us an' our weapons close by, we lay there listenin' to the whisper of flames, the sigh of wood as it settled an' the water as it lapped the narrow beach only a few steps away. The air now was still an' it seemed just then, at least to me, that we were the only two people left in the whole world. It was time to sleep, but we didn't because our ears 'ad to be keen for any sounds that might not belong. Well, Mister Peter, whatever sounds I at least might have expected were not what we next 'heard.'

"The horses," muttered Iolaus, leanin' forwards. "D'you hear – they're becoming restless. Something is worrying them."

'He was right. As we listened, the 'orses began to snort aloud, pullin' on their tethers, whinnyin' an' stampin'. We were on our feet, each with spear at the ready, each starin' at water that reflected quiverin' moonlight. There were splashes - splashes gettin' louder with each 'eartbeat. "There – look!" I said, pointin' into the night.'

"Yes I see it!" cried Iolaus. "It – maybe it's our Hydra!"

'As though attracted by our presence the thing was risin' up, loomin' against the stars, glintin' moonlight, a glistening black form sheddin' water, a great serpent squirmin' onto the beach on wide-splayed limbs with firelight reflected in the great, bulgin' eyes of its crested 'ead. Its white-fanged mouth was openin' wide, hissin', slobberin' in anticipation of a feast soon to be. Ourselves! And awkward movin' up from the water as it appeared to be, I suspected it might any moment dart forward with alarmin' suddenness. Thoughts flashed through my mind. There could be no escape on the island itself – no room for that, an' if we took to the water it would quickly be in there waitin'.

"At least it's only got one head," voiced Iolaus as we both stepped back.

"One's enough," I muttered, grippin' my spear.

Another ear-splittin' hiss and the thing arose to lunge at us! I jumped to the left, feelin', tastin' the foul waft of its rottin' fish breath, so close was I. Iolaus sprang to the right an' with his left hand he grabbed the firebrand. This he plunged into the glowin' embers of our fire where it ignited, burstin' into flarin' yellow. Each of us signalled to the other an' we backed further onto 'igher ground so as to be level with the Hydra's 'ead. The creature before us was all but clear of the water, hissin' aloud, risin' up with its tail thrashin' the surface, its great fearsome 'ead swingin' from side to side as if decidin' which of us it might seize first. We dashed at the thing. I thrust my spear 'ard into its body close behind the 'ead while Iolaus, wavin' the firebrand side to side about its eyes, plunged 'is spear into its throat, wrenched it out then thrust it deep into the creature's mouth. He pulled 'is right arm clear just in time as the jaws closed on his spear to cleave the shaft with a wood-splittin' crack. I wrenched out my spear, feelin' blood spatter over me, an' thrust it in a second an' a third time, causin' the 'ead to swing my way while Iolaus dodged by to the chariot where the 'orses were goin' wild. From there he grabbed another spear. Back in precious moments, he plunged his spear repeatedly into the Hydra opposite to where mine 'ad entered, then we leapt back further still to where we could go no 'igher. With a shout of, "Athena guide my blade!" I cast my spear 'arder than any time I ever did an' it entered one of the creature's eyes where it stayed swingin' about. Iolaus hurled 'is also to penetrate the forehead where it remained good an' deep. The Hydra was retreatin', writhin' violently from side to side, bleedin' 'ard from where we'd struck it but it 'ad no more voice other than a rattle from deep within. The sounds now were that of the horses stampin' an' cryin' out, still in a state of panic. But we figured the Hydra 'ad not long to live. We looked on as it settled part way into the water. We watched intently as it rolled slowly aside with a forelimb raised up to the sky. We waited a while longer then Iolaus announced, "I say it's dead – it *has* to be dead." And 'e was right - aye, we'd done for it!'

Heracles peered up at the sky an' I remarked, 'It still turned out easier than you might have expected, though – only one head to deal with instead of five or more, don't you think?'

'Alright, Mister Peter,' he responded, 'only one 'ead as you say an' not quite the beast the men of Lerna believed it to be. So then we'd to retrieve our spears an' cut its 'ead off. We laid aside our bloodied clothes an' boots an' got busy, Iolaus workin' through the flesh with 'is sword then me hackin' through the bone with the axe until we were both covered in gore. Once we'd done, the 'ead seemed smaller than it did when the creature was out to get us with its jaws wide but its body was still several times the size of mine. The 'ead was a mess; difficult to 'andle an' we couldn't 'ave taken it in our chariot even if there'd been room. We discussed what best to do then decided we'd remain on the island an' rest there until sunrise. But first we washed in the stream, gettin' rid of the blood that'd defiled our bodies an' saturated our clothes. After this Iolaus added more wood to the fire so that it burned up well enough to 'elp dry an' keep us warm.'

'But what if there'd been another Hydra,' I asked as Heracles hesitated to think on what he'd described.

'I expect the 'orses would 'ave warned us again but some'ow I was certain there was no other like it. At sunrise I left Iolaus on the island, half swum, half waded ashore an' walked back to the hut where some of the other men we'd spoken with the day before were again lingerin'. I told 'em we'd done for the Hydra but needed a strong sled, if they could provide one, to bring back one of its five 'eads. Why disappoint 'em, Mister Peter, by sayin' it only 'ad the one. They looked at me like they'd been blessed by Zeus 'imself an' did as I asked with a sled they might use for carryin' a couple of dead sheep. The sled I dragged back to where I managed to float it across to the island where Iolaus 'ad the 'orses an' chariot ready. With the sled 'itched to the chariot, the evidence of our deadly work was rolled over an' tied to it with ropes. After bathin' again we made our way back to dry land with some difficulty then carried on to the hut.

In our absence the men there 'ad sent word out to others an' now there 'ad appeared a large crowd includin' women an' children. Much of Lerna it seemed 'ad gathered in silence where they gaped at us and at the grisly' ead of what they claimed 'ad been the source of their misfortunes. We stopped amid them and I 'eld up a coiled length of silver, a fortune in their eyes, sayin', "Here is enough to get yourselves food an' decent weapons but this is what you must do! Guard your animals well! The Hydra

112

may be gone but it was not the sole cause of your problems. Have armed men stay out at night with firebrands to keep away wild beasts!"

"Promise in the name of Zeus you will do this," added Iolaus, now wearin' 'is cuirass and 'elmet upon which the mid-mornin' sun glinted, "and you may prosper once more!" We managed to get from 'em enough linen to cover an' conceal the severed 'ead an' keep away most of the flies that were swarmin' all about it. Then followed by almost all of the people who cheered' an' waved' at us we set off north on our slow return to Mycenae.'

Well, dear reader, that was Heracles' second labour over and done with and it seems this and the first were far less way-out than those writing centuries later than his days would have us believe. Might it be so for the rest of his tasks? But Heracles was once again to appear before Eurystheus to show evidence of his success. But his account had me wondering what really was the nature of the beast that had arisen out of the sea that night. Too large by far for the biggest of snakes and it didn't sound like some kind of killer whale. No, it didn't belong to any member of the animal kingdom I'd ever heard of. Was the creature they encountered sent by the gods, by the vindictive Hera, or was it a rare species long extinct and unknown to science even in my day? Whatever – I'm sure the world was better off without it.

'It was late mornin', the third day after our quttin' Lerna,' Heracles continued, 'an' very hot when we approached the city an' arrived back at the

Lion Gate. Heat or no, I took the lion skin out of the chariot an' pulled it on. That done I left Iolaus to deal with the 'orses an' chariot while I dragged the sledge with much difficulty through the gate. Once inside I requisitioned a slave to 'elp me get the sledge up the great ramp and around to the palace entrance. There I was challenged by the guards who of course recognised me. One of 'em went inside to inform Eurystheus of my arrival while three of the others insisted on seein' what was under the cover an' was cause of the overwhelmin' smell it was givin' off. They took one look at it, let drop the cover then stepped back squeezin' their noses and eyein' one another with expressions of disgust.'

'But why,' Mister Heracles, 'did you need to wear your lion skin again in the palace?'

'Well, Mister Peter, I though it'd make Eurystheus feel uneasy even before he'd 'ad sight an' smell of the new present I'd brought 'im.

A little later the guard they'd sent inside returned, sniffed the air, looked at me, puzzled, an' ordered me to follow. I'd by then got used to the smell. I 'auled the sled into the megaron an'around the fountain, not so difficult on the smooth tiled floor, then stopped before the throne where daintily attired Eurystheus sat with 'is gowned or armed cronies gathered casually either side. "Mighty One," I announced with the required bow, "I stand 'ere before you with proof that I've destroyed the Hydra." Some of 'em were already twitchin' their noses as I wafted away the sheet to find the 'ead crawlin' with maggots an' the intact eye of the thing starin' wide. It was quite one of the most 'orrible sites you'd ever want to look upon.

"It did 'ave five 'eads, all of 'em like this 'ere," I informed Eurystheus, 'but the rest were too much for me to carry. This one is big enough for Your Majesty to see what a strange creature it is, or was, an' so I now dedicate it to you." Even before I'd finished, Eurystheus was squirmin' in 'is seat. Most of those closest to 'im were lost for words with a few already holdin' their noses an' turnin' aside while several further away were sniggerin' discretely. Eurystheus, shuffled back 'ard into his cushions, raised one arm to cover 'is lower face, pointed with the other arm outstretched to the revoltin' object on the sled an' yelled, "Get that - that damnable object away from me! Get it *out* of here– now!"

'There was some confusion as to what *anyone* was goin' to do about the thing until they called for a couple of slaves to shift it out of the megaron. I 'ad to feel sorry for the poor buggers. Meanwhile I gave another bow, turned and 'urried from the megaron an' out of the palace, thinkin' how what was left of the Hydra had found a good 'ome. Aye, one stink dedicated to another.

I waited by the main gate with my lion skin folded but it wasn't long before Iolaus returned, grinnin' an' holdin' out my rolled-up parchment. While I'd been in the palace, however, Iolaus 'ad received a message delivered by courier from 'is home town an' he informed me, "Heracles, there are problems at Thebes and my return is needed."

'He was nevertheless eager to know what'd 'appened at the palace but we decided first to return my lion skin to our chariot then make our way to the city tavern for food an' beer, an' there to see what was set out for my next labour. As we chatted, as we studied the unrolled parchment, I asked 'im, "How soon must you return to Thebes?"

"I could set off today but I will instead take a small, lighter chariot in the morning to quicken my journey. I may be gone for quite some time but I hope to rejoin you once my business in Thebes is over and done with, then, sooner or later, I hope you and I will continue together as we intended."

'I considered my next task an' replied, "Then I'll get around this one on my own as it looks none too demandin' except for the journey, and I've no wish to stay 'ere with that idiot Eurystheus supposedly in charge." We returned our attention to the list and I said, "All it seems I've to do is capture a deer called the Golden Hind then bring it back to Mycenae. It doesn't say whether dead or alive so that shouldn't be too difficult. I'll take our big chariot since it'll contain many of my needs as well as plenty more rope. Whichever of us gets back to Mycenae first can 'ang about for the other, or we can 'ave a slave do the waitin' in case one of us is away longer than expected. I'll arrange it with our tavern keeper."

"Yes, I'll go along with that but looking at your fourth task I say two of us might be better than one if I can indeed join you."

Jeffrey Peter Clarke

'We agreed over that and havin' done so our minds turned to other things as we eyed the small group of ladies, gatherin' for business as they did in most city taverns frequented by men willin' and able to reward 'em for their services.'

Chapter 6 - The Golden Hind

Heracles and I set aside the main subject for a time – namely himself, and we left our courtyard table to take a welcome stroll outside. We wandered amidst the trees, shading ourselves from the hot sun and out again to gaze across the open countryside with me almost forgetting we were on the privileged top floor of hell. A scent of flowers graced the warm air, happily twittering birds flew from branch to branch in wooded spots and there was a gentle, passing buzz of insects. During this break he questioned me again about my own world, thinking, still, that it was somewhere out at sea beyond the Mediterranean, which of course it was – I mean, is. And I had to be somewhat circumspect. I also, while pretending to gaze out across to the hills, managed to switch off the recorder.

'D'you also worship Zeus and the rest of the gods like people do in Greece?' he asked as we loitered by the stream. Sunlight glinted on the busy water, the reeds swayed in a passing breeze and I thought for a few seconds before giving my answer.

'Many worship what they believe is a kind of almighty being who reigns alone. In different places he's got different names. Some think he looks down on them from above and has even performed miracles although nothing has ever been proven and he's never actually seen. Others claim, and always have, to follow his commands in order to justify their actions. His words are given in writing so may be interpreted by his followers in different ways. Because of this they have felt free to do in his name very much as they please and over the ages it has resulted in bloodshed and countless deaths.'

'So, Mister Peter, he doesn't visit your world to pick 'is women or take time off to create storms.'

'There are some who think he creates storms,' I informed Heracles as he grinned at my comments, 'but increasing numbers no longer believe that he, or it, exists at all.'

'Then give me Zeus any time,' he muttered. 'At least he listens to people and visits 'em at times even if it's mainly for their wives an' daughters.'

I felt it inappropriate to mention the immoral, unholy deviations practised by some of the sole god's preachers through past history and into my own times. 'The one many worship because they see it is really there,' I continued, 'is that which I mentioned yesterday, Helios. Many shed their clothes and prostrate themselves before him, especially by the sea. Others travel far from my land to find him as all to often he's not visible through our clouded skies.'

'Oh, Helios is *that* important is he, and not even one of the Olympians. But Athena – she came to you an' brought you 'ere so she must be well enough known.'

'Not so well known, really.'

'So, Mister Peter, in your land you're one of the chosen few, is that it? Are you then close to the king? Is 'e a good man or one like that sad bugger,

Eurystheus, a figure'ead to be manipulated by others?'

This was becoming awkward as I replied, 'I was chosen only by Athena, Mister Heracles, because I was considered worthy of recording – recording in my mind, that is, your own true words, when no one else had done so. I am not known to the king nor am I to those who hold onto real power in his name.'

We strolled along discussing incidentals and by the time we'd made our way back to the house, Helios declared himself to be past mid-afternoon. I walked behind Heracles, fumbling inside my shirt pocket to switch the voice recorder back on. We returned to the courtyard table where one of his attendants carried over a replenished jar of beer from which, in silence, he recharged our cups. Heracles drank deeply, issued a loud belch of satisfaction then began the account of his third labour.

'This time I'd to make my way over pretty rough country to a small town called Keryneia, in the region of Achaia, north-west of Mycenae. This was built on a steep 'ill between a mountain of that name and a river called the Ladon. In an extensive wooded area around there was said to live the Golden Hind, a great red deer claimed to possess golden antlers an' hooves of bronze. I found this much about it from those at Athena's shrine outside Mycenae because, apart from where the animal lived, all my instructions said was that I'd 'ave to go there, capture it an' get it back to Eurystheus. It'd take me within two days to reach the place.'

'Didn't sound dangerous did it, Mister Heracles,' I said. 'Nothing like the first two. I mean, being a deer it wouldn't have fangs or look upon you as its next meal.'

'Sound dangerous, Mister Peter? Not right then it didn't. I said goodbye to Iolaus that mornin' and watched him set off with the plume on his bronze 'elmet swayin' proud. What a good pair we'd made seein' to the Hydra but life for 'im now 'ad its own demands. I gathered all that I needed an' set off that same mornin' to Keryneia. I didn't know the place too well but I'd no trouble with bandits as Mycenae, bein' as powerful as she was, 'ad seen off most of 'em in the Peloponnese.

There's little to say about my journey to Keryneia other than that I arrived around mid afternoon the next day an' soon located a tavern with well provided stables where men would tend the 'orses an' keep a keen watch over the chariot. They'd 'eard of me but it 'elped to impress 'em when I walked in wearin' the lion skin and peerin' at 'em from it with the club restin' on my shoulder. Over good food that day I asked about this so-called golden 'ind an' where it was usually seen but was advised to visit the temple of Artemis, another of the twelve Olympians, and talk to 'em about it there. The so-called virgin Artemis was also a daughter of Zeus and armed with a silver bow was said to be a mighty huntress who sent 'er arrows to punish the wicked and impious. As a one devoted to the chase she was yet a protectress of all young animals where she roamed the mountains and the streams with 'er nymphs.'

'With her nymphs!' I quipped. 'Sounds like your luck was in this time around, Mister Heracles.'

'So you say, Mister Peter, but there was more to all of this than I'd been told at Mycenae. Artemis 'ad temples in many parts Greece, very famous, you see, an' there was an important shrine dedicated to 'er in Keryneia. I left the tavern without lion skin an' club as I'd no wish to intimidate those I was about to visit. Her temple was a stone structure set against a steep hill outside the town an' there I introduced myself to one of the girls who was busy keepin' the place tidy. Their high priestess came out, a tall, hook-nosed woman in 'er plain, long gown, and asked me what I wanted. "The Golden Hind," I replied, "where's it to be found?"

"It is seen often, close to here, drinking by the river Ladon," she answered as more of her acolytes appeared, "but this creature must never be disturbed. I hope you understand this, so why have you come here?"

"I am to capture an' take the hind to Mycenae," I responded. She an' those with 'er stared at me in disbelief.'

"You cannot do that!" cried one of them, raisin' 'er hands wide.

"No," added her superior, gazin' very sternly into my eyes, "the Golden Hind is sacred to Artemis and protected by her at all times. It is one of five golden hinds she possesses; four pull her chariot and the fifth, the one you speak of she allows to wander much as it pleases. Keep away, I implore you. Ignore our wishes and you will surely call down her wrath."

'So, Mister Peter, on hearin' that, what was I to do? I shrugged, thanked 'em, said goodbye an' walked away wonderin' what choice *did* I 'ave. If I obeyed the priestess I'd be defyin' Hera an' would doubtless pay the penalty – that I knew only too well so I didn't 'ave any choice at all did I. Then what I'd just been told might be no more than make-believe, but even if it wasn't I'd take my chance, try to capture the deer an' get it back to Mycenae one way or another. I returned to the tavern plannin' to collect my bow and arrows. The place was rowdy an' it sounded as if they were all havin' a good time. I left, thinkin' that if I saw a likely lookin' deer I'd bring it down easily enough - any deer for that matter since they all look much the same, except that males 'ave antlers an' females usually don't. But I'd first have to make sure there was no *real* Golden Hind and if there was I'd need to take it alive.

Late that afternoon found me wanderin' down to the river where I looked about to see if there was any clue, a few tracks maybe, where the 'ind might show up. I noticed a clear spot by the river bank – just the place where a large animal might stop to drink so I sat 'igh enough to get a clear view, leanin' against a tree, listenin' to the call of birds an' steady flow of the water.

The sun was dippin' below the 'orizon an' twilight not far away when I decided nothin' was going to 'appen so I upped, left and returned my bow and arrows to the chariot. I entered the tavern where amid loud raucous chatter of men, with just a few women present, someone was trying to make 'imself heard playin' the pipes – a losin' battle if ever there was one. I managed to get myself a jar of beer and a seat in the corner. Some of 'em knew who I was from earlier that day so I 'ad a few sideways nods an' glances. I'd not been sittin' there long when this fair-haired figure, 'ardly more than a young girl, pushes 'er way through what'd become little more than a noisy, non too sweet-smellin' crush. She leaned close to my ear, asked, "Not waitin' for anyone special, are you?" then squeezed down next to me. I don't think anyone 'ad told her who I was or if it would have meant anythin' anyway, but smilin' an' pretty as she was, I didn't consider myself quite the man for 'er an' said, "I'm just passin' through Keryneia an' need to be alone if you don't mind. Sorry."

'She was silent an' remained starin' down at 'er 'ands when a bearded, sour-faced man in a well-worn grey tunic, a man larger an' even rougher lookin' than most of 'em in there, stepped over. He gripped the girl's shoulder 'ard and over the noise bellowed, "What're you doin' with 'im? Get back over there with me an' the others!" He was obviously hurtin' 'er and she was leanin' aside with 'er eyes tight shut, tryin' to thrust his 'and away. I stood up to face 'im an' said, "Leave the girl alone, she's passin' time with me."

He released his 'old on 'er, stared 'ard at me, took a step back an' demanded loud as you like, "Who the fuck might you be?"

'The piper stopped playin', the chatter died, faces turned an' someone called over, "He's the famous 'Eracles! You not 'eard of 'im yet, Kyphos?"

"Famous is 'e!" the man responded, steppin' closer. "Well not in my part of the world an' not in 'ere 'e isn't!" He glanced at me and as he thrust 'is left hand forward to grasp the girl's arm I placed my 'and on 'is chest, rose up an' said, "Leave off 'er – try pullin' me about instead!"

'All of 'em in that room were waitin' to see what would 'appen next. The place was silent except for a brief ripple of murmurin'. All of 'em were shovin' back and all were starin' in anticipation.'

"I'll try pullin' you about alright an' more!" the man declared as the girl squeezed into the corner. He was quick but I was quicker. He swung 'is right fist an' caught me a glancin' blow as I dodged aside but I struck up and 'ard against his jaw, causin' 'im to stagger back with his arm raised for a second attempt. Others in the room looked on, shufflin' about uneasily as their man crouched low. He sprang at me with fists flyin' but again 'e wasn't quick enough; I blocked 'is intended blow an' landed a punch against 'is 'ead that sent him reelin' towards the tavern door. I was onto the bugger again an' struck 'im so 'ard that he crashed against the closed door, splintered it through an' fell clean outside into the night air. I followed 'im out but he was up on 'is feet, glarin' at me, mouthin' foul vengeance an' ready for more as others were spillin' out of the tavern to enjoy the show. P'raps I should've knocked 'im senseless an' let matters be but in those brief moments I knew he'd take it out on the girl an' maybe others once I was gone. In my anger I fell upon the man and in spite of his desperate efforts to better me I determined he would never bother the likes of 'er or anyone else again. Ever.'

'So you finished him off for good, Mister Heracles, is that what you're saying?'

'Aye, Mister Peter,' he responded, gesturing with his great fist, 'finished 'im off for good as you put it an' there were cheers a-plenty followin' so I figured their Kyphos wouldn't be missed by most of 'em.

Well before sunrise next day I set out with my spear an' a long coiled up rope, determined to sit by the river for as long as it took, in the same spot where I'd been the previous afternoon. I'd devised a lasso at one end of the rope so that I might catch the deer by its 'orns. It seemed a good way to go about it but this was somethin' I'd not attempted before. The sun was past its height when a rustlin' noise alerted me an' I saw below me, in a pool of sunlight, what I knew must be the Golden Hind. I didn't actually see it arrive, no, it was suddenly there and I reckoned I must 'ave dozed off a while before'and. I eased slowly to my feet an' stared at it while uncoilin' the rope. Aye, its mighty antlers did look to be of gold an' glistened in the sun as it lowered its 'ead to drink. As for its 'ooves – well they were difficult to see in the long grass but they didn't look like those of an ordinary deer. It was also somewhat bigger, as I'd been led to believe. I crouched an' moved forwards quiet as I could. It raised its 'ead an' peered about nervously. I froze. It waited, listenin', then continued to drink, so I crept closer still. Very close. This time it must've 'eard me because it was alerted an' was backin' away from the water. I sprang up an' threw the rope as it turned to dash off and as luck would 'ave it, and I do mean luck, the noose caught around those fearsome antlers an' I pulled my end around a tree trunk. The 'ind swung about, swayin' its 'ead, snortin', stampin' in its efforts to escape an' I could see those hooves of bronze - aye, they didn't just look like it, they *were* 'ard bronze, I swear!. The animal appeared very powerful, its 'orns would be deadly, an' I wasn't at all sure just 'ow I was to deal with it. An' dangerous as the males can be, they've big dark brown eyes with sweepin' lashes that make them look very expressive. Suddenly, it stopped. I secured firm my end of the rope. I stood watchin' for a while then carefully approached, wonderin' just how I'd get the animal to Mycenae an' what would 'appen after that. Though I was quite close now, the 'ind simply peered back at me, calm and makin' no move at all. I was thinkin' how I might arrange the rope best to take 'im in tow when I sensed somethin', a presence, behind me. I turned an' saw a kind of light shimmerin' amid trees that overlooked the edge of the clearin'. As I watched, it resolved itself into the long-gowned figure of a red-haired woman. In 'er right 'and she carried a long, gently curved bow and at 'er back was suspended an ornate quiver of arrows. She was not quite solid yet she was no ghost either, at least not as I might think of one – you know what I mean, Mister Peter, like a see-through mist. But she was real enough. She 'ad to be real because she spoke very clearly. "Heracles," she said in a voice that sang all about me. "Heracles, you have snared the Golden Hind, the one that I say must run where he will because he is most precious to me, and now you plan to take him away."

'I realised who she was - who she 'ad to be, an' I thought I was well an' truly in for it. I managed to compose myself an' said in the courtly manner you'd a while back asked me to speak, "I am challenged to take this hind before the King of Mycenae – challenged by Hera herself. I've – I have no desire to do this but I otherwise face whatever she chooses to inflict upon me and that could mean death."

"I know what you are obliged to do, Heracles, and I know Hera is permitted by Zeus himself to place this and other burdens upon you. She expected I would punish you but I, as does Athena, as do others among us, feel it unfair and so instead I will be of help to you."

"You – you will?" I responded, almost disbelievin' what I'd 'eard.

"Yes, Heracles, take my precious Golden Hind to Mycenae. He will no longer resist but you must care greatly for him on the journey with food and water, and look after him all the time he is with you. But do not let him into the city. When Eurystheus has witnessed his presence you must allow my Golden Hind to escape. He will return alone to where you found him, where you now are."

"Return alone?" I queried. "What if there are lions about or men out hunting?"

"None will see or sense him, I assure you. Go now."

'The pale image of Artemis was waverin', becomin' fainter, fragmentin' until there was nothin' more of 'er. I turned to the sacred deer an' found 'im quite willin' to trot behind me to where I left 'im tethered to a tree well away from pryin' eyes.

I returned to the tavern for my 'orses an' chariot, then to the Golden Hind. I attached 'im loosely by rope to the rear of the chariot an' set off on my way back to Mycenae. In spite of the time it took, I encountered no problems day or night though the few people who saw us pass by did stop an' stare. Many more of 'em did so as I neared the city wall, once more wearin' my lion skin. Soon I'd a followin' of chatterin' men women and kids who I 'ad to warn off from gettin' too close or trying to touch what was obvious to anyone as bein' no ordinary animal. The Golden Hind, though, didn't seem at all bothered. By the time I reached the Lion Gate the guards, who'd seen us draw close, stood with spears crossed to prevent me passin' through; somethin' I'd no intention whatsoever of attemptin'.'

"We saw your approach and 'ave informed the king of your arrival!" called one of 'em. "He says you're not to enter the city because of the displeasure you created last time! He will come down to see you!"

'Well that was somethin' we were in agreement over. Aye, an' displeasure - the sweet smell I'd left 'em with on my last visit came to mind. So I'd 'ang around for the royal appearance - and then what? At least the guards kept back the rabble. I was able to see through the gate an' some way up the ramp so I knew when Eurystheus was on his way. There was 'is company of guards an' courtiers but he was being carried by four men, two at the front an' two behind, in some fancy, gilded contraption that also kept the sun off 'im.'

'A sedan chair we'd call it,' I informed Heracles.

'Aye, whatever. Well they let 'is royal self down in front of the Lion Gate where 'e pushed aside a thin curtain an' peered out of 'is window at the Golden Hind, which I'm pleased to say remained placid an' took no notice of Eurystheus whatsoever. He stuck 'is hand out the window an' wiggled the royal finger at me to approach so I stepped from the chariot an' walked over to face

130

'im. He didn't appear too pleased at me starin' out through the lion's jaws so I stared a bit 'arder.

"So once more you have succeeded," he said as I dipped my 'ead in slight reverence, "and now you present me with something more acceptable by far. When my guards are ready, remove your rope from that animal and I will have it brought up to the megaron so others may look upon those golden horns." He leaned to the other side of the, whatever you called it, an' addressed two of the guards. "I will return now. Take the creature by its antlers and proceed back to the palace so it may walk directly behind me."

'Wonderin' if Artemis was keepin' an eye on all this I stepped over to release the rope, patted the deer's neck then moved back. Now don't laugh, Mister Peter, but I swear 'e fluttered one of those long eyelashes an' winked at me, aye, winked at me! The guards closed in as Eurystheus' fancy conveyance was bein' lifted up for turnin' around. The Golden Hind shook 'imself, snorted aloud, stamped 'is feet an' swung 'is head violently about. His antlers, pretty dangerous they now looked, caught one of the guards an' sent 'im spinnin' into the gawpin' crowd who reeled back in confusion, while 'e turned an' with one of 'is back legs 'e whacked the other guard where a man's most tender parts are. Then the Golden Hind was away! He sprang at the crowd who panicked to get clear of the antlers. All turned to watch as 'e galloped across an' down the rise at a mighty speed to disappear from sight around the city wall from where 'e would soon be on 'is way north-west an' back to Keryneia. That he'd get back there safely I knew full well and I was 'ighly pleased.

Eurystheus couldn't complain because I'd done as I'd been obliged to do. He'd witnessed how it wasn't me but his own men who'd let the hind escape. I left 'em to argue among 'emselves an' once I'd dealt with my 'orses and chariot I went up to the tavern, the Poseidon, where Iolaus and I had earlier stayed. There I was told by the keeper that the slave left waitin' there by Iolaus had already ridden off to Thebes to inform 'im of my arrival back in Mycenae. Good news that was, so it seemed at first a matter of stayin' where I was for a time in case he returned an' if he didn't then I'd carry on as expected.'

With Heracles' account of that episode ended, our conversation had become small-talk and a light meal of sliced poultry, green leaf vegetables and olives was placed before us by two of his attendants. This time there were no honey-topped wheat cakes though a jar of red wine and two gold goblets followed. From beyond the entrance I could see the sun split by the horizon so twilight would not be far away. Then night-time, the prospect of which had me thinking of Tiye and Mayet though they'd not put in an appearance for this evening's meal as they had on the previous night. Anyhow, I didn't think it appropriate to mention them but as our conversation no longer dwelt upon Heracles' labours there was something else of importance to bother me – the voice recorder. Heracles' attendants had busied themselves with lighting the numerous oil lamps around the courtyard and within the house so I excused myself, taking the opportunity to switch off the recorder on my way to that remarkable bathroom. On passing the bedroom I'd previously occupied I heard voices and laughter. Yes, Tiye and Mayet were there. I hesitated then carried on but before I turned, another figure was crossing the end of the corridor – a tall woman with long brown hair, a gold headband and dressed in a plain, white woollen gown. She hesitated, gave me a questioning stare then swept quickly out of sight. This, I concluded, must be Heracles' wife. I returned to the courtyard where we passed the time in light conversation until well after darkness had fallen. After a final swig of wine we arose and Heracles, with a wink and a broad smile said, 'I think your two little Egyptian friends will be waitin' Mister Peter.'

That, of course, I knew and I entered the bedroom where rich perfume enhanced the air to find them seated close together on the bed, holding hands. "Hello, Peter," their voices chimed as one.

Chapter 7 - Boar, Oxen and Birds

I awoke next morning to the sound of their chatter but I pretended to remain asleep. Once Tiye and Mayet left me I slid from the bed and pulled on my gown, planning to wait my turn until they'd done in the bathroom. I expected them to reappear soon to collect some of the possessions they'd left strewn at the end of the bed. My attention turned to the voice recorder that I'd concealed temporarily in the pocket of my gown. I figured it needed at least bright daylight if not direct sunlight to help top the battery up if only part way. Early light was already spilling around the leather flap over the window. I recalled there was a ledge there and I thought it a good place to leave the recorder as it would be out of sight when I went to the bathroom. It could remain there until I was due to meet with Heracles.

When Tiye and Mayet at last returned, fresh and smiling, it was getting late and I knew Heracles would soon be in the courtyard. The girls hugged and kissed me then off I went to sort myself out. When I returned wearing my freshly washed and dried clothes the two were still there, seated on the bed and chatting. I didn't expect they would be coming outside as they seemed to have eating and leisure arrangements of their own, but I needed to collect the voice recorder. I stepped around the bed to reach up and grab the thing then while attempting to push it into my shirt pocket I found them staring at me.

"What is that you have there?" asked Mayet. "It looks very strange; is it of great value?"

"Oh yes, Peter, do tell us please," added Tiye, part rising to take a closer look.

I crammed the recorder out of sight and was well pleased with the answer I came up with. "Forgive me but it is so sacred in my own land I am forbidden to let others gaze upon it." I don't know if they believed me as each looked puzzled at the other. Anyhow, I got out of that one and fumbled to switch the thing on as I hurried out to the courtyard where Heracles already waited. I imagine if they'd had watches in those days he'd have been glancing impatiently at his. As I sat down he forced a grin and said, 'Those two keep you busy did they, Mister Peter?'

I smiled and looked at the breakfast that appeared to be based upon dried figs, plus yet more olives while I fantasised about a lean, back-bacon sandwich on granary bread. There was some kind of bread but pretty crusty, dry stuff. I reached for the waiting beer as he began, 'Right, let's get on. I didn't care to spend my days 'angin' about Mycenae. The next task set out for me was to capture what the parchment referred to as the Erymanthean Boar; Erymanthos bein' the name of a mountain, sacred to Artemis, where a larger than life boar was claimed to roam about attackin' an' eatin' people. I'd never 'eard of a boar doin' that kind've thing but on thinkin' back to the Hydra I'd believe almost anythin'. As for bein' larger than life – well it would 'ave to be, wouldn't it.

Now Erymanthos wasn't too much further away from Mycenae than 'ad been Keryneia so I decided to 'ead back that way alone rather than wait for Iolaus though I'd leave a message for 'im with the tavern keeper. It didn't seem a job needin' two of us any more than did the Golden Hind. Apart from that, there was no tellin' how long before he'd be able to leave Thebes after the messenger reached 'im. But if he arrived at Mycenae before I returned, he'd find enough to do in discussin' trade and other affairs with the officials an' merchants there. Or he could ride out after me. Aye it was the boar an' as with the previous tasks I was supposed to bring it back to Mycenae to prove I'd succeeded. Now I knew somethin' about boars because in the past I'd hunted 'em. They're a kind of pig, aren't they, but muscular an' strong with more a mind of their own and *will* go for you with those nasty white tusks if they feel threatened. And can they run, aye, they'll easily outpace a man. They taste good when roasted, though, and as you may know, their tusks can be fixed interlocked to a leather skullcap to make a protective 'elmet for any warrior.

After another pretty uneventful journey I arrived in the afternoon at Erymanthos to find not a town or even a village but a group of farms, though there was a good sized tavern on an 'illside close to the mountain. The tavern was there because a nearby shrine to Artemis attracted visitors at certain times of the year. I decided I'd go an' leave a small offerin' at the shrine before darkness fell over the land. Meanwhile there were just five rustics in the tavern, drinkin' with the owner but no women to be seen. The tavern did 'ave facilities for keepin' my 'orses but I intended to stay with my chariot throughout the night, this time at the shrine of Artemis. In the tavern I wore no lion skin an' didn't carry the club as both seemed pointless. The men there appeared much preoccupied with 'emselves until I asked about the boar then all of 'em wanted to speak at once. Only one man swore he'd actually seen it but another insisted the boar 'ad seized an' taken off his daughter an' all agreed it'd accounted for a number of their sheep. All said it was to be found in the forest close by an' all agreed that it was unusually large.'

'Had you planned how to catch the boar,' I asked as Heracles gulped his beer, belched and banged down the cup.

'Aye, Mister Peter, I'd thought about that while talkin' to 'em. I offered 'em silver to make me a stout wooden cage with two good wheels and a swingin' shut end that would close tight – a cage large enough to contain the boar. This 'ad them thinkin' but after we'd shared a few drinks they agreed they'd go about it the followin' day if I would 'elp. I was with them early next mornin' an' their numbers 'ad grown. One of the men was expert in workin' with wood and all were busy gatherin' suitable lengths of timber. They didn't need much 'elp from me as it 'appened an' the cage was takin' shape nicely through that mornin', 'eld together by pegs and strengthened by windin's of rope. The solid wooden wheels went on last so all that was left for me to do was find an' trap the boar. Bein' familiar with boars I knew what they liked to eat which was, for normal boars that is, just about anythin' they can find around the forest floor.'

'Anything?' I queried, picking at the last of my figs and olives.

'Anythin',' he responded as he brushed the sleeve of his gown across his beard. 'That includes roots, bulbs, nuts, green plants, even bark and twigs. They'll also grab birds' eggs and any small animal they can catch, includin' snakes an' frogs. I really didn't believe any of 'em ate people at all, at least not live people, so any boar would do as long as it was large enough to convince the likes of Eurystheus. I'd set up my cage in the forest, under a tree, with a chunk of fresh mutton in it. I'd trail a length of rope over a branch to 'old the swivel end up an' I'd be hidin' some distance away graspin' the other end of the rope. If an unwelcome animal came snoopin' around I'd lower the end just enough to keep it out but if a decent sized boar turned up then -. Trouble with that was the time I might 'ave to wait. And wait I did, Mister Peter.'

Having at this early stage already consumed far more beer than I had, Heracles called for another jar full. I'd rather have done justice to a hot cappuccino but coffee was unknown to the Mycenaeans and I'd seen nothing of milk. During these brief moments I recalled the Erymanthean Boar episode as recounted by ancient writers, some of whom claimed Heracles carried the thing back live to Mycenae over his shoulder. That sounded ridiculous so the alternative *had* to be as he'd planned.

'Aye,' he continued, 'three full days I waited, 'idden behind a bush where I also took my food and drink. One thing the cage didn't keep out was flies an' long before that third day the bait was teemin' with 'em. But late that very day, with sunlight streamin' low through the branches, it 'appened. I was feelin' drowsy when I 'eard a rustlin' noise an' there it was, as good an' large a specimen of boar as ever I saw. I let slip an' readied my end of the rope from the branch next to me an' stiffened up to watch. The boar 'esitated, sniffed about, stuck its 'ead inside the cage then as it entered to grab the meat I let go the rope.'

He banged the table with his fist and cried, 'Yes – I'd got the bugger!' then reached for his beer. 'Aye, the end fell an' jammed shut. The boar thrashed about, tryin' to get free an' it looked for some moments like it would break out, but the cage 'eld. I hung back until it'd calmed down then I walked over to take a proper look at it. At the sight of me it fought once again to escape but after a while it gave up. Even as I towed the cage back to the tavern the boar remained pretty calm though its tusks poked out from the cage.

The locals came out to look at it, some askin' me if it was the one that had been giving 'em trouble. Well some at least must've realised a lion or wolves might really 'ave been the problem but I was nevertheless plied with food, beer an' the attentions of some of their women who I didn't find in the least appealin'. I hauled my cage to the shrine with the boar seemin' just then resigned to its fate an' there I took my sleep.

Only a hint of light showed that mornin' when I recovered the 'orses, hitched 'em up and set off in my chariot with the cage in tow. It was a long, slow journey back to Mycenae but feedin' the captive boar was no problem as it would eat anythin' I gave it, though often rattlin' its cage to try an' break free an' jammin' those tusks out at me through the slats. On the day I approached Mycenae the sun was past its 'ighest and I was wearin' my lion skin once more. People were stoppin' out of curiosity then followin' me all the way ro the Lion Gate where as before I was surrounded by an oglin' crowd. Our go-between messenger 'ad seen me approach an' before I'd encountered the guards he'd dashed out to inform me Iolaus 'ad arrived days before but that mornin' was out huntin' with some of 'is Mycenaean friends. That was good because we'd soon meet up again.

I'd to stay where I was until one of the guards reported my arrival to the palace but when the man returned it seems Eurystheus 'ad changed 'is mind over keepin' me outside and I was to drag the boar up to the megaron as I'd done with the Hydra's 'ead. I presumed then that he wouldn't regard the sight of a boar in a cage as too objectionable, even one as large an' as nasty lookin' as this was, but at least it wouldn't stink the place out. I carried on up the ramp with the guards ahead rather than behind me where the boar glared out and rattled its cage.

Before I crossed the megaron I could see the royal throne was unoccupied; unoccupied by Eurystheus, that is, but the royal crown was there restin' on it. Maybe, I thought, he was havin' 'is face done to look a bit prettier so on I went, stoppin' short to let down the rope attached to the cage. The royal attendants were gathered there just as before but still there was no sign of 'is majesty.

"Leave it there and go on your way," ordered one of the palace officials so I gave 'em all a big smile through the jaws of my hairy suit an' turned to clear off out. As I did so, somethin' caught my attention – somethin' I was surely not meant to notice but in that brief glance all was revealed.'

Heracles grinned broadly, leaned toward me and continued in a low voice, 'Get this, Mister Peter - to my left stood a row of patterned an' coloured chest-'igh storage jars, these bein' as common in Mycenae as in most other towns. Either side of one stood two slaves. The lid of this was raised slightly an' from beneath it a pair of eyes peered. Eurystheus, the mighty king, was watchin' from a safe place in case the boar got out but 'e was hopin' not to be seen by me.' Heracles leaned back, adding, 'It was all I could do not to break out laughin' there an' then but I winked at the poor bugger, 'esitated, reached behind to twirl my lion's tail around and 'eard the lid of the jar clink shut as I carried on out of the megaron. I imagined the two slaves tryin' to haul 'im from it once I'd gone, or maybe they lowered it onto to the floor so he could crawl out.'

141

'Now that sounds ever so funny, Mister Heracles,' I smiled, 'but what happened to the boar?'

'Oh, the boar, aye, I guess they'd 'ave roasted and eaten it later an' made use of the tusks. Havin' got to know it as I did on the way there I confess I'd rather 'ave seen it go free as did the deer. I walked out of the palace but instead of goin' down the ramp to the Lion Gate I strode up to a nearby section of the city wall to gaze across the afternoon countryside while thinkin' what I might do next. In the distance a group of 'orsemen was approachin' and as they drew closer I saw a white plume swaying above 'is bronze helmet. It was Iolaus and 'is party! I made my way down to the gate an' waited until they arrived. Comin' to a halt he saw me, dismounted an' strode over to where, graspin' arms, we greeted one another. "Uncle Heracles," he said, grinnin' wide, "it's been some time but you're still looking fit enough and I take it you have plenty to tell me!"

"I do, my friend," I assured 'im, "aye, I've much to tell, so when you're ready we must talk together in full at our tavern in the presence of well-filled goblets."

'And so it was. Iolaus recounted his dealings at Thebes and elsewhere and I described, without exaggeration, I hoped, my encounter with the fabulous Golden Hind an' with Artemis an' the – well, just a boar, even if others were convinced it was a man-eater. My account of Eurystheus peerin' from under the lid of a storage jar had Iolaus rockin' with laughter. Soon, though, the subject of my next task arose, the goblets of wine were set aside an' the parchment unrolled on our table close by a window. As we stared at it, Iolaus said, "Oh, I see this one is over in Elis, at the town of Epeus."

'Aye, he was right and Elis was due west on the other side of the Peloponnese where ruled Augeas, king of the Epeans. I knew a little about 'em but that far away would take me, or us if Iolaus came along, four days journey – maybe more as much of it was rough country. And the task I was given was to clean out the king's stables where the oxen are kept. That was all it said.'

"Nothing dangerous to capture or kill, then," remarked Iolaus, peerin' at the document. "Sounds too easy, don't you think?"

"Too right it does," I responded, "but if it was goin' to be easy it wouldn't be set out 'ere, would it."

"Well, Heracles, I'll be with you so we'll find out more once we reach Epeus."

On reading this you'll be glad to know the time-consuming journey undertaken by Heracles and Iolaus to Epeus offered no dangers and no problems other than that of finding somewhere to make their fire and rest each night. I therefore had him say no more about it and begin instead with an account of their arrival.

'The afternoon sky was cloudy but clearin' when we first 'ad sight of Augeas' town. It was surrounded by a defensive wall but it was no Mycenae or Thebes. No, not impressive at all though the wall displayed some of the spaced-out, carved stone bulls' 'orns in simplified form you'd see at Mycenae and at Knossos. It also 'ad a modest sized river flowin' close by with many people on its banks tryin' to catch fish an others just bathin'. There were people comin' and goin' from the town as expected an' we attracted the usual attention as our chariot drew close with me in my lion skin and young Iolaus lookin' ready to enter battle in plumed 'elmet and polished breastplate. Had it been earlier we'd 'ave located a tavern first but I was impatient. At the modest main gate I ordered the guards, "Inform King Augeas Heracles has arrived from Mycenae an' wishes to present 'imself." They must 'ave been impressed because one of 'em dashed off straight away an' we didn't wait long before the man returned an' gestured for us to follow through the gate in our chariot. The palace stood straight ahead but we were first shown a secure place for the chariot an' someone to take care of an' groom the 'orses. There were two men in attendance at the royal stables and I asked one of them, "The stables where your king keeps 'is oxen – they far from 'ere?"

"Far enough, aye," he responded, "until the wind changes, then they're not far enough away."

"No they're not," agreed his companion as he squeezed finger an' thumb to his nose an' lifted up 'is gaze.

"Oh, really," grinned Iolaus, "and why is this? Are you saying there's an unpleasant smell?"

"Unpleasant smell!" voiced the first man. "Some days they stink to 'eaven! Augeas inherited all three thousand of 'em from 'is father, now dead, though he claims 'is old man was Helios 'imself, and he's no interest in them oxen whatsoever. We're told local farmers feed 'em but that's all. We 'ear the stables never get cleaned out an' they say the very air around 'em is poisonous."

"Three thousand oxen," I said, "that sounds impossible.

"Quite so," agreed Iolaus. He regarded the man with amusement, saying, "So you have counted them all have you?"

"Er, no," he replied, "but that *is* what most others say."

"Well we'll find out soon enough, won't we," I said and we strode off to enter the palace. I'd already removed the lion skin and Iolaus his breastplate and 'elmet, though we retained swords at our tunics as might be expected. We passed through an anteroom where storage jars, similar to those at Mycenae, were lined up then into the megaron where ahead of us stood Augeas' marble throne with the robed, slenderly built king seated on it and guards lounging either side. Augeas was a thin-faced, dark 'aired, sallow lookin' man without a beard. I noticed on his lap there rested a baked clay tablet. Since nobody'd ordered us to bow, neither of us did, though we stood in silence waitin' to be addressed.

"So you are the famous Heracles," he said in a crisp voice. "And who is this man with you?"

"Iolaus is a good friend of mine," I answered, "and a member of the Theban royal house. We go huntin' together."

Augeas stared at both of us a while with dark, unsmiling eyes then still harder at me, sayin', "Heracles, I am requested by a messenger from Eurystheus, King of Mycenae, to give you these instructions." He lifted an' gazed closely at the clay tablet then informed me, "You are to clean out stables some way from the city where our oxen are kept." Well I knew that, didn't I, but then he added, "This says the work is to be completed in one day, between sunrise and sunset and if this is done to my satisfaction I am to offer you the value of ten oxen or a tenth of their number, whatever that might be. Is this supposed to be an incentive? I think not. I think it more Eurystheus' sense of humour, but it is no concern of mine. You may leave us now."

'As no further conversation was required we nodded in a manner we considered duly respectful an' made our way from the megaron in silence. Once outside in late afternoon sun I said, "What a cheerful old bugger 'e was. What say we retain just our tunics, nothin' fancy, an' take a look at those outside stables with the oxen while there's enough daylight left, then find ourselves a tavern." Iolaus agreed so we consulted the two palace hands where our horses were bein' kept on the location of stables an' tavern.'

"Turn due right outside the city gate," offered the first man, "then walk over to the river. Follow that and yer nose and you'll find the stables close between the two rivers that join up to make the main one." The second man informed us also that when we returned we'd find a decent tavern to the rear of the palace. So first we set off out from the city gate to 'ave ourselves sight of Augeas' neglected oxen; a fair way it was as well, until reachin' where two busy but shallow lookin' rivers met. We strode on, aware of a most foul smell carried by the breeze. Closer still and it was obvious the extensive range of neglected lookin' stables set between the smaller rivers were the ones housin' the oxen an' some way from both rivers stood a group of farmhouses.

"Somewhat exaggerated don't you think," said Iolaus. He eyed the stables from where we could hear grunts an' other cattle-soundin' noises. "I mean, three thousand oxen. There's not room even for three hundred as far as I can see and maybe far less."

"Still enough from the looks of it though," I said, "This task is designed by that damned woman above to demean me, to get me shovellin' shit 'till I'm covered in it an' she'll know it won't be possible to do it all in one day, not even for the two of us. There 'as to be another way. There are five men workin' over the other side of the main river; let's 'ave a word with them." We were able to wade across the river but the water, comin' as it did from quite high up, was very cold. We approached the group of men to find them befouled by their labour in diggin' 'ard to widen an irrigation ditch. Seein' this gave me an idea. But was the idea I'm about to reveal really mine, Mister Peter? The men'd stopped work, climbed out of the ditch an' leaned on their spades as we stood before 'em to ask about the stables an their livin' contents.

"Augeas gave us the land we farm an' in return 'e expects us to feed 'is beasts," said one, laying aside his spade. "But it's not enough to 'ave us keep everythin' in good order as well so only once a month do our men try an' clean 'em out an' that's only if we're not taken up with too much work of our own, which at present we are."

"Aye," added another, "we've more than enough of our own work right now."

"The shit may be good for our soil," continued the first man, "but there's far more than we'd ever need. Be that so, we've not seen Augeas or anyone else from the palace up 'ere, never, except at the very beginnin' when a couple of 'is men turned up with 'is instructions."

'Well at least, so I thought, a once in a while clean-out was better than none at all, as others claimed.'

"So if Augeas doesn't care about them why d'you not let some of the oxen go?" queried Iolaus. "Or why not make use of them yourselves, or sell them perhaps?"

"Or eat a few of 'em," I quipped.

"Daren't do any of that, dare we," put in one of the others. "Augeas will still think they're 'is even if he doesn't want anythin' to do with 'em. It's said by some they're immortal an' we're beginnin' to

148

think so. Those oxen, you see, don't do nothin', don't go anywhere at all. Just eat an' shit."

"How very odd," Iolaus remarked.

"Very odd's right enough, sir," said another, "and we never know if the king'll change 'is mind over 'em and then if we'd done what you said we'd be in for it good an' proper."

"Aye, good an' fuckin' proper," agreed one, pickin' up 'is spade, "so we leave things as they are an' try to get on with our daily work."

'As we spoke I was lookin' back at the stables an' to where the two smaller rivers joined as one on their way to Epeus. "Now then," I asked, "how many men are there around 'ere who can dig as 'ard as you?"

"Another four or five who're fit enough," shrugged the first man, peering around at the others who nodded their agreement. Iolaus was grinning at me. It seemed he suspected what I 'ad in mind.

"Now look," I said, "if enough of you got together an' dug a channel diagonally from the furthest river to one side of the stables the water'd wash right into it, yes?" After some thought an' peerin' across at the stables they agreed that it would. "Then if you continued the trench on from the stables to the nearer river it'd wash all the shit out of there an' take it along to where that river joins the first. That one river would then carry on down to Epeus."

"We'd not dare do that - no!" cried one of the men.

"Augeas would 'ave our arses!" declared another.

"We'll pay you in silver," I assured him, "and if needs be you can tell Augeas we did it alone because that's what we'll have 'im think."

"And how would Augeas know otherwise if he never sends anyone out here?" asked Iolaus. By now the sun was touching the horizon and I felt an agreement was much needed. The five men shuffled away from us to talk among themselves. When they returned the first man said, "Aye, but it'll 'ave to be enough silver for us to move on soon after with our kids an' our women in case Augeas does find out we were a part of it. We're free men, y'know, not the slaves we'd end up as."

'Iolaus and I stepped back to discuss the men's proposition. We 'ad between us more than these people would regard as a true fortune an' so we agreed we'd have 'em go ahead. "Very well," I concluded, turnin' to the men, "we'll be 'ere with you before sunrise an' let you have sight of the silver you'll be needin' if you'll be ready to start work at once." With that confirmed Iolaus and I returned to Epeus where we located the tavern. There we ate, drank an' the diversions on offer by the women below served to quell any concerns we might 'ave 'ad about the followin' day.'

'But you were still taking a risk, Mister Heracles' I said 'What if Augeas after all had sent someone to watch you or even turned up himself, no matter how unlikely that might've been?'

'Aye, a risk as you say, Mister Peter, but I don't think he was at all interested other than just doin' as he was asked by Mycenae who 'e looked upon as an ally.

The followin' day we set off back in our chariot to meet up with the farmers well before sunrise hopin' not to attract too much attention. We were dressed as when we arrived that previous day at Epeus but this time I'd got the club over me shoulder and Iolaus was fully armed. We needed to create an impression so the men'd know we meant business an' there'd be no trickery. When we arrived, nine of 'em were ready and waitin' with spades an' pick axes. Some of their women were standin' around to watch while others also carried spades. They wanted to see what we were offerin' before they'd begin work but the sight of coiled silver an' some fancy trinkets they could sell on seemed to satisfy 'em.'

Heracles was interrupted by the arrival of more beer an' some food so I said, 'I imagine looking at you and Iolaus would have discouraged any argument.'

'Aye, Mister Peter, and it did. They got to work, first on the down side of the trench from the stables to the second river. They were at least used to the stink around there but they disturbed the oxen who were snortin' and shufflin' about. They laboured 'ard but that part of their work was completed before midday when women an' kids brought out food and all of 'em stopped to eat. The next part of their work was diggin' outwards from the stables to the first river – risky it was as they got closer to the water though this was all but done before sunset. They clambered out of the near completed trench then dug at the remainin' ground from each side until it started to give way. Then it 'appened – the earth still blockin' the upper river collapsed altogether an' a gush of foamin' water threw down that final barrier to become a torrent. It poured in to wash through the stables, burstin' out the other end, causin' such a commotion, such a panic among the oxen with 'em crashin' against the timbers it looked like they'd soon break out. The flood continued into the second river loaded with – aye, with all the foulness you can imagine until both rivers joined on their way to Epeus. When all the shit and soil began floatin' by 'is town this'd be proof I'd done as I'd been ordered to do.'

'But Augeas wouldn't be too pleased about that, would he,' I remarked as Heracles downed his beer.

'No, he wouldn't,' Heracles laughed as he banged his cup on the table, 'but it was too late for that. We paid what we'd promised to those who did the 'ard work, took ourselves back to the palace stables, secured the 'orses chariot an' changed to make ourselves look ordinary for the tavern.'

"I'll pay you nothing!" declared Augeas that next mornin' as we stood before 'im. "I don't know how you did it but the river, with many of my people bathing in it, was completely fouled!" He had at least prepared a baked clay tablet bearing a written confirmation of what I'd supposedly done.

This he gave to one of his guards who in turn handed it to me. "Very sorry, Your 'Ighness," I said, "but where else could all the shit possibly go?"

"My good friend Heracles is right, sir, if I may say so," voiced Iolaus, "where else *could* it go? You as King of Epeus ought to honour your word and give to him in silver what was promised."

'Augeas gripped the sides of 'is throne an' glanced at 'is guards as if about to give orders. He said nothin' an' glared back at us. I drew breath but kept quiet. Iolaus, as a member of the Theban royal house could talk to Augeas like that an' get away with it. Or maybe *just* about. The King of Epeus sat for a time as though frozen solid then spoke in a low voice, "I will have silver sent around to the tavern where you both are staying."

'It was time for us to leave – sooner the better. "Now get out!" Augeas bellowed, risin' from 'is throne. "Now! Out of my sight!"

'Iolaus gave a slight bow an' so did I. Maybe the poor bugger deserved it. Even so, 'ad I not been under orders from Mycenae an' had Iolaus not 'eld the status he did, I reckon the people of Epeus would 'ave seen our severed 'eads on display above the city gate later that day. But well before sunlight the followin' day we'd got ourselves, our horses, all our possessions an' our chariot ready. We left Epeus quick as we could with Augeas' grudging payment of silver added to our own an' were on our tiresome journey back to Mycenae with proof of labour number five accomplished.'

'And what,' I asked, 'did your favourite person, Eurystheus, have to say about it when he read the tablet?'

'Well Iolaus was to go off on business with others in the city so when we'd dealt with our horses an' chariot I walked up to the palace. Would Eurystheus believe I'd done the impossible on my own? He'd obviously no fear of baked clay tablets when one of his attendants presented it to 'im. He looked down at the tablet then up at me several times as I stood there and I began to wonder if he believed what was inscribed on it. The tablet was only a confirmation but I knew the details of what'd 'appened must reach 'im sooner or later, by which time I'd most likely be occupied elsewhere.

The parchment 'ad been left at our tavern so when I met up with Iolaus again he'd want to take another look at it. I of course already knew what next was expected of me. Aye, it was at a town north-west of Mycenae called Stymphalos, where Artemis was also celebrated, as well as Hera, and it was only around a quarter the distance away as Epeus 'ad been. All the parchment told me was to rid the people of carnivorous birds that had taken to livin' close by. That at least sounded better than the last challenge. No evil smell an' no shit involved, or so I thought. Later that day Iolaus informed me he was for the time bein' free to be my companion once more, especially as the next task was not so far away. After that he must return to Thebes.

There was some kind of party goin' on in our tavern late that night. Very busy it was with girls

154

dancin' to the rhythm of pipes an' drums until their activities, by which I mean their behaviour, became temptin'ly freer. Iolaus and I took no advantage of this as we wanted to be settin' of at the first glimmer of light next day. We intended to reach Stymphalos by sunset.

After another uneventful journey we arrived at the modest town within the time planned an' there we located a suitable tavern with good stables. I'd been to Stymphalos some years before an' I recalled it was located close to a marshy lake from the far side of which spread a dense forest. We 'ad the landlord's men deal with our 'orses an' chariot as usual an' entered the place dressed in our tunics, that worn by Iolaus somewhat more refined than my simple attire. Iolaus an' I as usual retained our swords. The dim interior was rendered less so by numerous oil lamps arrayed on tables and on shelves above. The conversation quietened, 'eads turned and from their looks it seemed a number of 'em recognised me. Thinkin' to obtain food an' wine I also asked the landlord an' some of those men close by to tell us of their problem with the birds. This served well to liven up the conversation.

"You're 'Eracles!" declared one man, pointin' at me. "I've seen you walkin' around Mycenae in yer lion skin an' with that there club, an' your as big a man as I ever saw."

"That's who he is," agreed some of the others while two of the few women seated together there were eyein' up stubble-faced Iolaus.

"So you know all about our troubles with those bird things then," said the portly, bushy-bearded landlord.

"Come to sort 'em out 'ave you?" asked another man.

"Someone 'as to," declared one. "We've made sacrifice to Artemis and also to Hera at all three of 'er shrines in Stymphalos but we say they're not listnin' to us."

"Sacrifices to Hera," I muttered. "Well thanks for tellin' me that."

'I noticed a fleeting smile cross Iolaus' features as he asked them, "But do you not have a temple dedicated to Athena?"

"Aye we do," replied the landlord, "over the opposite side of our town from the lake."

'I decided we'd visit her shrine in the mornin' so then I asked 'im, "Tell us, what's been happenin' 'ere so we might understand an' help you?"

'Everyone listened intently as the landlord explained, "They began to appear earlier this year when our sheep were bearin' their young."

"Some say they come from out of the forest," interrupted a man close by him, "others say it's overgrown parts of the lake they live in."

"Aye," said another, "they've got bronze beaks an' bronze wings that catch the sun an' glitter like..."

'The stern look given 'im by the landlord rendered the man at once silent. Not surprisin' was it Mister Peter; how could anythin' with bronze wings possibly fly. Far too 'eavy I'd say.'

156

'Er, yes, Mister Heracles, you're right – a metal bird could never rise into the air.' Passing through my mind as I glanced up at the ceiling was an image of numerous vapour trails that promptly vanished as Heracles continued his tale.

"Well whatever they're made of," said the landlord, "they're the biggest birds I ever saw – big enough to seize our sheep an' I've watched 'em do it so I 'ave."

"An' some of our little children 'ave gone!" called out one of the women. "That'll be them birds alright!"

"Aye," the landlord continued, "even some of our children so I've 'eard. The things fly so low over our 'eds they scare the life out of us but we've not the means to deal with 'em."

"An' they foul our crops when they shit on 'em so there you 'ave it." said another. "So tell us now you're 'ear, what's to be done?"

"By Zeus, not more shit?" I groaned, then I told 'em, "Well we'll look at the way things are tomorrow."

Iolaus an' I sat with food an' beer to think about 'ow we might deal with these aggressive birds. "We could look for where they nest durin' the day," I suggested, "but whether it's in the lake or the forest they 'ide 'emselves I doubt that'd be too easy."

"So we hang around until they come flying out," said Iolaus. "I'm pretty good with bow and arrow and you're not so bad, Uncle Heracles, or so I hear."

"Not so bad!" I exclaimed as he grinned at me. "I'll 'it any target you aim for, so aye, we catch 'em in the air if they're really low enough an' see which of us brings the first of 'em down. I wager it'll be me so how about that?"

"Yes but we don't know how long we'll have to wait, do we; it could be days as I'm sure you appreciate."

"Aye then, we'll need to be patient, somethin' I've become used to of late, an' see what else these people 'ere can tell us about 'em." But there was little more we could learn that evenin' other than that with each passin' account, the birds seemed to grow larger and ever more ferocious.'

"I wonder why the people of Stymphalos themselves didn't try 'arder to fight those birds off," I remarked once Iolaus and I were alone. "One of 'em them said they'd not the means but they must've 'ad somethin' they could use as weapons if not spears – pitchforks or axes maybe?"

"It could be they only have basic weapons of a sort," said Iolaus, "spears to fend off wolves, bears or even lions, but they're farmers who make a living from the land, not warriors in the service of someone high up. They'd seldom if ever have seen the weapons such as we use."

Long before sunrise next mornin' in cool, clear air, we set out with our bows an' arrows to see what if anythin' might show up. Iolaus also had 'is spear an' me my club. There were certainly no giant birds flyin' around, no, just ordinary ones, so first we'd visit Athena's shrine. We came upon a modest

158

temple that was in darkness an' utterly silent when we entered. We stood thinkin' perhaps there was no priestess in attendance, then as if from nowhere a figure appeared, wearin' a long, multi-layered an' delicately patterned woollen gown. Her 'ead was enclosed by a cowl so that in the gloom 'er features, except for 'er bright eyes, were barely visible. She waited for one of us to speak so I said, "We are come 'ere out of respect to leave an offerin' of silver." On 'er lips I could make out a broadenin' smile as we reached into the pockets of our tunics to place onto her small altar clippings of the precious metal.'

"I thank you," she responded softly, while lookin' at each of us in turn with a searchin' gaze. "You have been called here have you not to destroy the flying creatures."

"Aye, that we have," I answered, thinkin' that on seein' our bows, our arrows and the rest of what we carried, she must 'ave guessed our intentions. What's more, she referred to the birds as creatures. But there was a surprise in store for us. She stooped behind the altar an' retrieved an object that she placed next to our offerin's.'

"Take this," she said, "you will find it serves you well today."

'I picked the object up, recognised it as a bronze rattle, the kind children played with, only a lot larger, and no doubt it would be very much noisier. Iolaus an' I must 'ave looked puzzled until she spoke once more. "Go with it close to the lake and to the forest and use it there in the manner for which it was intended. The noise it makes will have the creatures you seek take to the air." With that she reached to pick up our offerin's, turned and, driftin' into the darkness at the rear of the temple, left us as if she'd never been. For a time we waited in a kind of silent awe.'

"So let's get along to the lake," declared Iolaus, breakin' the silence in his enthusiasm an' proppin' aside 'is spear so as to adjust the quiver of arrows at his back. We left an' I was convinced that should we return, we would find there was no longer anyone in that temple. I know what you're thinkin', Mister Peter, an' so was I; per'aps the priestess 'ad never been there.

Heracles was right about that but I didn't wish to interrupt him.

'The air was warmer, the breeze mild and the lake ripplin' gently when we arrived at the deserted shore close to where the reeds grew plentiful and green and with the dark forest spread wide a fair way to our left. Needless to say, there was no one else thereabouts, no small boats out on the water an' no one fishin'. The newly risen sun was warmin' our backs as we placed our quivers on the ground with arrows part spilled out at the ready. "Lets see what 'appens when I use this," I said as I lifted the rattle arm's length an' spun it 'ard. An' what a shatterin' racket it gave out. Over the lake an' land thereabout, numbers of small birds scattered in panic, fluttered around an' circled 'igh above us. I put the rattle down an' we waited, graspin' our bows with an arrow fitted loosely in each. For a time that I thought would never end we stared across the reeds an' to the forest. In those moments I wondered, as did Iolaus, if anythin' was ever to 'appen. Then came sounds from the direction of the forest – a kind of guttural squarkin', a swishin' an' swayin' of upper branches. At last we saw the first of 'em – large black forms risin' from amid the trees and gainin' just enough height to clear the upper branches. These first of these circled an' as others rose to join 'em, they set off flappin', weavin' in and out, switchin' from side to side, low an' slow across the lake, headin' in our direction with a few set to pass right over us. It looked to me that from wingtip to wingtip they'd measure almost twice the height of a man.'

"Are they a kind of bird?" Iolaus queried as we raised an' drew back our bows.

"They look more like bats or flyin' reptiles to me," I responded - and by now we could see they 'ad short necks, long, copper or bronze-coloured beaks - or were they not beaks but pointed jaws. "I'll take that first one!" Iolaus called. They were well within our range, some hoverin' close over us when we took aim and released our first shots with me choosin' the one close behind Iolaus' target. All the while lookin' up we reached for our second arrows, seein' as we did that our first two'd struck 'ome. One of the creatures fell, screechin'an' twistin' about as it hit the water while the other dropped straight to the shore close by us with an arrow embedded in its body. That got 'em rattled for others joined those circlin' over us and one, its

161

wings spread wide an' its beak-like jaws agape, looked about to strike at us. We dropped our bows. I grabbed for my club and Iolaus stepped aside with 'is spear at the ready. The bird-thing descended with a snarl, its wings hissin', makin' for Iolaus with dagger-claws spread to rip into 'is flesh. Another followed from above with its eyes 'ard on me. Iolaus leaped up with his spear at the first of 'em, rammin' the blade straight into its throat as it swung a vicious claw, missin' his face by a whisker as he dipped aside to avoid it. He was staggerin' forward to dislodge the creature from 'is spear over the water when in the screechin' chaos I felt the draught from the next one as it closed on me, all but blockin' out the sun. I dodged its claws, or so I thought, by smashin' 'em back with my club then I swung the club again, damned 'ard, strikin' its 'ead with a mighty crack that 'ad it attemptin' to rise up, beatin' the air to gain height before it faltered an' plunged squealin' into the lake. Three or four of 'em still circled over'ead as if to see what was happenin' but they were too close for their own good. Iolaus and I 'ad again grabbed for our bows, fitted our arrows, let fly an' scored our third an' fourth hits with both victims plungin' down to the lake, one floatin' close to us, thrashin' the water as we let fly again at those above. But as we loosed further shots, most were wheelin' away, cacklin' to each other an' soon were crossin' over the far edge of the lake. Even so a fifth 'ad been struck in the wing an' spiralled down onto land. I couldn't say for sure which of us 'ad loosed that arrow. Had we not been so quick and agile we'd 'ave been dead men, aye, with those things feedin' on our guts. Even so, Iolaus turned to me an' said, "Heracles, there's blood on your face." He was right but I 'adn't noticed at all until I raised my 'and to find my left cheek bleedin' down over my shoulder. That bird's claw had caught me after all though I'd felt nothin' at the time – that's how razor sharp it was. I'd rinse it with water from the village well and a honey poultice would do the trick.'

"It's fortunate there weren't too many of them," said Iolaus in his usual, easy-going manner as I wiped much of the blood from my face with the edge of my tunic an' we shouldered our quivers. "Did you manage to count them?" he asked. "The way they were drifting around confused me."

"And me," I responded, "but I'd guess around twenty somethin' – no more than that for sure, with a few less now."

You may recall, dear reader, when first introduced to Heracles, I mentioned seeing the scar on Heracles' face and I suspected he might sooner or later reveal its origin. So now he has, I'll have him continue.

'We looked toward Stymphalos an' there were men approachin' the lake. They must've 'eard our rattle an' seen the birds take to the air. We walked around the shoreline to meet 'em an' found they'd stopped to look at the last of the fallen birds. Aye, I was now callin' 'em birds though they didn't look like any bird I'd seen before. Other men, women and kids were gatherin' with the first lot when we

got there. Joinin' 'em also was an ancient, stoopin'
man with a walkin' stick. They informed us he was
a priest of Artemis and a well respected soothsayer.
He led 'em all in thankin' us, claimin' Artemis 'ad
sent us an' assured us the birds would never visit
'em again. "How d'you know that?" I asked 'im.
"He *knows*," insisted one, an' those hearin' what
was said all agreed. "They'll not come back to
trouble us no more," confirmed another close by 'is
side.

Neither Iolaus nor I felt inclined to question
their supposed authority or tell the old man it was
Athena we looked to, but I for one assumed the
priest must have a success record in predictin' the
future to 'is credit. The fallen creature close to 'em
was still twitchin' but the townspeople agreed
they'd retain it as a trophy until it began to rot, as
soon it must. One of the dead ones we'd 'ave
bundled in straw an' dragged on a sledge back to
Eurystheus as evidence of our, or as far as 'e was
concerned, of my, success. In an act of gratitude the
people agreed they'd 'ave both bird an' sledge
ready for us before we left next day for Mycenae.
First, though, the rattle 'ad to go back to Athena's
shrine. We turned up there to find the place as we
expected, deserted an' silent, so with not a word
passin' between us, I placed the rattle carefully back
behind the altar.'

'Another victory, Mister Heracles,' I said.
Upon which he downed a mighty swig of beer as if
to emphasise the success of his latest related task.

'Aye, Mister Peter,' he responded, 'but I learned later about those what we thought of as birds an' the old man was right; they'd descend upon others as a curse, often in a form other than we witnessed, but once driven away they'd not return.'

'So,' I asked him, 'what was it that brought the curse down upon those people?'

'As I recall they'd somehow upset Hera,' he replied, 'but then, I knew how easily that might be done.'

Then dear reader, what, we may ask, was the nature of the so-called Stymphalian birds? It had flitted through my mind that we perhaps had witnessed a miraculously enduring species of the otherwise long-extinct pterosaurs. But had this been so their existence would surely have been better noted and documented. I must admit at present, with my credulity much relaxed, that before the monotheistic religions condemned them to the realms of pagan mythology, the major and minor gods and goddesses really did interact closely with people when and where they chose to. And still did in my case.

'Iolaus an' I,' Heracles continued, 'were on our way back to Mycenae with the latest offerin' for Eurystheus. At least it 'adn't attracted too many flies and 'adn't begun to stink too much. We arrived at the Lion Gate when the sun was goin' down an' there I detached the sledge from our chariot. This and our 'orses Iolaus would again deal with an' we agreed we'd meet later at our city tavern. For now I'd not bother wearin' the lion skin. As before, the guards, this time five of 'em, needed to know what I'd brought to take before their illustrious king. One of 'em, havin' parted the straw to gaze in disgust at its contents, as next did the others, set off to the palace. On 'is eventual reappearance, with the sky already darkenin', I was informed that the king 'ad taken early to 'is royal bed. This prompted a none too discrete round of sniggerin' from the other men.

"Then I'll leave it with you," I informed 'em, givin' the sled a goodbye kick. "I've obeyed the orders of Eurystheus, I've returned with the evidence demanded of me an' that's all I'm obliged to do." I pushed by 'em, club over me shoulder, an' walked beneath the gate, leavin' 'em to think about it, then I 'eaded for the tavern where Iolaus, food, wine an' a log fire waited. Waitin' also was the parchment that outlined my next labour. I'd known all along where I'd next be expected to go but I'd continually shoved it to the back of my mind an' said nothin' to Iolaus because I'd no desire to think about it. Iolaus must've realised that was so because he'd not mentioned it either. But now I *did* 'ave to face it an' I knew, because of his commitment to matters in Thebes, Iolaus would not be with me. I was to visit Crete an' there go before King Minos at Knossos.'

"You may be on your travels for quite some time," said Iolaus as we poured our wine from a vessel adorned with flowing an' colourful images of sea creatures – this perhaps from the workshops of Knossos itself. "I have visited the palace of Minos on a number of occasions and it's a wonderful experience indeed, so I regret that I'm unable to share your – well, whatever your next challenge is to be."

"I'd been to Knossos also, when I was younger," I informed him, "but that was for reasons of trade and I saw too little of the palace. But one thing I'll tell you, my friend, obliged as I am to go there again, that bitch of a woman will *not* get the better of me, though your good companionship I will sorely miss."

"And I yours, Heracles, yet I know you will succeed, and I hope to ride out with you again when you return."

'We recalled an' compared our memories of Knossos, his of far greater interest, an' we drank well. Later that night, although we'd savoured female company to the full, at the back of my mind lingered what the purpose of my going to Crete might be.

The next mornin' Iolaus was to depart. Outside the Lion Gate we grasped arms an' shook 'ands then the one who'd so willingly an' with such good humour shared in full those dangers with me, rode off in the smaller chariot, 'is helmet plume swayin' proud. With Iolaus vanished into the distance I now 'ad to address my own affairs. I'd 'ave the larger chariot with two 'orses but leave behind at Athena's temple anythin' not necessary for me to carry on my way to the southern tip of the Peloponnese from where I'd board a vessel to Crete. Silver I 'ad aplenty an' I'd be well armed. So there you 'ave it, Mister Peter, I was on my own once more.'

As he relaxed in contemplation, gazing up at the sky, I knew in outline all Heracles was claimed to have faced. That was, of course, set out in translations of ancient sources I'd consulted back home but once again I expected, or hoped, his forthcoming account would reveal unexpected truths and lay aside less credible claims.

'I say we eat now,' he announced at last, 'then I've matters to deal with indoors. When we've fed ourselves you can take a break from listenin' to me until later this afternoon. Those two Egyptian girls will be in the garden at the rear of the 'ouse if you're interested. They've taken a likin' to it since they arrived. Lots of flowers growin' there they've never seen before and I've a man takin' care to keep the garden lookin' good.'

I enjoyed, if that's the right word, the Mycenaean fare, but I did need some free time alone. At that point a loud cry burst from within the house. "Heracles!"

It was his Hittite wife. I grinned to myself as he rattled back the chair, shuffled hurriedly about and left the table. When he'd gone inside I upped and set off out to the wooded area where I first had been introduced to the great man. Overhead sunlight flooded through the branches where in the fully illuminated clearing stood the deserted table and chairs. Good, I really *was* alone. I stepped over, sat down, pulled out the voice recorder and checked to ensure all was okay by playing back the very end of our last conversation. Then I placed it on the table to gain more charge from the sun. Even if it didn't top up completely there'd have to be further opportunities. I relaxed, listening to the pleasant ripple of the nearby stream and the call of birds as they fluttered from tree to tree. When eventually Heracles summoned me back to the house, it would be to relate the seventh, perhaps one of the greatest of his labours.

Chapter 8 - The Bull of Minos

Heracles called me back to the portico on that pleasantly warm afternoon when the sun was well past its zenith. I made my way along the path, pushing the voice recorder back into my shirt pocket, switching it on and feeling pleased now it held a healthy charge. He was back in the courtyard when I joined him, seated at the table upon which rested a jar of beer and two cups; both already filled.

'Had a good break, 'ave you?' he asked me, raising his cup.

'Yes thank you,' I responded, reaching for my drink.

'Then we can get on with number seven of my…'

He hesitated, stared hard at me, put aside his cup then said, 'Mister Peter, you've listened to me with great patience, havin' assured me earlier that all of my words will be related to those in your land just as I've spoken 'em but – but how can the mind, the memory of any man be *that* good? What I mean is, bards in the places I once knew, like those I met in my years at Thebes, told of events in their own manner and as they each recalled 'em. They varied in their tellin' an' the further back in time the events they drew upon, the more their accounts differed one from the other. What I'm askin' is – how d'you do it, an' are you able to relate some of my earlier words back to me just as I said 'em?'

This was a request I dreaded. We were half way through his labours yet it was a situation I'd but vaguely foreseen and I hadn't planned quite how I might deal with it. I had to do so then and pretty quick! I took a gulp of beer, almost spluttered, then said, 'Yes - one of the gods of our land resides within me but is himself sightless, a god of darkness that may be heard only in the dark. He will utter your words in your voice but until I am returned to his shrine he will do so most unwillingly and will cause me much discomfort.'

'Aye, well, maybe tonight an' I'll much look forward to it.'

'Tonight, Mister Heracles. In the room you've given me or that close by but with the two girls excluded.'

'Right, then, tonight, whenever you're ready.' He drained his cup of beer in one go then began, 'I set of from Mycenae with chariot and 'orses, knowin' it'd take me under 'alf a day to reach Argos. Now Argos is thought by some to be the oldest city in Greece an', would you believe, yet another sacred to Hera. And 'er people also claim she was born there! Felt as if I couldn't get clear of the bitch so I wasn't stoppin' there. No, I carried on south to the mightily fortified city of Tiryns, built on a low, rocky hill risin' above the plain of Argolis. Like Mycenae, the people there made out its defensive walls 'ad been built by the Cyclops'. It'd been an easy journey though - no problems. In the town I found a tavern, stabled the 'orses, secured the chariot an' stayed the night. Most important though, Tiryns was close to the sea, on the Gulf of Argolis, an' from there, carryin' with me what I needed in a strong canvas bag but wearin' the lion skin with the club restin' over my right shoulder, I took myself next mornin' down to a likely lookin' boat. She was a long, graceful vessel with 'er hull an' single large sail coloured bright an' she was roomy enough for a good amount of cargo. The captain assured me he'd be sailin' shortly for the north shore of Crete where lay the port of Amnissos, the 'arbour town of Knossos. It seemed 'e wanted to charge me a lot more silver than it was worth for the trip but thought better of it as I stepped on board an' scowled at 'im through the lion jaws. The weather was fair so mainly under sail, with the 'elp of her thirty-somethin' oars as needed, she was soon on 'er way. I stood much of the time in her bow enjoyin' the cool sea breeze, sometimes watchin' 'er crew at work, sometimes gazin' out over the blue, open waters. In other words, Mister Peter, I was lovin' every bit of it.'

'Was there no danger from pirates?' I asked on recalling how this was a serious problem in parts of the Mediterranean throughout much of its history. His answer was much as I'd expected: 'There were no pirates in those days, not in those parts of the sea where Minos' navy ruled the waters. He'd cleared 'em all out as far west as Sicily an' many said he treated the sea as 'is own. Aye, in times of conflict Minos' ships would carry armed men ready to board an enemy vessel once they'd rammed it so you can imagine the 'and to 'and fightin' with their decks awash with blood. But back to my own affairs; we sighted Amnissos and were pullin' into the 'arbour long before sundown. Amnissos town was a busy place full of traders, its large 'arbour filled with vessels of all shapes an' sizes from Greece an' many other places includin' Egypt, but it also 'eld the king's own fleet. From it led a well prepared road, crowded with people, carts and animals goin' to an' from the city which spread over a series of low hills above the Vlychia stream. With some trouble I found a good tavern but 'ad to go outside Amnissos for it.

Next mornin' I set out minus the lion skin an' club to go into the city, thinkin' it better to look less threatenin' in this, a more sophisticated an' peaceable part of the world. Even left the sword behind. I 'elped myself to space on a large, ox-drawn cart carryin' goods up there from another ship and took in the sight of the place on my way. To reach Knossos I passed over the Vlychia stream via a massive stone viaduct supported by nine great arches. Along it went all of the traffic travellin' between the northern ports that traded with the Aegean world. Aye, it wasn't the first time I'd been, as I said earlier, but still, as we drew closer, I found Knossos a wonder to behold. It appeared as a vast spread of colourful, angular buildings, clustered together in terraces on risin' land many several floors 'igh with storage magazines ranged outside the main area full of great jars like the one Eurystheus 'ad hid inside when I dragged in the boar. There were parks an' gardens beyond where stood cypress trees and olive groves. And you know what, Mister Peter, so secure did they consider 'emselves, there were no defensive walls – no, nothin' at all like Mycenae, Tiryns or Thebes. Seems that in controllin' the seas as they did, the Cretans weren't afraid of anyone. Who on the Greek mainland could claim that when so many of 'em were all too often at each other's throats or under siege. And I 'oped next day to meet the great man, the ruler of Knossos 'imself, the one who claimed to be a descendent of Zeus, no less. One of several others, that is, who made the same claim.

I made my way along, entered through the southern gate then continued up a stepped passage decorated with colourful frescoes, this leadin' to a wide staircase. This in turn opened out into the great ceremonial courtyard surrounded by magnificent buildin's of varyin' size an' height but nearly all with those same columns below an' bulls' 'orns runnin' along the tops. I'd seen too little of the city all those years back but I knew the palace of Minos itself was to be found at its very centre. There were plenty of people millin' around or hurryin' about their business; better off citizens from the looks of 'em as well as a number of outsiders such as me. Even the slaves looked respectable so you might sometimes be unable to tell if a man was a slave or not. Most of the Cretan men dressed in a plain loincloth with bright patterned waistband but the women – well – you'd see 'em bare-breasted in the courts of most Mycenaean cities but far more so throughout Knossos, and lookin' fancier in their multi-layered flounced skirts an' open bodices with cap sleeves. They dressed their hair with pins an' jewels or let it fall curlin' loose about their shoulders. All very nice, an' thinkin' about it, some of the wealthier men's hair styles didn't look much different.'

You, dear reader, may on having reached this point, be inclined to think Heracles had become little more than a tourist, so impressed he was by Knossos. I couldn't blame him, though, even if all I saw of it when I went there was an almost total ruin with displays showing how it all was once believed to have been. Soon enough he'd have to relate the real reason for his journey but I didn't care to interrupt. Perhaps just then he sensed my thoughts because he gulped down his beer, looked hard at me and said, 'Mister Peter, I'm goin' on about the place when I should be tellin' you what that damned woman was lettin' me in for!'

'Please,' I assured him, 'I'm interested to hear about all you witnessed at Knossos.' Through my mind wafted the possibility that once back home I could add to or even refute what was accepted as known about Minoan Crete. But then, in trying to explain how such knowledge was acquired, I would, of course, attract only ridicule. Even should the recording go public it would be … No, wait - I could make it into a novel! My flight of fancy evaporated as he downed more beer, belched hard and resumed his tale.

'More and more people 'ad begun to gather either side of the court as if somethin' important was about to take place. Like most people, I'd 'eard about the bull-leapin' ceremony that took place there from time to time but they'd need to clear the entire area for such a spectacle so that wasn't about to 'appen. I carried on then stopped on the shaded side just over 'alf way along. Opposite me was a fine lookin' buildin' with wide steps leadin' up into it and a wider, decorated gallery above where people were gatherin', people of more than just courtly attire; these were royals. An' there was a fancy chair – no a throne, bein' set up. A man in rich regalia stepped around to sit in it an' I knew I was seein' King Minos 'imself! In a plainer gallery above that were assembled those I imagined to be lesser worthies.

People were movin' aside so it looked like we were in for some kind of parade so all I could do was stand an' wait for it to pass by. After that I knew exactly where I'd be headin' – aye, up those stairs! There was much noise from the direction where I'd entered the court. Men attired mainly in loincloths of varying colours were enterin', paradin' along, shoutin' an' singin'. These were led by a grey-'aired, long-bearded old man in a coloured smock who was obviously of some importance. As he drew level with me he turned with a steep bow to those in the lower gallery then continued on. Some of those caperin' behind 'im carried above 'em sheaves of grain or, by their sides, small implements from their farms. A good few of 'em looked to 'ave been at the beer or maybe it was wine, an' were not quite able to walk straight, while one fell over and 'ad to be hauled to his feet and 'elped along by others. It all looked very 'appy, in spite of a certain problem besettin' 'em that was to involve me. I looked on amused, then above the noise came a voice close to my ear: "It's the harvesters' procession – a ceremony of thanksgiving for a rewarding season and it's a chance to be seen by the king."

'I glanced around to be confronted by a rough lookin' character with loose cape over 'is well-worn tunic, a mop of unkempt black hair an' mid-length beard.

"Oh, thanks," I acknowledged, not intent upon pursuing further conversation.

"You're Heracles," said the man and suddenly I was listenin'. I looked down at 'im and not recognisin' the face I responded, "That I am, so who are you?"

"I'm called Amyntor nowadays and I remember you from Thebes but when there I was known as Dorus. I spent some time in the palace translating foreign language tablets with Creon's scribes. I didn't look quite like this, though; not until I came back here."

'His manner of speech was considerably more refined than mine; more like yours, Mister Peter, I'll readily admit, though his appearance was decidedly not. "So why," I asked, "are you 'ere now instead of Thebes an' why under a different name?" But people passing close in the procession were beating drums an' clashin' cymbals so conversation had become difficult.'

177

"Down there," he said aloud, gesturin' to a narrow back alley. We entered to find the noise of the procession less intrusive. "Let's find a tavern where we can talk," he suggested, "unless you want to wait this out. It might be getting on for midday before they're gone by and I have a tale to tell you."

"Aye, talk with you I will, but not now," I replied. "I've yet to go before Minos."

"You are to see the king, yes. Has he yet summoned you?"

"So you've 'eard have you. Well he's expectin' me an' knows who I am but you an' I can meet later in the day."

"We can meet shortly before sundown where we were standing just now. There's a tavern by the north gate with good wine if that's your preference."

'I agreed to that but as we were to step out into the open he said, "Heracles, mention nothing of me or my name to Minos, I beg you."

'I assured 'im I wouldn't an' so we parted company. Then I returned to watch the rest of the procession, stayin' until it began to thin out. As it ended, as the sounds an' tail-end retreated, the people on the galleries opposite disappeared inside an' the great square returned to normal. I crossed over to the stairs an' made my way up to what I found was a small anteroom with cushioned seats and richly frescoed walls. On them was well represented the double-headed axe I'd noticed elsewhere – a symbol of Minos' power. The place was well lit because there were light wells throughout all the main buildings of Knossos. Three guards approached me an' wanted to know who I was an' what was my business. With my brief answer one of them left the hall an' returned shortly after with a gesture for me to follow. We entered a stone flagged room; not one as grand as I'd expected so I imagined 'is great hall, the megaron, must be elsewhere for large gatherings an' this area for less formal ones or 'is chosen few. Before me, set on the floor, was a wide alabaster basin an' close beyond it, flanked by two armed guards, sat Minos, on a tall alabaster throne with carved scalloped back, little different to those I'd seen occupied by the rulers of Mycenae, Thebes and other royal cities. He was a stocky, round-faced, red 'aired man with a frownin' expression but unlike most other people I'd seen around since enterin' Knossos he'd got a full, meticulously trimmed beard. Across his cheek, runnin' diagonally under his right eye, was an ugly scar. On 'is head rested a shallow, upwardly flared copper crown set with precious stones of various colours an' topped with a red plume. A torque bearin' more valuable stones crossed his broad, naked chest while 'is heavily belted kilt of pale linen was richly embroidered about its lower edges. All this I took in before offerin' my bow an' straightenin' up again. Below two of the russet coloured walls, decorated with mythical griffins, ran well-cushioned stone benches. I glanced briefly aside at these. They were occupied by those I imagined must be priests an' maybe officials of a sort – all of 'em starin' at me. It appeared a conference 'ad been in progress but not so important that the king couldn't summon me. At last Minos broke what was becomin', at least for me, an awkward silence.'

"Heracles, I have heard much of you and your presence is welcomed. Eurystheus, ruler of Mycenae, informs me you are cunning and capable and will undertake a most necessary task here in my kingdom. This is so, is it not?"

'He appeared relaxed but spoke with a commanding yet calm confidence that confirmed 'is status. "I hope to be of service," I answered, an' not bein' sure whether to address 'im as 'Sire' 'My Lord,' or somethin' similar, I decided to risk not botherin' an' so added, "But the full nature of what I'm called here to do is not yet revealed to me." Great an' powerful a man as he was, quite ruthless many said, he showed no sign of anger at my lapse in offerin' a correct title though others gathered there didn't 'ide their expressions of disapproval an' the armed guards glanced at 'im in expectation of instructions to do with me whatever he ordered. Maybe he felt 'e needed my services more than petty formalities, or per'aps I flattered me'self.'

"What I require of you," he went on, "is to capture then remove from our lands hereabouts a great white bull that roams wild to menace our farmers, though you might not have thought anything was amiss when standing down there with that peasant to watch the procession. The bull treads down their crops and plays havoc with their cattle and it has gored to death some of those who attempted to contain it. You are to capture then take it to the port of Amnissos where a vessel will be readied for its transportation to the Peloponnese. There you must deliver it to King Eurystheus who will do with it as he pleases. I will provide you with men and the means to contain the beast and you will be rewarded should you succeed. If you do not succeed, Eurystheus requests that you be put to death. Is that understood?"

"Aye, sir, it is," I responded with that added courtesy, while wishing once again I could get my 'ands around that bastard Eurystheus' scrawny throat.

"Return for directions when you are ready to begin your task," he continued. "Inform one of my men and the means of transport will be made available. You may leave us now."

'It's no exaggeration, Mister Peter, if I say I was taken aback. Why would Minos think Eurystheus would want somethin' that'd caused so many problems? Or maybe Eurystheus didn't know about such problems but 'ad 'eard the bull was good for breedin' purposes.'

I asked him, 'D'you think, Mister Heracles, that Minos would've had you executed if you'd failed?'

'Can't be sure, can I, but as I left the buildin' I considered Hera must be behind it all to bolster 'er crass entertainment at my expense. Anyhow, as I'd time to spare until sunset I wandered around to admire the grand buildin's of Knossos, then before returnin' to the great square where I'd find Amyntor waitin' I located Athena's shrine an' there made my offerin'.

"Minos did see you talkin' to me," I informed Amyntor as soon as we met. "He thought you were a peasant."

"Hope I don't smell like one," he grinned. "Let's get ourselves to the tavern."

'I followed Amyntor who was now lookin' cleaner and tidier than before, along to the tavern which as I expected, bein' where it was, proved a better place than any I'd encountered outside Knossos, includin' Mycenae an' even Thebes. With a lute player earnin' 'is keep in one corner, it was moderately busy but lacked the shoutin' an' raucous laughter you'd expect in most other places. We sat in comfort with good food an' good wine, an' now the sky was darkenin' there were plenty of fancy oil lamps placed about so people could still admire the frescoed walls. As we began to eat I said, "I take it you wish to explain somethin' to me, am I right?"

'He remained silent for a while, as if unsure 'ow to respond, then replied, "Your fame and your exploits are known to many but I gathered knowledge of your present situation by listening to the words of traders who loiter a while and exchange news at Amnissos. Some of what I hear may be nonsense but I understand you are allotted numerous tasks by Eurystheus, King of Mycenae and that one concerns capture of the bull that is a serious cause for concern in the farmlands around here. There is much I wish to tell you, Heracles, in part because you are to become involved in something of which I know a great deal and because it's an account I need to get off my chest and give to a man who will keep my words to himself alone."

"This does sound interestin'," I told 'im as I tasted good Cretan wine. "And I'll keep your confidence, my friend, that I promise."

"Have you heard people speak of the Minotaur?" he asked.

"Yes, I recall somethin' of it" I replied. "I think a good few people 'ave 'eard of it but only as a vague rumour an' there's plenty of those about. Why d'you mention it?"

"Well," he replied, lowerin' 'is voice as though to avoid bein' overheard, "It exists, it lives, and it is the reason why my name and my identity had to be changed before I returned to Crete."

'Darkness 'ad fallen beyond the tavern window an' stars were brightenin'. The oil lamp flame on our table swayed as he poured more wine an' havin' now my full attention he leaned closer to say,' "As the evening is ours I'll relate my tale from the beginning. As you must know, Minos claims descent from Zeus himself, direct descent that is, and as we know, most people will believe anything if it's repeated often enough, especially by someone like a great leader who holds the power of life and death over his subjects. Though not by nature a spiteful man, he ousted two of his brothers to gain sole rule over Knossos, with its seaports. For this he thanked and offered sacrifice to Poseidon, as god of the sea and shaker of the land. He made this city greater than any other on Crete; he established his power over the whole island and well beyond with his navy, for which he often thanked Poseidon for looking with favour upon him. To prove his god-given right to rule, he boasted that any prayer to the gods would be answered if considered worthy, and so it was. On one occasion when sacrificing to Poseidon, he prayed that a bull might emerge from the sea and promised that if so, he would then sacrifice it in public ceremony to the god himself for his continued blessing.

There was one night a great storm with immense waves pounding our shores. Fishermen standing around that morning with nothing to do until the weather calmed saw a great white bull emerge from the waves and go galloping off in the direction of Knossos. It's said to have scared the wits out of those who saw it but when word got around that it seemed less dangerous than bulls usually are, Minos had it brought to the city, no doubt intending to fulfil his promise to Poseidon. Having taken a good look at it, though, and knowing Poseidon was not in the habit of coming ashore, he decided the bull would be better off let loose among his own cattle for a time to help breed better stock. In the open ceremonial area west of the palace he arranged to sacrifice a different bull in its place. So people wouldn't notice the difference he chose the largest bull anyone could find and had it coloured with a paste made out of fish glue and chalk. In all of this Minos, from the very beginning, was encouraged by his wife, Pasiphae, who pulled Daedalus in to help them - yes, Daedalus, regarded as the cleverest and greatest craftsman this land ever saw. Over the years he'd overseen improvements to water delivery and sewage disposal throughout Knossos and even found time in applying his skills to make the cleverest of toys for Pasiphae's children. But I'll return to Pasiphae and Daedalus shortly unless you feel my tale is wearing thin."

'No, I didn't feel the man's tale was wearin' thin and I told 'im so. I hope, Mister Peter, you don't feel it's wearin' thin, either.'

'No, Mister Heracles,' I responded as he topped up our drinks to overflowing. 'I find it most interesting. But didn't they risk anyone noticing the difference with the substitute bull? The fish glue and chalk must have stunk a bit.'

Heracles found my comment most amusing. 'Aye,' he grinned, 'and that's what I asked Amyntor an' he replied, "Yes and that's where we came in, myself and another slave."

"Another slave?" I queried. "You mean you both were...?"

"Yes," 'e answered, "we were personal slaves to Minos and sworn to secrecy. We helped prepare the substitute bull and dressed as priests we led it out of the city to the open area outside the town where thousands had gathered to watch. It was sacrificed without a fuss and that was that. Except it wasn't. No, it wasn't the kind of thing you could keep entirely secret and it soon became known throughout his household and beyond. Poseidon, of course, found out what had happened and took his revenge, first dealing with Pasiphae. Queen or no,

she'd always been free with her favours throughout
the palace and any number of the guards had left her
presence with a smile on his face, as well as, er, yes,
as well as a number of others. Minos must've been
aware of this but as he enjoyed the attentions of
young women kept about the palace at least in part
for that reason, both saw the situation as a case of
live and let live. But what happened later really was
intended to be secret as far as Pasiphae was
concerned – or so she hoped. Poseidon caused her
lust for physical gratification to intensify beyond all
reason. She tried to control her urges but could not
and developed a quite unnatural craving when she
saw the white bull sent by Poseidon."

'An' that, Mister Peter, is another story but not
one involvin' me.'

'But Mister Heracles,' I insisted, 'you've taken
the tale this far. Can't we step aside and follow what
you were told of the whole affair concerning
Pasiphae.' I really didn't want to miss out on the
words of people so closely involved in what after all
had been related in one way or another in my own
time without the wonderful source here at my
disposal.

'A small diversion,' he muttered, glancing at
me in disapproval. Then he relented and said, 'Oh,
very well, Mister Peter, I'll do that.' And so
Heracles continued in his own words with the tale
Amyntor had begun.

'Pasiphae approached Daedalus once more an'
demanded that 'e construct a life-sized model cow.
This she intended to climb inside so as to receive

the attentions of the bull. For the bull to mount it, 'owever, the false cow would 'ave to be utterly convincin' and only Daedalus might work out how to achieve this. Daedalus told Amyntor later he'd been appalled at the thought, an' the consequences should Minos find out, but she'd persuaded him one way or another to undertake the task. He also avoided one of 'er well-known rages that'd determined the fate of others. In a disused part of the palace below ground level but with easy access to outside, Daedalus went to work with Amyntor an' a companion slave called Oxylus; both ordered by Pasiphae to 'elp 'im with the job. At first the two weren't sure what it was all about because Daedalus wouldn't say but Pasiphae made it clear that if either of 'em mentioned what he was workin' on to anyone, anywhere, any time, they'd both be done for. The result, after many long days of effort, was more than just a model. It was clad in genuine cowhide, it 'ad realistic false eyes an' Daedalus 'ad concocted some kind of animal scent that made it smell right. Its side hinged upward so by then Amyntor and Oxylus 'ad realised what the cow was designed for.'

'Pretty obvious wasn't it, Mister Heracles,' I put in.

'Aye, Mister Peter, pretty obvious. Anyhow, Daedalus 'ad done what was asked of 'im an' left Amyntor and Oxylus that last afternoon with Pasiphae remainin' to appraise their 'andiwork. A day later she ordered Amyntor an' Oxylus to meet 'er after dark with the bull, which 'ad been allocated a compound close outside, an' to take it to where the false cow was kept. They thought at first they were pretty skilled in keepin' the animal under control but soon worked out there must also be another, unseen 'and, in charge of it. On that warm evenin' they entered the chamber to find it illuminated by just one oil lamp an' Pasiphae standin' almost naked before 'em, except for 'er precious bodily decorations. Utterly shameless they said, with a kind of defiant smile on 'er face. She then demanded Amyntor an' Oxylus to leave 'er alone. The bull would do its business with 'er inside the cow and afterwards the two men were to go back an' return it to the enclosure. Listenin' from a discreet distance they 'eard the bull doin' what it was intended to do with considerable snortin' and 'er cries from in there were loud enough for both of 'em to 'ear above that. For 'er future encounters she'd no longer need Amyntor an' Oxylus except to take the bull away again after she'd left via the internal passage to the palace.

This continued over numerous evenin's for almost a month, but one night the bull broke loose from its compound an' disappeared. Minos eventually 'eard somethin' of Pasiphae's nocturnal activities but for a time ignored it as the palace was always awash with gossip of one kind or another. By the time he got to thinkin' he ought to take more notice, the bull was gone an' 'is devious wife'd ordered Amyntor an' Oxylus to destroy the false cow, which they did by burnin' it to ashes. Nothin' more was said so at last the two men thought this was the end of the affair an' maybe they no longer needed to fear for their lives. But it wasn't the end at all – it was the beginnin' of somethin' far worse.

Unfortunately for both of 'em, Oxylus, after too many beers in the tavern when Amyntor wasn't there with 'im, couldn't keep 'is mouth shut about the cow. Minos or Pasiphae some'ow got to know what he'd been on about an' ordered Amyntor and Oxylus executed. Amyntor was warned by one of Minos' palace women he'd befriended so he got out of Knossos that night and 'eaded for Thebes where, because of 'is skills, he took up the work I already mentioned. What 'appened to Oxylus, Amyntor could only guess at but he's never set eyes on 'im since.

Aye, Mister Peter, it was a rare tale but on hearin' it I 'ad to ask 'im why, in the end, did he return to Knossos? Even in disguise he must 'ave been takin' a risk. He grinned wide as you like an' said, it was simple enough; Thebes wasn't too bad a place in those days - better than Mycenae, but life in Knossos he found more satisfyin'. The place was bright, open an' clean, the food an' wine were better an' the women, well -!

Once returned to Knossos Amyntor made contact with one of the palace slaves, Dorus, who he'd known well, to find out what'd 'appened in 'is absence. This Dorus 'ad not been one of Minos' personal slaves but one who'd 'elped keep allocated areas of the palace clean. After plyin' the man with enough wine Dorus went on to tell Amyntor what must've been known throughout the palace at the time as well as what wasn't supposed to be known.

A priest of Poseidon 'ad informed Dorus how, on discoverin' the bull he'd sent to Minos for sacrifice was still around an' doing its duty with selected cows as well as with Pasiphae, Poseidon 'ad caused it to break out an' go runnin' wild. The bull 'ad learned enough about people to be crafty an' was provin' too difficult to catch. In spite of complaints from those who earned their livin' outside the city an' their threat to march on Knossos in protest, Minos, hopin' to get the bull back, 'ad taken little notice until matters worsened and I, Heracles, was called across to sort things out. Dorus told 'im also that as Pasiphae 'ad been with child she'd not been seen around for some time. She already 'ad four sons an' two daughters, an' some claim there were more, so no one 'ad thought 'er absence unusual, although there was the inevitable secretive whisperin' about who the father on this occasion might be.

When this latest child was delivered there'd been the usual celebrations expected but after a while all 'ad gone quiet an' the little one, they'd called 'im Asterion, wasn't paraded around or outside the palace for public admiration as might've otherwise been expected. Dorus 'imself 'ad never actually seen the child but word got out in those early days, from one of the few who 'ad, that it looked more like a pig an' snarled rather than cried. He'd gathered from continuin' innuendo that somethin' was very wrong. Word from one of the kitchen staff 'ad got around that little Asterion was growin' bigger almost by the day an' already as large as a ten year old. Worse still, either side of 'is 'ead were growin' two lumps that gradually, as people witnessed, began to get longer. Dorus one day sneaked into the kitchens where 'e saw Asterion eatin' raw meat from the floor, then word got out that it'd 'appened several times already. Eventually only slaves were to attend 'im an' they admitted to Dorus that they'd dreaded doin' so because of 'is appearance – as much animal as human they said an' they feared he might bite one of 'em.

What no one could 'ope to play down was the day Asterion attacked a female slave in the kitchen when she tried to rescue the meat he'd stolen. He leaped at 'er, tore out the girl's throat an' was tryin' to eat 'er until they pulled 'im off! Minos ordered 'im taken by armed guards an' slaves to a secluded room in a little used area at the northern edge of the palace. Dorus was ordered to discontinue any duties 'e might've been given in that part of the palace an' to stay well away.

But Dorus, out of curiosity an' with less work to do, 'ad on occasion hung about the area. On earlier visits, he'd seen Pasiphae goin' along the corridor on 'er way to the forbidden area with armed guards an' slaves, some of 'em carryin' raw meat. He'd each time dodged behind a column so as not to be seen an' from there he'd 'eard agitated conversation an' the loud snarlin' of Asterion. One day a small dog belongin' to Pasiphae's daughters, Ariadne and Phaedra, scampered by. He told how he'd 'eard the dog barkin' furiously, then squealin' in terror. Next, there was only silence. Then along came Ariadne, forbidden to be there but anxious to find the dog. Moments later he'd 'eard her screams an' she came dashin' back along the corridor in a wild panic, to be met by 'er brothers who'd set out in turn to find 'er. Dorus had decided then an' there it was no place for 'im to be an' as he left he narrowly escaped bein' seen by a group of armed guards an' slaves makin' their way to where Asterion was kept.

Now that's as much as Dorus was able to tell Amyntor but as time passed, rumours materialised as if from mid air until the truth could no longer be concealed. But he'd go no further than this. I'd need to talk with Daedalus himself as he knew more than almost everyone about the affairs of Knossos in general an' what later 'appened. I would most likely find 'im in 'is workshop to the east of the palace where it was much quieter and Amyntor would show me the way.

We left the tavern an' he took me through a number of alleyways an' smaller squares that led us out to a lower buildin' where seated in the shade before a small table was dark-'aired an' bearded Daedalus, a sharp-eyed man of middle years, in a loose-fittin' woollen smock. On this well-worn garment I noticed a number of stains of various colours, paint stains, maybe, an' I wondered briefly what he'd been workin' on. Amyntor introduced me an' Daedalus, part risin' from his seat, stared at me 'ard an' said in a soft voice, "Ah, so I meet at last the notorious Heracles. I've heard much about you these past years and I know why Minos has summoned you here to Knossos. Do sit down won't you but please try not to break my chair with your weight."

'I eased carefully down then as I sat he looked up at Amyntor to ask, "And will you be joining us? If so there is another chair in my workroom."

"I'll not stay," Amyntor replied, but he outlined to Daedalus in the briefest terms what he'd explained to me. Daedalus ran a hand down 'is beard an' nodded as Amyntor finished speakin'. With final niceties Amyntor strode off an' left us alone to talk. Daedalus 'ad heard more than I expected about my life at Thebes an' my subsequent troubles but he was curious to know more. I described in greater detail what I'd faced up to through the curse of Hera, includin' the 'elp I'd received from Athena an' my friend Iolaus, an' as the shiftin' sun began to cast light over the area we occupied he listened intently, questionin' me from time to time. Talkin' with 'im I felt this was a man whose modest appearance an' situation belied a knowledge and an understandin' far beyond that of anyone else.

"You've been quite busy, then," he smiled when I was done. Turning to his workshop he called for a youth who I took to be an apprentice, to bring us wine. This was set before us in a colourfully decorated jar together with a pair of ornate silver goblets an' as the youth left us, Daedalus said, "He's hardly any older than my own son, Icarus, you know." I didn't know because I knew nothin' at the time about Icarus. Anyhow, Daedalus poured an' the wine was very good indeed. We relaxed a while then he set about to relate those happenin's I was so keen to know about. Aye, it's all fresh in my mind, Mister Peter.

Minos an' his dear wife 'eld out for much too long before recognisin' the fact, obvious to everyone else at Knossos who'd set eyes on 'im, that Asterion was a monster in the makin', if not already made. He 'ad to be removed from sight as well as contact with all others, except for slaves who took 'is food an' the armed guards who let it be known that they wanted only to kill 'im before 'e went for one of 'em.

So what 'appened next, Daedalus 'ad me wonderin' as he swirled 'is wine about. Well though it was no secret to anyone familiar with Knossos, still existin' below a part of the city are the remains of an earlier palace, known as the Labyrinth, upon which the present one was built. It's a maze of chambers an' passages, forbiddin' an' most of it utterly dark, though in one of the oldest chambers there's a fresh water spring that drains away through a channel into the 'illside.

Some areas were once used for storage, later the livin' quarters for slaves an' after that for the imprisonment of criminals. But its use 'ad to change because they wanted Asterion confined there. There was only one entrance to it from within the palace itself an' that needed to be much altered. All of this work was left to Daedalus an' he 'ad 'em rebuild this passage with the first part leadin' to an anteroom. From the anteroom an inner passage led to the Labyrinth. This second passage Daedalus 'ad made too small for Asterion, or the beast he'd soon end up as, to escape through, well before he – it, 'ad grown with bull's 'orns to full size – aye, that's what they in time became. Through this inner passage a pair of slaves, havin no choice in the matter, were sent stoopin' low each day, one carryin a firebrand, the other with raw meat which they were to pass through the innermost door. The reason for the firebrand, apart from enablin' them to see their way, was that they peer into the Labyrinth an' report back if they'd 'ad sight of the Minotaur, as Asterion was becomin' known, though who thought of it was a mystery.

In case anyone was wonderin' why it continued to be fed, the priests of Poseidon had convinced Minos that if he allowed the thing to starve or to die by other means, this would bring upon Knossos further retribution from the god 'imself. There'd been a number of minor earthquakes that the priests assured 'im were a forewarnin'. Well it served to make 'em sound credible. Asterion still 'ad to be given food but no slave any longer would go through the remainin' entrance to do that, no matter how 'arsh or real was the prospect of punishment for disobedience. Two lots of slaves, he told me, 'ad never returned. After that, food was passed down a steep slopin' chute situated in a small courtyard close to the palace. This was already in place from the days when prisoners were kept below there.

Daedalus 'ad it protected by an 'inged bronze grille he'd devised. Asterion would never have gotten through it anyway because his 'orns 'ad grown too big.

But it was human flesh the Minotaur desired more than anythin' an' people in the palace above, an' others beyond, could 'ear it bellow durin' the night. Minos' daughters, Ariadne and Phaedra would lie awake in the dark fearful of the beast somehow breakin' out an' findin' its way up in the darkness to enter their room, even though it never could 'ave. To placate the thing a condemned man, a criminal, a slave or even sometimes a woman might be cast down into its lair from the coutyard above or forced to go through the passage inside the palace. People would gather around the grille outside an' wait to 'ear their screams but the Minotaur's victims might 'ide an' evade 'im for days in the darkness before he came upon the poor buggers. Daedalus much regretted that he'd used 'is skills in the affair an' feared that Minos one day might 'old him ever more responsible for it all through 'im constructing the false cow. One day, he believed someone must enter the Labyrinth an' destroy the beast because it seemed to cast its shadow over all of Knossos.

D'you believe much of this, Mister Peter,' Heracles asked me, 'now you've 'ad me go over it?'

'Sounds pretty dreadful but yes, I do,' was all I could think of saying as we each left the table to take a necessary, or should I say, natural, break. His tale of the Minotaur could all have been bullshit, if you'll pardon the term, but being immortal Heracles must have known that some time later, a man would go down there and slay the beast. That man would be Theseus the Athenian - but that's another story. But wait! I'd never asked how long Heracles himself had been where he now was, in the Elysian Fields. Perhaps for him the event I mentioned was yet to happen.

During those moments alone, I checked all was well with the voice recorder. When back in the courtyard I asked Heracles what more he'd learned from his meeting with Daedalus.

'Well, Mister Peter, he'd kind of brought me up to date but I was surprised Hera didn't 'ave Minos send *me* into the Labyrinth. Maybe but for the presence of Athena's influence with Zeus she would 'ave an maybe I'd 'ave done for the bugger with my old club. Anyhow, I'd like to 'ave spent more time in Daedalus' company but my next move was a return to the palace where I'd get instructions for roundin' up the big white bull sent by Poseidon.'

Heracles looked beyond the courtyard entrance and said, 'The sun's gettin' low, Mister Peter. Remember you were goin' to give me a sample of that amazin' memory you possess – in a darkened room, wasn't it, aye, that's what you said.'

'Yes, after sunset,' I replied, having worked out how I hoped to manage it.

'Then let's watch the sun go down,' he said, refilling our goblets, 'an' finish the wine before we go inside.' His attendants had already been out to light the oil lamps when we arose from the table and

I said, 'Mister Heracles, I must first contemplate and prepare myself in the darkness of my room before I do as you ask. It takes me great effort to do this when not at my own home. I will go inside now and call you when I'm ready.'

Feeling pretty nervous I went straight into the bedroom and pulled out the recorder. By the light of oil lamps I was able to run back the recording to a convenient spot. This was to his first labour, the part where he related how he'd gone to the cave to find the Nemean lion and he'd hurled a stone into the cave where it lay hidden and how, when it emerged to leap at him, he'd single-handedly killed it. Once I was prepared I blew out the lamps and in complete darkness I groped my way to the door and called out, 'Ready, Mister Heracles!'

When he arrived, a dark form merging from the unlit corridor beyond, my hand was shoved into my shirt pocket with a finger twitching over the 'Play' button. 'Right,' I said, 'now we'll hear you speak.' I held my breath and pressed the button. A short pause. Then his voice! The term, 'bag of nerves,' certainly applied to me as his words spilled clearly into the room. Neither of us moved or made a sound during the time he narrated his tale, so on it went with my finger stroking the 'Stop' button until his account reached the point where he arrived back at the village with his prize in tow. I heard as well as felt the click and then – silence.

'Don't know what to say, Mister Peter,' he breathed at last. 'I don't understand how you 'ave my voice within you. I'm bewildered – I can 'ardly

believe what I just 'eard. It's as if the gods were …
Aye, who are these gods? Can I 'ear more?'

'It exhausts and confuses me,' I replied. 'Only
when I return home can I reveal in full what I hold
inside for our gods are not here in the Elysian
Fields. You must accept this, Mister Heracles.
Within me, really, is all you have said. Every single
word.'

Again a silence, now charged with uncertainty.
Would he *demand* more? Sounds, and female
chatter drifted from the direction of the bathroom.
Tiye and Mayet, and I sighed inwardly with relief.
Now footsteps and the light of wavering oil lamps
began dimly to invade the darkness of the wall
outside the bedroom. Heracles turned aside to look
back at me, saying in a subdued manner, 'Them two
girls are headin' this way, Mister Peter, so I'll not
see you again 'till sunrise. Meanwhile, 'ave a good
night.'

He left the room and as the two approaching
stopped to watch him leave, I managed to yank out
and reset the voice recorder. The light outside my
door was brightening, the chatter getting closer, so
quick as I could I got around the bed to push up the
leather blind and place the recorder onto the
window ledge where it would catch next morning's
light.

- and Its Capture

'So,' began Heracles next morning as we sat
once more in the courtyard with food and drink, 'I

was out early next day to let Minos know I was ready to set out after the bull. I wasn't wearin' the lion skin, nor did I carry my trusty club, but the guards told me there was no need for me to meet the great man again because they knew what was needed for this, my latest task. They advised me to return to the stables area below the south gate by midday and everythin' would be ready for me to leave, so with time to spare I decided I'd revisit Daedalus for further enlightenin' conversation. I found my way there only to discover 'is workshop was closed up an' there was nobody around who could tell me where he was. I strolled back to the great square hopin' on the off-chance I might see Amyntor but as there was no sign of 'im either I spent a while in the tavern where we'd been the previous day thinkin' perhaps he'd show up there, but 'e didn't. Next I returned to the tavern at Amnissos to collect those items I'd need, includin' the obvious. A good time for the lion skin, I thought, then people would know for sure who they were dealin' with. So I set off back, peerin' out through a pair of jaws, a spear in one 'and, sword at my waist, my club in the other with it restin' on my right shoulder. I wasn't sure what I'd find waitin' for me outside Knossos but it became clear enough as I approached the stables. There was a large, 'eavy, four-wheeled cart with high, sturdily railed sides, a rear gate an' a hinged ramp. The cart, with four 'orses attached, was obviously intended to contain the bull but didn't appear suitable for rough country. Inside the cart were three men, one bein' the driver, together with provisions an' coils of rope. Close by the cart stood a pair of two 'orse chariots, each containin' two men. One of the men in the cart jumped down to greet me. "Heracles without a doubt!" he grinned. "I am Harmonides; I'm in charge of these men and by order of King Minos we are to capture, contain and give over to you the white bull that is roaming our land."

'I was much impressed by the preparations Minos 'ad ordered for my benefit an' this man, well spoken as he was, must 'ave been a member of the king's court. But an important question I needed to ask - "Does anyone know where this bull is to be found?" If none of 'em did know, then we might wander for many days without a sight of it.

"We know from where most complaints arise," replied Harmonides. "They're from level farming lands south of the city, owned largely by King Minos himself, so that's where we first must search."

'It was pretty 'ot by then, Mister Peter, with the sun blazin' from a cloudless blue sky an' no sign of a breeze. With nods from the men, I clambered into the cart, its gate was swung shut an' our party set off south with some shoutin', a crack of whips, rattlin' wheels an' snorting 'orses. As the afternoon went on we passed through olive groves an' vineyards until findin' ourselves in more open country with wheat fields and grazin' land spread all about.'

"D'you know this area, Heracles?" Harmonides asked.

"No," I answered, "only Knossos an' close thereabouts."

"Well if we kept going we'd reach cedar and cypress forests and later on next day we'd have sight of the sea. But of course we go no further than the farmland we see around us because this is where the bull wanders. As the afternoon has drawn on this far I think now we should stop here and keep our eyes open."

'I and the men gathered on or around the cart. Each of us glanced about from time to time until one of the men pointed aside an' called, "Look out!" But it wasn't the bull I 'oped he'd spotted. Two men were approachin', both, from their rustic dress were obviously farm workers. They drew close an' one called out angrily, "What's all this?" an' from the other, "Aye, what's goin' on?" Their attention soon switched to me in my strange to them attire but it was Harmonides who answered, "We are here to find and to capture the white bull. Has it been seen of late?"

"Has it been seen 'e asks!" responded the first man, angrily. "Aye it 'as been seen – it tramped across my fields earlier this mornin'. Pity it is you weren't 'ere then."

"An' it scattered my cows!" added the other. "Its been stampin' around 'ere for two days now an' doesn't look to be finished with us yet!"

"Then," replied Harmonides, "lead us to where the bull was last seen and there we'll continue our search."

'Our small group carried on, our cart rattlin' behind the two men with our chariots followin'. After travellin' no great distance we approached their small 'amlet an' its surroundin' wooden barns. There we stopped on land indicated by them an' watched the pair leave without another word to carry on with their work. Harmonides' next move would 'ave been to send out the two chariots in an effort to locate the bull but the sun was gettin' low and even if the bull was spotted it might be dusk before we could get near enough an' too dark for the attempted roundin' up.'

"Alright, lads," he called, "we settle here for the night! We've logs for a fire, food to cook and beer aplenty. In the morning, soon as the sky begins to lighten, we unload the cart then set off with it to find our bull." It seemed this was to be our base for a while. Soon enough one man was twirlin' his little bow to raise enough flame for startin' a fire. By the time the sun went down two of 'em 'ad the fire goin' steady with meat sizzlin' on a bronze grill above it, one was ladlin' out the beer an' another playin' a double flute. Those with less to do were chantin' and singin'. After we'd eaten an' as the fire was dyin' each set out 'is place to rest – some in the cart, others, as well as me, on a grassy rise. Peace for a time would be ours. As I gazed up at a benevolent sky with a crescent moon an' a spread of brilliant stars, somethin' passed close over'ead. I gazed wide-eyed as it circled then swept low an' slow above me before soarin' into the night. A white owl!'

'So the goddess was sill keeping an eye on you, Mister Heracles,' I said.

'Aye, it felt to me like she was. When I an' the rest of 'em awoke there was barely a glimmer of light on the 'orizon an' the air was chilled. While I looked on, two of the men began clearin' stuff out of the cart, except for coils of rope an' their spears, while another was set about startin' a fire. The sky was brightenin' an' others were soon occupied with preparin' food – figs an' cheese with barley bread dipped in red wine. Maybe an odd start to the day but I wasn't complainin'. With the sun risen we were on our way with the chariots goin' well ahead, parted from each other but each within our sight. The cart rumbled on with the rest of us takin' an easy ride.

Mid-mornin' found us crossin' a stream with more wheat sown fields and grazin' pastures ahead. It was then one of the chariots stopped on a shallow rise an' one of the men aboard it began to wave at us. We carried on as the second chariot joined the first an' then we saw the white bull. It was grazin' peacefully. We in the cart jumped out. The two chariots approached with me an' the men on foot followin', two with coils of rope over their shoulders an' all of em' carryin' spears planned to act as goads. Even as we drew closer the bull at first took little notice. One of the men remarked 'ow it appeared to be used to humans. Well it would be, wouldn't it, Mister Peter, as you know. But now it stopped chewin' grass an' raised its 'ead to watch us approach. We were quite close when the two men with ropes let down their spears an' the two chariots once more spread apart to proceed slowly, not too close, on either side of the bull. Once stopped, their four men jumped down with one of their number, who also carried rope, lettin' this part way out an' ready to cast its lasso end, as did the other two from the cart.

I'd contributed nothin' to this effort so far but now readied my spear also to act as a goad if needed. The bull watched us, glancin' this way an' that as if any moment to make a dash for it. One of the rope men from our cart was closest to the bull an' was first to make his cast, followed right after by the other two who'd dashed forward while the bull was distracted. Two of the lassoes 'ad caught its 'orns while the third passed over his back. The men were careerin' about with shouts flyin' from one to the other. In a whirl of snortin' and stampin' the bull tried to escape, tuggin' violently, scatterin' earth as the two men whose ropes 'ad caught, closed together an' pulled 'ard towards the waitin' cart, heavin' away without success. Others moved to its sides with spears levelled. The third rope man recovered 'is lasso an' was about to throw again when I thought now to become fully involved.

I dropped my club, wrenched off the lion skin an' dashed at the bull, 'ardly thinkin' what I was about. Approachin' it side-on I grabbed its left 'orn an' swung up onto its back. Holdin' both 'orns I was thinkin' what next was to 'appen. I wondered if the bull would wrench free an' dash off with me astride so I was surprised, as were the rest of 'em, when it calmed down. With me still perched up there it allowed itself to be drawn towards the cart. There the two men in charge there stepped into the cart an' at its front they fed out their rope ends to those outside before makin' their way out past the bull, which stood there as if puzzled an' doin' nothin'. Once I'd dismounted, the bull could be drawn from outside into the cart, an' so it was, clatterin' into it without any sign of a fuss. Only the 'orses seemed worried as the ramp was raised an' the gate slammed shut. I recovered the lion skin an' my club then all we 'ad to do was set off back to our base camp. It was late in the afternoon when we arrived there so they debated over whether we should set off straightaway to reach Knossos in the dead of night or leave at daybreak. Daybreak won out so as some of 'em took fresh wood to rebuild the fire, others made ready to prepare food once it was lit. The rest of us sat around chatterin' an' drinkin'. I admit they'd had little need for me most of that day.'

'A busy labour for others this time around, Mister Heracles,' I said.

'So it was but don't forget I'd to take our prize all the way back over the sea to Tiryns then on to Mycenae, feedin' it and cleanin' out shit on the way until I'd present the bull to 'is glorious majesty. Anyhow we set off in the mornin' as planned but on the way we called into a couple of the farms to collect hay for the bull. On seein' we'd caught it they could 'ardly begrudge us that, could they. Aye, they were pretty impressed an' glad they were to see the last of it. Before reachin' Knossos' later that afternoon I left the bull an' men lookin' after it closer to Amnissos, so avoidin' an awkward climb to the palace. The bull attracted a crowd of chatterin' people with their kids runnin' about the cart an' tryin' to poke at the bull with sticks. Harmonides' men managed to drive 'em all away while I went up to 'ave one of the guards inform Minos of our arrival. He returned to tell me Minos was not interested in goin' down in person to see the bull, he'd instead sent a man along to report on it and 'is wife 'ad made no comment. All Minos wanted was that we get the bull away from Crete and that would be in the mornin' when a vessel to take the cart would be available at Amnissos. Harmonides an' three of his men were to make sure our bull went onto the ship then they'd sail with us an' see it left our vessel at the other end.'

'Minos was certainly making sure he got rid of it, wasn't he,' I remarked.

'Too right he was,' Heracles responded, 'and it may be his dear, lovin' wife had somethin' to do with that.'

'Though it could be,' I remarked, 'that with her unnatural urges less pressing, Pasiphae felt too embarrassed to comment.'

'Aye, could be,' he muttered. 'Anyhow, Mister Peter, Minos agreed to 'ave more of his own guards look after the cart so those men with me could get a proper night's rest and I'd return to the tavern at Amnissos. Minos, meanwhile, 'ad sent to me a leather pouch, heavy an' about the size of a man's shoe, its opening fastened with a cord that in turn was sealed with 'ardened wax that bore the royal stamp. At the tavern I opened this to find it contained coiled up lengths of gold an' silver that for a time would make me a wealthy man.

At first light next day we were down at the 'arbour where ramps 'ad been prepared to 'elp get the cart safely onto the stern of a large vessel. Minos 'ad ordered it to carry no other cargo unless it was essential an' sail as soon as the cart was in position. The bull snorted an' stamped for all it was worth but that didn't stop us doin' what we 'ad to do. The ship set out with 'er large square sail billowin', while the captain bawled 'is orders an' fifty oarsmen pulled 'ard. But uneventful as the voyage otherwise was, we didn't make such good time as I'd 'oped. A blusterin' wind from the north was what slowed us. It was dark when we approached our destination with firebrands lit at our bow to let 'em know we were on our way in. Fires were burnin' ashore to help guide us and men with firebrands were gathered at the 'arbour. When we docked our captain ordered the cart unshipped at once. The four horses were attached to it so it could be taken away from the 'arbour with most of my own possessions safe in their bag an' slung from the rear gate. Harmonides and his men stayed with me as far as Tiryns where my own chariot an' two 'orses were bein' kept. With their job done they said their farewells, took their own 'orses an' returned to their boat. The bull 'ad to stay where it was but the owner of the tavern, after due payment, ensured two

of his men would stay the night to keep watch over
it.

Early the followin' day, after I'd eaten an' seen
to feedin' the bull, I bought two 'orses from stables
outside the town and 'ad these hitched to the cart
together with my original pair. My chariot would
need to be towed behind, loaded with hay. But
before I left I cut off an; offered a piece of silver at
Athena's shrine an' was given a blessin' by 'er
priestess for good measure.

With such a cumbersome charge an' the
demands it imposed I reckoned it would take me a
good part of the day over rough ground to reach
Mycenae. Now an' then I'd attract attention with
people hurryin' over to gaze at the bull an' more so
as, by mid afternoon, I drew close to Mycenae.
When I'd reached the Lion Gate, by which I
stopped close, I was surrounded by a crowd of noisy
people, some shoutin' questions I'd not the time or
inclination to answer. Except for one who yelled,
"How d'you get the bull 'ere - in that cart was it?"

"No!" I responded, almost without thinkin' as I
unhooked my canvas bag, "It swam from Crete with
me on its back then I rode it all the way 'ere until
findin' this cart!" Little could I have known, Mister
Peter, how seriously some of 'em were to take what
I'd said and 'ow quickly it got about. Their clamour
'ad the bull snortin', stampin' and twistin' about.
One of the guards, on seein' my approach, 'ad
already gone to inform the king. When the man
reappeared it was to tell me Eurystheus wanted the
bull takin' up the ramp. That I assumed was so he

could get up off 'is pretty arse an' step out to see it. I told the guard, no, it couldn't be dragged up the cobbled slope an' couldn't be turned around at the top to get back down. Off the man went again an' when 'e reappeared a second time I expected 'im to tell me Eurystheus would gape at the bull from the city wall. But no. "Lord Eurystheus," he declared, "has decided he will appear in person and will arrive here in due course." More spear-carryin' guards came out to clear those gathered well away from the gate an' from around the cart. And so I waited in sultry afternoon heat. Yes, I waited. Eventually there was a rattle of drums from within the gate, gettin' louder as it approached. Then it stopped. First appeared his courtiers then the fancy contraption carried by four slaves as I'd described earlier – what did you call it, Mister Peter?'

'A sedan chair, Mister Heracles.'

'Aye, it was one of those. They put it down so Eurystheus, movin' his little curtain aside, 'ad a good view of the bull. He didn't call me over because I was wearin' the lion skin and 'e wouldn't be very 'appy about that. He was starin' not this time at an agile deer with gilded 'orns but a damned great bull that was none too pleased about bein' caged up where it was. The crowd, kept well back, was altogether silent an' one of the courtiers was leanin' close to Eurystheus, speakin' to him an' pointin' at the bull. The subject of their conversation I guessed would be the courtier tellin' 'im what a good animal for breedin' with his own flocks the bull would be. Eurystheus was noddin'

210

then I 'eard 'im order the four slaves to lift the chair up again an' take 'im around the cart with the courtier to explain the bull's finer points. I didn't believe he'd be all that interested but imagined his presence might impress the onlookers, who still were quiet. The bull 'ad calmed down an' Eurystheus was passin' close behind the cart when it 'appened. The bull blew off loudly from its rear end then crapped a steamin' pile onto the floor of the cart. This was too much for the crowd who on seein' what'd happened right in front of Eurystheus, burst into an uproar of laughter, cheerin', clappin' an' diggin'one another. Some of the guards an' courtiers obviously 'ad difficulty in controllin' themselves an' I was almost in tears. The window flap snapped across an' Eurystheus' chair continued around the cart somewhat quicker then before, then it un-ceremoniously disappeared through the Lion Gate with guards followin'. I tried to imagine the expression on Eurystheus' face while the crowd was awash with chatter, some of 'em still laughin' as they began to disperse. One of the courtiers 'ad remained outside the gate an' he, with two of the guards, stepped over to me. "I'm to tell you," he began, "that you are to appear before the king at sunset when he will announce the instructions for your next task."

"Don't need to," I responded. "Remind 'im I've got a copy of the parchment so I'll know where I'm goin' next, won't I!"

"But our king demands it and ..." he began.

211

I leaned towards the man, starin' through the
lion's jaws as I rolled the club on my shoulder. He
stepped back an' so did the two guards as I growled,
"You 'eard what I said – now bugger off, the three
of you!" They looked at each other then headed to
the gateway. Well I'd fulfilled what was expected of
me; Eurystheus 'ad the bull plus a pile of fresh shit
an' I needed a drink. First, though, I'd see to the
'orses, 'ave 'em stabled an' with the two from Crete
offered for sale next day. I sent a young lad, one of
the few people still hangin' around, to 'ave the
stables send over men to detach an' take back the
'orses. They'd also keep my chariot safe. That
would leave the bull where it was until Eurystheus's
men turned up to deal with what was now their
problem. Even so, lookin' back on it, I 'oped the
bull would be given over to its intended task before
long as I was beginnin' to feel sorry for it. I was
about to go up to the tavern when a hand fell on my
left shoulder an' a voice spoke my name. A voice I
knew. I spun about, dropped the club an' grasped 'is
hand. The smile I knew as well an' there he was in
plumed helmet an' polished breastplate over a
leopard-patterned, tunic, a prince among men an' a
welcome friend. "Iolaus!" I exclaimed, "Once again
we meet 'ere in Mycenae!"

A short way behind 'im stood a younger, dark-
'aired man in patterned tunic, also clean-shaven.
From his finely decorated leather belt hung a sword
not unlike that worn by Iolaus himself. Iolaus turned
to gesture 'im forward an' said, "Heracles, let me
introduce my companion, Abderus. He comes from

a family of horse breeders working close to Thebes and is himself an expert rider and tamer of the very wildest breed. This I can vouch for from when we go hunting together." Abderus and I shook 'ands an' I said, "Pleased to meet you, Abderus, and any friend of Iolaus 'as to be a friend of mine."

"I'm honoured, Heracles," he responded, "I've heard much about you, mainly from Iolaus, and always hoped we would one day meet so I'd see you wearing your famous lion skin."

"Oh, aye," I laughed. "It's not every day I wear it but it 'as its uses, especially when confrontin' the likes of Eurystheus an' some others. And you, Iolaus, what've you been doin' since we last got together?"

"I've been back and forth across the Peloponnese between here and Thebes," he replied. "It's mainly trade and mutual interests that have occupied my time but now other matters have arisen so I must return very soon to Thebes. We saw Eurystheus carried from the palace and followed his party down. When I saw the bull I knew you had returned from Crete. We watched what happened and like the rest of them gathered around there we couldn't help laughing – then I spotted you with the stable men. What are your plans now?"

"I was off to the tavern to eat, drink an' think over what I was to do next," I informed him. "You'll both join me of course - won't you?"

"You'll not keep us away!" he declared, "We'll have you tell us how you fared on Crete and what your next task is to be."

Chapter 9 - The Black Mares

'So we headed for the city tavern where my room an' some of my belongin's 'ad been kept an' there we sat with food, goblets, a flagon of good wine an' the rolled parchment set to one side. My description of my own an' other matters at Knossos 'ad Iolaus' an' Abderus' full attention, after which Iolaus related to me affairs of interest at Thebes an' whispers of a plot or an uprising against Creon that would take 'im on 'is way back at sunrise next day. By then darkness was fallin' and I called for oil lamps. With these as our source of light I unrolled the parchment, peered down at my eighth labour an' said, "It tells me I've to steal the mares of Diomedes in Thrace – that's a long way east of the Peloponnese. Don't know anythin' about the man – do either of you?"

"Diomedes of Thrace," Iolaus mused. "I know something of his reputation but little else. He's a petty ruler, so it's said, but of exactly what or where I'm not sure. In an area like that borders are often changing. I recall a traveller telling me he trains horses, not for normal use but for sheer aggression. I'm told he'll challenge a man to ride any one of those horses for a considerable reward but no one ever has because the horses attack and have been known to kill them. That's as much as I can say on the subject, I'm afraid."

"Well," I said, starin' down at the parchment, "accordin' to this I'm to get those killer 'orses back

215

'ere to show Eurystheus. He won't know how many there were so maybe two or three at most will do. Or maybe just their tails or manes."

"But Hera will know how many, won't she," Iolaus pointed out.

"Aye, maybe she will. But I 'ave to do whatever I can."

"I've also heard of this man, Diomedes," said Abderus, "but the rumours about his horses sound very odd indeed."

"So they do," agreed Iolaus, "and I very much wish I could join Heracles once more."

"But," said Abderus, "*I* could go with him, if you both are in agreement. I have, after all, much experience with horses."

'Iolaus downed his wine, looked at us both in turn then said, "Yes - why not. So plan together how you're to go about it, beginning with the journey." The journey to Thrace I was yet to give more thought to but there was no point in our speculatin' about it until later.

"Then," smiled Abderus, turning to me, "as it would please you to have me, a stranger, by your side I will gladly join you, though I have one more day for duties with Iolaus here in Mycenae. I'm trading horses' would you believe."

'You can imagine, Mister Peter, that the offer of Abderus' company, an expert with 'orses, cheered me up. "Damned right you can join me," I responded, "an' I'll wait as long as you wish!" With this decided, the sounds of music an' laughter from down below turned our minds to things of more immediate interest so it was to there we took ourselves for the rest of the evenin'.

The next day found me with little to do so I strolled out of the town minus lion skin an' club to find, as I expected, the cart an' the bull were gone from where I'd abandoned them outside the Lion Gate. I'd time enough to take one of the 'orses an' ride down to the fortified port of Mycenae where I could watch the boats comin' in an' out from near an' distant places. To make better use of my time I inquired about the possibility of makin' it to Thrace via the Pelasgian sea as I suspected this might be easier than over the mountains an' rivers we'd have to cross if goin' by land. Aye, my trip to Crete 'ad been easy enough so I spoke to some who'd taken the route to Thrace. I drank an' talked long with them an' I was soon convinced that goin' by sea *was* the better way. As for the time such a journey might take I could find no definite answer. It would depend upon the winds, the size of the vessel, 'er cargo, the number of islands she'd call into an' the length of her stay.

Sorry, dear reader, to interrupt Heracles' words, but the Pelasgian Sea, as he would have known had he given it some thought, was later named the Aegean after Aegeus, the great and respected King of Athens who threw himself to death from the Acropolis into the valley below. But that's part of yet another story and some way later in the course of events, so now let's allow Heracles to continue.

'I negotiated with the captain of a large vessel who was to load goods the followin' mornin' and who assured me his stopovers would be no longer than necessary. He'd take our chariot and 'orses but couldn't understand why we wanted to go to Thrace where he'd be tradin' mainly for slaves an' furs. Thrace, he informed me, was a wild country with small towns where anyone could be king until deposed or murdered by a would-be successor. He'd also 'eard of Diomedes an' the mad 'orses but they were further inland so he'd seen nothin' of 'em.

I'd learned a bit about ships in my time, Mister Peter but never spent too long at sea; d'you know much about 'em yourself – ships I mean?'

I answered him in the only way I could. 'Not really, Mister Heracles – not the ships of your world, so please do explain.' I had done some research in the past, of course, but here was contemporary knowledge.

'Well most ships at the port were **shallow-draught** to cope with sandy bays. They bore sails an' oars, sometimes for the big ships as many as fifty oarsmen. Dependin' on their routes they might carry anythin' from olive oil, wine an' grain to fabrics, ceramics, ivory, copper, tin, weapons an' much else, includin' luxury goods for palaces an' temples. Minos' navy didn't reach as far as the Pelasgian so there was a risk of piracy to consider. Even some tradin' ships turned to that when business was slow. It wasn't too difficult since any ship large enough would carry fightin' men as part of its crew. On my way back to the city I spotted three of Eurystheus' courtiers takin' a walk in the late afternoon sun so I stopped an' dismounted to talk with 'em. Now away from Eurystheus they were free enough with their words an' manners to admit they'd seen the humour of his encounter with the bull. I asked 'em if the bull 'ad now been taken an' released to where Eurystheus' cattle grazed but they said no, it'd not. To where then, I asked, 'ad it gone. They were a bit shy over answerin' the question but one admitted that the encounter 'ad greatly embarrassed Eurystheus an' that anyone seein' the bull afterwards would be reminded of it. He'd therefore ordered the bull sent east an' let loose in Attica, to wander the Plain of Marathon whish is north of Athens an' far south of Thebes. Well, I thought, bringin' it all the way over from Crete wasn't 'is decision anyway since he was no more than Hera's lackey, so now someone else would suffer the problems Minos once 'ad.'

At that point one of Heracles' attendants walked over, excused himself for the interruption and informed his master that his presence was required within the house. Heracles appeared to understand what the request was for, arose from his seat, turned to me and said, 'I'll be a while, Mister Peter so amuse y'self as you please – time for a walk, maybe. More beer an' food will be comin' when I'm back.'

I wondered if he'd been summoned by his elusive wife and for how long but I wasn't going to hang around. I left the courtyard and hurried through the trees straight for the clearing where we'd first met. You'll recall how I'd previously sat alone at the table there and used that opportunity to top up the charge in my voice recorder as the late morning sun was shining through. I intended now to do the same again. I withdrew the recorder from my shirt pocket, wound the recording back a little to where Heracles had finished speaking, placed it face up on the table then settled down, thinking, once back home I'd have a lot of editing to do.

Having no watch I was trying to guess the time, I figured from the position of the sun that it was past midday, when I heard voices from the direction of the stream - the unmistakeable, singing voices of Tiye and Mayet. Reaching to lay a hand on the recorder I peered through the trees to see which way they were going but it was to the house with bunches of flowers they'd been busy picking. I closed my eyes and once more relaxed in the pleasant warmth thinking how I would have welcomed their company just then since I hardly ever saw them except at night. I must have dozed off because the next voices I heard were male and heading my way. One of them was Heracles and in a minor panic I managed to grab and conceal the recorder as they entered the clearing. The other man was his attendant carrying a tray of food together with a jug and two cups. He placed these before me as Heracles said, "We'll stay out 'ere for a while, Mister Peter, yes?"

'Fine by me,' I responded. As the attendant departed I brushed a hand across my shirt pocket for reassurance while Heracles' attention was elsewhere. He sat to pour beer with one hand while fingers of the other jostled to pick up figs.

'Now where were we?' he began. 'Aye, I'd met up with Abderus first light at the Lion Gate. I already 'ad the chariot an' two 'orses waitin' with my canvas bag slung over one of 'em an' two round shields over the other. There was room in the chariot for our weapons includin' my club as well as my bow an' arrows. As for armour – I possessed none, though Abderus wore a bronze 'elmet and cuirass of boiled leather over a thick tunic. He didn't consider anythin' 'eavier for the nature of our journey in spite of Thrace's reputation for cooler weather. The lion skin would keep me warm. Any risk from pirates was not of much account since most of our considerable crew could become 'ard fightin' men at short notice. We boarded the ship as arranged, 'er name was *Triton*, and she was soon under way, leavin' the 'arbour with coloured pennants flyin', 'er big sail catchin' the wind and 'er sun-glintin' oars strikin' water as one. I stood with Abderus at the stern to watch people, mainly friends an' wives with their kids, wave farewell to those on board our vessel. As we cleared the 'harbour our captain poured a cup of red wine over the side as his offerin' to Poseidon.'

Heracles gulped beer then asked me, 'You ever been far out to sea, Mister Peter?'

'Er, yes, now and again.

'Big ships are they, where you come from?'

'Oh, some are quite big, yes. Very big, in fact.' I had in mind some of those floating hotels, seagoing monsters that turn up to disgorge thousands of passengers.

'They've lots of oars then 'ave they – fifty, sixty an' more?'

'I, er, well I never bothered to count them so I can't really say.'

He downed more beer, wiped his mouth as so oftem before on the sleeve of his gown, looked to see my cup was still half full and said, 'Aye then, let's get on with what you're waitin' to 'ear.'

While everything he told me was duly recorded I was less concerned with his sea voyage than I was with his various calls on the way. He described the passage around Attica, stopping to trade, take on supplies and stay overnight at the tip of Euboea. Then on to Chios, one of several islands claiming to be the birthplace of Homer, which in the time of Heracles life on Earth lay some four hundred or more years in the future. Next there was Lesbos with its later connections still at that time unfounded. As for his time at sea, the winds were varied; sometimes with *Triton*, sometimes not but his comments on their penultimate port of call I found of greater interest.

'The crew of *Triton* appeared more keen on our arrivin' at Lemnos than anywhere else. It's a hilly but fertile island with a good 'arbour an' it's known for its hot springs. There we took on pigs an' some grain an' traded salt for the preservation of food, together with a few fancy goods from the workshops at Knossos among other places. The main attraction at Lemnos, 'owever, was its women, supposed to be ruled over by one called, Hypsipyle – Aye, Hyp-sip-y-le they said she was called. Our

222

captain told us how, years back, their men 'ad raided the mainland of Thrace an' returned with lots of slaves. The young women captives they insisted 'ad to share their beds.

This didn't work out too well because their own wives conspired to 'ave their 'usbands murdered in their sleep one night throughout the town after druggin' their wine. The captain didn't believe quite all of it but reckoned the women trained an' armed 'emselves to keep those men who survived an' fled elsewhere away from the island, takin' with them all their possessions of value an' even their slaves. A number of slaves escaped an' they were allowed back on Lemnos where they tended abandoned farms well away from the town. It's said the women call in selected few of 'em on certain days, fettered an' stark naked, to do their duty, if you see what I mean.'

'But there must be male as well as female offspring,' I remarked. 'What happens to them?'

'Accordin' to the captain, girls are brought up to defend 'emselves an' keep the men out, an' boys are trained from birth to be subservient. As they come of age a small number are kept as slaves with their balls cut off an' the rest sent to join the farmers. When vessels like *Triton* enter 'arbour none of their crews are allowed beyond the dockside ware'ouses because these are guarded by armed women who'll stand no nonesense. You might wonder, then, why they were so keen to make port at Lemnos. Well, Mister Peter, it strikes me they were livin' in hope and imaginin' what might be possible when they got there. You'll not be surprised to learn that three men did find their way past the guards at night but as they never returned no one knows what 'appened to 'em. Maybe they're livin' a life of pleasure or maybe they're dead. Anyhow, when our vessel left the island next mornin', Abderus an' I took to the oars to fill the places of two of those who'd cleared off.

Stoppin' only a short time at the island of Samothrace, a wild, rocky place, our next call was Thrace itself where our own items, includin' of course the chariot and 'orses' had to be got ashore an' up to dry land. With days an' nights spent in port it'd taken Abderus an' me fourteen days to arrive at Thrace. The climate there is changeable, often with grey skies an' the natives said to be an unruly lot. Here was a dock with little storage space an' no back-up town. *Triton*'s captain traded salt an' assorted goods mainly for grain but also furs an' a small number of male slaves – these delivered by cart an' guarded by armed men. We'd to find this Diomedes but first we needed food an' shelter. On the advice of the captain we followed the direction from which the carts 'ad come until we arrived at an 'amlet of sorts where some of the men drifted over to stand an' stare at us. No, Mister Peter, this was *not* a welcomin' place. The language of those who lived there was not easy to understand but the, peasants, for that's all I could regard 'em as, pointed out to us an empty barn where we could spend the night, stay warm an' keep an eye on everythin' of ours.

In the mornin' we asked where we might locate Diomedes an' were told it was further along the coast to where the land appeared level. Mention of the man's name did nothin' to cheer 'em up. The rest of 'em, six or more men, remained there eyein' us in silence as if we were up to no good. The watchers began to disperse as we connected our 'orses an' stepped into the chariot. It wasn't far to go before we entered wheat fields an' grazin' land, intersected by a gushin' stream. There was one large but plain stone buildin' an' several wooden out'ouses an' barns. There were people at work in the fields, men, women an' children. One of the few men on 'orseback, armed an' seemin' like he'd some authority, came trottin' over to meet us. He demanded in passable Greek to know who we were but lion skin or no it seemed he'd never 'eard of me. I informed 'im we were to see Diomedes so he led us along to the stone 'ouse where we stepped from the chariot. He went inside an' soon reappeared, movin' to one side of the doorway so we were face to face with a stout, course-lookin' man of middle age with a long, black, unkempt beard an' hair 'angin' at the sides of 'is head to leave the rest bald. Oddly, the long woollen gown he wore, delicately embroidered an' fringed, could only 'ave originated somewhere more civilized. That applied also to the long-bladed knife at one side of 'is belt an' on the other side to the finely crafted sword with gold banded 'ilt an' jewelled pommel protrudin' from an engraved an' gilded bronze scabbard. No, Mister Peter, they didn't belong with the man before us or to 'is world. He took a step back, ignored Abderus, looked me up and down then declared, "I've 'eard a bit about you 'aven't I – lion skin an' all that. You're that 'Ercales aren't you! What d'you want out 'ere?" It was far from the most welcome reception I'd experienced.

'Diomedes knowing about you, Mister Heracles, is the price of fame,' I quipped, 'He could never have met you personally until then - or could he?'

'No, Mister Peter, 'e couldn't because I would've remembered. Word must 'ave got around from those payin' him a visit by sea. Anyway, in answer to 'is question I said, "We'd like to see those famous black mares of yours."

"We most certainly would," confirmed Abderus. "We're told no one was ever able to ride any of them without being thrown off. Is that right?"

'It seemed a good time to check that with the man. You know how rumours can mislead through what *I've* already told you. Diomedes smiled like he'd just discovered somethin' of value he didn't care to reveal and muttered, "Aye, you will soon enough," then gestured for us to follow 'im inside. It occurred to me then, as it must've done to Abderus, that this Diomedes and 'is men 'ad full control of the land an' its people, which explained why we'd 'ad such a cool reception on arrival. The place we entered looked as plain inside as it did out, with no frescoes, not a trace of Minoan finesse about it. But one big surprise awaited Abderus an' I

226

when we were shown inside 'is main room. It may've been smaller by far than a palace megaron but it was treated as one so as to display what he was sure would impress any visitors. All about the walls were 'ung various kinds of weapons an' armour, some of recognisable origin an' some not. Many pieces bore a metallic gleam even in the dull light that entered from outside. Layin' around as if dumped wherever space was available were assorted items that well equipped people might carry with 'em on their travels with some appearin' to be of considerable value. I'm talkin' mainly of clothin' an items of ornamentation worn about the body. The room was a showplace an' Diomedes wanted us to take our time in admirin' it. What lay through a plain, curtained-off doorway to one side of it I assumed must 'ave been 'is private quarters. If the rumours then were true, most if not all of what this man was showin' us must've been obtained from those who'd taken up 'is challenge an' paid the price, maybe with their lives.'

"I'll take you now to see the mares," Diomedes said as we gazed over 'is hoard of dubiously acquired possessions. "This way if you will."

'I sensed Abderus' enthusiasm as we followed 'im outside beneath a cloud-thickenin' sky. We walked around to the far side of the buildin' to where the mares came into view. There were five of 'em contained within a high-fenced enclosure. They were magnificent alright – sleek an' jet black from their manes to their tails. Abderus was more impressed than I was, an' strode ahead to take a closer look. The 'orses milled about, stampin' and whinnyin' like they were agitated an' as we joined Abderus he declared "Heracles, just look at them! Never did I see finer horses than we have here!"

"Nor will you anywhere!" declared Diomedes with an irregular-toothed grin, "I see 'em as a gift of the gods. Tame an' ride just one of 'em an' anythin' of value in that room I showed you is yours for the askin'."

'To Diomedes' surprise and mine, Abderus walked back to the chariot an' there un-tethered our two 'orses'. These he led over to the corral where 'e had 'em peer through at the black mares. The mares calmed down as they gathered an' approached to look out at our 'orses. Abderus was up close an' appeared to be talkin' softly to the mares so we couldn't 'ear 'is words.'

"What's he up to?" asked Diomedes, starin' hard at Abderus.

"Can't really say," I answered, "but he's expert with 'orses an' trains them for other people. Aye, he wanted above all to see your mares."

"Oh, did 'e now," muttered Diomedes.

'Abderus stepped around to the corral gate an' lifted aside the iron bar that secured it. "Don't do that!" yelled Diomedes. He started forwards with one arm raised 'igh but I grabbed 'is shoulder an' stopped 'im dead. He turned about, shoutin' full in my face, "He'll let my fuckin' 'orses out – get yer 'ands off of me!" but I 'eld on tight an' assured him, calm as I could, "He won't let 'em out – he knows what he's doin'." I didn't know for sure what

228

Abderus intended but I was certain he wasn't about to release any of those five mares. Meanwhile, as Diomedes gazed wide-eyed, Abderus 'ad pushed through an' closed the gate. I released Diomedes an' we walked over to stop short of the corral where, inside, Abderus stood amidst the 'orses.'

'Your new-found pal, Diomedes, really must've been confused,' I said.

'Maybe 'e was, Mister Peter, but my new-found pal 'e was not. From the start I'd disliked 'im an' I felt certain the bugger was up to no good. Abderus 'ad 'is arm over the neck of one of the mares an' was whisperin' into its ear while the four others stood by, lettin' out the odd snort. He stepped about, talkin' to an' pattin' each of 'em in turn an' I was aware of their owner, close by me, gettin' ever more agitated. He'd cheated a lot of people out of what was theirs by challengin' 'em to ride any of those mares of 'is an' maybe thought Abderus would succeed an' we'd be takin' some of those ill-gotten gains back off 'im. Abderus stood back an' I knew what he was plannin' to do. I was sure he'd be pretty good at it an' I wasn't too bad at that kind of thing myself as you know, Mister Peter. He was steadyin' 'imself to leap onto the back of the nearest 'orse when Diomedes dashed suddenly forward as if 'e trod on burnin' rocks. He was yellin' out loud, wavin' 'is arms like a madman as he reached the fence. What then 'appened was all too quick. The 'orses turned suddenly wild, screamed, panicked, jumped about an' started to kick. One of 'em caught Abderus in the thigh with its back leg as 'e ran for

the gate, bringin' the lad down with a cry. He tried
to rise to 'is feet but the mares circled about 'im.
One struck im' 'ard in the side, then another with
yet greater violence against 'is head. He was down,
layin' still, an' those damned 'orses reared an'
pranced over 'im I swear in triumph. I rushed to the
gate, club in 'and, thinkin' to get in there an' try to
beat 'em back so Abderus could make 'is escape. I
reached the gate an' saw 'im sprawled out a short
way inside with blood pourin' from 'is ear an'
where 'is cheek bone was exposed. I'd seen plenty
of dead men in my time an' I knew straight away
Abderus was beyond 'elp. His bronze 'elmet, layin'
close by, hadn't saved 'im. Then I 'eard a sound I
knew well – the hiss of a blade bein' drawn from its
scabbard. I turned to see Diomedes advancin'
toward me with deadly intent, sword raised as 'e
shouted' "You'll 'ave nothin' of mine but cold
bronze!" I dodged aside as the bugger took a swing.
I felt the wind of it, but I was ready for 'im. I swung
my club across to strike 'is sword arm, knockin' 'im
off balance an' as he cursed aloud I raised an'
brought the club down against 'is skull so 'ard an'
with such a crack it split bone. He was dead before
'e hit the ground with bloodied eyes starin' up at the
sky.'

Heracles sighed with hands pressed to his face.
He was thinking hard about poor Abderus, the one
who'd set off with him as a true friend, full of
enthusiasm to help him through a part of his
troubles. He recovered his posture, slowly refilled
our cups then continued.

Jeffrey Peter Clarke

'I realised now that other people were watchin'
from closer to Diomedes' 'ouse what'd 'appened.
There were some of 'is guards an' a number of 'is
slaves but none of 'em cared to approach me or
their dead master. I looked again at Abderus' body
sprawled in the grass an' at the black mares, still
snortin' an' trottin' around in circles. I strode over
to the watchers, some of whom took a step or two
back as I glared at 'em from between lion jaws.
"Who's in charge 'ere now?" I demanded.
"Diomedes' son," came the reply.

"But he's been raidin' inland these last two
days with most of our armed men," added another.

"Once he gets back 'e'll want to know why 'is
father got killed," informed the first.

"Well you all now 'ave a choice," I told 'em.
"But before anythin' else, two of you can 'elp me
bury my dead friend so I can make due sacrifice
over 'is grave. I take it you've a priest somewhere
around 'ere, so one of you call 'em over right now.
I'll then take charge of Diomedes' 'ouse an' when
'is son returns I'll clear off. You'll all take the
blame for lettin' this 'appen, unless…!" They
looked on in silence waitin' for me to speak further.
"Unless," said I, "we make up our minds to do
somethin' else before that 'appens. Those of you
able to deal with Diomedes' 'orses can 'arness four
of 'em soundly to my chariot. My two 'orses I leave
with you. Before I'm ready to leave, you set about
'elpin' yourselves to everythin' Diomedes collected
in there an' make off with your families richer than
ever you could 'ave imagined. I'll want none of it!"

231

That gave 'em somethin' to think about. They shuffled about, movin' closer together an' mutterin' among 'emselves but they didn't think about it for long. They elected a speaker, the guard who'd rode up to challenge us when we arrived, an' after further discussion 'e agreed on everyone's behalf with my last proposal.'

'But, Mister Heracles,' I said, 'you still had to see Abderus buried.'

'Aye, that I did because there was no way I could take 'is body all the way back to Thebes. When the priestess turned up, advanced in years an' not lookin' much like a priestess in 'er tatty gown, I 'ad the two men who'd stepped forward push into the corral an' 'elp me carry Abderus' body out while Diomedes' mares looked on. We took Abderus to a grove of trees some way from the 'ouse an' there, out of sight, the diggin' began. When we'd finished, 'e was lowered to dark earth wearin' 'is cuirass, 'elmet an' sword while the priestess uttered 'er incantations. Unfortunately she represented some god I'd never 'eard of but I'd no choice in that. She at least informed the two with me that should they return to the grave or reveal its location to any other, the wrath of whatever she represented would fall upon 'em. Aye, it sounded like the wrath of Hera that I was all too familiar with. I nevertheless made 'em disguise the grave so no one, hopefully, would later recognise it as such an' they assured me it would soon be overgrown anyway. As for Diomedes body, they could do with that whatever they wanted.

232

While most of the men were settin' out to the fields to call in their wives an' kids I inquired with the priestess if there was a shrine to Athena so I could 'ave 'er priestess also visit Abderus' grave to offer sacrifice. There was none. Their god or goddesses own shrine, when her priestess pointed it out, looked an unpretentious affair in one of the wooden outhouses an' in the time I'd left she explained to me how some of the people thereabouts followed other deities that I'd likewise never 'eard of. Meanwhile, four of the black mares 'ad been tethered to my chariot but appeared restless, havin' me wonder how the men 'ad managed it. The fifth mare 'ad been let out to roam anywhere she pleased.

As their wives an' kids were bein' called in from the fields I asked some of the men if they knew when another large vessel might turn up at the inlet where Abderus an' I 'ad arrived. It would need to be big enough to take me, my chariot an' the 'orses back to somewhere convenient in Greece. Maybe they thought I was jokin' but if so the joke was on me. No one could say when or even if another boat like *Triton* was due in any time soon. So I'd no option. But would I be able to 'andle all four of those 'orses for the long an' difficult journey overland? It was not a prospect I cared to think upon. But I'd got my precious silver an' gold as well as those items of value poor Abderus 'ad left behind in my canvas bag. Yes, Mister Peter, I'd to make use of the black mares an' try to get em' all

233

the way to Mycenae so Eurystheus could set 'is beady eyes on 'em.

As I walked over to the chariot I found waitin' there a young, bushy-'aired lad in a plain but clean lookin' woollen smock.

"Lord Heracles," he blurted, claspin' 'is hands together at 'is chest as he dropped to one knee, "allow me to serve you."

"Serve *me*?" I responded, "I need no one to serve me unless you can show me 'ow to fly through the air. I've a hard journey ahead an' that's all there is to it."

"Lord Heracles," he pressed, standin' up to place a hand about the neck of the nearest 'orse, "I was help to Master Diomedes with these horses as I've been just now in getting them here and tethered to your chariot. I would be with the lord when feeding them and he showed me, as he did his own son, how to mount and ride them. When both were away I would tend and talk to them because they trusted me and did as I wished. I think you alone will not have them do that."

'I hesitated, wonderin' how 'is Greek was so good, then I asked the boy 'is name,'

"I am called Ardomir," he answered.

"And why, Ardomir, d'you wish to leave your friends an' family behind an' set off to somewhere you know little or nothin' of, though you speak Greek almost better than I do - 'ow is this?"

'I watched 'im stroke the 'orse's neck, an' it seemed as much contented at his touch as they all 'ad been with Abderus. "Diomedes had a Greek slave who taught me," he replied. "I also am a slave and have no parents I know of. When the people here leave, which soon they must, none will wish to take me with them because I was a part of Diomedes' house and I did not mix with those outside."

"So," I responded, "you're sayin' they'll reject you."

"Yes Lord Heracles, that they will."

'So there we are, Mister Peter; I was more than willin' take 'im with me. He'd no longer be a slave, I'd 'ave someone able to deal with the black mares better than I could an' I'd ensure young Ardomir was rewarded at the end. A bit of luck under the circumstances, don't you think?'

'Sounds that way, Mister Heracles, and he thought of you as a Lord.'

'Aye, well I'd let 'im think so for a while. Before gettin' away we stocked up with as much food an' fresh water, this in leather flasks, as we could manage in the chariot but more of what we'd need was placed in satchels draped over the two closest 'orses together with the two shields, so far not needed. By late mornin' everyone around there was informed of Diomedes' death. Even more people were arrivin' from the direction of the docks to 'elp 'emselves to whatever they could get their 'ands upon. The outcome I should 'ave foreseen; all were intent on lootin' the 'ouse an' swarmed about it like ants, but only so many could get inside an' from in there came a lot of shoutin'. Some of those who'd managed to get out with anythin' of value found 'emselves set upon by others who wanted what they'd managed to grab. Men were fightin', women were screamin' and people were layin' on the ground. As we set off the area around the place 'ad become a scene of total disorder an' ever risin' violence. I let Ardomir take charge of the black mares, which 'e did with enthusiasm while askin' me, "What direction must we take?"

"We follow the coast west," I told 'im as we left the turmoil behind an' passed close to the woodland where lay Abderus. "We carry on west or south-west until we enter Greek speakin' country then maybe we'll find out more or less where we are."

We'd stopped for something to eat after which Heracles had walked back to the house, saying he'd be gone for a while. This gave me a chance to sneak out the voice recorder and place it on the table for a battery boost. It was a thoroughly pleasant and warm afternoon. They'd so far been like that in the Elysian Fields, and very restful, but I this time avoided the temptation of closing my eyes. As he'd explained, Heracles and his new companion, Ardomir, were just beginning their long journey to Greece and he'd promised to relate most of this, his eighth labour, on his return to the clearing. I spotted him well in advance as he approached so I grabbed and pocketed the recorder in good time. He sat down, poured fresh beer then said, 'Well now, Mister Peter, we 'ad a long journey back over good as well as rough country with the occasional stream or river gettin' in the way. I lost count of the many days we passed; as many if not more than the boat trip out to Thrace. Early on we 'ad to camp each night an' on two occasions under the stars we were approached by wolves, though nothin' worse. With sufficient moonlight to see by I used my bow an' a few arrows to drive away the wolves, killin' at least one of 'em, but no people were around to bother us. Eventually there was the odd village to stop at an' a few people who spoke Greek. We skirted Mount Pangaeus an' eventually found the coast droppin' away to the south. We kept on west, passin' a number of lakes until we reached a gulf of what turned out to be the Pelasgian Sea again. There we learned that Mount Olympus lay to the south so all we needed then was follow the coast, keepin' due south over hills an' valleys until we'd find ourselves enterin' Greece proper. Aye, we were back in my own, familiar land. From now on we'd come upon villages an' small towns where we'd find a tavern for comfort, then on we went, now away from the sea, ever south until passin' another inlet where we turned south-east to 'ead for Thebes.

I tell you, Mister Peter, without young Ardomir to deal with those 'orses I'd never 'ave made it. He cared for each of 'em day an' night, feedin' and waterin' - even brushin' down their coats. I wondered if 'is presence an' willingness to join me in Thrace was in part Athena's doing. Durin' that time, though, my confidence in handlin' the black mares 'ad grown considerably so now an' again I'd take charge of 'em.

Mycenae, not Thebes should 'ave been my goal but I'd first to contact Iolaus an' explain to 'im what 'ad occurred in Thrace an' the death of his close friend, Abderus.

On arrivin' at the city gate shortly before sunrise I put aside the lion skin, gave silver to Ardomir as promised an' stepped down from the chariot. Ardomir, with chariot and 'orses, would stand by outside the gate by which I'd entered. Many would know who I was an' I 'oped I'd soon be speakin' with' Iolaus. At the palace entrance I informed the guards that I wished to see 'im an' I didn't 'ave to wait long. He appeared at the palace steps in courtly attire, grinnin' wide, as always, as he strode over to me where we clasped arms in friendship. "Heracles," he said, "so you're back at long last!" He demanded to know how Abderus an' I had fared an' glanced by me, wonderin' why I stood there alone. Trouble is, Mister Peter, I now 'ad to reveal the bad news. Iolaus realised somethin' was not right when I didn't return the smile he offered me but instead held back for some moments in silence. I then outlined what'd happened an' why, an' though he tried to conceal it, I knew how distressed 'e was at the news. And although Abderus 'ad willingly offered his services, I felt myself touched by the 'and of guilt. Iolaus stood by me in thought for a time, gazin' down at the ground, then said, "Very well, Heracles, it's a cruel world we live in and I will surely miss one who was a dear friend. For now, let me take a look at those black mares and meet the lad who you say helped you with them."

Guards at the gate stood to attention as we passed through to where the chariot and 'orses waited with Ardomir standin' dutifully by them. The boy shuffled back, offerin' a short but nervous bow as Iolaus walked slowly around to appraise the black mares which stood givin' an occasional snort an' hoof tap. He turned to me, sayin', "Never before have I seen their like. A pity they must be shown before Eurystheus. I wonder what he will do with them. And you, Ardomir – Heracles tells me you made his return here with them possible. What will you do when the horses are taken to Mycenae?"

Ardomir looked from me to Iolaus an' replied, "Er, I do not know, Lord Iolaus, but I can never return to Thrace. Perhaps I will serve another – perhaps I will…"

"No - wait!" cut in Iolaus. "The services of another Abderus, one skilled as was he with horses will be needed here at Thebes. If you care to offer us your skills, as a free man of course, there are our own horses in want of them."

I nodded encouragement to Ardomir an' he, glancin' at me then back to Iolaus, answered, "I – I would be honoured, my Lord, and I would serve with gratitude."

Iolaus an' I talked little as he once more inspected the mares but at the back of my mind were thoughts of Mycenae. I would need soon to leave Thebes an' I let this be known to Iolaus, who readily understood. The young Thracian boy was about to take his former place in the chariot when I called, "No, Ardomir! You've given me confidence to go on alone. This is no difficult journey I'm to make an' your place now is 'ere at Thebes." I stepped into the chariot, pulled on my lion skin an' as I positioned myself with the reigns, Iolaus raisin' a hand, said, "May Athena be with you and may I – we, see you back here at Thebes all the sooner."

I manoeuvred the chariot around, cracked the long whip an' with a backward wave I set off with my four 'orses goin' at a steady pace. Yes, I reckoned I'd arrive at my destination before sunset. This time no woman carryin' a burden was goin' to stop me as 'appened last time I crossed the Isthmus of Corinth on my way to Mycenae.

I made good time, now an' then at a gallop, an' was attractin' attention, or at least the black mares were, as I approached the rise upon which the city stood. Already, though, I was askin' myself, "Where next after Mycenae am I to end up?" Bein' conspicuous as I was, they must 'ave spotted me from the city wall long before I turned up at the Lion Gate because three guards an' a courtier were there waitin'. "Our king is informed of your arrival," announced the courtier, "and you are to await his pleasure."

So Eurystheus might keep me waitin' might he. Well I'd make it look as though it didn't matter in the least. I took up the brush used by Ardomir to groom the 'orses an' began to go over their coats as they snorted gently. I was still at it, surrounded by onlookers, when Eurystheus' fancy box was carried out to be let down before the gate. I'd 'eard the drums announce 'is approach but pretended I'd not noticed. Only when a guard started gesturin' at me did I turn about an' say, "Oh, your 'ighness, I do 'ope these magnificent black mares are to your likin'."

Eurystheus, havin' lifted the flap that covered his little window, peered out an' said, "We are most pleased you have brought them to us, Heracles, but there are only four of them. Were there not more?"

"There were more," I answered, "but the Thracians 'ad eaten 'em."

"Eaten them!" exclaimed the courtier, "Eaten such fine horses as these? Never!"

"Aye, what I tell you is true," I responded, "the Thracians will eat anythin' that moves an' a few things that don't when they're 'ungry – an' they were very short of food. But I did rescue these for 'is Majesty who could ride any one of 'em in complete safety." I turned to ask Eurystheus, "Shall I take them now to the stables, Your 'Ighness where they may be retained for your personal use?"

"Yes, do that," he answered, "that is where they must at once go. And now you have your next task to perform." With that he poked out a hand, twitched fingers at the courtier an' pulled down his window flap.

The courtier indicated with a palm-down gesture that I should wait until Eurystheus was lifted by his attendants an' taken back inside the gate before I made a move. I moved off anyway. On my way to the stables, this time leadin' the four

mares by 'and, I imagined someone helpin'
Eurystheus up onto one of the mares then standin'
back. The 'orse would buck, throw 'im sky high
then with a bit of luck stamp 'ard on the bugger. But
no, he'd not dare to try an' ride one of these, or any
other. The stable would, as earlier, look after my
chariot an' I, with one of the stable 'ands, escorted
the black mares around to a small enclosure at the
rear, where already they were showin' signs of
restlessness. If they decided to escape, the lower
fences would never stop 'em but that was no longer
my concern.'

'Quite an adventure you'd had, Mister
Heracles,' I said. 'And such a pity about Abderus.'

"Aye it was," he agreed, "and I was glad to see
the end of it. I was starvin' an' my thoughts turned
to the town tavern."

The Elysian Fields afternoon was wearing on
when Heracles and I decided to take a walk by the
river rather than have him embark upon the next
episode of his long and complicated tale. As he
strode before me I managed to reach and switch off
the recorder, then I followed him close. I wondered
if Tiye and Mayet might have walked back this way
unnoticed but there was no sign of them.

Did Heracles have designs on either or both of
those Egyptian girls who'd been so thoughtfully
allocated to me? I doubted it; he was too robust for
their more comely forms and lacking the refinement
to which they would doubtless be accustomed. And
perhaps he'd be too wary of his wife finding out. As
night closed in we were back once more in the

courtyard with a fire burning, oil lamps lit and wine to accompany a modest meal. He asked me again about my own world, awkward questions such as the number of horses I didn't have and the raids by bandits I'd never been subjected to. With a generous degree of imagination I once again managed to deal with most of his questions without too many slips. Rescue was at hand when his wife shouted for him from inside the house. He arose promptly and called back, "Comin' sweet one!"

I nearly choked on my wine, spilling some of it and trying not to laugh as he upped and left without so much as a "Good night, Mister Peter."

You may be wondering, as did I, How his Hittite wife ended up with him in the Elysian Fields. I hadn't bothered to ask as I preferred to stay with accounts of his obligatory tasks. Perhaps it would be revealed later.

The sky above was dark with a spread of gleaming stars unlike anything I could recall back home. I didn't yet want to go indoors, no, I wanted to rest right there alone in silence and muse over the amazing tales so far rendered by Heracles. But if Tiye and Mayet reached the bedroom before me I'd not have chance to sneak the voice recorder onto the window ledge. I listened hard. There were no voices from within the house so I jumped up, hurried inside, found the bedroom unoccupied, placed the recorder where it needed to be and let fall the leather flap. There was still silence so I returned to my seat in the courtyard where I relaxed and closed my eyes. There I pondered over the incredible world

I had entered only days ago but seeming now like a lifetime. I must have dozed off because I heard nothing until a hand gently squeezed my shoulder and a warm voice whispered close to my ear. 'Hello, Peter, we were waiting for you but here you are asleep all on your own.'

I opened my eyes to the lovely smiling faces of Tiye and Mayet and I thought I was still dreaming. But no, it *was* time to go inside. Well don't blame me – I hadn't planned any of this had I.

Chapter 10 - The Argonauts

I showed up at the courtyard next morning with the recorder switched on. The sun was peering over the hills like an inquisitive eye and the air I found refreshingly cool. Heracles, there ahead of me, gestured to the waiting food and jar of beer. "Another good night, I 'ope, Mister Peter," he grinned as I sat opposite him. I smiled back but wasn't going to respond further.

'Right,' he began slopping beer into our cups, 'I was once again free for a time in Mycenae so off I went to the tavern where I'd dump the lion skin an' club before lookin' once more at the parchment roll to see what next I was in for. It said I was to steal the girdle of Hippolyta, Queen of the Amazons, an' present it to Eurystheus. Now we've all 'eard of the Amazons, fierce warrior women, it was said, livin' way over to the east, beyond the Pelasgian Sea, past Troy, through the straits an' into what some call the Black Sea. I'd never been quite that far but I knew it was a much greater distance than Thrace so I was not well pleased. Right then I didn't want to think about it so I rolled the parchment an' placed it aside.

There was noise an' music from below so I decided to lose myself with the rest of 'em. I chatted with some of those who knew me from my earlier stays there an' went on to drink more wine than I ought. Then I noticed starin' at me was someone I'd not seen before, someone who seemed quite out of place; a clean-shaven, short-'aired young man in leather-belted tunic with a short sword at 'is side. He seemed keen on speakin' with me an' pushed closer to get my full attention. I was interested enough to 'ear what he wanted to say so we pushed our way over to the door an' let ourselves out from the noise to where we stood face to face in fresh nighttime air. "My name, sir, is Hylas," he began, "I am in the service of Lord Jason, prince of Iolcus in Thessaly."

'Now, Mister Peter, I knew somethin' of Iolcus and 'er famous harbour of Pagasae. These stood someway north of Delphi, but I'd never actually been there. I'd 'eard also of Pelias, its king, an' of 'is stepson, Jason, but 'ad a feelin' I was soon to learn more as he spoke.'

"I saw you enter the tavern when you were wearing your lion skin so I knew you were Heracles. You are known of through much of Greece and are credited with many great deeds, claimed to be ever more amazing, I must say, by those who have never met you. When my father, Thiodamus, was killed by someone unknown, many claimed the deed was yours."

"Well," I responded, "I've never 'eard of this Thiodamus an' I've been credited with the deaths of a good few others I'd never 'eard of, either, on top of those I 'ave. That's rumours for you, isn't it. An' in some people's memories will 'ave been the killin' of my two sons all those years ago in Thebes. Somethin' I wasn't aware I'd done until I came to my senses. Ever since then, if you didn't know it, 'er ladyship Hera's 'ad me runnin' all over Greece an' beyond to do 'er biddin' with that puffed-up bugger sittin' 'ere on the throne of Mycenae as 'er mouthpiece. So, now then, tell me what you want with me."

"Lord Jason," he answered, "is tasked with recovering the Golden Fleece from Colchis and..."

"The Golden what from where?" I cut in.

"I will not enter into any great detail for now, sir," he replied. "It is said to be a fleece of pure gold from a winged ram taken out of Greece and sent by Hermes to Colchis where it was sacrificed to Zeus. The precious fleece is kept in a cave and guarded, so we are told, by a fearsome creature that never sleeps. The gods say Jason must seize the fleece and bring it to Iolcus in order to prove his worth and gain the throne from Pelias, his stepfather who has no true son. The King of Colchis, Aeëtes, however, is said to be a powerful man and so values the fleece that he will stop at nothing to prevent it being taken from him. He believes it protects his kingdom from all of his enemies. For Jason to succeed he must have fit and brave warriors to crew his vessel and I, among others, am commanded to seek out such men but in particular yourself, sir. I learned you were often to be found here at Mycenae and so I came to ask if you would join Lord Jason on his venture. I have waited here for many days."

"Oh 'ave you now, an' where is this 'ere Colchis?"

"Colchis, sir, is far beyond the Pelasgian Sea, through narrower waters at its east then estwards to the furthest end of what many call the Black Sea."

"An' d'you know exactly where the Amazons live?"

He appeared puzzled by my question but answered, "The Amazons, so I hear, occupy a land called Thermodon by a river of the same name. This is on the coast but quite some way before we reach Colchis."

'Well now, I *was* listenin'. What d'you think of that, Mister Peter?'

'It sounded to me, Mister Heracles, that if you wanted, you were in for a free ride and you could skip off Jason's boat at Thermodon before reaching Colchis.'

'Aye, that I could, but if I made this Jason a promise an' stayed with it I could just as easily leave the boat on the way back, couldn't I. So I decided to go with young Hylas to Iolcus where he assured me the vessel was bein' readied with the blessings of Athena an' that Hera had nothin', absolutely nothin' whatsoever to do with it. So I agreed we would meet up at first light an' quit Mycenae.

He was waitin' dutifully for me that mornin' with a good-sized cart an' two 'orses. He might 'ave been prepared to carry more than one passenger but as there was only me, I could easily take along whatever I felt necessary. Unless we met with 'ostility this was to be yet another time-consumin' journey, much of it over rough country. And so it proved to be, with two nights passed at village taverns. We'd plenty of time for conversation, durin' which Hylas would often address me as "Sir." He was certainly no slave but it seemed he'd been brought up to show a deal of respect that to me appeared quite genuine. Or was it only for me? I'd find out later.

In bright afternoon sun we arrived at Iolcus, a city that occupied a steeply risin' site above the seashore. Below lay the busy 'arbour of **Pagasae** an' after a much-needed break for food an' beer, that is where we 'eaded - at least far enough along the path above to look down on the vessel. "And there she is!" declared Hylas, wavin' out 'is arm. "Her name is *Argo*. She is named after Argos, the man who designed her and at present oversees her completion. Although long in years he will also be our captain; Jason insists upon it, and he'll also have trusted men of his own in our crew."

'I tell you, Mister Peter, I was duly impressed at the sight of *Argo*. From bow to stern, the ship was swarmin' with men and boys goin' about their final tasks with their calls driftin' up to us on the warm air. We stayed a while to watch but I was to get no closer that day. On a level field near to the city wall lay an encampment that Hylas explained 'ad been set up by Jason to accommodate those men who were to sail with 'im. They called 'emselves the Argonauts. So now, with the sun gettin' low, we made our way to the encampment where spread a field full of colourful tents; some of 'em with pennants wavin' above. A few men wandered about.

There was pipe music playin' an' from some of the tents came the laughter of women. Hylas conducted me to a tent that when shown inside looked comfortable enough for two people. "This, sir, is for yourself and me," he announced. "Once you had decided to join us I was instructed by Jason to act as your squire so unless you decide otherwise I will from now on be at your call. I am hardly known to anyone else dealing with the vessel so if you wish to have them think I arrived with you then I will act accordingly and play my part."

'So I 'ad a servant, or squire, as Hylas was pleased to call 'imself. Well what's in a name. "That'll do fine," I informed 'im, "an' when am I to meet this Jason?"

"He will be here in the morning before he returns to the ship, as will the rest of those men who will be manning her. They are men who have experienced much hardship on land and sea and choose to boast of it openly."

"Oh, do they now," I responded. "But it's gettin' late an' soon I must find a tavern an' 'ave my belongin's secured there."

"That will not be necessary," Hylas responded, "I will take them into the city with our cart and there they will be safely guarded, Your canvas bag will be in the tent."

"Well I must find a tavern anyway," I said, "if you care to come along. I'll make my own introduction 'ere in the mornin' as soon as the sun's up. When we returned late to the tents, cookin' fires, though dyin' down, still gave forth rising smoke an' a few men from the arbour' gathered in conversation with people of the town. Present that evenin' were a small number of women waitin' to engage with the men for a payment of silver. Followed by Hylas, I slipped into our tent unnoticed.

I slept well that night an' when I awoke daylight was reachin' in. I could smell smoke and 'ear loud voices. I looked around for Hylas but he'd gone off somewhere so I dressed an' peered through the gap. Close to my tent was the group of fires, newly lit, where meat was bein' cooked on spits an' gathered about the fires were those men, more than I could at the time count, who would crew *Argo*. I spent some time listenin', not wantin' yet to make myself known. They were boastin' an' cheerin' to each other across the fires, most of it for a laugh so it seemed, an' the women were eggin' 'em on. One man I 'eard shoutin' out how he'd, "matched the deeds of 'Eracles," so I 'elped myself to a goblet of wine, donned my lion skin with its 'ead pulled over mine, took up my club an' stepped out carryin' also my bow an' arrows which I set down on the ground. On seein' me *as* I was, a good many of 'em began to realise *who* I was. "By Zeus it's really 'im!" someone called out.'

'There's once more fame for you, Mister Heracles,' I remarked as we both hesitated to take a drink.

'Aye, Mister Peter, I suppose it was. An' as I stood there starin' through the lion's jaws I was unaware of Hylas creepin' back to the tent. "So tell

us what you've been up to!" called one man. That
was an invitation I couldn't resist so I pushed back
the lion's 'ead an' began with, "First thing I did was
take on this lion not far from Mycenae – strangled
it, I did." They were murmurin' among 'emselves,
glancin' at one another then back at me as I added,
"And that's how I got this." I shook open an' closed
the front of the skin though many, I'm sure, didn't
believe a word of what I'd just told 'em. They
seemed more convinced by a brief account of the
Golden Hind an' the Erymanthian Boar so I shook
the club, thumped it on the ground an' went on,
"...an' then the King of Crete an' ruler of Knossos,
aye, the great Minos 'imself, 'ad me go out an'
catch the creature single 'anded. This was the
biggest bull you ever saw, damn great white beast
with 'orns like scythes! But I mastered it, oh yes,
then I got it on board a Cretan vessel and back over
to the mainland where we landed at night. I tethered
it to a tree and in the mornin' I let it go, aye, it
scared the shit out of people when they saw it. They
asked me 'ow I'd got it there because the Cretan
ship 'ad earlier left so I told 'em I'd 'ad it swim
over with me on its back. They still believed that
an' ..." I'd decided not to mention Eurystheus when
I was interrupted by the arrival of one who was
obviously more important than the rest of 'em. He
was fair - 'aired, blue-eyed, clean shaven an' stood
before me, arms folded an' a grin on 'is face. He
was dressed in plain, leather-belted linen tunic with
sword at his side that boasted a finely crafted,
ornate hilt an' pommel set with a gemstone. "And

who's this," I asked as they all turned to look at 'im, "that finds my account so amusin'?"

"I am Jason, son of Chiron," he replied, "and do I take it you are -?" He was interrupted by a burst of laughter from some of the men so I let drop my club, pulled the lion's 'ead up an' over my own again, peered at 'im through the open jaws, thumped my chest an' called out, "I'm 'Eracles,' that's exactly who I am! An' what's more I've volunteered of my own free will an' brought over one of my lads to 'elp you out – yes you, since I'm told it's you, the son of Chiron, leadin' us all to find this Golden Fleece thing an' whatever else we pick up while we're about it!"

"Yes, I realized you must be the famous Heracles," said Jason, "but I had to ask. My father and others have told me about you but I understand you are committed to undertake a number of tasks by King Eurystheus of Mycenae and -."

"Yes, alright, so I am," I responded. "There's twelve of 'em, aye, twelve so-called labours an' I've passed the eighth. When I 'eard about your scheme I decided I was overdue for a break an' so I left off 'em."

"I'm sure you are most welcome, my friend,' Jason assured me, 'and when my father knows you're here with us he will make his way over to greet you."

"Aye, good," I responded then turned to my tent an' called, 'Hylas, a drop more wine out 'ere!' To my audience I added, "He's my squire if y'please." Hylas emerged from the tent with a brimming silver goblet that he handed me. Jason did not acknowledge him as I downed the wine but strolled away, still smilin'. The men wanted to 'ear more so I accounted the most recent, the mares of Diomedes, then made out I'd gone on far enough. Some of the men were gatherin' together in close conversation an' one of 'em stepped forward, followed by others who stood before me an' said, "You. Heracles, would be the right man to lead us in times of conflict should any such arise. Will you do so if Jason agrees?"

"No," I responded, "that's the sole responsibility of your leader an' not my purpose in bein' 'ere." They said no more and began makin' their way down to the vessel. After returnin' my lion skin, club, bow and arrows to the tent it was to *Argo* I also would head while Hylas could keep 'is eye on our belongins'. On approachin' the 'arbour I stopped to take in the sight. My knowledge of ships bein' by then reasonable for a landsman I understood most of what was goin' on. Smoke drifted across an' I sniffed the odour of pitch applied to the ship almost up to the gunwale an' stanchions, these latter to support the upper bank of those rowin' who I reckoned as bein' twenty-five each side when *Argo* wasn't under sail. Above the black pitch 'er timbers were painted bright red an' above 'er cutwater bow arose a railed platform with curvin' 'igh over this, a slim an' delicate device in the shape of a horn. A similar device was positioned above 'er stern, also curvin' toward the mast which was stepped through the narrow, central deck. As I approached, 'er yardarm was bein' hoisted with the broad, white sail bearin' an image in black of Poseidon's trident. I climbed onto the busy deck an' was greeted by Jason who grinned at me an' said "Welcome aboard, Heracles – your lion skin ran off, did it?"

"Aye it did," I answered, "but if I whistle loud enough it'll soon come trottin' back." As I spoke we were approached by a stout, balding, bushy-bearded figure in leather kilt who walked with a swayin' gate. "Ah, here is the man I have appointed as captain," said Jason, gesturing for him to hesitate so he could introduce us. Exposing gappy, discoloured teeth, Argos beamed broadly an' once we'd shook 'ands he looked me up an' down an' said, "Nice to meet you, Heracles; a man such as you will do good work at the oars."

"Aye, I'll do my bit," I assured 'im, then he went about 'is business among the clatterin', callin, an' clamberin'.

"He's a good man," said Jason. "He's spent much of his life at sea and he'll know the route well. He told me how, after dark yesterday, he saw a white owl perched on the bow of this vessel. He watched it take to the air, circle a while then vanish into the night. He feels strongly Lady Athena has blessed our boat."

'That, Mister Peter, I found most reassurin', so I asked Jason, when we were to sail. He told me the ship would be floated early next day with the crew on board to check things over. The day after that, if

all was well, she'd be loaded with essentials at first
light an' ready to sail.

'Much of the followin' day I spent on board
Argo to find out more about the ship an' talk to
many of the men I'd be sailin' with. Their arms and
armour would be stowed on sackin' with some of
their supplies beneath the narrow deck. Mine, in the
canvas bag, would be with them. There'd be fifty
men to take the oars an' around twenty for other
duties. I learned more about my own tasks an'
where I'd be takin' my place when oarsmen were
needed an' so did Hylas. I talked with Argos for a
time then was introduced to Tiphys, the sun-
bronzed 'elmsman, a man well travelled as the
captain 'imself. He tried to convince me he was a
son of Poseidon so I guessed he didn't know who
'is real father was. There was another on the deck, a
clean-shaven man, of similar years to Argo 'imself,
seated on a three-legged stool an' playing a lyre. It
was no ordinary lyre but an instrument of exotic an'
valuable appearance. His shoulder-length fair hair
was 'eld in place by a gilded, leaf-patterned band,
the edges of his Egyptian cotton tunic colourfully
embroidered. On seein' me draw close, he stopped
playin', placed the lyre aside an' raised up from his
seat. This was Orpheus. I'd many years ago listened
to 'im and 'ad slain Linus, one of 'is pupils. He
must 'ave remembered it but still 'e managed a
smile.

Not long after sunrise next day we were leavin'
the 'arbour of Pagasae with oars strikin' the water
as they swept back and forth to the captain's

drumbeat. Those twenty or more of our crew not mannin' the oars, clambered about her deck and riggin', callin' to one another as they raised the yard arm an' deployed the big, square sail. People 'ad come down from the city an' gathered about the quay from where they cheered and waved. Drums an' pipes played, children dashed to an' fro with some climbin' on wall an' parapet to gain better sight of a vessel larger an' more colourfully arrayed with pennants than any they'd ever seen. Before reachin' open water, heavin' away as I was, I saw Jason pour a cup of red wine over the side of our vessel as the customary offerin' to Poseidon.

We were well clear of Pagasae by late mornin' with our oars shipped an' a steady breeze fillin' the sail. Now I'd time to go about an' talk to some of the others, or should I say stagger about as the boat swayed an' I grasped whatever I could to keep steady. Goin to Crete 'ad been much smoother. But where next would we stop? Well, it was to be Lesbos where we took on supplies, then Lemnos, of which I spoke earlier. You'll recall that, Mister Peter – or I 'ope you do,'

Heracles eyed me with suspicion as he poured more beer and I wondered if a second demonstration from my hidden recorder might be a good idea after dark. 'Why Lemnos?' I asked.

'Well we'd with us a few luxury goods the women weren't able to produce on Lemnos, some from Crete, an' they, or their slaves at the dockside, would supply us with good wines, fresh fruits, spring water an' the finest of fabrics, woven by themselves, to trade on or take back to Iolcus. Per'aps they 'oped our men might 'ave themselves to offer as well. Anyhow, couple more days would see us there. One of our crew, Telamon, had with 'im somethin' I'd not seen before - a pebble shaped piece of rock crystal he called a 'Firestone.' Watched intently by those close to 'im, he'd hold this steady as he could to concentrate the sun's rays an' ignite tinder within the small braziers over which we cooked our catches. When ashore he was also to prove a man of considerable skill with the bronze razor for those, includin' Jason, who'd no wish to grow face hair.

When we arrived at Lemnos' 'arbour and moored our vessel, no one ashore appeared to notice even though the town an' palace was in view. Jason left the boat wearin' his ornate helmet of gleamin' bronze with red horsehair plume swayin' above it. With 'im went six armed men. I stayed put when others of our men began to leave the boat and assemble on the quayside. By then I guessed we wouldn't be leavin' the island any time soon.'

'But you, Mister Heracles, chose to stay onboard *Argo*,' I commented.

'Too right, Mister Peter. I'd no intention of goin' ashore, believe it or not. More than all else I needed to get on with what was demanded of me and I 'oped I'd not be waitin' long for Jason an' those men who'd gone with 'im to return. Understand, Mister Peter, what else that damnable woman up above might 'ave inflicted upon me if I'd joined the rest of 'em. Jason did show up later that day but with three young women who he brought down to take a look at our ship. He 'ad a few words then made 'is way back with the remainder of our men followin'. That included Hylas an' even Orpheus. Well lookin' at those slim beauties by Jason's side you could 'ardly blame 'em an' for a time I was sorely tempted.'

'But, Mister Heracles, you had given Hylas permission.'

'Aye, Mister Peter, I Imagine the looks of resentment I'd 'ave otherwise been gettin'. But Jason didn't return next day, nor the day after, nor the day after that did any of 'em. Days began to pass; fifteen in all, though much later on I 'eard there were those who'd made it out to be a year. Throughout those passin' days, to keep me-self busy, I'd go huntin' with bow an' arrows, thinkin' often that the men might never reappear an' wonderin' how I'd ever get on my way. After the fifth day though, an' once each evenin' after that, Argo 'imself showed up to check over the vessel an' make sure all was as it should be. We discussed the situation on Lemnos an' both agreed that it 'ad got to end. Apart from anythin' else, you can't leave a wooden vessel all but abandoned because it will begin to deteriorate. One night a voice reached into my mind, tellin' me it was me an' only me that 'eld the answer. Was it Aphrodite wantin' to 'elp or was it Hera keen to get me movin' to the next labour? Whatever, I awoke determined to sort things out that very mornin'. I decided also, because the time

I'd lost, that I wouldn't remain with Jason on 'is mission to steal the Golden Fleece.

After a bite to eat an' a beer on board *Argo* I recovered my lion skin an' club, then in the warm rays of a risen sun I set off ashore. I made my way through the small town to the palace entrance where a couple of slaves thought to prevent me enterin'. They quickly realised it was best not to try. I pushed by 'em an' wandered into a kitchen where a woman in blemished grey smock stared at me in 'orror as three others with 'er fled in panic. I pushed back the lion's 'ead an' demanded she take me to Jason. In followin' her upstairs I noted how luxurious the place was, Minoan style if you see what I mean. We entered a short passage an' stopped before a door. The woman tapped 'ard but as nothing 'appened she tapped 'arder still. I backed away before the door opened an' there stood Jason with the woman who'd been keepin' 'im happy durin' the night – he in tunic with sword belt tugged on an' she in patterned gown, pushin' past 'im to demand, "What is the reason for this?" One look at me an' she froze. Jason's sword was part drawn as the woman who'd guided me blurted out, "there's a man out 'ere seekin' Lord Jason; a big man dressed like a lion an' armed with a club! Almost scared the life outa me 'e did! He came bargin' into the kitchens while we was seein' to the food an' -."

"Wait!" Jason exclaimed, "I'll deal with this!" He pushed by both women into the passage to find me standin' there an' asked, "Heracles, my friend, what's this all about?"

'I rested on my club and answered, "Sorry to break in on you, sir, I'm sure, but we 'ave problems brewin' that need your attention."

"What problems?" he asked.

"Some of our men," I answered, "say the demands made on 'em by these women are too great, if you see what I mean, and -."

"Oh, really," he grinned. He knew I was lyin'. "Not too many of them I imagine - and what else?"

"No, sir," I went on, "maybe not *too* many but our captain worries also about the neglect of 'is boat, as should we all since it seems there are no other vessels on the island – at least none that's seaworthy. Then there's no guards to keep an eye on things."

"Let's discuss this outside before I go and bathe," said Jason, glancing back at an apprehensive Hypsipyle who clutched at her gown. Aye, that's who it was, the very Queen of Lemnos. We made our way down a flight of steps then into the still shadowed courtyard where a fountain danced 'igh. There we stood face to face an' Jason said, "I hear what you say; much as we find it so compelling to remain on this island we have soon to leave and what you have told me may offer an answer. Those of our men still obsessed by what is on offer here must be persuaded by you, Argo an' myself to sail on but we must not stir their anger to the point where they confront us with refusal. I hope all of them will see good sense and depart Lemnos with us."

"Well, sir, they'll be takin' their mornin' food now," I declared, thumpin' my club on 'ard flagstones an' causin' Jason to step back abruptly as I swung it over me shoulder, "so I'll go an' put it to 'em in a more direct manner than maybe you'd care to do, with yourself an' our captain followin' up to talk more sense. I've faced far greater tasks, that I 'ave!"

Jason thought over what I'd said then replied, "Yes, as you say, we have to act but we'll allow them one more night to prepare themselves for what to many will be an agonizing decision."

"Agonisin', your Lordship – when we're at sea I'll show 'em a bit of agonisin' - I'll show 'em what 'ard work at the oar really is so we win back a bit'f lost time!"

'I was as good as my word, Mister Peter. When the cooking fires burned an' smoke swirled all about the clustered 'ouses and alleyways where the Argonauts resided, I strolled among 'em with me lion's 'ead in place. A couple of crewmen walked ahead of me with rams' 'orns blarin'. They hesitated from time to time for me to order aloud, "Gather before the palace at midday, lads! Before the palace at midday if y'please an' even if y'don't please!"

'They 'eard my message to a man but seein' my expression as I glowered at 'em through the open, white-toothed jaws of the lion's 'ead, an' the way I 'eld high the club, none of 'em seemed willin' to interrupt or to ask why. When the sun was at its 'ighest they began to gather in uneasy silence about the open space between palace an' quay where I stood beside Jason and Argos on the steps. There we could easily be seen and 'eard. A short way behind me awaited Hylas. "On the orders of Lord Jason, our leader," I went on in a voice that rang across to the quayside, "we leave to continue our voyage at first light tomorrow! That's the orders I and all of you 'ave to follow as 'ell now confirm!"

'Mutterin' an' disquiet spread among the men as Jason declared, "I understand your reluctance but we must leave this island for all your sakes and not just mine. We have a great journey ahead so ask yourselves how long most of you can afford to be away from your homes and what troubles could next arise there in your absence. You all gave your word to my father! Dishonour will fall forever upon any who break that promise and the gods above know it!"

"We catch fish an' 'unt for food durin' the day!" called one man. "Some of us could live out the rest of our days 'ere!"

'No, my friend!' Jason responded as the men shuffled about, looking from one to the other, "the novelty would eventually wear off and when it did you'd find there was no way of leaving without the skills you would need to repair or build a vessel!"

"That is so," declared Argos, "ours is the only seaworthy vessel on Lemnos an' she demands a worthy crew!"

"Continue with me as you have sworn you would," said Jason, "and if you so wish, on our journey back with our task completed, you may return to the pleasures of this island!"

Clever, dear reader, I thought, as Heracles tipped out more beer, because it helped avoid Jason being seen as a selfish killjoy intent on spoiling their fun to serve his own ends.

'There was further mutterin' an' shufflin' among the crew,' Heracles continued, 'but when this subsided there was no voice of dissent. "I'll muster our men before sunrise tomorrow, sir!" I announced, ensurin' as I spoke that my voice was 'eard by all. The women of the palace watched an' listened from above an' lookin' up at 'em, I shouldered my club an' growled, "Huh, women – all right in their place they are but this is a man's world an' it suits me that way."

'Did you really feel that way, Mister Heracles?' I asked him.

'Aye, well maybe I was just puttin' on a show. Maybe I was regrettin' after all that I never went ashore with the rest of 'em. Anyhow, before sunrise next day the women of Lemnos town, some young, some not so young, lined the quay to watch our vessel depart with 'er sail filled an' pennants flyin'. Most were silent though a few wept while others clung to a friend or to a sister for consolation. One stood aside from the rest, part way up the steps to 'er palace; Hypsipyle, in plain white gown with 'er hair fallen loose about 'er shoulders, raised a hand to Jason who acknowledged her with a wave of 'is arm. She'd given 'im an expensive lookin' cloak, left behind by a noble of Lemnos when he an' others of the men cleared off. Jason now wore this. The majority of men, strainin' at their oars, yelled

264

back their goodbyes while those not at the benches waved from mast an' riggin'. Tiphys, seated once more at his steerin' oar, twisted about to wave an arm at the women, perhaps one he cherished an' who he'd promised to find again on the Argonauts' return. Hylas was lookin' pleased with 'imself until he caught my eye. As we 'eaded out into the open bay to eventually turn east, our captain stood by Jason in the bow. Argos told me as I joined 'em that there were only four men he couldn't account for. He reckoned they'd 'idden away or been 'eld there by the women. Aye, some of those women – well who could blame 'em'

"That still leaves us with over sixty fit and able men," Jason remarked. "Quite enough for the task ahead I'd say."

"Quite enough, young sir," agreed Argos. "But those missin' four will sooner or later see the error of their ways. What's more, though, I expect our time there will result in an increase to the island's population before too long and give those women somethin' more to get on with."

"Oh, perhaps it will," muttered Jason. "And once we're clear of the island I'll make our offer of wine to Poseidon."

"And to Athena," I added. "Yes and to Athena," he agreed.

'This day,' continued Heracles, 'offered calmer seas than on our journey from Pagasae, an' once beyond Lemnos' southern bay an' passin' around the island more vessels, mainly those out fishin' were to be seen. *Argo*, sometimes propelled by oars but usually under sail in a steady breeze with Tiphys steerin', proceeded eastwards. When rowin' to the beat of 'er captain's drum the men sang loud to sea an' sky with me joinin' in. When the winds favoured our progress an' the oars were drawn in we cast our fishin' lines. A few men 'ad gamin' boards to occupy their time and wagers were made. Orpheus, due to 'is age was not suited to 'ard work an' so stayed out of the way until 'is true skills were needed and 'e could be 'eard. The men also boasted among 'emselves over their encounters with the women of Lemnos, each maintainin' 'is so-called conquest had been greater than that of others.

By mid afternoon the channel ahead was gettin' narrower and Argos stood to address us all, "Over there if you've not sailed this way before," he announced, gesturin' to the right, "is the mighty city of Troy. An' as it's the Hellespont we're soon to enter, we'll get by the city quick as we can in case they think we're traders with goods to exchange for grain an' try to charge us for the privilege."

"I've heard many people speak of Troy," said Jason. "Those who sail to cities beyond the Hellespont are said to resent her control of passing trade and the taxes she imposes. My father tells me there's been talk of war over past years with the great cities of the mainland combining against her but it seems nothing has happened so far."

Argos turned to Jason, sayin', "Yes, I've 'eard that also. Maybe sooner or later somethin' will 'appen to light the spark of conflict. For now we'll row an' use what wind there is to get clear. Hah, what wind there is, I said, but now it seems there's 'ardly any at all and soon may be even less. The lads will 'ave to pull 'ard as they can."

'Hearin' those words, I part rose an' called out from my bench located close to the bow, "Let's see you match my stroke, you idle buggers! Come on - match it now!"

"Aye they'll 'ave to," I 'eard the captain say as he took charge of 'is drum. "They won't want to break it if 'e's determined the speed will they. I'll 'ave to match 'is beat, that I will, and not 'e mine I reckon." The oarsmen were pullin' 'ard, all strainin' to match their strokes with mine as we entered the channel with Troy passin' slowly to our stern. No Trojan vessel seemed to be approachin' us but I wasn't about to ease up and instead I cried out, "C'mon! Keep it up! Let's show 'em over there what we can do!" I think Argo wanted us to slow down before some of our lads gave in to fatigue. But as he stood to call out there was a loud crack, the sound of splittin' wood 'ad the men at the benches ease back and raise their oars as the blade end of a shattered oar bobbed by. Aye, Mister Peter, *my* shattered oar. Cursin' aloud, I rose up, swung up the remaining length of oar and 'urled it spinnin' into the sea. "Look at that!" I called out to Jason and Argos, 'There's no damned strength in the thing!"

"Congratulations!" responded the captain, "Now you've busted it we're an oar short an' we don't carry no spares!"

"So what d'you have to say?" demanded Jason, steppin' down onto the strip of deck. "You've had a great deal to say about many things, my friend, so how about this?"

The crewmen turned their 'eads, the boat swayed as I glared at 'im. I was in disgrace but not feelin' inclined to show it. "Very well, your 'ighness," I declared, "when we put ashore I'll take an axe an' I'll seek out good timber wherever there's any to be 'ad an' I'll carve out a new oar. Aye, an' a better an' a stronger one than that you gave me!" Jason was joined by Argos, who addressed the crew. "All right, lads, keep us on course 'till we're clear of other vessels. After sunset we'll put ashore an' see what the mornin' 'as to bring."

'I sat starin' into space with arms folded as though the broken oar was no fault of mine. We were into the Hellespont with the sun gettin' low. Those at the oars were pullin' 'ard but with darkness not far away an' the sea gettin' rougher in an increasin' wind we put into a bay where Jason and a few of 'is men went ashore to visit a petty king Argos knew called, Cyzicus; someone I'd never 'eard of. I'd no intention of goin' with 'em so the oar I'd promised would 'ave to wait. They were back late the followin' mornin' but the wind was still strong, the waters yet rougher an' the sky vergin' on twilight. I 'eard Argos tellin' Jason it wasn't a good idea to sail out, but under oars we did because Jason was impatient an' so was I. Trouble was the weather got even worse an' we could go no further. Argos ordered the boat turned about and as early darkness fell we were once more back in the bay we'd earlier left. Jason and 'is few men went ashore, leavin' the rest of 'is crew on board, me included. I wondered if he intended to find us somewhere to shelter for the night but by then the sky was clearin' an' the air becomin' calmer so we managed sleep wherever we could. There was barely a glimmer of daylight when Jason's party returned an' we prepared to cast off at once, rowin' out of the bay in haste as the sail was bein' unfurled. Somethin' was amiss an' I found out soon after from one of 'is party what'd passed. In the dark, Cyzicus 'ad mistaken Jason's returnin' men as brigands. A fight ad' broken out and Cyzicus 'imself 'ad been killed. Jason ordered 'is men not to speak of what 'appened once on board.

'Soon in open water under a brightenin' sky the air became still an' I rowed with the rest of 'em, but no 'arder – just in case. Didn't want to break another oar did I, though the current was against us an' we weren't makin' good progress. As the day wore on the channel was narrowin', the wind pickin' up in our favour an' our sail billowin'. With the oars pulled in I stepped along the deck to ask Argos how we were doin'.'

"The channel will open out as we enter the Propontis an' from there we sail on to the Euxine Sea where lies our destination – Colchis. The mainland we approach to our right is Mysia an' as daylight will soon begin to fade I'll 'ave us pull in there. Some of our men will find brushwood for our

269

fires an' maybe you'll locate timber suitable for makin' the replacement oar you boasted of doin'. There are freshwater springs if we wanted to take on more water."

'*Argo* was manoeuvred into a sheltered cove an' once the vessel was secured, 'er crew disembarked, takin' with 'em their arms as did I. I'd also put on the lion skin to make things more comfortable as we'd be sleepin' on the ground there an' I'd taken with me my canvas bag. I wandered about lookin' at suitable tree branches while Hylas was with the other men 'elpin' to find brushwood. Before dark there was enough gathered for cookin' with fires ignited from a small brazier that had been relit on board the vessel after the weather calmed. Hylas joined me, Orpheus played 'is lyre, the men chatted, ate, drank beer an' laughed into the warm night while reminiscin' further about their stay on Lemnos. One of 'em asked me more about my own goin's on under Hera's curse. I rose to the occasion with club in 'and but there didn't seem as much interest as I'd expected so I sat down with Hylas an' we roasted some skewered boar meat.

When the fires 'ad died an' stars dominated the blackness above, the men were unable to find sufficient space about the cove for all to sleep in comfort. Some returned to the vessel, preferrin' to find rest at their benches or on deck. Jason and 'is captain remained sat in conversation on an embankment. They spoke of gettin' underway soon as possible next day an' it seemed to me Jason's impatience was grown large. I approached to inform 'em, "I'll be off at first light. I'll carve an oar same size as the others though it'll not be quite so fancy – still, I'll be the one usin' it."

"Very good," said Argos.

"And I look forward to seeing what a splendid job you make of it," grinned Jason. I stepped away grumblin' to myself an' rejoined Hylas. The night passed without incident but in the mornin', with the sky lightenin', Jason, Argos an' their crew were well awake an' busy with others already returned to the boat. "We didn't keep any fire for the mornin'," remarked one. "We've nothin' to light the brushwood with."

"We'll 'ave to wait until we're aboard with the sun well up," responded another, "then Telamon can use 'is magic pebble to light one."

'But, Mister Heracles,' I said, 'You still hadn't started that replacement oar.'

'No, Mister Peter, no I 'and't, though I'd seen a few likely lengths of wood. I looked round for Hylas but there was no sign of 'im. I called out loud. No reply. I called out again, "Hylas, you bugger, where are you 'idin'?" I peered around the men by the water then over at the boat. "Hylas!" I called again. This time came a reply from the boat itself so I shouted, "Hylas, bring over an empty water jug an' get one of the others to fetch me an axe!"

With copper, two-handled jug swingin' from one 'and, Hylas eased 'imself over the side of the boat an' called back, "All right, I'm coming!" an', waist-deep in the water he waded ashore as I called, "Is one of 'em bringin' me that axe?"

"I don't know if anyone heard me," came the reply as he trod towards me. "They're all very busy so maybe they didn't."

"Well leave the damned jug 'ere an' go back for the axe," I said. "I should've been 'ard at it by now!"

'Hylas ran back to the ship an' after some delay returned, bronze axe in 'and. "Will that be all?" he muttered, handin' over the axe.

"No it won't!" I answered. "Bring that jug an' follow me. While I'm choosin' a decent length of wood you can get us some fresh spring water to refill our flasks, if y'don't mind."

'I 'ope you can understand, Mister Peter, how impatient I was feelin' though I admit I'd wasted more time than I ought. They'd be readyin' the boat to leave an' maybe no longer worryin' too much about the oar. Hylas wandered off into the woods with the jug an' I set to work with one of the fallen branchs I'd already come across. I kept busy hackin' away until the oar was not far off finished when I realised Hylas still 'adn't returned. I looked around an' called 'is name but while the birds kept singin' there was no reply from him. I put aside the axe an' set off to find my so-called squire. The vessel would've been ready and 'er crew waitin' for me but as I'd 'eard no one call my name I assumed they'd still 'ave other things to do. Cursin' Hylas aloud. I searched 'ere an' there until I came upon a large pool. It was there I spotted the empty jug layin' close by in the bushes. I stood gazin' about, thinkin' there was an odd, unworldly feel about the place, then concluded Hylas must've run off somewhere, maybe fed up of his role in life, or fallen into the pool an' drowned, though without a body floatin' there in calm water, that seemed unlikely. I grabbed up the abandoned jug, made my way back, still lookin' 'ear an' there, then 'urriedly finished the oar. I called out several times more then set off to join the others at the ship thinkin' that's where Hylas must be. If so, I intended to make the bugger account for the neglect of 'is duties. Well, Mister Peter, I arrived to find the cove deserted an' lookin' seaward I spotted *Argo,* well out into the channel, her sail filled and 'er oars glintin' sunlight with each stroke. "Damn the lot of you!" I yelled at the recedin' vessel then I flung the roughly finished oar to the ground an' smashed it into pieces with my club. Aye, maybe they 'ad called for me but I'd been too far away to notice. But what did it matter now. Fortunately my canvas bag still rested on the embankment where I'd left it with the contents untouched.'

'So you were well and truly abandoned, Mister Heracles,' I said.

'Well and truly as you say, my friend, an' I knew almost nothin' of Mysia. So now I'd follow the coast until I came upon a harbour town or even a village, unless I meanwhile spotted another boat I could jump onto.'

He peered up at the cloudless sky and said, "Now then, Mister Peter, lets you and I get back to the courtyard and 'ave ourselves somethin' to eat. Per'aps we can come back 'ere later an' I'll go on about the Amazons."

That seemed a good idea so I followed him through the woods and back to the house while fiddling to switch off the recorder. We'd finished eating when his wife called his name from along the corridor. Heracles shrugged, got up from his seat and said, "Shouldn't be too long." Once he'd gone, I hurried to the bedroom and placed the recorder up onto the window ledge. With the sun still high overhead even a short time there would give it a decent boost and I'd hear him coming back along the corridor in time to grab and switch it back on.

Chapter 11 - The Amazon Queen

I was on my way back to the clearing but I'd not after all had a chance to switch on the recorder without the risk of being noticed. Tiye and Mayet had returned to the bedroom moments before Heracles clumped by in his heavy boots so I'd grabbed the recorder from beneath the window and stuffed it into my pocket. But planning a walk by the stream the girls had accompanied me to where Heracles waited before carrying on together. One of his attendants, following behind with a fresh jar of beer, distracted him briefly and gave me the opportunity I needed to switch the recorder back on. We settled down, Heracles watched his man pour beer into the waiting cups then continued his epic tale.

'By mid-afternoon I'd come upon a large village with mainly fishin' boats in its cove. I was wearin' the lion skin with the 'ead pushed back, mainly because it was easier than to carry it in the bag. I straightaway got the attention I wanted with people starin' and some followin' me. It didn't appear to be a great tradin' town because there were only two boats that looked like they'd be goin' anywhere far. I stepped down to the larger of 'em whose captain clambered over the side to meet me. He was a sturdy lookin', weather-beaten old character an' stood waitin' for me to speak first. I told 'im that I wanted to reach Thermodon an' its river an' I'd pay my way. "I've 'eard somethin' of you," he said, eyein' me slowly up an' down. "There are traders from west of 'ere who've described you. It's 'Eracles, am I right?"

"You are right, my friend," I answered, "that's who I am. Now what about this boat?"

He went on to inform me that next day he'd be headin' out into the Black Sea through what 'e called the Clashin' Rocks an' stoppin' at an island called Thynia. Then he'd continue along the southern coast to Sinope, which was not too far from Thermodon. "The Clashin' Rocks," I asked, "What're those?"

"Oh, they're the 'igh rock walls each side of the narrow passage we pass through into' the Black Sea. It's said that in the past they'd sometimes close in an' crush ships tryin' to sail through. Well I've been in an' out through there over more years than I can remember as 'ave many others so I tell you it isn't true. A big, fancy-lookin' ship passed this way only two days ago with sail as well as oars pushin' 'er on but both were needed because the currents are changeable an' the water can get a bit rough."

'So he'd seen *Argo*. I paid the man but insisted I spend the night on 'is vessel with somethin' to eat an' drink as I didn't care to get involved with anythin' in the village an' miss sailin' a second time. I was awake next mornin' before the crew turned up to load cargo for the tradin' he'd planned ahead so I kept out of their way in the stern. There I remained, close by the steersman whose knowledge of Greek was not so good that I was able to understand everythin' he said but he stopped talkin' so as to concentrate as we approached the narrows. Aye, the water *was* on the rough side an' the boat rolled. I could imagine how the idea must 'ave come about that the sides once closed in but after a time the channel opened out an' before us lay calmer open water. The oars were shipped an' we proceeded east under sail only, keepin' the coast well within sight.

By late afternoon we reached the small, steep island the 'elmsman informed me was Thynia an' there we tied up to a tree stump at the only inlet. As there wasn't any village there I opted once again to remain with my belongin's on the boat. The captain went ashore but returned before dark to stay the night on board together with most of 'is crew. He'd spent some time talkin' with one of the few people on the island, men who went there to catch fish an' he'd a tale to tell. A large vessel, the very one our captain ad' already told me about sailin' past 'is village, 'ad called in there two days previous. One of their crew 'ad died an' they brought 'im ashore wrapped in sailcloth then carried 'im up to level ground close to an old, abandoned temple of Apollo surrounded by laurel trees. The island men stayed close by but remained 'idden. They watched the ship's crew gather brushwood an' make a pyre to burn the body. They watched 'em before the temple sacrifice a wild goat in the man's name."

"Did you 'ear 'dead man's name spoken?" I asked.'

"Aye, I did," he replied, "They spoke it aloud to Apollo. He was called Tiphys. Many stayed up there the night while the rest went back to their boat They sailed away at sunrise yesterday."

'That surprised me, about Tiphys, Mister Peter, an' I was much saddened. But next day we cast off at first light an' continued on our way in a good breeze to the peninsula where lay the town of Sinope, which we sighted as darkness was fallin'. I'd only one thing in mind after sayin' goodbye to the captain an' leavin' the boat, an' that was to locate a decent tavern, which was none too difficult as this was a large town. The lion skin I'd packed away as I didn't want to risk bein' recognized so my canvas bag was bulgin' and 'eavy. I carried on through the old town an' away from the 'arbour until I found a tavern with a stable an' chariots nearby. The tavern was as dim as most taverns were in spite of all the oil lamps but bein' away from the port it was more for those with silver to spare. I'd a clean place to sleep but before that I sat below with food an' wine in a shadowed area.

It was quite soon after I'd eaten when she came over to sit close by me with a goblet of wine in 'er 'and. I 'ave to say, Mister Peter, she was as fine lookin' a woman as I ever saw; wide-eyed an' with full red lips. Her dress was colourful an' close fittin' about 'er slim figure but it was not Mycenaean or Minoan court style with 'er breasts exposed. She'd jewelled clips to keep 'er long dark hair in place an' even in the dim light, gold glinted in 'er earrings an' necklace. She placed gold-ringed fingers on my arm an' asked me where I was from. She spoke excellent

Greek an' I tell you, Mister Peter, I shivered at 'er touch. "I'm from Mycenae," I told 'er.'

'I noted how one of the men standin' not far away grinned an' winked at me an' it looked like I'd got 'er company for as long as I wanted.'

'Your lucky day, Mister Heracles,' I said.

'My lucky night don't you mean, Mister Peter,' he grinned, downing his beer.

"Are you a trader from one of the harbour vessels?" she asked, movin' closer 'till 'er warm breath touched my ear. "You don't look like a trader. Are you here alone?"

'I told 'er I was then I got us more wine an' informed 'er also I was to set off next day, before dawn, to find the Amazons.'

"The Amazons!" she responded an' she looked quite shocked. "They're wild vicious women ruled by a queen. It's said men do most of the work while the women hunt for game and make war on anyone who tries to take what they claim is theirs. Sinope sometimes has conflict with them. You'd better be careful – sorry, er, I don't know your name - mine is Circe."

'Well I doubted that was 'er real name so I told 'er mine was Delphus, one thought by many to be a son of Poseidon.'

'D'you think she believed you?' I asked him.

'I've no idea,' he smiled, 'an' I really didn't care because I'd better things to think about as we made our way upstairs. The night didn't end too well for the woman though. You see, Mister Peter, I'm a light sleeper an' woke up as she slipped quiet as she could out of our bed. I watched 'er pull on 'er clothes without makin' a sound. There was still one small oil lamp burnin' in a corner of the room where my tunic an' the canvas bag with my belongings in 'em lay. She glanced at me then stepped over to 'em an' lifted up the tunic which must 'ave seemed 'eavy because I'd got many pieces of silver in there. She'd been reachin' inside the pocket when she sensed I was creepin' up close behind. She turned around an' let drop some of my silver. She knew there was no point in makin' excuses or creatin' a fuss as I grabbed up my leather belt an' dragged 'er across the room to the bed. I sat on the corner, got 'er over my knee, pulled up 'er gown an' gave 'er pretty arse a bit of a thrashin' – enough to cause 'er embarrassment rather than any real hurt. I let 'er up, sobbin 'er eyes out an' insistin' she meant no 'arm so I gave 'er a piece of silver for the pleasures she'd earlier given me an' shoved 'er out the door.'

'A foolish thing for her to do, Mister Heracles,' I said, 'especially as she appeared to be quite well off already from what you told me.'

'Aye, Mister Peter, but maybe that's 'ow she got to be well off – by robbin' those who passed through Sinope, 'idin' away until they'd gone an' movin' elsewhere from time to time. And knowin' where I was 'eaded I reckon she was sure I'd not be comin' back. Anyhow the tavern 'ad a fresh water pool at the rear so after I'd bathed an' eaten I set off for the stable an' paid for use of 'orse an' small chariot. When the two men in charge learned where

I intended to go they demanded I bought their 'orse an' chariot outright. That I didn't care to do but made 'em accept a bit of extra silver and 'ave them tell me how long I might need to travel before reachin' the Thermodon river.

Once away from Sinope I pulled on the lion skin. For much of that hot day I carried on east through rough country with the sea to my left an' crossin' the occasional stream. Inland I'd seen a small village as well as farms an' orchards but by early afternoon there was no sign of 'abitation. That remained so by the time I'd passed through open spaces an' mixed woodland to reach the banks of a wide, slow-movin' river I guessed must be the Thermodon, in part because of the time it'd taken me to get there. I peered around an' could see no one but realised later that someone must've been watchin' me. I followed the river bank, passin' through woodland until the land opened out further with isolated dense copses of trees.

I was passin' close by one of those copses when it 'appened. There was a sharp thud at the side of my chariot. I slowed my 'orse an' glanced over to see an arrow embedded there. I stopped an' saw people steppin' from amid the trees, five or six on each side, some of 'em carryin' a bow with arrow loosely fitted but ready for use an' a quiver over their backs; others holdin' a long spear. Then two more emerged from behind the trees on 'orseback. All of 'em were variously attired as warriors; I noted some with cuirasses, worn over decorated smocks, others with greaves or long boots. Some wore metal 'elmets an' one of the two mounted, boasted a swayin' red plume. They approached me with the plumed rider callin' out in a language I didn't understand but the voice I 'eard was that of a woman. It looked like I'd found the Amazons, or should I say, they'd found me!'

'A tricky situation, Mister Heracles and you were well outnumbered.'

'Aye, well outnumbered I was, Mister Peter, an' surrounded, so all I could do was wait. I pulled the lion's 'ead over my own on the off chance it might 'elp me bein' recognized by one of 'em. The rider came closer an' stopped in front to look me up an' down.'

"I've heard of a man such as you they call Heracles," she announced, "a man said to perform his antics while strutting around in a lion's skin. I take it you are that man."

'I understood 'er words now as she was speakin' good Greek an' replied, "I am Heracles an' I'm ordered by King Eurystheus of Mycenae to call upon your queen."

"I know something of Mycenae" she responded, "but this land is Thermodon and it is forbidden to outsiders such as you, famous or not. Also, we observed a large vessel with pennants at its masts sailing eastwards beyond the river mouth two days ago. Were the people aboard her known to you and do they intend to come ashore here?"

"They're known to me but they'll not come 'ere," I told her as my 'orse an' hers stamped an' snorted at each other. "They've business only in

282

Colchis, further to the east." She continued to stare at me then gestured to the arrow lodged in the side of my chariot. "You see how accurate we are with bow and arrow, as intruders find to their cost. That arrow struck exactly where it was intended but it could just as well have been you. You now will return with us and Queen Hippolyte will be informed in advance."

'She gestured to the second rider an' spoke in 'er own language, tellin' 'er, so I gathered, to inform their queen of my arrival. I was already thinkin', as she rode off, how I might get away from there, with or without the precious girdle, should the woman in charge not care to see me. So I went on with them ridin' either side. Once clear of the trees the land opened out to reveal fenced-off sheep an' cattle to one side with further to the other, fields of grain with irrigation ditches leadin' to the river. There were men labourin' in the fields an' they glanced up in surprise as I passed by though they didn't stop what they were about for long. They appeared more like slaves rather than owners or tenants of the land they worked an' there were armed women on 'orseback overseein' them.

Directly ahead lay what looked like orchards an' beyond these, smoke was risin', though I could see no sign of a town or city. Soon there appeared closely spaced groups of 'ouses, some of stone, others mainly wood, none spreadin' back very far from the river bank. It looked more a very large village than a proper town. Everywhere appeared well ordered with no animals runnin' around but I could see no tavern. There were well groomed young women goin' about their business, most seemin' to 'ave a short sword at the belt of 'er patterned tunic an' many with their hair knotted up at the top. An' very odd it was, Mister Peter, they an' the ones who'd escorted me over there all looked about the same age – reasonably young, I reckoned. The few men I saw, each dressed in no more than a plain kilt, looked to be menials, undertakin' 'ard work or involved with a beast. None of 'em possessed a weapon an' I could see no kids runnin' about anywhere.

The village now was openin' out into a large square with at the far side a more substantial stone buildin' with an upper floor. It looked to be of great age an' once may've been some kind of fortress. To one side of the buildin', between it and ourselves, was a wooden frame from which was suspended a dead pig. Facin' it on the other side of the square, a small group of women with bows an' arrows were usin' the pig for target practice. As we approached we stopped to see one of 'em let fly. Her arrow struck the pig but then the pig was already bristlin' with arrows so they'd all struck it to prove 'ow good they were. Maybe good as me for what that was worth. They hesitated to let us pass between 'emselves an' the target where the woman in charge of my female escort informed me, "Today you see a pig but anyone foolish enough to threaten our ways or do us harm might be seen there instead."

'Well that wasn't too encouragin', Mister Peter, as you can imagine since their victim would most probably be a man, or so I concluded. But we carried on to the front of the big buildin' where I spotted on the roof a small number of armed women peerin' down at us. To the left of the buildin' stood what looked like a modest temple. Before the guarded entrance she in charge ordered me to step down from the chariot. I did but then one of the women on foot jumped on to take my place an' grabbed the 'orse's reigns. "Where're you takin' that?" I demanded as my bag an' my club were still in it. Some of those on foot moved threatenin'ly close to me as she answered, "It will be placed with our queen's chariot over there." She gestured with a thumb to a wooden barn to my right, pointed to the main buildin's entrance then added, "Now you will be taken before our queen and there you must kneel and remain silent."

'Aye, that's what she said; I was expected to kneel. Five of those carryin' a spear levelled their blades at me so, not wantin' to be prodded too 'ard with a sharp point through the lion's pelt, I walked up the short flight of steps an' entered through imposin' doors. We passed along a windowless corridor where firebrands, mounted on the walls, supplied light. This passage turned aside then opened into a large chamber with windows at one wall an' a light well passin' up through to the roof to give the place a fair amount of extra light. About its smooth walls I made out what must've have been frescoes depicting trees, birds and animals, except that they were all but obscured by round shields an' others of varyin' design, all interspaced by assorted, bronze-glintin' weapons of a number that even Mycenae or Thebes might've been proud to display. These included swords, spears, maces an' axes as well as a few things I'd never before seen. Aye, this was in its way a larger version of that I'd seen at the 'ouse of Diomedes, a pretty disorganised collection of arms an' armour that once belonged to others.

But all of this, Mister Peter, I took in with the briefest of glances. A carved alabaster throne with tasseled blue cushion stood on a low plinth close to the back of the chamber and upon it, in more modest splendor by far than the pretentious Eurystheus, sat Queen Hippolyte. Keepin' 'er long raven hair in place was a gold 'eadband glintin' jewels. Her hair framed a face of sculpted rather than tender beauty but 'er wide brown eyes 'eld not the bewitchin' gaze I recalled from the girl at Sinope who'd tried to rob me, but one of calculatin' coolness. She wore a white tunic that appeared as embroidered with gold wire an' even though she was seated, much of the girdle, or sash if you like, was visible. To one side of 'er stood a slightly younger, very pretty an' not so 'ard-faced woman in a pale blue gown who also wore a girdle. Her arms were bare an' though she wore jeweled bands, these appeared no more pretentious than might be worn by a courtier elsewhere. Both of 'em weighed me up an' down an' I swear the younger one managed a fleetin' smile.

"Kneel before our queen!" hissed a voice close to my ear as one of 'er women prodded me in the back. I resisted the urge to swing about an' send 'er sprawlin' with a punch.

"I kneel to nobody!" I responded loud, an what I tell you now, Mister Peter, flashed through my mind as I spoke. I was 'emmed in by those five with their spears pointed at me but if I spun around, the lion skin, swishin' out might confuse 'em, might've 'ad 'em back off while I grabbed one of their spears an' made a stand or dashed forward to threaten their almighty queen. But Hippolyte, as if sensin' my thoughts, raised a hand an' those with the spears 'esitated, lowered their blades an' took one step away. I glanced around, turned back to face Hippolyte an' gave 'er the kind of reluctant bow I'd given to Eurystheus, though maybe this time it lasted a moment or so longer. I even mumbled, "Your 'Ighness," but I'm not sure if she 'eard. She raised up slowly, 'er eyes all the time 'ard on me, an' in their own language she dismissed the five women. She descended from the plinth to face me with the girl in blue a step or two behind. I'd now full view of the girdle I'd been ordered to steal. It appeared one of rare silk with lots of colours woven in. "This is my younger sister, Penthesilia," she began in cool but near perfect Greek as the girl moved to her side. "We know of you, Heracles, by the words of those traders who are granted permission to visit us at certain times of the year. They are questioned over affairs in Greece and thus we have heard something of your deeds. But we must know what brings you alone and uninvited to our land. What interest can King Eurystheus have with us?"

'Now that *was* a tricky one, Mister Peter. I couldn't tell 'er Eurystheus 'ad ordered me to steal some of 'er clothin', could I, but I did need a quick answer an' said, "I am ordered to take back to 'im proof that I came 'ere but it's Hera speakin' though 'im." I wasn't sure how she expected to be addressed but it didn't seem right then to matter.'

"What sort of proof?" she asked.

"Er, somethin' of yours," I replied. "Maybe somethin' personal to convince 'im."

The smile she managed was hardly one of good humour as she responded, "Oh, really - something personal. Well now, Heracles, I will have to think about that should you eventually be permitted to leave our land."

'Hippolyte and her sister seem to have been very trusting, Mister Heracles,' I said.'

"Ow's that?" he responded, topping up our beers.

'Well they'd been left alone with you, not knowing how much of a threat to them you might be.'

'No, Mister Peter, I think she knew her an' Penthesilia wouldn't come to any 'arm an' I knew if they did I'd never get out of there alive. I'd glimpsed 'er armed guards hoverin' just inside the doorway by which I'd entered an' another lurkin' behind 'er throne. Aye, I might 'ave ended up in that square where I'd seen that pig 'ung up, bristlin' with arrows. "Who is that shrine outside dedicated

288

to." I asked, thinkin' it best to change the subject of 'er possessions.'

"It is indeed dedicated to Hera, she of Olympus, wife of Zeus and mightiest of women. She helps each of us to maintain our strength and our – and our appearances."

"So they worship that bitch even 'ere do they," I muttered under my breath.

"And who do you most often favour with your offerings?" she asked.

"Athena," I replied, "aye, definitely Athena."

"Well at least it's another woman," she responded. She turned to 'er silent sister an' said, "Have them prepare food and wine in our courtyard for myself and this man." Penthesilia hurried off, still without a word, an' vanished through the door to the rear of the throne. Hippolyte turned to me, sayin', "There are matters I will discuss with you, Heracles."

'I was taken aback, Mister Peter. Here was a woman and 'er armed population with total power over 'er kingdom, if kingdom was the right word, an' all the men in it. She'd power of life an' death, but was addressin' me without any formality, aye, as someone she was already familiar with. Yet I sensed it wasn't really like that at all an' the situation might change quickly if it suited 'er. "Follow me," she said, an' havin' no option, I did so. We passed through a frescoed anteroom with unobstructed walls. Whoever 'ad painted these must've seen the ones in Knossos or some other part of Greece but 'ad never quite attained the skills I'd observed there. After passin' through features that reminded me of where I'm livin' now, we ended up in a small courtyard where wine an' cold food already waited on the table. There were two armed woman attendants there as well but these she dismissed. The air was warm but the sun too low to shine in. We sat, she 'erself poured the wine into fancy gold goblets so I waited for 'er to drink or to say somethin'. It felt like I was driftin' through a dream.'

"You are not a young man, Heracles," she began, "but I see you are fit and strong. This I consider good for breeding purposes – to maintain our own numbers, that is." I was lost for words, Mister Peter, so I took a gulp of wine an' let 'er get on with it. "Our female children are taken well away from here to train in the use of arms. Male children, those who we consider to be of use and able to understand their purpose, are kept elsewhere until fit enough to toil on our lands."

'I was beginnin' to work out what she meant by 'er reference to male children but I wasn't inclined to question 'er on it. She asked me to say more about what was happenin' in Greece then about the tasks, the labours that'd been imposed on me. As the shadows were deepenin' firebrands were brought in an' fitted to brackets on the courtyard walls an' I could see oil lamps bein' lit inside. As brief as it 'ad to be in finer details, this conversation kept us goin' until well after dark. The air was quite cool by then an' I was thinkin' I was fortunate to 'ave the lion skin about me when she said, "We must now go inside."

'I was first shown upstairs to witness the kind of set-up you've seen 'ere, then 'er bedroom where she said we were to meet when I was ready. When I arrived there were two of 'er armed women set to stand outside the room should she need 'em. Very reassurin' that was. Her bedroom wasn't the plush affair you'd think a queen would want but somehow that didn't surprise me. Aye, I really did go to bed with Queen Hippolyte an' got on with the business. I'll say this, Mister Peter, she did soften up for a while an' she be'aved like a woman's expected to be'ave at such times except she was more in charge.

When I woke up in the mornin' she'd gone like a fleein' spirit. The window was uncovered an' the sky lightened enough for me to peer about the room. Draped over a wooden chest by the bed was 'er girdle. In those moments alone, with the door pushed almost shut, I yielded to temptation, pushed the girdle aside an' lifted open the lid of the chest. Little enough light as it was, I was inwardly dazzled at what I saw. Here were cut gemstones of all sizes mixed together with small objects, includin' bodily adornments in bejeweled precious metals. But little in the way of bodily adornments seemed of interest to any of the women I'd encountered except for Hippolyte and 'er sister. I could 'ear lowered voices outside. I knew they were waitin' for me so I closed the lid an' drew the girdle back over it.

I left the bedroom to do my necessaries, followed as far as the entrance by the two armed guards. Good lookin' they were as well but it 'ad me thinkin', aye, but give me Lemnos any time. I wondered if she was goin' to keep me under watch everywhere I went an' if so, how was I to get away from Thermodon. After I'd finished bathin' an' dressed the two women were joined by a third guard an' I was escorted down to the courtyard where food an' beer waited. But Hippolyte wasn't there. While eatin' alone under the watch of those three I was joined by Penthesilia, whose voice I 'eard for the first time – soft an' musical it was as well. "I am to be with you most of today," she informed me, sittin' down opposite where she managed a smile. She was fair 'aired an' blue-eyed – a different father, maybe than the queen. "Where's your big sister?" I asked.'

"She is gone first to make sacrifice at our temple. Do you wish for us to join her? You will see there also how a fire is kept ever burning in her name so others may obtain theirs from it. You also may offer sacrifice."

"Sacrifice to Hera!" I exclaimed. "Maybe another day." We finished our food an' drink an' I asked, "Is there a shrine to Athena hereabouts?"

"Yes, it is on the edge of our settlement. It is very small and there is no priestess. Some of the men who work our fields and tend the animals go there but it is as close as they are allowed to approach us without permission. Do you wish to visit the shrine?"

'I told 'er I would like to visit it but before we left the courtyard she was keen to ask me many of the questions Hippolyte 'ad about myself an' so for some time I found I was goin' through much the same answers. By then the sun'd risen high enough to flood light over the courtyard wall. We left the courtyard followed, naturally, by the three with their spears an' made our way through to the front of the buildin'. I could 'ear what sounded like a commotion before we reached the main entrance but the cause of it became obvious as soon as we stepped out. There looked to be some 'undreds of women there, gathered mainly on the far an' nearer to us sides of the square with the in-between area almost empty. Almost, I say, an' we, bein' higher up on the steps, 'ad a view clear across. To our right, where I'd earlier seen the dead pig, there was a youngish lookin', short-bearded man strung up naked. Over to our left were gathered three women readyin' their bows with a purpose I couldn't doubt. Hippolyte stood a short way to one side of 'em. Now, Mister Peter, I'd seen plenty of men killed – a good few by me durin' one conflict or another but this didn't seem right. "What's 'e done to deserve this?" I asked Penthesilia. She shrugged an' replied, "I don't know. He must have transgressed. Perhaps he was caught stealing from us – it sometimes happens."

As she spoke, one of the archers drew back an' took careful aim at their human target. The sea of chatter ebbed to an expectant silence. The woman released her arrow which, speedin' across the square, struck the poor bugger above 'is left thigh. A sudden clappin' an' cheerin' arose then just as

293

quickly faltered as the second woman readied to shoot. I was 'opin' this would do the trick as the man was obviously still alive an' twistin' about in agony. The second arrow flew an' penetrated 'is stomach. It was still not fatal an' again a short-lived acclaim erupted from the crowd. It was time for the third shot. She drew the bow tight, let it slacken, changed 'er position slightly, drew again then sent 'er arrow on its way. It struck deep into their victim's chest, into 'is heart I 'oped, to release 'im from further sufferin'. The crowd was goin' wild, some of 'em shriekin' for a time then they quietened an' started to disperse.'

"We can continue to that old shrine, now," said Penthesilia.

'Hearin' the girl speak, it seemed she was quite indifferent to what we'd witnessed. Why, I thought, make such a spectacle of it. If a man's got to die then at least let it be in defence of 'imself. Give 'im a sword, a spear an' a shield. We were crossin' the square where I glanced at the dead man, slumped forwards, an' asked Penthesilia, "Who'll take 'im away?"

"Oh, slaves will put the body in a frequently used place far from here so his people will collect it. It will serve as an example to them."

"An example," she'd said an' as we took a path from the square I wondered if she ever 'ad feelin's for anyone.'

'So *you* were stricken with compassion rather than *her*, Mister Heracles,' I remarked as he drained the jar of beer into our cups and called for another.

294

'Aye, Mister Peter,' he responded, 'Maybe for once I was – but not for long. I'd to think very seriously about gettin' away from there and as we walked along with the warrior-women close behind I was formin' a plan. We reached Athena's shrine, further away than I'd expected, an old, freestandin' stone enclosure little taller than I could've reached up to with my arm. It stood neglected an' sad, overgrown with weeds but mostly intact. Within the dim space was an altar for offerin's. This was covered in a layer of grit which I removed with a few sweeps of my 'and, while wonderin' who last had visited the place. I 'ad no offerin' to make other than a piece of silver. I was reachin' inside my tunic but seein' this, Penthesilia told me anythin' of value I left would sooner or later be stolen by one of the men but still I left it. Strange, you know, but for a moment I felt there was a presence, a presence that stirred deep within those stones, a presence that knew me.

All five of us 'eaded back to what I now thought of as Hippolyte's palace but in the square the dead man's body 'ad been removed. I told Penthesilia I wanted to fetch somethin' from my chariot so all of us walked over to where, on the previous day, one of those women 'ad indicated where it was to be kept. It was a kind of stable with my 'orse in another close by it. One of our guards opened the door to let me in. I pretended to poke around the chariot, really to check the 'arness lay coiled inside it an' that my club an' the bag containin' my valuables were there. All were as I wished so I made an excuse about bein' mistaken.'

One of Heracles' attendants approached us with fresh beer, refilled our cups and placed the jar before us. We drank and he continued his tale.

'There was an afternoon ahead of us so after passin' back through the buildin' to take food an' beer in the courtyard, I asked Penthesilia if we, or I, really needed to be followed everywhere by the guards since if I wanted to escape I'd not get far before I was caught an' I wasn't armed since my club, my dagger, sword, spear, bow and arrows were still in the chariot. She thought for a while then agreed we might 'ave only one to follow us at a more discrete distance but the woman would carry a rattle to summon 'elp should it be needed. She suggested we spend a part of the afternoon watchin' the women practise in the use of weapons an' I agreed to that.

When we set off out again it was opposite the direction of the shrine we'd visited that mornin'. In an open field the women were at it in groups with sword, spear an' shield. Most wore armour to a varyin' degree so the clash of bronze upon bronze as well as their cries rang out loud across the open field. I 'ave to say, Mister Peter, they looked to me as skilled, as formidable as any fightin' men I ever saw an' I doubted any of their subjugated men would ever gain advantage over those women even if someone gave 'em arms of their own. Beyond the field I could see 'em trainin' on 'orseback an' with chariots as well. The sun was gettin' low when the women an' those watchin' 'em were preparin' to leave an' as we set off back I told Penthesilia I'd changed my mind about Hera's temple an' really would like to see it. On the way back I noted which buildin's were mainly of wood an' which were not.

We crossed the open space to where the modest temple to Hera stood an' went inside to be greeted by 'er priestess, an 'ard-faced woman in a plain white gown with a cowl over 'er head. Bein' familiar as I was with Knossos I always, without thinkin', tended to judge such places as this by the standards I'd seen on Crete. Bein' old as the main buildin' an' no better cared for, this didn't compare well. I was expected, of course, to place an offerin' onto the stone altar which I did, a piece of silver, an' believe me, Mister Peter, that 'urt me deep inside! But it was their ever burnin' fire I wanted to see. I could smell smoke so I asked where it was comin' from. I was taken behind the altar to where a narrow passage opened onto a small, walled-off garden-like area sheltered by trees that rendered the place gloomy. At its center a large fire cracked an' burned with smoke risin' through the leaves above. Against the low wall beyond, in which there was a sturdy gate, were piled cut logs an' smaller lengths of timber.'

"One of the permitted menials," informed Penthesilia, "will come here regularly, day, night or whenever summoned to maintain and to replenish the fire as necessary, though they are forbidden to enter the shrine itself. It is a duty he or one of his family must perform in the name of Hera and goes back very many years. The dwelling they occupy is a short distance beyond the trees you see before you. They are punished if this duty is not maintained.

'I didn't care to ask what their punishment might be but my own plans now were more or less formed. The light was fadin' when we returned to the courtyard for food an' wine where I expected I'd be joinin' Hippolyte once more. She was still not there an' it soon became clear that 'er younger sister was to remain with me for the night. I made no comment but wondered if they intended to use me in turns until each got what she wanted – a strong female child.

The firebrands 'ad been lit an' after we'd eaten I convinced Penthesilia I'd please 'er all the more if we were freer with the wine, which was unwatered, so we accounted for our one jar then 'ad one of the attendants fetch another. Now I'm well used to my drink but after a while it became clear, as I 'oped it would, that Penthesilia wasn't. I also was fillin' 'er cup to the brim but tippin' less into mine. She was already chattin' an' mumblin' when I persuaded 'er to order a third jar. We touched 'ardly a drop of it because by then she was almost outside 'erself. I 'auled 'er up from the chair, held on to keep 'er steady an' guided 'er from the courtyard to where, in the corridor, the two who were supposed to keep an eye on me waited. They looked at both of us, puzzled, while Penthesilia grinned back. "There's wine out there for both of you," I told 'em, gesturin' to the courtyard. Don't know if they understood my exact words but they did get the message.

Once in the bedroom where lamps 'ad been lit for us, I tugged away Penthesilia's girdle an' laid 'er on the bed. She came around, though, just enough to slip open 'er gown an' demand my full attention, so who was I to deny us both the pleasure. After that she relaxed an' closed 'er eyes so I pulled a woolen blanket over 'er. Aye, Mister Peter, she'd be out good an' proper for the night.

I could 'ear the pair in the corridor talkin' in low voices but it no longer sounded as if they were close to the bedroom door so I pulled on my boots. My attention was drawn a second time to the wooden chest which I again opened. I glanced inside then I grabbed Penthesilia's girdle, laid it by the chest and 'elped myself to a good number of gemstones as well as a few smaller objects of gold an' silver. All of these I laid on the girdle which I gathered up like a bag to carry what I'd collected – and it was so 'eavy I worried that the material of the sash might not be strong enough to contain it. I blew out all the bedroom lamps, crept to the door an' peered out through the gap. The two guards 'ad stepped along to the courtyard where one 'ad picked up the jar of wine an' was busy fillin' the cups we'd left. I watched 'em downin' the wine but several times they glanced in my direction. I 'eld back from leavin' the room but kept an eye open. They must've downed all the wine an' now were headin' slowly back arm in arm, whisperin' to each other with the spears restin' on their shoulders. I eased

down the weighted girdle, thinkin' I might jump out
an' floor 'em both by bangin' their 'eads together
since they weren't wearin' 'elmets. On the other
'and I 'oped that standin' outside our door through
the night after drinkin' wine wouldn't appeal to
either an' so it turned out. Satisfied I was in bed
with Penthesilia they passed by the door. I opened it
far enough to watch 'em step inside another room
further along the corridor. I waited, 'earin'
Penthesilia snore quietly, so I lifted up the girdle
with its contents. If I got away with it, if I got back
to Mycenae, I'd be an even wealthier man than I'd
been for some time an' I'd pass Penthesilia's girdle
off as 'er older sister's as it was almost as fancy.
Eurystheus wouldn't know, would 'e, but then, I
thought, how would 'e know I'd been as far as
Thermodon at all an' not come by the girdle
somewhere closer to Greece? I decided I'd need to
find more evidence once I got to Sinope. *If* I got to
Sinope.

It seemed like an age I'd stood thinkin' and
listenin' before I stepped outside the room. I could
'ear the two of 'em laughin' an' makin noises like
they were enjoyin' 'emselves – enjoyin' each other,
if you know what I mean. I crept on past their door
until reachin' Hippolyte's throne room. Again I
waited but there was only silence with lights from
the oil lamps burnin' steady. Luck so far was with
me as long as neither of those two went back to peer
into the bedroom. I made it to the main entrance an'
breathed easier when I found there was nothin' to
stop me easin' open the main door. No guards, you

see, Mister Peter, that's how secure they must've felt 'emselves. I stepped out into cool night air with a three quarter moon 'angin' amid a sea of stars. I 'eaded left to the stables where I'd seen my chariot, glanced about an' pulled open the door. It was dark but I eased the girdle carefully with its precious contents into the chariot, dragged the thing out then opened the door where the 'orses were kept. There were only four in there an' mine was in the first stall. Where the rest of their 'orses were to be found I'd no idea but there must've been 'undreds of 'em, maybe kept closer at 'and by their owners. I took mine outside an' set about connectin' the 'arness. With that done I was breathin' easier an' tempted to clear off at once. But what if one of those women *did* return to check on me? The rest of 'em would be out in full force, knowin' the land far better than I did in the darkness.

I took up my club, left the 'orse an' chariot where it was an' legged it along to the temple where they sacrificed to Hera. I knew what I'd 'ave to do if anyone was there but my luck 'eld because the place was deserted. I got through to the garden where the fire burned an' I saw new wood 'ad recently been placed on it. I picked up a burnin' length an' took this out to the front. Fearin' I might attract attention I 'urried back to the stable. Close by it was a storage barn full of straw. I threw my club back into the chariot an' holdin' up the torch I set free an' drove the remainin' three 'orses out. With them well clear I threw the torch into the straw barn. It began to burn at once an' was spreadin'

301

quicker than I expected. The 'orses I'd set free were prancin' about an' mine was gettin' agitated. I jumped into the chariot, took the reigns then I was off as fast as I dared into darkness with only the moon as a guide. I knew the direction I'd to take but the ground ahead was 'ardly visible.

It was the river I needed to find an' once there I'd follow it before 'eadin' along the coast back to Sinope. If they guessed I'd do that then they could cut me off. I 'eard a crash behind me like somethin' collapsed so I slowed to look over my shoulder. I could see the fire was well ablaze amid those wooden buildin's with embers soarin' high into the night an' there was lots of shoutin'. Where my chariot 'ad been kept would by then be so consumed by the flames that they'd maybe not realise it'd been taken. I continued on, determined not to stop until I'd reached Sinope.

Well, Mister Peter, when mornin' came, I'd reached the river estuary. I was well on my way west and there were no howlin' women chasin' after me an' no swarms of arrows flyin' my way.'

'A great escape you had, Mister Heracles, but I wonder what Hippolyte and Penthesilia would have made of it.'

'Hippolyte would've guessed the truth soon enough, I'm sure of that, an' someone would've suffered for it; most likely the two women she'd left to keep an eye on me an' 'er sister that night. As for Penthesilia, well she wouldn't 'ave known what was goin' on until she sobered up after sunrise.'

'But you said you needed proof, didn't you, proof that you'd been as far as Thermodon where the Amazons ruled.'

'Aye, Mister Peter, so I did. When I reached Sinope later the next day I bought a good sized leather satchel into which I tipped the valuables I'd 'elped myself to in that bedroom. Maybe while in Sinope I'd sell much of 'em for gold and silver that'd be easier to carry on my person. I returned to the tavern I'd first visited, took food an' drink there then left most of my belongin's in the room except for the lion skin, my knife an' my sword.'

'Not your club?' I queried.

'No, I wasn't expectin' trouble but 'ad there been any, swingin' the club around in a crowded place like the 'arbour' may not 'ave been so easy. I first returned the 'orse an' chariot to the owners, who were mighty surprised to see me back alive, then I continued down to the 'arbour where most of the tradin' took place. I wandered around lookin' for somethin' unusual – somethin' unique to that part of the world. I was havin' no luck until I came upon a stall set up in front of a stone buildin'; a stall laid out with various weapons. In charge of this was a lone woman; unusual in such a place with so many people comin' an' goin an' where things could get a bit rough. She was a tall, attractive woman of early middle age in a dark, woollen gown an' with long brown 'air clipped back at the sides. She stared at me a while then said in slightly accented Greek, "I believe I know of you – are you not Heracles or simply one looking like him? My father had business with Thebes many years ago when he ruled there and I later learned from others trading here something of what became of him. Many spoke of his famous lion skin."

'Well, Mister Peter, I didn't remember the woman as she must at the time 'ave been a young girl, but comin' upon 'er right then an' there I found most pleasin' and I assured 'er that it was really me. I felt straight away it was someone I'd been destined to meet so I told 'er I was on my travels and asked 'er more about 'erself. She said 'er name was Kilushepa, an' I recognized this as a Hittite name. She explained how 'er 'usband 'ad died at sea a while back an' she'd been tryin' to continue alone with what was essentially a man's business, though she'd got very much a will of 'er own. While we were talkin' I spotted an unusual lookin' sword. The blade wasn't made of bronze but a sort of polished grey metal. On seein' my interest she picked it up to show me an' explained that it was a metal bein' used by the Hittites whose territory bordered upon that of the Amazons. It was, she said, more difficult to make but stronger than bronze an' would pierce bronze armour but the Hittites kept secret the method of its makin'. I'd no knowledge of such a metal as this bein' used anywhere in Greece so we agreed a value an' I paid 'er in silver. That sword an' the girdle would 'ave to prove to Eurystheus how far afield I'd been.

We carried on talkin' and as the sun was goin' down I 'elped 'er secure 'er goods inside the buildin' for safety then suggested we go to my tavern for a bite to eat an' a goblet or two of wine. Getting' to know as much of me as she did, she was amenable to this an' once there she told me 'ow she was thinkin' to make a break from what she was doin' but 'ad no idea how that might come about. I couldn't go into anythin' other than the most basic particulars over what'd 'appened to me, but she got the general idea. The goblet or two of wine became more than that an' we'd become so at ease with one another I felt a bond was formin' between us. Maybe the gods, one in particular, had intended it so. When I asked 'er if she'd consider returnin' to Greece with me she gave me a smile an' said she would like that. I assured 'er it wasn't drink talk an' later escorted 'er back down to where she lived alone above 'er stall. There I promised I'd rejoin 'er at sunrise next day.'

'That was quick work, Mister Heracles,' I said.

'Aye, well, Mister Peter, we were both alone an' maybe lookin' for a way out. Once more in the tavern I examined the sword by lamplight. Its wooden hilt was bound with copper wire for a sound grip but it was otherwise a plain weapon, designed for action, not for show. The blade was sharp but could still be flexed an' I wondered if I'd get the chance to use it.

I at last pulled out the parchment to see what I was in for next an' was sorry I'd not done so earlier. It said I was to go all the way to Erythea an' seize the cattle of Geryon. Now I'd 'eard about Erythea when I was at Knossos from men who'd been there. They'd all agreed the remote island of Erythea was very far to the west, far beyond Sicily to the very end of our great sea, to a passage that opened out to an unendin' ocean that led to the edge of the world. I'd given Kilushepa so much 'ope in 'er life but it looked now as if I'd no chance ever of deliverin' it. And though I'd 'ardly got to know 'er, I was stricken with regret, Mister Peter, really I was.

Next day we met again before Kilushepa was open for business. We went up into 'er place where it was quieter an' I explained the situation as best as I was able. She remained silent but couldn't hide 'er disappointment as she stared at me. Then I took 'er hand an' said, "Look, when I return to Mycenae I've a long journey ahead, many months I'm certain, but if you'll come with me I'll take all you own to nearby Thebes where I'll see you set up there for business. What you've got to sell could be worth more there than it is 'ere in Sinope an' I will return. In the name of Athena, in the name of all the gods, I *will* return to you."

In my mind, all the gods did not include Hera.

She continued to look at me then said, "Very well, Heracles, I find Sinope oppressive and noisy and I will put my trust in you. I will take all I have and go with you to Greece. I will not be a burden because I have no children and I possess all the wealth left to me by my husband in silver as well as goods."

'Her decision cheered me no end an' I intended to make sure no one took advantage of Kilushepa when disposin' of 'er property. But there was more to this I needed to tell 'er: "In charge at Thebes is

Iolaus, my nephew an' a good friend of mine. While I'm gone, he'll see to it that you're set up as it best pleases you and 'e'll make you feel you belong."

All of this I said an' I wanted Kilushepa to believe me. Aye, Mister Peter, she needed a new life an' I felt it was time to 'ave someone sharin' mine since losin' Megara all those years ago. Ours was a meetin' of souls an' for that I thanked Athena.

Over the next few days I 'elped Kilushepa dispose of her property. I learned then she didn't stand any messin' from anyone and it 'ad me wonderin' if she might've made a good Amazon. She in turn 'elped me find the right people to trade in those items I preferred to get rid of so most of what I brought in turn I'd find easier to 'ang on to.

We located a large Minoan vessel named after Palaemon, a sea divinity. She was headin' for Greece an' would eventually call at Anthedon, the main port of Thebes. We hired slaves to box up an' carry all Kilushepa's trade goods as cargo on the ship. Her captain 'ad a sailcloth spread well over the stern area of the ship as a shade for the payin' passengers. It wasn't to be a comfortable journey, time at sea as far as I'm concerned never was, though most nights we'd go ashore somewhere to rest. Kilushepa 'ad been to sea before so she took the voyage well enough. If anythin' that journey brought us even closer.'

So, dear reader, this at last explains Heracles' Hittite wife. He suggested he wouldn't go into much detail over their long journey from Sinope to Greece as nothing much out of the ordinary happened so I told him that was fine by me. The afternoon was drawing on and next morning I'd be most enthusiastic to hear about his next labour. We agreed over this and so he went on to conclude his present tale.

'On arrivin' at Anthedon we paid for the use of two 'orses and a wagon large enough to take all 'er possessions. Once more wearin' my lion skin, I drove us from the 'arbour to the city where we stopped before the palace, hopin' Iolaus would be there. Most of the guards an' officials knew me or of me, of course, an' havin' been assured Iolaus was in residence, we were taken to the anteroom outside the megaron,. We were not kept waitin'. He stepped into the anteroom, a smile lit up 'is face an' he strode over to grab me by the arms, sayin', "Heracles, you're with us again after all this time! And this lady – please introduce me to her."

'I did so but before I could explain much else to 'im, we were conducted through the great hall an' to Iolaus' private chambers where we were allowed time to get ourselves lookin' and feelin' respectable. His attendants were ordered to offer us whatever we, mainly Kilushepa, needed an' when we were back with 'im Iolaus would 'ave food an' wine ready for us as well as a waitin' ear to know what'd passed since we'd last met.

We could not 'ave had a better welcome anywhere at any time, Mister Peter, an' over the next few days Iolaus did all that was necessary to 'ave Kilushepa set up as she wished with she an' me together in all the comfort we could ask for. But it couldn't last because I'd to carry on back to Mycenae where I'd once again stand before Eurystheus an' present the bugger with the proof he'd be expectin'.'

The mornin' I left Thebes was cool an' hazy but was brightenin' up as I departed in a two-'orse chariot, its space part taken up by the satchel bag containin' what I'd 'elped myself to in that bedroom - my loot, aye, that's what it was.'

'But Mister Heracles,' I asked, why didn't you leave your Amazon loot safe at Thebes?"

'Because,' he replied, raising his beer, 'I was runnin' my affairs from within Mycenae and 'avin' to return there after each task. I already 'ad possessions an' valuables lodged at Athena's temple so what I'd brought from Thermodon could stay there also for me to draw upon if an' when necessary.'

His explanation seemed reasonable enough so I let him continue.

'The last I'd seen of Iolaus an' Kilushepa was when they' stood at the main gate of Thebes to see me off. I crossed the isthmus to the Peloponnese but their images were still in my mind as I entered the territory of Mycenae. Once closer to the walled city I 'eaded to Athena's temple where I was welcomed by the priestess who was mightily pleased at my generous offerin' an' accepted all that I needed to 'ave placed safe an' sound in their treasury. While I was there I talked a while with the priestess who said somethin' that seemed odd at the time. She said

I must return to speak with 'er again after I'd finished in the city.

Before makin' my way into Mycenae I stopped at the usual stables to secure the 'orses an' chariot. There I pulled on the lion skin, determined to wear it again when facin' Eurystheus where I'd stare out at 'im through the open jaws. Before approachin' the Lion Gate I wrapped the sword carefully inside the girdle, in case the sight of it worried any of 'em in the palace. At the gate, where I'd already attracted the usual attention of a small crowd, the guards sent their messenger off to tell 'Is Majesty I'd arrived back from Thermodon. Would I be graced with 'is appearance at the gate or would I be summoned inside to stand before 'im.

It turned out to be the latter since what I was takin' could easily be carried up to the palace. It wasn't stinkin' rotten, it wouldn't foul the air an' it wouldn't be dangerous because I'd not be close to Eurystheus with the sword when I revealed it. I was escorted beneath the gate, up the ramp an' through into the megaron. There, with guards either side of me I stood my permitted distance from the fancifully adorned Eurystheus and 'is gathered courtiers an' offered my grudgin' bow.

"So, Heracles," he began, all the time eyein' the rolled up object restin' in my arms, "you may or you may not have travelled far from Greece but if so have you proof of what we demanded - the girdle of this – this Amazon woman?"

I unwound the sash, let it fall open an' held it up with my left 'and while holdin' out the sword with my right. "The girdle 'ere is my proof!" I declared. "An' the likes of this sword I obtained from the same area is not yet to be found in our own lands." I was 'opin' that was true an' that no one in there by chance knew of one. Eurystheus seemed not as interested in the sword as were his guards an' replied, "Perhaps so but unless there is identification on that garment how may we know it is genuine?"

"Oh, that's easy," I replied, "just send one of your own men over there to visit Hippolyte an' if he gets back alive he'll tell you she's got another girdle very like it!"

Eurystheus gazed in silence for a time while some of 'is courtiers grinned at me an' I gave over what I'd brought to one of the guards. At that point Eurystheus raised 'is hand an' from my right appeared the robed an' cowled, stern-faced woman, the priestess of Hera, who'd shown up with the parchment when I'd stood before Eurystheus to be given my first task. She gestured for me to follow 'er, which I did, while not botherin' to await permission from their esteemed ruler. We made our way through an' out of the megaron but stepped aside into a small bare chamber before reachin' where the guards were posted. From within 'er gown she produced a rolled-up parchment. This she offered to me, sayin', "I am required by our king to present this to you for it contains in greater detail what you must do. And while I know you can read I will nevertheless say it."

311

'Well I already knew how far I was supposed to go next but not all that was expected of me when I got there. She unrolled the parchment, stared down at it, rolled it back up an' shoved it into my 'ands. Then she told me, "When you reach Erythea you are to capture the cattle of Geryon and send them back to Mycenae. When that is done you must cross the water to the coast of Africa where you are to steal the golden apples of the Hesperides, that are sacred to Hera herself because they were a present from her to Zeus when the two were married."

'Now I tell you, Mister Peter, this sounded crazy to me an' I told 'er so. I asked 'er what would be the point of sendin' cattle all that way back to Eurystheus when there's more than enough cows there in the Peloponnese. As for these golden apples – what chance would I 'ave in tryin' to grab what's sacred to those on high Olympus who rule heaven an' earth? She backed away from me, sayin' "I cannot assist you. I cannot say more. It is Hera herself I serve and no one else."

'With that she turned an' hurried out of the chamber. I left also but once outside I could see no sign of the woman. I was to return to Athena's temple, wasn't I, so that's where I 'eaded next – back out through the main gate after leavin' my prized lion pelt in the tavern but keepin' the parchment with me. Once there, the priestess 'ad me follow 'er to a quiet spot at the rear of the temple where wine awaited us. She was aware I 'ad the parchment and asked to look over it as we drank. "You should know," she said at last, liftin' 'er gaze, "and from Athena herself it was passed to me, that the real challenges lie not at the end of your journey but with the long journey itself. Hera knows well the dangers and she expects you will not return alive."

'Well that was encouraging wasn't it, Mister Heracles.' I offered.

'Aye, Mister Peter, that it was. Very encouragin', I don't think. I left the temple but as I strolled in late afternoon sun below the city wall, an idea was blossomin' large in my mind, as if the seeds of it'd been planted there in Athena's shrine. But maybe I'll go on with this in the mornin'.

That, dear reader, would have us see Heracles planning his tenth and eleventh labours, if labours they proved to be, for both would take him in the same direction. But I was in for a surprise because as our day was coming to an end he decided he wanted further reassurance that all he'd so far told me would be sound in my memory. This was again awkward but as before I'd arrange to have a completely dark room so he couldn't catch sight of the recorder. Again I had first to ensure it was ready to play back an episode selected from all that he'd so far related.

He remained a while in the clearing after I made my excuse to hurry off to the house. That gave me the opportunity I needed to have ready what I thought suitable to impress him. After checking the battery power was sufficient, and thankfully it was, I selected his account of the bandits' attack upon him when on his way to

Delphi. I'd play that but would, as previously, ensure that it ended before my own voice followed.

To my immense relief all went well and Heracles was much pleased. We ate in the courtyard under starry skies then retired for the night. Kilushepa would be waiting for him with Tiye and Mayet expecting me. I dared not let them see me place the recorder on the window ledge to catch the next day's sun but there was the empty room further along the passage from our bedroom where I managed to leave it unseen at the window.

Chapter 12 - The Ends of the Earth

Tiye and Mayet were still asleep that morning when I eased out of our bed with great care in the darkened room from where I crept out in silence. On groping my way along to the bathroom I saw from the window that the sky was beginning to lighten. The place was deserted but oil lamps were still lit but as the water was already heated I undertook all my necessaries, dressed and made my way to the courtyard. It was too early to recover the voice recorder as the day was yet to brighten and sunrise still some way off. I hurried out into cool air, crossed the courtyard and made for the clearing where I'd sit a while with the dawn sound of the birds as my company.

So why was I up and about so early? Well I needed to be alone, to reassess my situation and to think over all Heracles had been telling me. Accounts of his life originating from the Classical world ascribed to Heracles a totally impossible existence. His own accounts were much more acceptable by comparison but still utterly fantastic. So could I believe all or much of what he'd been telling me? Well I had to make out that I did since I myself had become very much a part of his life – or at least the tail end. Or should it be the *tale* end? I was living in a world and with characters that people in my own time would never have taken seriously and I'd been conducted there by a goddess from the distant past who no one would believe ever existed.

So what next? With the sun now peering over distant hills beyond I reckoned the bright sky would have given my voice recorder a reasonable top-up so I made my way back to the courtyard where I expected Heracles to be waiting with food and beer at the ready. He was there but the food and beer were yet to arrive. I hurried by him to recover the recorder, wondering if he'd want to know the reason for my morning excursion. I entered the room, grabbed and pocketed the recorder, then found Tiye and Mayet waiting outside the door. "Oh, Peter," cried Mayet, "we thought you had deserted us!"

"Why is this?" asked Tiye, grasping my arm and tingling my cheek with her warm breath and her soft lips. They both looked ready to grace a pharaoh's court and I wondered yet again how they filled their day.

'Look,' I responded, 'I haven't deserted you, but Mister Heracles is waiting for me outside.' I pulled away, thinking, 'I'd referred to him as, 'Mister', in front of them. 'What does it matter,' I asked myself, 'perhaps they don't exist anyway.'

But it did matter; they certainly existed at night and Heracles was definitely waiting for me. I hesitated at the entrance to the courtyard. The food and beer had arrived and his attendant passed by me offering a polite nod. I fumbled to switch on the recorder then joined Heracles at the table. He didn't ask where I'd been but as we ate he resumed his ongoing account.

'Aye, as I walked back through Mycenae that evenin' things were becomin' clearer. I stopped at the tavern a while for somethin' to eat but the noise was easin' off as I went upstairs. I was thinkin' 'ard. I was a wealthier man ever since my visit to Thermodon an' those Amazon women. I'd trade what was heft of those gemstones for silver because that would be easier to add to what I already carried with me. I'd sail to Crete, to the port of Amnissos, an' there I'd negotiate for a worthy vessel with a crew of fightin' men. Minos 'ad a powerful navy so I was sure there'd be experienced men to spare. There'd also be the prospect of plunder to whet their appetites.

As I'd done for my seventh task I set off early mornin' from Tiryns in the south Peloponnese an' took a tradin' vessel to Crete. The voyage was uneventful as before an' late that afternoon we docked at Amnissos. After food an' beer amid many of the traders an' with a view of the vessels, the fadin' day had me makin' for the tavern outside Amnissos. I'd a notion that one of the women hangin' about in there might 'elp round off my evenin' but the need to think 'ard over the next day an' what lay ahead overcame temptation. I remained alone instead to take another look at the more detailed parchment.

Sunrise next day found me back at the port with lion skin an' club to 'elp attract attention. I was soon chattin' to sailors in the tavern, a rough but cheerful lot, the kind who looked like they'd be ready an' able to deal with pirates or anyone lookin' for trouble. Some of 'em maybe were pirates when they could get away with it. I explained how I'd a task to undertake at the far end of the great sea but I didn't go into the finer details. More joined in to listen until we'd much of the tavern to ourselves so I bought all of 'em beers. There were those among 'em well familiar with the seas far west of Sicily and a small number who claimed to 'ave gone to the very end, even beyond into the limitless ocean where they'd traded north an' south along the coasts where they also encountered 'ostile peoples.

Word got around and on the followin' day I was talkin' with many more of 'em in warm sun by the 'arbour. There were soon fifty an' more seemin' keen to follow me an' with their numbers I figured I'd men enough to crew a good sized vessel. A stocky, short 'aired, weather beaten man with sharp eyes an' short beard stepped up to me an' announced 'imself as Phorbas. Until that moment he'd not spoken but 'ad stood to take in what I said. As others quietened down he told me he was captain of a vessel there in the port, 'er name, *Polemos*. She'd recently been re-caulked an' re-masted an' with 'er patch sewn linen sail renewed she was ready once more to set out. I asked 'im if she was not called upon at present to serve in King Minos' navy, in keepin' down pirates, and 'e said that she at times 'ad been but because of Minos' success in drivin' 'em out of our waters, *Polemos* and 'er crew, as well as some other ships, spent most of their time at sea wanderin' about with little else to do other than carry goods. A few 'ad sailed west of Sicily to become pirates themselves. The thought of shared plunder as well as what they received from Mimos fired their enthusiasm an' though I wasn't sure where most of the plunder would come from, a good few of 'em would 'ave their own ideas.

After our gatherin' broke up Phorbas took me along to explain somethin' more of his vessel. "She's a fine boat," he assured me with pride as we stood lookin' across at 'er from the quayside, "aye, one of the best. She'll take twenty-four men rowin' each side an' she's two steerin' oars. She's slim, maneuverable an' she'll carry all the arms needed for every man on board, includin' a number of smaller goods from Knossos to trade in places where such are 'ighly valued. She's sailed far an' seen us to the very end of our sea. Some might take us only for a tradin' ship and 'ope to seize our cargo but we'd give 'em a nasty surprise."

'I was mightily impressed by his confident manner an' sight of the vessel. All that remained was to do the deal an' though they'd still be in the pay of Minos I'd contribute enough extra to keep 'em happy. We'd agree a day for settin' sale an' I'd take my part in workin' the ship.'

'Mister Heracles,' I asked, 'would you by any chance be rowing?'

'I reckon I would,' he grinned, seeing the point of my question, 'but I'd try my best not to snap one of their oars in 'alf. Phorbas an' I wandered up to my tavern away from the port for a beer or two an' there I asked 'im, "Have you been ashore at a place called Erythea an' d'you know anythin' about this Geryon who I'm told lives there?"

"No," he answered, "in sailin' by the place I recall seein' odd, reddish-'aired cattle in the fields but no sign of any town other than a small port. It looks like this Geryon's business is no more than raisin' and tradin' cattle so he's been of no interest to us."

"And what about the Hesperides?" I asked.

"They're said to exist on the opposite side of the strait," he informed me, "that is the north coast of Africa. They're claimed by some to be three sisters lookin' after a temple of Hera somewhere inland that's believed to contain much of value – though I never met anyone who actually went there. The inhabitants thereabouts are known to be a wild lot an' charged with protectin' the temple. What's really in any of this for you when we get there?"

'I decided to keep it simple so I told Phorbas I was doin' it just for Eurystheus who wanted some of the cattle an' then some object or other from Hera's most distant shrine to show off in 'is palace, but I avoided sayin' much else. It seemed Phorbas did know somethin' of me but what little he'd 'eard about my labours was vague an' exaggerated.'

"But as for your cattle goin' back to Mycenae," he said, "we'll not 'ave room for any of 'em on my boat so you'll need someone else to do it. If there are any suitable boats at Erythea maybe you can work a deal with one of them."

"I'll manage somehow," I responded, then we went on to discuss sailin' time and 'e agreed this

would be at sunrise the followin' day. That left me
with the rest of my day to do as I pleased so I
decided to leave the lion skin an' club at my tavern
then 'ead off into Knossos where I thought to find
Daedalus. He wasn't there but 'is boy told me he
was workin' on some job at the palace – the drains I
think he said. Aye, Mister Peter, the drains! So for
me, then, it was an afternoon for wanderin' the
streets and alleyways of Knossos.

First light next day I was down at the 'arbour
with all I needed to take with me on board *Polemos*.
Supplies 'ad been loaded, includin' those for trade,
an' all of the crew were present with most already
seated at their oars. Phorbas welcomed me an'
agreed I could 'elp out at the oars if needs be once
we were out at sea. There was no ceremony as we
left the 'arbour as few would know this was not a
regular patrol.

Once we were in open water the big square sail,
patterned blue an' red, was unfurled an' soon
swollen with wind. When the oars were shipped,
Phorbas, havin' poured a cup of red wine into the
sea as an offerin', explained to me how this an'
other vessels like it were sometimes allowed to
behave like merchant ships so as to lure in an' trap
pirates. "There's few if any pirates in this part of the
world nowadays," he confirmed. "And unless the
wind eases, as it often does, we'll 'ave it with us
from the south-east as far as Trinacria, then it may
at times be against us."

Sorry, dear reader, but I need to explain
something right now and for shortly ahead. When

Phorbas used the term, 'Trinacria,' he referred to the island we now call Sicily, which in those days was credited with strange tales of its own. He'll mention Sardinia as, 'Sardo,' and the coast of Spain he will refer to as 'Tartessos,' not to be confused with that least desirable part of hell – 'Tartarus.'

'Well, Mister Peter,' Heracles continued, 'I won't go through the very many stages of our voyage since nothin' what you might call out of the ordinary took place. Out from Crete we put in first at the south west of the Peloponnese to renew supplies, stayed overnight then crossed direct west with favourable winds day an' night takin' three days to reach Trinacria. Phorbas knew the stars alright. Durin' the day, with little need of the oars, the men chanted, sang, sometimes danced on the deck, gambled or caught fish as there was a brazier kept alight on board for cookin'.

We took on more essentials at Trinacria an' spent two days there tradin' Minoan goods. We followed the south coast of Trinacria then continued on to the south coast of Sardo in two days with varyin' winds an' much rowin'. When not busy at the oar I also tried my 'and at fishin'. We stayed overnight then sailed on further for the same time to a small group of islands whose several names I forgot but there we took on more provisions an' rested. Again west for a day but now with winds not so much in our favour meant 'arder work at the oars. I tell you, Mister Peter, I put some of 'em to shame but managed not to break anythin'.

322

Throughout this journey we'd encountered only small tradin' vessels an' fishin' boats in calm to moderate seas. Aye, this voyage 'ad me wonderin' if the pirates really existed but Phorbas assured me they did. We arrived at night on the coast of Tartessos but with a near full moon to guide us an' the skills of Phorbas we located an inlet where the good ship *Polemos* was secured an' most of us could make camp ashore. Next mornin' we'd obtain fresh water. When layin' on a rise under the stars that night my thoughts turned to Geryon an' that part of Erythea where 'e was said to 'ang out. I was dozin' off when I heard it, or thought I did. The cry of an owl close above.

Early next mornin' we we'd set out under threatenin' skies to follow south the rugged coast of Tartessos for two days with nights spent ashore an' well away from anywhere that looked to be inhabited. On the third day, when it rained an' our boat rocked 'ard, we were followin' the coast west, rowin' for much of the time, then once again ashore for the night though we could light no fires to keep ourselves warm an' dry.

It was well into the fourth day off the coast of Tartessos that Phorbas called me forward to the bow an' pointed ahead to say, "There is Erythea." An' though we were some distance off our destination it appeared more an archipelago rather than a true island but what did that matter, we'd be there around midday with the sky once again clear an' the sun bright.

"You may not find anyone who understands Greek," said Phorbas, gesturin' aside to a figure I'd 'ad no contact with until then, "but we've someone who possesses knowledge of their language." With that, a short, swarthy man with walnut complexion, curly black 'air an' long, droopin' moustache stepped over an' stared up at me with sharp brown eyes. I'd seen 'im on an' off since we left Crete, hurryin' around, always busy an' seemin' very agile, but never passin' time with other people apart from Phorbas, an' usually out of sight when we were ashore.'

"He came on board some years back as an escaped slave, when we were last this way," Phorbas went on. "He rows well in spite of 'is size an' climbs the mast like a monkey but seldom speaks to anyone. His name is Maro." Phorbas went on to inform me that Maro believed Geryon to be a monster of a man who employed another of almost like size, Eurytion, to guard 'is much prized cattle, for much prized everywhere they were said to be. This Eurytion has a great dog, big as a pony so Maro claimed, and with it 'is men will fall upon an' butcher anyone who dares approach the cattle without 'is permission no matter who they are. "We'd better take armed men with us," Phorbas advised, "but you've to decide sooner or later what to do with any of those cows even if you get 'old of only one."

'I looked toward Erythea as we drew closer in the settin' sun. The so-called island arose high an' steep so it was the mainland bay to the left of it that we were 'eaded. "There are a few boats in the port – that's clear enough," I remarked, "and further inland I can make out what must be some of Geryon's cattle. I'll go ashore with Maro, no lion skin an' no club, just my sword an' knife. I'll see if any larger boat's got a captain who understands Greek."

Phorbas' men 'ad taken down the sail an' we were rowed slowly through lappin' water to the stone jetty where *Polemos* would be secured. Phorbas 'ad ordered most of our weapons to remain concealed. Though of modest size, a port is still a port but this one 'ad only the sound of vessels bein' worked an' looked as if a part of it was somehow always in shadow beneath a long, overhangin' ledge. There were few raised voices an' no sign of a tavern among the group of plain wooden 'ouses overlookin' the port. If I was questioned, I'd tell 'em we were there only to take on fresh water an' a few supplies that if needs be we'd pay for in silver.

I jumped onto the jetty with Maro followin' an' we looked across at the vessels. Some were settin' out to catch fish and 'ad lanterns lit at their sterns while a few men were still readyin' to leave. Others glanced at us without a word or even a nod. One vessel, larger than the rest an' nearly the size of our own, struck me as familiar in appearance so we made our way over an' stepped down onto 'er deck where we were confronted by the captain, a rugged clean-shaven man of middle years. I asked if he spoke Greek and 'e replied that 'e *was* Greek, so I asked what 'is business was on Erythea and 'e told me it wasn't business with anyone there but just takin' on basic supplies as there was no trade to be 'ad at the port an' they'd been warned off elsewhere. He'd been told also by someone who spoke a little Greek that everyone at the port felt they somehow were bein' watched by Geryon, who they much feared. They said he comes out at night an' prowls the land, lookin' for anyone foolish enough to be wanderin' out there. "When d'you intend to leave?" I asked 'im, because I'd already formed my plan.'

"We leave at first light to head back east where there's plenty of trade. And you – whatever brings you here?"

"We're to steal two or three of Geryon's precious cattle but don't 'ave space for 'em on our own vessel whereas it looks as if you do." He gazed at me in disbelief, laughed an' said, "Why should I want to take any of his lousy, I mean, precious cattle on my ship – do tell me."

"Well for a start," I answered, "As you seem to be lackin' trade I'll pay you well in silver or gold." I then went on to explain who I was, as he'd not recognized me, an' how proof of my havin' been to Erythea was demanded by King Eurystheus of Mycenae. "You can offer to sell the cows to Eurystheus," I went on, "but should 'e not want to keep these you can sell 'em elsewhere as they're said to be valuable." He thought over my words, peered along 'is ship, glanced at the ever silent Maro then back at me an' said, "How d'you propose we go about this? I don't want my ship at risk if this Geryon finds out what we're up to. I'm not a warship but a trader though I've a fast enough vessel and all my men are armed in case we encounter pirates."

'I explained what I intended to do with the 'elp of our fully armed warriors an' that he should be prepared next day to make a quick departure from Erythea together with our own vessel. We both saw the 'arbour appeared not to 'ave any boats able to challenge or to pursue 'im an' so we reached an agreement. On returnin' to *Polemos* I imparted my plan to Phorbas who'd no objections other than that we'd no clear idea of what we'd be up against on land. Still, he wasn't one to be deterred. In descendin' twilight he sent out a man to look over any route we might need to take next day. The man returned to say there seemed to be no problems. It was almost dark when we all settled down to sleep or at least rest the night in the confines of our boat.

The 'orizon was lightenin' an' we'd all snatched a quick bite to eat. Phorbas 'ad over twenty men lined up on the jetty, each with sword an' spear, two of 'em with coiled ropes 'ung over their shoulders while each of the rest carried a small circular shield. Except for Maro, who possessed only 'is sword and a curved dagger. I of course wore my lion skin an' carried a spear as well as my club an' sword.

Some of the fishin' boats were returnin' with their lanterns extinguished, but none of 'em, as they tied up, were of a mind to question what we were about. In a cool mornin' breeze we set off in loose order to the rise above the 'arbour an' once at the top with the sun startin' to appear, we could see way across to the fields. We tramped down to a narrow path an' there, beyond a stout wooden fence at the far end, grazed some of Geryon's cattle. I didn't bother to count 'em but there must've been gettin' on for thirty, maybe more, an' they were the oddest I ever saw. All were a dull reddish colour with long, very long, wavy coats an' fringes that all but covered their eyes. As we followed the path I saw that one, a fair bit lager than the rest, must be a bull. Its 'orns were thick an' curved forwards whereas those of the rest were thinner an' curved upward. We reached the fence to be faced by 'eavy wooden gate. Two men clambered over, removed a solid bar an' dragged the gate aside then the rest of us, sayin' little, made our way through. Just then one of the two lads turned to call, "There's a man watchin' us!" He gestured to a wooded area beyond where the cattle stood but the rest of us could see no one. He insisted, though, that 'e had seen someone.

We spread out an' approached the cattle, none of which seemed in the least concerned at our presence, except the bull snorted an' plodded around a bit. As we moved closer, the two men with ropes unhitched an' uncoiled these, each ready to lasso one of the still placid cows. This they did with ease then as we watched, each began to tow 'is captive beast toward the open gate. I was thinkin' this was easier by far than catchin' the Cretan bull since neither animal resisted, then sounds further away, hoof-beats, 'ad me turn an' call, "Watch out - 'ere they come!"

'They were headin' towards us from around the trees, not as many as ourselves but all were on 'orseback and carryin' spears. "Get those cows on the boat!" shouted Phorbas after 'is two men. The riders slowed to make out how many we were an' how we were armed then spurred on their 'orses, causin' the cattle to scatter.

"Closer to the fence so they can't get around us!" I called out. It was pretty obvious that only a few of us would get through the gate in time though our two men with their cows already 'ad. The men approachin' slowed again, were shoutin' to each other an' spreadin' out. One was movin' ahead of the rest, a big, ugly man, bigger than me an' next to 'is horse loped a dog unlike any I'd ever seen. The man, I'd no doubt, was Geryon's shepherd Eurytion and 'is dog. The thing was a darkish brown, thick-furred, heavy an' looked to be over 'alf the height of a man. Eurytion gestured 'is men to stop just beyond spear-throwin' distance. He'd spotted me in my lion skin an' so e' pointed an' ordered the dog to go for me. It leapt from 'is side, growlin' loud an' bounded my way. Some of Phorbas' men closest by readied their spears but I took a step forward, laid aside my club, rammed the butt end of my spear 'ard into soft earth, crouched an' held the shaft at a low level with one foot on the end to 'elp keep it in position. The dog was almost on me, growlin' like thunder, its jaws wide. It leapt an' as it did I raised part up an' yanked the spear at an angle to meet it. The dog struck an' sent me staggerin' back 'ard against the fence but its own weight an' momentum 'ad caused it to impale deep through the neck on sharp bronze so now, yelpin' an' chokin' blood, it fell aside, rolled over onto its back an' thrashed about with my spear wavin' from side to side. I grabbed for the spear an' wrenched it free. The great dog was still alive, but not for long.

To a loudenin' thud of 'orses Eurytion and 'is men were closin' in on us an' spears began to cleave the air. They'd got mobility an' we were stood mainly with our backs not far from the fence. A man near me was struck through the chest an' tumbled onto 'is own shield. In the growin' confusion, amid the shoutin' I saw one of their riders and 'is 'orse go down then I let fly my already bloodied spear. Aye, it was a good shot. The man I struck was 'imself about to cast and 'as he turned about with 'is arm raised my spear caught 'im in the side. Phorbas was in the middle of it all and 'ad just dispatched a man with 'is spear when I spotted little Maro. He went dashin' among the riders, avoidin' spear thrusts an' at least one sword swipe. He leapt like a cat onto one man's 'orse where reachin' round with 'is knife he slashed the man's throat an' heaved 'im out of the saddle. But 'e wasn't stayin' up there, no, 'e was back on 'is feet runnin' among an' dodgin' underneath some of the riders while creatin' confusion an' avoidin' their sword strikes while runnin' 'is blade into their 'orses to bring the riders down. Aye, Mister Peter, the gods were surely with 'im!

Our men, shields an' weapons at the ready were stridin' forward but in the clash of arms Eurytion still had 'is eyes on me an' was headin' my way. I picked up my club an' the shield of our own fallen man, who was obviously dead, an' I prepared to meet Eurytion, a wide 'eaded giant of a man with bushy black eyebrows an' plaited beard, an' like most of 'is men he was wearin' no 'elmet. His 'orse reared and 'e hurled 'is spear down at me from close to. As I dodged aside it struck my shield a glancin' blow, so 'ard it made me stumble aside. Now 'is sword was drawn but he was havin' trouble controllin' the horse with 'is left arm so I was at 'im with my club raised. I saw the man was wearin' scale armour over 'is tunic but that didn't matter an' yellin' aloud I swung the club 'ard against 'is left arm. With a shout he let go the reins an' the 'orse reared up, throwin' Eurytion over its back so 'e fell crashin' to the ground with 'is arm broken. He was still graspin' the sword, cursin' an' strugglin' to get up when my club paid a visit to 'is 'ead with a bone-splittin' crack. Aye, an' I do mean bone-splittin', Mister Peter, for 'is 'ead no longer looked quite the same as it 'ad before. I rejoined the clamour all around me. I saw another of our men 'ad been wounded an' was clutchin' the fence but those attackin' us 'ad fared much worse. Maro was still causin' havoc, four of their 'orses were down and at least four or five were prancin' about riderless. I let drop the club, picked up one of their own spears, rushed forward, hurled it an' caught another of their men who'd lost 'is mount an' was stridin' towards one of our men with 'is sword raised. They'd witnessed Eurytion an' the dog killed so were now pullin' back from the confusion with two retreatin' on foot.

Phorbas stepped over to me, sheathin' 'is sword 'an said, "Damn good work, Heracles though we've two dead and one wounded, but the man will likely recover. Our men will collect for themselves the arms of their fallen an' we've got what we came for, or at least you 'ave. Now what about this Geryon? Our men will be wantin' more than a couple of cows out of this."

'I was lookin' around for Maro an' saw him wipin' 'is sword clean on one of the fallen enemy. "Aye," I said, "so maybe we should bring up more men an' see what's beyond the trees over there. You said Maro knows the language spoken around 'ere so that'll help."

"That he does, so I'll call for another twelve men to join us and we'll see what there is to see. Our remainin' men can keep an eye on *Polemos* and the other boat."

'While Phorbas was gone, taking the injured man with 'im, our two dead were hastily buried an' once he'd returned an' we were reinforced we set of in the direction Geryon's men 'ad retreated. A kind of peace 'ad returned to the fields the long-'aired cattle re-gathered and began to graze among the bodies of dead men and 'orses. Didn't give a damn, did they.'

'Did you not expect more resistance, Mister Heracles?' I asked him.

'I dunno, Mister Peter,' he answered. 'Does it take a whole army to look after a few cattle, valuable as they are? Maybe if someone 'ad been sent out to parley with us I could've made 'em an offer for those we took, but that didn't 'appen. We marched on in loose order, passin' the trees to find the land openin' out again. There were more cattle an' beyond 'em, farmland with men visible in the fields, unaware of what'd been goin' on over our side. Closer to us stood a group of wooden buildin's, at their centre a long 'ouse where those close to the owner must 'ave gathered. There was near to it another buildin', more elaborate, that I took to be a temple of sorts. It 'ad small windows an' there was a stream runnin' close behind. Gathered before the temple were the remnants of those who'd attacked us. There were no women in sight. They appeared ready to defend 'emselves if we approached any closer so I called for Maro an' asked 'im to tell 'em we intended no more violence but that we wanted to talk with Geryon. What I 'ad in mind was tribute for our captain and 'is men. Maro walked forward with Phorbas an' me close behind. The sight of Maro in particular had those still in possession of a weapon tighten their grip as 'e spoke. One of 'em, unarmed, stepped to face us and answered Maro at length in their strange-soundin' tongue. Maro turned to us, sayin', "He tells me Geryon rules above them all and is ordained to protect them and guard their treasures as long as he is obeyed."

'Geryon wasn't doin' too good a job of it that day, I thought, as the man continued to speak an' Maro translated further. "He says it's through their sins they've been punished this day but that you must go away now for none from outside may look upon Geryon and live."

"Tell 'im," I said, "that we worship almighty Zeus, the true lord of heaven an' earth who will strike 'em with death from the skies if we don't carry out 'is will." I adjusted the club restin' on my shoulder an' Phorbas' hand dropped none too discreetly to 'is sword hilt. The Erythean looked startled, turned an' dashed back to 'is comrades with our message. They began to shout an' argue with one another, all the time glancin' at us. Phorbas called some of 'is men forward with their spears at the ready. A few of those standin' before the temple appeared ready to defend it but as we closed in they 'urried away with the rest. We stood in expectant silence before the copper-banded but otherwise plain solid door. I took 'old of the big bronze ring attached to it an' pulled. I expected it might resist my efforts but it didn't an' the door began to swing open with a long, eerie sighin' sound.'

Now then, dear reader, at what I regarded as an ill-chosen point, Heracles stopped talking to lift the jar and replenish our beers. He took a long gulp and dragged his tunic sleeve across his mouth before resuming his tale.

'I stepped inside, followed by Maro an' Phorbas, to where we found ourselves in a semi-darkened area an' faced by two long-bearded, red-cowled an' gowned priests, their faces clouded with anger. The air was warm, humid an' carried a foul smell as if somethin' 'ad gone rotten or was decomposin' in there. Behind the priests, hangin' from a roof beam down to the floor, was a wide, 'eavy red curtain and either side there were weapons mounted on the plain walls. Both priests issued what could only be taken as a verbal warnin', though I didn't understand a word of it. "What're the buggers sayin'?" I asked Maro.'

"They say as did the others; we must leave now. If we enter the shrine of Geryon we face only death."

'Well, Mister Peter, I was used to facin' death an' they weren't about to stand in *my* way! Even so, as I pushed one of 'em aside I'd a feelin' this was no place any sane man ought to be. As I took 'old of the curtain the second priest reached into 'is gown an' pulled out a long, double-edged knife. He'd raised it up next to me when Phorbas grabbed 'is arm, dragged 'im back an' slammed a fist to the side of 'is head, a blow that sent 'im sprawlin' to the stone floor where 'e lay still. The first priest backed away and I 'esitated. From behind the curtain we could 'ear somethin' growlin' and movin' as if the sound of our voices 'ad disturbed it. I grasped 'ard on my club, raisin' it while Phorbas an' Maro drew their swords, then I grasped an' wrenched the curtain aside. In the dim light where oil lamps wavered, as hideous a scene as you can imagine met my gaze. I froze for a moment. Phorbas drew back with a gasp but Maro just looked on. Only paces from us in that cavern-like den, sprawled Geryon. Aye, this was, a man of sorts but a man of

nightmares. He was bigger even than Eurytion an'
might somehow 'ave been related to 'im. His
protrudin' jaw was wide open, 'is discoloured,
uneven teeth bared, 'is pale an' too wide-apart,
over-sized eyes glarin' from beneath a back-slopin',
squarish forehead topped with a tangle of black 'air.
The smock 'e wore looked to be streaked with fresh
bloodstains. Aye, he'd dropped a part eaten human
arm aside as we entered. Behind 'im lay a straw
mattress covered in 'eavy cloth of some sort an' to
one side was a stone altar on which lay
unmistakably human limbs that looked to be fresh.
Geryon rose to 'is full height, glared with a burnin'
malice at the three of us, growled aloud an' spat
bloodied mucus, just missin' me as I jerked aside.
He was starin' 'ard at me, reachin' out with arms
seemin' too long for even 'is body. Huge 'ands with
long' blood-tainted nails were about to seize me.
Maro an' I backed away, Phorbas 'ad pulled down a
spear from the wall an' pushed it to me but I didn't
take it. Maro an' Phorbas, swords raised, must've
wondered in those 'orrific moments what I'd do but
it was clear that one or more of us wasn't goin' to
get out of there alive if Geryon sprang. His right
'and reached suddenly out, touched an' closed 'ard
on me with nails diggin' through the lion skin an'
into my flesh. But another force was possessin' me.
I closed on Geryon with my club raised an' before
he could stop me I brought it down 'arder than I
knew I ever could against that great an' fearsome
skull while shoutin', "Athena is with us!" Phorbas
an' Maro pushed by me, drivin' their blades into 'is

sides as I raised the club high an' struck again. That second blow split open Geryon's fore'ead and it was to be the end of 'im. His grip loosened an' slipped from me. We backed away as 'e slumped aside an' fell back with a rattlin' growl, mouth and eyes wide, onto the mattress. We stared for some moments in silence, transfixed within that fetid grotto of death then on backin' clear we became aware of the priest who stood pressed against the wall with 'ands clasped to 'is face. "Let's get 'im outside," I said. Phorbas an' Maro needed no persuadin'. They grabbed 'old of the man and stepped out into sweet-tastin', late mornin' air an' welcome sunlight to where our men waited. Breathin' free again I slammed shut the door by which we'd entered while Phorbas an' Maro kept 'old of the priest. His pal, still in there, was due for quite a surprise when he woke up.

Phorbas said to Maro, "Ask this man where Eurytion's valuables are to be found and 'ave 'im tell us more about Geryon."

After Maro's questioning the priest looked at Phorbas, to me then back to Maro an' began to speak. He went on at length while the men we'd fought with watched from a safe distance, joined now by their women. Our men, ever alert, chatted among 'emselves. When the priest 'ad finished talkin', Maro looked up at us, sayin, "He doesn't understand what we mean about Eurytion's valuables unless we refer to their weapons because it's the cattle and farm produce they value above all else. He thinks Geryon was sent long ago by their gods as a punishment but would protect them in return for human flesh. He emerges at night to prowl the darkness, to wait unseen and seize anyone who tries to approach the cattle. Sometimes he'll even visit the port. Eurytion, they say, appeared long ago as his son, sent to lead their men and ensure no one enters their land during the day. Their bards insist it's always been that way and always will be."

"Not any more it won't," I remarked, and Maro imparted that to the priest, who we then let free.'

'But, Mister Heracles,' I said, 'there'd been no plunder for Phorbas' men and the Erytheans had lost the religion they'd been condemned to obey.'

'Aye, Mister Peter, they 'ad, but there was more to follow. We returned to the port where I persuaded Phorbas to 'ave some of 'is men go ashore to grab another of the late Geryon's valuable cows together with enough straw to keep 'em fed until the next landfall. Maybe the men of the other vessel out from Greece who'd be takin' 'em back there would make a good profit from them in Mycenae when Eurystheus had seen 'em an' been told how I'd played my part out 'ere. The captain of that vessel informed us they'd leave Erythea that afternoon as they'd be keepin' close to the land we ourselves 'ad followed but as we'd no need to get away as quick as we'd earlier planned it was decided we'd rest where we were for the night but keep a good lookout. Needless to say, thoughts of Geryon loomed large that night. Maro, however, 'ad ideas of 'is own which we part discussed on board

Polemos after the other boat 'ad sailed. He'd leave us that afternoon, go back alone to meet the Erytheans then return to us before we sailed next day. Phorbas wasn't keen on the idea but I didn't think by then that Maro would come to any 'arm.

Before sunrise the followin' day, as we were preparin' to leave, he was back with us an' eager to explain what'd 'appened.'

"I met the two priests and some of the older men. I persuaded them they'd nothing more to fear from the likes of Geryon or Eurytion and his dog but must understand the true beliefs of the Greeks and the gods of Olympus if they were to find a better way in this world. I explained how we served our gods, how almighty Zeus ruled above all and how the gods made themselves known to us and gave us strength. They listened and took what I said as true for it was through our gods that we had destroyed Geryon. I promised them others would come out from Greece and show them how to build a temple for proper worship so for this I rely upon you, Heracles, when you return home."

'Well there was confidence in me, Mister Peter, don't you think?'

'Definitely, Mister Heracles,' I responded as he continued Maro's message.

"Before I left the Erytheans this morning I had them set fire to the place where Geryon had died so there would be no more of him to haunt them day or night except in their dreams. I'll say farewell now. I'll return to the Erytheans and I'll begin to teach them all I an able of our ways."

'Phorbas much regretted Maro's decision but didn't try to talk 'im out of it. Once he'd left us we set out to cross the strait to Africa'.

So, dear reader you might, as have I, be wondering what Geryon and Eurytion really were. They could be a result of gross exaggeration of course, or they might have been the final remnants of bizarre species of humanity that still remains in our own time unknown. After all, the final remnants of Homo neanderthalensis, Neanderthal Man, are said to have persisted in that very area during the late Ice Age.

But the beer was finished and before we had something to eat Heracles went to rejoin Kilushepa. I left the courtyard to go for a stroll and a chance to have the voice recorder topped up with another dose of Elysian sunshine.

Chapter 13 - And Beyond

I returned to the courtyard to find Tiye and Mayet had joined Heracles so his attendants had brought out food and beer for all four of us. The inclusion of wheat cakes topped with honey I much appreciated though it failed to exclude from my mind the image of breaded cod, mushy peas and French fries.

We indulged in small talk with the girls who, at my request, enlarged upon aspects of their life in Egypt. However, I felt Heracles was becoming impatient and wanted only to continue with the account of his penultimate challenge. Soon enough Tiye and Mayet prepared to leave, both smiling at me with Mayet giving my shoulder an affectionate squeeze. I stood to watch the girls exit the courtyard and facing away from Heracles I reached to switch back on the recorder.

Seated now in the midday sun we drank more beer and Heracles began, "We cast off from the jetty that mornin', passed the towerin' rock to our left an' made our way into open sea where we turned south. There was land ahead but as the day wore on it was beginnin' to look too steep for any vessel to moor safely so Phorbas decided to follow the coast by turnin' west, as sailin' east would 'ave us headin' back towards Trinacria. Unfortunately the wind was comin' from the west so our men, me included, were at the oars an' our sail was furled.

We'd seen no other boats an' we were beginnin' to wonder where we'd be able to make land but as the sun was settin' we could see ahead a more level shoreline and a shallow bay. Into this we rowed an' there spent the night. Over a fire in the mornin' where our food was cooked, it was already clear that steeply risin' hills inland didn't appear to offer much so Phorbas an' I agreed we'd continue west in spite of the prevailin' wind. This we did for the best part of another day, by which time the strait was growin' wider with empty water ahead. But we were by then followin' a long bay with more level land further in so we made our way there an' moored with some difficulty though the sea was calm, relyin' on our stone anchor to prevent the ship driftin' off.

Once ashore Phorbas pointed west to the open water that glittered bright in the settin' sun an' told me, "Out there begins the endless ocean. Some believe it goes on forever but we may never know. Men have sailed out thinkin' there may be a land with great treasures to be taken but I never heard of anyone returnin'. This, then, is as far as I go."

'And it's as far as *I* want to go, I told 'im. So that was that an' we agreed we would set off inland next day with some of our men, fully armed, an' see if there were signs of life. Over our fire, one of several that'd been lit, Phorbas an' I talked about the people, about the horror we'd encountered an' overcome in Erythea and 'e wondered if he'd ever meet up with Maro again.

By sunrise Phorbas an' I, with twelve of our men, were ready to set off up the gentle rise from where we 'oped to gain a good view of whatever lay beyond. Naturally I'd presented myself as you'd expect, though with the lion's 'ead pushed over at my back. As well as my club I also carried bow an' arrows. I'd a strange feelin' about the place. I felt I was meant to go the way we planned an' no other but once on our way I decided this was only wistful thinkin'. We trudged up the grassy slope in warm, humid air until the land opened out before us, green but lookin' barren further toward a rugged horizon. It was one of our men who spotted it. Pointin' out to a low, mid-distance rise he cried, "Look over there – what's that?"

We peered across to where light of the risen sun was fallin' upon a small group of stone buildin's and I some'ow knew I 'ad to go there even if I went alone. But I wouldn't be goin' alone because Phorbas told 'is men to look out for trouble as we 'eaded for the rise.

It took longer to walk there than we expected an' we'd to cross a small stream, but as we approached in silence, much became clearer. The low buildin's couldn't 'ave been used by more than ten or twelve people an' these, what might've been dwellin's, looked in places neglected. But there were well-tended vegetable gardens, olive trees an' a fenced-off area for geese. Chickens could be 'eard cluckin' from somewhere nearby an' from one of the buildin's smoke was risin'. There was no one to be seen so we stopped an' looked about. Then voices. From behind the buildin's a woman appeared, followed two others. She was holdin' a narrow spade. They stopped, lined up an' stared at us but none of 'em spoke, though their attention was soon on me because of the way I was dressed. Each of 'em wore a smock an' short boots suited to farm work. "We mean you no harm!" called out Phorbas. But havin' no idea of what language they might speak we were surprised when the first of 'em called back in our own tongue, "Oh, you are Greek!"

"Aye we are!" I answered, steppin' out from Phorbas' men to stand before the three women, each of whom looked to be in 'er later years. Their dark 'air hung loose an' untidy. "Why are you here and what do you want?" asked the woman with the spade. "We've got nothing of value."

"I am Heracles," I replied. "I am from Mycenae. I seek the temple of Hera an' the three Hesperides."

"Oh, he seeks the temple of Hera!" exclaimed the second woman. "*And* the Hesperides,"

"The three Hesperides," added the third.

"Well you've found us," said the woman with the spade. "And this," she gestured back with her thumb, "is, or was, the temple of Hera and next to it is our home. Are you pleased now you have found us?" The three of 'em were smilin' up at me and Phorbas' men 'ad begun chatterin' among 'emselves – some of 'em soundin' amused at what we'd come upon. I wasn't at all amused, Mister Peter, but I was mightily puzzled at what we'd

Jeffrey Peter Clarke

found. I peered about an' muttered, "I don't understand. What 'as happened 'ere?"

'They looked at me for a time then the first woman answered, "Hera wanted to express her power beyond those lands ruled over by the Olympians – yes, to express it beyond Greece to the ends of the earth. Armed men were sent out to construct what you see here and with their support we were to serve as Hera's priestesses. Those who wandered these lands knew nothing of our gods so we were to learn their language, to spread the word and to enhance Hera's prestige above that of all others. So confident, so proud was she of her plans that she entrusted us with the golden apples that had been a marriage gift from her to Zeus himself. Symbolic they were because she so loved apples and these would last forever as a reminder of her affections in those days as well as affirming her presence here."

'I much needed to talk with these women further but I sensed Phorbas' men were becomin' restless. There was nothin' for 'em to do but stand around an' Phorbas said, "Perhaps I should take my men back to the ship and await your return."

'I agreed that was a good idea an' so they ambled off back to *Polemos* where they'd no doubt eat, drink and entertain 'emselves or set out on foot huntin' for goats or whatever else might be found in this part of the world that could be cooked an' eaten. I turned to the women and asked 'em to tell me more. They appeared uncertain for a time then gestured me over to one of their small plots where we could sit on stool or stone wall facin' each other. Beer was brought out in plain earthenware cups, aye, they made their own, an' the first woman began, "The local tribesmen were at first friendly to us. They made offerings, and their men would help our own look after some of the larger animals we then kept as growing herds. Then things changed. It seems Hera and almighty Zeus quarreled – why, we cannot say for certain but we think it was over another of his female conquests. Whatever the cause, we think he accused her of overstepping her role as his wife. To him our presence here was a waste of time, the natives too primitive and warlike and the place being too distant with nothing of value to attract any more Greeks. And so she gave in to him and withdrew her influence altogether from us."

"That she did," agreed the second woman, "and then things began to change. The local tribesmen started to treat us with suspicion, then hostility, as if they felt our gods and our teachings were no longer of worth."

"Of no importance at all," put in the third woman, "and soon we felt threatened. They began to steal from us. Our men tried to stop them but were too few in number so we took the golden apples from Hera's shrine, all six of them, and one moonless night we went out unseen and buried them beneath a tree. We did this without telling even our own men."

"Things got worse," resumed the first woman. "One of our men was stabbed to death in an argument and others threatened with death unless the tribesmen were allowed to take from us whatever they pleased, including the golden apples, which they realised were hidden. We had a large dog, kept to warn us or help to keep away predators, but they killed that also. We three fled before light one morning into woodlands far enough from here to feel safe and with enough food to survive for a few days. There was also the fresh water stream that flowed down by our temple. But we could not remain where we were for long. One morning, when the sky was beginning to brighten, we set off back, all the time listening for voices. We could hear none."

"Closer to our home and Hera's shrine we came," continued the third woman, "and still we could see or hear no one. The sun was beginning to rise but there was no smoke and there was no one moving about. We could hear our geese and our chickens but of our larger beasts there was no sign. All had gone, together with the tribesmen. Our own few men we found dead, their bodies abandoned outside the temple and attended only by wild birds."

"They had been tortured," informed the second woman. The tribesmen would have wanted to find where the golden apples were hidden but those poor men had not known."

"The tribesmen had gone, leaving us to bury our dead," declared the first woman. "They had taken with them everything of ours they thought to be of value."

"At least they'd not found the golden apples," I said.

"They had not," responded the second woman, "The apples remained untouched where we left them. They are of no value to us. But, please, you must tell us about yourself and what brings you and your men here."

'I explained to 'em much about me an' what'd brought me all the way from Greece. They'd 'eard nothin' of what'd been goin' on in the rest of the world for many years. I wasn't sure they believed all I said an' who could blame 'em. Through my mind was runnin' one question: why'd I been obliged to find this place when there was no challenge an' nothin' of value to be 'ad? Well not quite nothin'. I bet, Mister Peter, you're thinkin' my mind was on those golden apples.'

'Oh, would I think that, Mister Heracles,' I responded as we both hesitated to down more of our beer.

'No, I'm sure you wouldn't,' he grinned, wiping an arm across his beard, 'but I did 'ave a proposition for the women. I suggested they return with us to Greece an' bring the golden apples with 'em. They looked at one an' other as if each knew what the other was thinkin' then the first woman said, "No, we have our lives here. It is peaceful now all others are gone and it is where we belong."

"But this man also has been a victim of Hera's contempt," announced the second woman gesturin' at me, "should he not take her golden apples with him now he is to leave us?" The third woman nodded her approval an' the first said, "Yes he must take them for no one else ever will." All three arose with the first woman takin' up her spade an' gesturin' for me to follow. We walked from the 'ouse, past their flutterin' chickens an' cacklin' geese over to a group of olive trees some distance away. At one of these they stopped an' the fist woman, pointin' down at its base, 'anded me the spade, sayin', "Now then - dig right there." I did, with care, an' found them clustered together not so deep in the soil. I picked 'em out, one by one an' when I knocked the dirt off they glinted gold in the sun. I gathered up a side of my lion skin to make a large pocket an' placed all six in there. They were smallish apple-sized an' were 'eavy. In the growin' heat of that day we returned to where we'd talked together. Now they sat an' looked up at me but said nothin' so I asked, "Will you come back to Greece with us?"

"No," replied the first woman and the other two nodded in agreement, "we would just be curiosities whereas here we have harmony and all we need."

'Their answer didn't surprise me. "Then I'll return to the ship," I said, "but is there anythin' I or we can do for you before we leave?" I had no idea what they might want but the first woman replied, "There is nothing. You should go now but we wish you well. We will continue until we have done all we can here and - and one day, when Helios rises to bless the land, we will awaken no more."

'So that was it, Mister Peter. I headed off in the direction of the bay but never looked back. I wondered, if I did, would there be anyone there. An' I'd never asked their names.'

'But you'd got something of enormous value, Mister Heracles' I said, 'and without a fight.'

'Aye, that I had, an' they were proof of my havin' been there. I told Phorbas what'd 'appened and we secured the golden apples safe beneath the deck. With me back on board Phorbas took on fresh water an' readied the ship to sail. After makin' his wine offer to Poseidon he planned to leave the strait an' turn north to follow the coast of Tartessos until nightfall when we'd go ashore for the night.

I'd long since lost count of the time I'd been away from Thebes. It would be months before I'd need to consider my final challenge. In the days followin' we'd set the course that'd brought us out 'ere until we eventually reached Crete, then I'd make my way back to Mycenae where I'd face Eurystheus once more an' after that to Thebes and to Kilushepa, the woman who for so long I'd abandoned after she'd given me new life.

The wind from Tartessos to Trinacria, Phorbas knew would be more in our favour so our oars would be drawn in an' our big sail would serve its purpose. After passin' the island group east of Tartessos in lively seas, Phorbas planned once again to stay in open waters day an' night, headin' due east, livin' on supplies we still 'ad an' fish we caught until we made land at Sardo. Once ashore at a port on the south of the island we rested up for two nights, did some tradin' an' took on more supplies. After sailin' from the port at Sardo we'd seen only one other tradin' vessel and a few fishin' boats nearer the coasts. I expected from there to Trinacria would be another long but uneventful voyage.

Aye, but how wrong that'd prove to be.

I was standin' with Phorbas at the bow, gazin' ahead at a sprightly sea. We'd sailed south-east with a keen wind behind us and 'ad the north African coast in view at a distance when one of the men at our bow informed Phorbas an' me that another vessel headin' out from the direction of the coast looked as if it might cut close across us. Phorbas peered 'ard an' long at it before sayin' to me, "Could be they mean us trouble."

'As we closed I could see it was a vessel not unlike our own but its crew were rowin 'ard to match our course and drawin' ever closer by intent. Phorbas 'ad already ordered our men to arm as discreetly as possible, if to do so was possible. I reached out my lion skin an' soon 'ad it ready with shield, spear an' club. The lion's 'ead, though, I left 'angin' at my back in part to see about me better.

For a time there was silence, except for hull-slappin' water, the creak of our timbers an' gentle thud of our sail. The other boat was almost within shoutin' distance, 'er oars were bein' drawn in and Phorbas informed me they'd now be steerin' by rudder. Most of 'er crew were standin' an' starin' over at us with spears at the ready. Phorbas called for our men to prepare for 'em then said to me, "They'll grapple and try to board us but they must by now 'ave realised we'll be ready for 'em."

'Aye, it seemed they'd thought us only a tradin' ship just as they 'oped maybe we'd think them. Both boats were rollin, their masts swayin'. We were close enough now for spear castin' an' that's what many of the pirates did. Our men crouched with shields raised. Some spears were stopped by our shields, includin' mine, with the impact nearly throwin' me off balance. A few passed over'ead or hit only our boat but two of our men were struck. Lettin' drop our shields, Phorbas an' our crew arose to hurl their spears an' in those brief moments, as shoutin' an' insults flew from both sides, all in Greek, I 'ad my first proper view of our enemy. A rough lookin' lot they were, variously dressed, some in gaudy or padded tunics, some with bronze, others with boiled hide corselet. Head protection, like that of our own men, was bronze or interlockin' boars' tusk 'elmet but many 'ad these decorated with fancy plumes or 'orns. One thing I was sure of, they numbered more than we did. But that was all I could make out as our men cast their spears with more hits as the brigands, prefferin' attack to defence, 'ad not raised their own shields. My own spear found its mark in a man preparin' to leap onto us who then tumbled into the sea between our vessels. There were screams an' curses as some of our attackers reeled back into their boat. With much shoutin', they threw bronze grapples, snaggin' us at bow an' stern as our ships, heavin' up an' down, crashed together with yardarms clatterin' and sails flappin'. They meant to board an' take *Polemos*, Mister Peter, while our men were strugglin' to hold their own an' keep 'em back. But very soon numbers were beginnin' to count as the pirates yelled an' fought to clamber over an' gain advantage of us. I wasn't goin' to stand by long enough to see that 'appen. "Board us will they!" I called out to our men, "Well I'm boardin' them so follow me!" Club in 'and I grabbed a forestay, called out. "Athena is with us!" an' heaved up onto the edge of our vessel where I dealt with one bone-crackin' blow the skull of the first man who came at me with sword raised. Then while our boats rocked an' their sides ground together I was onto the brigand's deck. I swept the club across to shatter the arm of the next swordsman who fell sprawlin' then struck another's 'elmet so 'ard with my club that the boar's tusks must've entered 'is brain. To a frantic clashin' of bronze against bronze I waded in with others of our crew close behind. We were cuttin' an' strikin' down those who'd been tryin' to board our ship but now were obliged to turn an' face us. This confusion gave Phorbas and others more opportunity to cut down an' drive' em back from our deck an' board theirs. Aye, cheerin' each other on, they were fightin' their way over an' onto the brigand's boat closer to the stern while stricken men were reelin' from their narrow blood-soaked central deck onto the rowin' benches or fallin' overboard.

I'd reached their mast, almost slippin' on the deck an' clutchin' on a halyard when the man I knew 'ad to be their captain, havin' just run through an' killed one of our lads, turned on me. A big, fearsome-lookin' bugger 'e was, with plaited, gold-laced black beard, horned bronze 'elmet an' fancily decorated, boiled 'ide corselet. He'd one thing only in mind – my sudden an' violent death. And bein' used to the sea, 'e was keepin' steadier than I could. As our boats rolled an' pitched, others nearby ceased fightin' to watch as 'e glared furnace eyes at me. Cursin' aloud he raised 'is sword intendin' to sweep it across an' render me 'eadless as I lurched forwards. Still grippin' the halyard I stooped, heaved an' swung myself around the mast as 'is sword hissed. His blade struck the mast so 'ard 'it entered deep enough to jam solid. He cursed an' growled loud, tryin' to wrench out the sword while I raised up an' swung my club 'ard as ever I did to strike the side of 'is 'ead with a crack. He went down gaspin' and clawin' at the planks then e' was dead. The effect on 'is own crew was all but instant. They were backin' away an' leapin' into the water as it churned around our vessels, expectin' no doubt to evade death an' to regain their ship once we'd quit 'er.

But our captain wasn't in any 'urry to do that. Havin' won the vessel he an' several others got down between the benches where they groped under the deck to look for what our brigands 'ad got hidden under there. As it turned out their curiosity was worth the effort. They pulled out canvas bags, wet with blood an' seawater to find with a glance they contained an assortment of precious objects, includin' temple offerin's an' personal jewellery. Phorbas 'ad most of the pirates' weapons collected as well as their dead captain's fancy sword, which he there an' then offered to me. I didn't want it. He also 'ad their oars thrown into the sea. We clambered back onto our vessel, leavin' the surrendered pirates remainin' aboard theirs to 'elp their men out of the water an' deal with their many dead an' wounded. From our own crew we'd lost but six.

I tell you now, Mister Peter, I couldn't 'elp but wonder if a certain person 'igh up didn't 'ave a hand in guidin' that shipload of brigands in our direction.

Back on board *Polemos,* Phorbas said to me, "They must 'ave attacked an' looted one of the coastal towns or ships then on their way out they spotted us an' thought we'd be an easy catch." He was right, I'm sure, though my main concern once we ere under way again was the days ahead of us before we'd reach Trinacria. As we'd already been long at sea and with the African coast still within sight Phorbas decided we'd go ashore to rest, replenish our supplies an' bury our dead, though we'd make it somewhat further along from where the pirates 'ad paid their last visit. The followin' day we'd carry on eastwards to Trinacria.'

Heracles relaxed, took up his cup and downed the remains of his beer. That done he let out a belch and turned to me, saying, 'So let's call it a day then we can pick up where I left off tomorrow mornin'.'

That suited me even though the sun was still hovering over the hills so I wandered off in the cool, late afternoon air. I sat alone in the clearing, away from the house, to check over the voice recorder, allow it a dose of daylight while trying to take in fully all that Heracles had told me that day. As the sun was disappearing I heard their voices - Tiye and Mayet, and spotted their alluring forms. They were returning from one of their walks by the stream and as they passed the opening between the trees they saw me. They stepped into the clearing with smiles on their faces as I slipped the recorder out of sight. "Ah, Peter," said Tiye in her soft, beguiling voice, "you are alone but now we are here to keep you company.".

"I think really he was waiting for us," said Mayet, bending close with a hand caressing my shoulder. The only other place to sit out there was the sturdy chair used by Heracles so I stood and suggested we return to the courtyard where I'd take it upon myself to have one of his attendants bring the three of us wine. We'd remain there until the stars were out and when one of them started tugging on my sleeve.

The voice recorder, never far from my thoughts, if you hadn't noticed, I would sneak onto the window ledge of the spare room while Tiye and Mayet busied themselves further along in the bathroom.

Chapter 14 - The Hound of Hell

Meeting Heracles in the courtyard each morning had become almost routine but this day would have him relate to me his final challenge which, as I knew, occurred back in Greece. We took our places later than usual well after the sun had risen, with food and beer set before us.

'Aye, Mister Peter,' he began, 'havin' left the coast of North Africa before the stars 'ad faded we set out to sail north-east as Phorbas considered this the shortest route to the coast of Trinacria. Even so, even with a lively wind behind us part of the time, there was much rowin' to do in squally waters. We didn't reach land before nightfall but Phorbas once more 'ad proved what a capable sailor 'e was. We 'eaded along the coast, turned an' followed it north with the wind once more behind us. We kept on along to the next stretch of coast then east, across to Greece where we'd turn south, even though the wind might often be against us. But that was still a very long way from Mycenae. Phorbas knew this an' suggested I might remain with 'is crew. He agreed we'd sail down the west coast of Greece, all the way around south of the Pelopnnese then back north up the bay to Tiryns. It made sense; I'd too much in the way of valuables to keep by me, includin' the golden apples to consider any way overland. He and 'is men 'ad also done well out of the pirate ship's plunder. I'd been offered my share but gave some of this back to 'im for 'is troubles in

357

divertin' to Tiryns when 'is intended destination was Crete. With the golden apples an' the valuable items I already owned, I felt like I might be one of the richest men in all of Greece.

I did my fair share of work at the rowin' bench but maybe tellin' any more of our long journey to the port of Tiryns then back by chariot to Mycenae would be an unnecessary strain on your memory, Mister Peter, good as you've proven so far that it is. Nothin' to get worked up over 'appened anyway.'

'A brilliant idea, Mister Heracles,' I responded, 'so let's pick up the tale from when you actually reached Mycenae.'

'Aye, let's do that. After we docked in mid afternoon, Phorbas 'ad two of 'is men 'elp take my valued possessions an' my weapons up to the tavern above the 'arbour where I'd once before stayed. I'd said farewell to Phorbas and 'is crew, and to *Polemos*, the vessel that'd taken us such a great distance, yes, to the end of our world an' back. Now alone in my room my thoughts turned to Eurystheus an' the golden apples.

One thing, though; after we'd killed Geryon we'd promised Maro an' the Erytheans that we'd send out priests to teach 'em about the Olympians an' our ways. I'd deal with that next day after I'd paid what I 'oped would be my all but one visit to Eurystheus. My thoughts turned to the final task imposed upon me by Hera; my descent into Hades to capture the great dog, Cerberus, that guarded its entrance. I was certain that woman 'oped the dog would kill me so I'd be down there as a wanderin' soul for good.

But the sky was darkenin' beyond my window an' there was laughter downstairs, some of it female. It was time to concern myself with the present an' worry about tomorrow when the sun 'ad returned to the sky.

So next day I pulled on the lion skin an' set off from the tavern with the golden apples clustered in a canvas bag. I passed through the Lion Gate unopposed though two of the guards followed a few steps behind. I'd been away from Mycenae for a very long time but the guards there could 'ardly fail to recognize who I was when I showed up at the palace entrance. One of 'em went inside to inform of my arrival and it wasn't long before the summons came for me to attend the royal presence. I walked into the buildin' an' through the palace until stoppin' the regulation distance from 'im.'

"So you have returned at long last," he announced, as if that wasn't obvious. "And have you completed your latest task as required? Have you visited the Hesperides and have you acquired the golden apples?"

'I assumed, rightly as it turned out, Mister Peter, that as he'd not said anythin' about Geryon and 'is cattle, they'd been delivered some time previous. I reached into the bag an' replied, "Aye, your greatness, I've all six of 'em and 'ere is proof." I pulled out one of the apples an' rolled it towards 'im. Eurystheus shrank back into 'is fancy-cushioned throne as if some creature or other was scuttlin' at 'im while one of 'is armed guards strode forward to pick the apple up an' hold it in full view. Eurystheus peered at it, shuffled about uneasily then said, "Yes, I see, but they can be none of our business as these still belong to Hera." He turned to one of 'is attendants an' called, "Summon the priestess from Hera's shrine to come here at once." He then pointed at the apple an' muttered to the guard, who picked it up an' walked over to me with a grin on 'is face. He 'anded the apple back, sayin', "You've to remain where you are until the priestess arrives." I wondered if the man 'ad any idea of the apple's worth but then neither did I. As I waited I asked Eurystheus, "Mightiness, if I succeed in capturin' Cerberus from the gates of hell, where would you wish to inspect 'im?" Well, Mister Peter, it might've been a nonsensical question but it touched a raw nerve an' the bugger replied, "That is no longer my concern and neither are you. It is to Hera's priestess you must address yourself and with her you are to leave those golden apples." I imagined if Eurystheus was confronted with what I thought Cerberus would look like, he'd shit 'imself. But that could never 'appen because Cerberus could never be captured an' Hera knew it.

I waited an' when the priestess turned up I could see, cowl or no, that it was the woman I'd dealt with those many months ago. With a slightest nod to Eurystheus, who pretended no longer to notice me, I followed 'er out of the palace an' to the temple of Hera. We didn't enter the shrine but in the portico, where I deposited the apples, she said in a low voice, "Heracles, I can confide in you because the Lady Hera is beginning to lose interest in your labours and has much else on her mind. She never expected you would return alive but was certain that if by chance you did return, and if you confronted Cerberus, the great dog would finally kill you."

'That sounded tricky, Mister Peter, don't you think? What *was* I supposed to do if I couldn't kill or capture it? If so then I'd 'ave failed my last challenge an' she'd 'ave me for sure.

'Very tricky, Mister Heracles,' I nodded and we both sat back to take advantage of figs, olives and the honeyed wheat cakes I so enjoyed – and of course the warm beer I'd become used to but still didn't care for.

'Aye,' he began, 'as you well know, Mister Peter, there are other ways into Hades for those who've been chosen but that wouldn't involve defeatin' the great dog. As I slept fitfully that night, Athena came to me in all 'er glory. "Heracles," she said, "I have spoken with almighty Zeus and he says even though you have so far overcome all the perils his vindictive wife sent against you, she hopes you may still succumb to defeat or death with this last. You must confront Cerberus and you must find your way to him beneath the earth. That will be final proof and Zeus will assert himself – he will ensure Hera accepts whatever is the outcome."

'So you see, I'd that one more peril to confront an' though it remained within the Peloponnese it was located at a long peninsula in the extreme south at a place called Taenarus, an' would be no easy

361

journey. I'd take a two 'orse chariot with the few provisions I needed an' on my way I'd stop at Sparta a city ruled by the great Menelaus and 'is wife, Helen, said to be the most beautiful woman in the world. I'd see neither as I'd arrive late in the day an' I'd be off at first light the next. Didn't wear the lion skin either as I didn't want to be recognized. I'd 'eard about Taenarus, about the caves where it was said anyone enterin' too far inside would never be seen again because it was a way into Hades that led to where Cerberus waited. Others maintain some of 'em simply got lost an' never found their way out an' so died down there.

The second day I passed through hilly country before reachin' Taenarus and a small fishin' village of that name. At the only tavern thereabouts I inquired about a long-lastin' firebrand. They soon realised where I intended to go an' said they thought I was mad. Their remark about madness brought back memories I could've done without. But on hearin' what I'd planned along came a wizened old character by the name of Norax who claimed 'e knew a part way inside the caves, would supply us each with a firebrand an' take me so far down there to where he'd wait. Wearin' my lion skin an' carryin' my club an' sword I met the man at dawn an' we set off along a rough path leadin' into a deep valley where, at the base of a cliff, we approached a cave entrance that looked none too invitin', more like gapin' jaws with stone teeth pokin' down from the roof further inside.'

Jeffrey Peter Clarke

'Pity it wasn't just a garden shed,' I muttered under my breath as he continued.

'I wondered how Norax was to light the brands as he didn't talk much but he'd another of those flattish gemstones that concentrated the sun's rays an' by then the sun was far up enough to be shinin' down the valley. He did what was needed an' soon both brands were well lit. He stepped inside with me followin' an' suddenly the air was cooler. We went on down an irregular passage, our boots dislogin' small stones that rattled ahead of us an' disappeared echoin' into the blackness beyond our swayin' lights. There were side galleries slopin' away into oblivion but where our passage steepened we 'ad to keep the torches 'igh an' scramble on our arses. When it levelled out I asked 'im, 'ow many people 'ad disappeared down there. Steadyin' 'imself with one 'and against a juttin' rock, 'e answered, "Can't say but it's usually been those who wander in with no more than an oil lamp that aren't seen again."

'The gallery opened an' levelled out a little with one main an' two smaller passages leadin' from it an' Norax said, "It's that left side one you take, I'm sure of it. I 'eard sounds from in there once but couldn't make 'em out. A voice or maybe some animal."

'Well, Mister Peter, he'd said the firebrands were long-lastin' but that didn't tell me for 'ow long a long-lastin' torch would burn. For as long, I hoped, as those used in our palaces an' temples. But I 'ad to go on. I entered the passage an' for some

363

way I needed to lower my 'ead an' keep the firebrand out straight in front of me. The passage was openin' out a bit when I smelled somethin' unpleasant. At the entrance to a side gallery my torch illuminated the body of a man. Aye, you could make out It'd been a man though it looked like somethin' 'ad been eatin' at it and it was on the way to becomin' a rottin' skeleton. I'd seen plenty of dead men before but not like this. By 'is side lay a broken oil lamp.

But still I went on an' now the passage was openin' out. Aye, it was gettin' wider an' eventually I found myself enterin' a cavern, a great domed space with a strange light of its own – a dim light that came from nowhere an' everywhere. An' there was water ahead. Shimmerin' water. I found a couple of 'eavy rocks where I could jam the firebrand upright an' save myself carryin' it further, then I peered about. Apart from the occasional splutter of my torch there was an eerie, all pervadin' silence. Some way to my left I could make out what looked like the remains of another body layin' there but now there were sounds. Somethin' stirred. Somethin' was risin' up ahead of me, close by the water. Maybe it'd been there all the time – crouchin', waitin'. It was a dark, fearsome form, gettin' ever bigger an' its eyes were 'ard upon me. Aye, the great black dog, Cerberus, was on 'is feet, almost tall as me and 'ad me wishin' I'd with me a good strong spear. While the dog barred those most wantin' to enter or leave Hades by their own means, it was intended I should never quit the place alive.

Aye, Cerberus was about to make sure of it by chewin' on my guts. The dog was lopin' towards me, slobberin' at the mouth, his eyes glintin' the light of my torch,. His growls rolled back an' forth about the cavern as thunder as he swayed from side to side an' the many shadows he cast seemed to rise up with 'im. There was no escapin'. None! I strode forward, callin' once more the name of Athena, hearin' echoes of my own voice as I lifted high the club. Cerberus raised higher an' opened wide 'is white-toothed jaws. I was feelin' 'is breath on my face as I swung with a strength I didn't know I 'ad to strike the side of 'is jaw with a bone-splittin' crack. Cerberus yelped, 'is cries echoin' all about the cavern so I struck 'im again. He backed off an' sank to 'is knees, glarin' at me, so I landed a third blow. He growled an' rolled over an' though 'e remained still I could 'ardly believe what I was seein'. But I knew Cerberus wasn't dead. He couldn't be dead because 'e was tended by the gods, yet I, a man, 'ad floored 'im. I'd been given a chance. Aye, Zeus 'ad let it 'appen. I backed away an' grabbed up my torch. I needed to get out quick before Cerberus was back on 'is feet as I didn't expect a second chance, but on turnin' around I was faced by not one but three passages an' I couldn't be sure through which of 'em I'd entered the cavern. I hesitated then went for the nearest. This 'ad to be it! I started back up with my boots clatterin' an' slippin' on loose stones. I 'eared a growl. I imagined Cerberus paddin' up behind with 'is breath fallin' on my neck. I went on, gaspin' hard, but it seemed I was takin' longer to get away from there than I ought, even as I was passin' that rotted body. Further still an' I saw light flickerin' on the walls ahead. Then a figure. As I stumbled close, Norax stared at me with light dancin' on 'is face an' said, "So you made it back – nothin' much 'appened then?"

"No, nothin' much," was my answer and I didn't want to say more. As we clattered our way to the top, Norax hesitated an' said, "When you walked off down there alone I sensed someone, somethin' pass by me, followin' you, but I saw nothin'. Scared me it did."

"Just your imagination," I told 'im as none too soon daylight appeared ahead. Once outside in welcome sunlight, Norax shoved both torches against the ground to extinguish 'em an' we carried on back to the village where I revealed what'd 'appened, rewarded 'im an' asked where I might find a shrine to Athena. He said there was none around there so I took to my chariot an' left.'

'So you'd finally triumphed, Mister Heracles,' I said. 'You'd overcome all Hera had thrown at you. Did you not feel proud?'

'Proud, Mister Peter? Aye, but per'aps relieved would better describe 'ow I felt – and all of a sudden knowin' I was free of endless wanderin'. He drank the remainder of his beer, called for another jar then said, 'A year an' more 'ad passed since I'd said goodbye to Kilushepa an' my old friend Iolaus. I would make my way back an' any man who chose to get in my way would wish 'e 'adn't. I set off north, stoppin' for a night at Sparta, then at Tiryns. I rode 'ard wherever the land was level enough though found my time lengthened when gettin' across rivers an' streams. Next came Mycenae where at the shrine to Athena I'd secured many of my belongin's. There I left a gift of silver on the altar before 'er priestess. I planned to leave generous offerin's at one or more of Athena's shrines on my way but so many towns in the Peloponnese 'were devoted more to Hera I decided I would not. There was one place better by far than any of 'em an' that's where I'd go next.

I crossed the isthmus of Corinth and 'eaded south to Athens where the goddess 'erself was most revered an' celebrated by the name of 'er city. Aye, and Athens was no great distance from Thebes. I was in Athens for a day and a night an' there visited 'er temple on the acropolis 'igh above the city. There I spent time in conversation with 'er chief priestess who was delighted to hear how devotion to the goddess 'ad been of such 'elp through my many trials. It was at Athena's main shrine where I left a good proportion of the valuables I still carried.

By sunrise next day I'd left Athens an' was ridin' north to Thebes under a clear blue sky. Rough country it might've been but I'd arrive there by midday. They must've seen me comin' from the city wall – at least recognized the lion skin, for by the time I'd drawn close to the main gate, guards an' ordinary people were gatherin' outside. People were millin' about me when the guards started movin' them aside from the gate. Iolaus appeared in 'is courtly robes together with three of 'is attendants an' two more guards. He was smilin' wide an' rushed over to grab my arm as I stepped down from the chariot. "Heracles," 'e grinned, lookin' me up an' down, "you're back with us and still in one piece! Praise be to the gods!"

"I'm very glad to be with you again," I assured 'im, but before I could mention 'er name Iolaus said, "I've sent a messenger to Kilushepa and she'll soon be joining us. Come with me now – these men will see to your chariot and horses and my guards will follow with your possessions. Oh, but do hold onto your famous club until you're settled."

Well, Mister Peter, I 'ad as fine a reception as any man could wish for an' more – much more. We went to that part of the palace were Kilushepa and I 'ad been set up before I'd made off west to Erythea, an' there she was waitin' for me in 'er finest gown. She was in tears as we kissed an' she admitted later that evenin' that there were times when she thought I'd never return. It was 'er business kept 'er occupied in mind an' body an' it'd kept 'er fully independent. Celebrations were ordered throughout Thebes an' I felt overwhelmed by it all.'

'Did you see Megara?' I asked him.

'My first wife y'mean – aye, Mister Peter, I spotted 'er in the megaron next day but she kept well away from me. I reckon she came out of curiosity and nothin' more. I learned later she'd married a man from the rulin' 'ouse of Corinth to 'elp keep relationships sound between them an'

Thebes. I was told by Iolaus she was 'appy and I was glad about that. Aye, very much I was.

Soon enough I joined with Iolaus as once I 'ad to go out huntin' an' Kilushepa would often be with us. Now an' again there'd be trouble on our borders, disputes an' incursions to deal with but with most people we managed good relations, especially with Athens where Kilushepa an' I would stay from time to time. It was there I learned of how Theseus, a prince of the city, 'ad sailed to Crete an' gone to Knossos where, with the 'elp of Daedalus and Minos' daughter, Ariadne, who'd cleared off with 'im later. He'd descended alone into the Labyrinth below the palace of Minos an' slain the Minotaur, the beast that lived on human flesh. But that's another tale in itself.'

'Perhaps you could have done for it with your club, Mister Heracles,' I said.

'Aye, maybe. Anyhow, while my nephew an' dear friend Iolaus was makin' a name for 'imself Kilushepa an' I were growin' old, drawin' in upon ourselves an' away from others. It was one night she, Athena, came to me as an ethereal figure, as she must 'ave done to you when you were 'alf asleep at 'ome. Almighty Zeus 'imself 'ad of course followed the challenges, the twelve labours enforced upon me by 'is dear wife, Hera. He'd 'ad to go along with it to placate 'er as you know, but now 'e wanted to make amends with the ultimate gift - immortality in the Elysian Fields. Athena, because of my devotion to her, brought that message and would await my response. Well,

Mister Peter, I wasn't goin' to argue but Kilushepa would 'ave to be with me. Athena said she would return the followin' night to confirm this.

She was true to 'er word and understood Kilushepa did not want to be left alone any more. We aged an' we died only days apart. They burned our bodies with great ceremony but these were but empty husks as our essential bein's 'ad already departed. We awoke 'ere, where we are now, with years taken from our true ages. We could live again in a modest version of Knossos with all 'er comforts.'

'And,' I put it to him, 'you have your attendants, your lyre player, those who work in your kitchen and the fields.' He stared at me, puzzled, then said, 'Aye, they've always been 'ere but – but when I don't see them it's like they don't exist at all. D'you understand what I mean, Mister Peter?'

As I'd long since reached the point where I thought anything might be possible, I replied, 'Oh, yes, I do understand. But what about Tiye and Mayet?'

'Well they were not brought 'ere for me, Mister Peter, delightful a sight as I found 'em both. They're real enough as far as I know – real enough at night I'd 'ave thought – aren't they? Don't tell me they're not.'

'Er, yes, Mister Heracles, they most certainly are but I've not seen them very often during the day.'

370

'No, they've usually been in the garden, goin' for a walk or passin' time with Kilushepa. They're a couple of my visitors she's taken a likin' to.'

There was silence for a time while we drank more beer then I asked him, 'The parchment given to you at the very beginning by Hera's priestess – did you keep it?'

'No, Mister Peter, I didn't, I burned it. I wanted no reminder.'

I looked across at the lion skin displayed there on the courtyard wall, at his club propped up in one corner then at his bow and arrows laying nearby. All these symbols, reminders of his fortitude, his bravery and his triumphs. 'Immortality must mean eternity,' I said at last. 'Is it something you and Kilushepa ever talk about?'

'Immortality - never gettin' any older – aye, we've talked about it an' we both agree - what else now does immortality 'ave to offer? The time will come, and I'm thinkin' of late it already 'as, when I – we, 'ave nothin' left to talk about or even think about an' our very memories will 'ave become distant relics. Even the moon an' the stars at night seem no longer to matter. Aye, we'll be fed up with bein' ourselves - even lookin' at one-another an' that I don't want. Talkin' to you about my past 'as livened me up a lot, Mister Peter, really it 'as but after this – well, I can't say. What else is there to do that we've not done a thousand times already.'

He became pensive, looking down and circling his now empty beer cup slowly on the table. The sun was past its highest, food and more beer were brought to us by the usual male and female attendants. I tried not to stare at them while telling myself they appeared real enough. Heracles and I indulged in small talk; he asking yet again about the world to which I belonged with me being as circumspect as I could and letting my imagination step in as necessity demanded. He was being polite because much of it we'd gone over before.

When Tiye and Mayet passed us by on their way out for a stroll Heracles said, 'Now then, Mister Peter, why don't you catch up an' keep those girls company for the rest of the afternoon; I'm sure they wouldn't mind.' We parted company and I left the courtyard, not hurrying but thinking as I went how Heracles, having related so much outwardly to me, accounts full of life and adventure, was turning in upon himself and would prefer the company of Kilushepa. Perhaps they would lie together, sigh together, and think of what there was yet to do, if anything, after I had departed.

I caught up with Tiye and Mayet past the clearing on their way to the stream where we sat on the gently sloping bank with myself as centre of their affections. They were so present and warm, their touch so real. There we talked about my world and theirs with my recorder switched off. It was easier for me to describe my world without confusing them because their gods and goddesses were so utterly different to those of Heracles, so varied, so fantastic in purpose and manifestation, that they found it easier to accept more of what I felt able relate. And I, of course, was fascinated to hear more about their life under a pharaoh who in their land was considered a god.

When the sun was low in the sky they excused themselves and I found myself alone with the sounds of rippling water, birds and insects as pleasant and fulfilling company. I was content to remain where I was, deep in thought, and time seemed no longer to matter. The sun was dipping below the horizon and soon was gone. I arose to sense someone standing by me. She was as I recalled her from that visit in my own home, a warmly illuminated, golden-haired young woman in a pale, flowing gown. Her voice touched my ear like warm breeze. "Peter, the sky will soon darken over the Elysian Fields. It is time for you to depart. Heracles will know and he will understand."

I looked around and asked, 'Can I not say goodbye to Tiye and Mayet?'

"They are gone but they will remember you always in their dreams."

As she stepped slowly away I was stricken with regret. I wanted to remain a while longer but I knew it couldn't be so. I followed her through the deserted clearing and hesitated by the table where I'd first spoken to Heracles. There were two empty beer cups still waiting there, one of them mine. We continued on, retracing our steps through the trees and to the passage from which I'd so anxiously emerged those uncounted days ago, then into the gallery which her presence gently illuminated. When at last I emerged into my own garden in near darkness my mind was bursting with questions I wanted to ask her but I turned to find myself alone.

It had been raining. The air was cold on my face as I trod the wet path by the lawn. I pushed open the kitchen door, I re-entered the house, passed through the kitchen and there I stood a while, waiting in the dark hallway where I tried to come to terms with reality. The house was silent, as it had been when I left. Utterly impersonal. I switched on the light, took off my wet shoes, went upstairs, feeling oddly tired, and entered the bedroom. At least the central heating was on, if only low. I placed the precious voice recorder into a drawer on my side of the empty bed where the clock indicated almost twelve-thirty. There was little else for me to do other than undress, dump my clothes into the wash-basket and slide into the cold bed.

As I gained a degree of warmth and comfort my thoughts returned to Heracles and the sunlit Elysian Fields. How much of what he told me was I to believe – how much of it true? So what in the end is truth? Truth is what people are led or told to think is true or what they want the truth to be. Perhaps both. I was beginning to wonder if I'd just awoken from a long dream.

Then I slept deeply.

I was out of bed a little later than I usually am at home and rain was beating against the window. My mind was a turmoil of memories as I had a much-needed shave that was definitely real. I was showered and almost dressed when I heard the stairs creaking. I held my breath. The bedroom door opened and there stood my wife looking decidedly anxious.

'What *have* you been up to?' she demanded. 'The back door was left wide open and so was the shed. I went along to see if you were in there but you weren't. It looks as if someone's made off with the bloody lawnmower, and there's muck from the garden trodden over the kitchen floor. What *have* you been up to?'

Yes, I was home. Oh, joy!

My thanks to Lynda Buxton for her invaluable assistance in reading through and identifying the textural and other deficiencies in my work.